EVERYMAN, I will go with thee,

and be thy guide,

In thy most need to go by thy side

ANTON TCHEKHOV

Born at Taganrog on the Sea of Azov, in 1860.
Began writing when he was twenty under the
pseudonym of Antosha Tchekhonté. Qualified
as a doctor of medicine in 1884. Awarded the
Pushkin prize by the Imperial Academy of
Sciences, Petersburg, in 1888. Travelled in
Asia and western Europe during 1890 and 1891.
Doctors diagnosed consumption in 1897, and
on their advice he moved to the Crimea in 1899.
In 1901 married Olga Knipper, an actress of
the Moscow Art Theatre. Died at Badenweiler
in Germany in 1904. Buried in Moscow.

TCHEKHOV

Plays and Stories

TRANSLATED BY
S. S. KOTELIANSKY

INTRODUCTION BY
DAVID MAGARSHACK

DENT: LONDON
EVERYMAN'S LIBRARY
DUTTON: NEW YORK

No. 941   Hardback ISBN 0 460 00941 9
No. 1941   Paperback ISBN 0 460 01941 4

ACKNOWLEDGMENTS

Acknowledgment is due to Chatto & Windus for *The Wood Demon*, and George Routledge & Sons Ltd for 'Chronological Table,' 'Tatyana Riepin,' 'On the Harmfulness of Tobacco,' 'A Moscow Hamlet,' 'At the Cemetery,' 'At the Post Office,' 'Schulz,' 'Life is Wonderful,' and 'A Fairy Tale' from Tchekhov's *Literary and Theatrical Reminiscences*.

ACKNOWLEDGMENTS

Acknowledgment is due to "Chitra" *&* "Sacrifice" for *Two Plays* by Tagore; and George Routledge & Son Ltd. for "Transplanted Flute"; Literary Digest for "On the Trimilngham of Telegra"; ... M. ... Timothy ... On Campbell for "Mula ..." for *Outer Bondue* Film ... "Memorial, and "A Clergy ..." from *Routledge's Diatoge* and *Original Reminiscences*.

All rights in the plays in this volume are reserved, and inquiries regarding their production rights should be addressed to R. P. S. Lowrie & Partners, Publishers, London, S.W.1.

INTRODUCTION

ANTON TCHEKHOV'S connection with the theatre goes back to his schooldays in his native town of Taganrog when he made quite frequent appearances on the amateur and professional stage and earned general recognition as a talented actor. It is significant that his first major work before he became known as a short-story writer was a play of inordinate length which he tried unsuccessfully to get performed after his arrival in Moscow in 1880. (The play was first published in 1923, nineteen years after Tchekhov's death, and republished in 1949.) This play represents Tchekhov's first attempt to paint a large canvas of the social forces that were moulding Russian life during the last two decades of the nineteenth century. Its characters represent the different strata of Russian society and its action hinges on the struggle between the social and economic forces that was growing more and more acute just then. Platonov, the hero of the play, falls a victim in this struggle. He represents Tchekhov's first attempt to depict 'the superfluous man' in Russian society, the idealist who is aware of the folly, laziness, and ineptitude of the people around him but who is too weak to do anything about it. He is the typical victim of his environment. 'Nothing will come of us,' he cries in despair. 'We are the lichens of the earth. We are done for. We are utterly worthless.'

Ivanov, the hero of the second full-length play which Tchekhov wrote eight years later, is a direct descendant of Platonov. It was performed for the first time in Moscow in November 1887 and in Petersburg in January 1889, and on both occasions it was a great success. The play certainly shows a great advance on *Platonov*. It is much more compact, its characters come to life and their indulgence in exhibitionism is not driven to such extreme length as in the earlier play. But its faults, as Tchekhov saw them, were none the less fundamental. They consisted chiefly in overdramatized situations and in the too obvious 'literary' derivation of the characters, particularly the character of Ivanov himself, which offended Tchekhov's sense of truth to life and tended to make his drama a drama of frustration. Technically, too, the play struck Tchekhov as too conventional, and in his next play, *The Wood Demon*, he hoped to challenge the accepted conventions of the stage by presenting life shorn of its 'dramatically effective' trappings. 'On the stage,' he wrote, 'everything should be as complex and as simple as in real life. People are having dinner and, while they are having it, their future happiness may be decided or their lives may be about to be shattered.'

Ivanov closes the first period of Tchekhov's work as a playwright. In addition to *Platonov* and *Ivanov*, this period includes his one-act naturalistic drama *On the Highway*, written in 1885 and banned by the censors as 'sordid,' six one-act comedies, and his dramatic 'leg-pull,' *Tatyana Repina* (1899), his version of the last act of his friend Suvorin's play. In all these plays the main dramatic action takes place on the stage in full view of the audience, while in the four great plays of his second period the main dramatic action takes place off stage, the action on the stage mainly turning on the reaction of the characters to the dramatic moments of their lives.

The Wood Demon (1888–90) does not strictly belong to any of these categories of direct or indirect action plays. It represents a transition stage between the two. It was written during the period of his life when Tchekhov was under the influence of Tolstoi's teachings and it is essentially a morality play on Tolstoian lines. In it vice is *converted* to virtue, the vicious characters first defeating the virtuous ones and then realizing the heinousness of their offence. Tchekhov's chief idea in writing this play was to show life on the stage as 'it really is' and not as it is contrived by the professional playwright. In this he failed. For what he produced was a revival of the romantic convention of a bygone age with all its incongruous crudities. It is true that he did his best to stick to his formula that in a play, as in life, there should be coming and going, eating and drinking, talking and making love, while the happiness or the ruin of the characters was working itself out unbeknown to themselves. His characters eat and drink, come and go, talk and make love, and so on. But in spite of this Tchekhov never succeeds in creating the illusion of real life. There is not a single situation in *The Wood Demon* in which the characters act independently of the playwright. Their entrances and exits may seem haphazard, but they actually occur just when Tchekhov wants them to occur. There is no dramatic necessity for them. The play, in fact, teems with coincidences and *deus ex machina* situations. A hawk flies across just when Helen looks up at the sky; Voynitsky takes it into his head to write a compromising letter and then unaccountably leaves it lying about in the garden for anyone to pick up; Fyodor turns up just at the right moment for Helen to fall into his arms; a diary nobody ever heard about turns up providentially to vindicate Helen's character; a wood catches fire simply because Tchekhov wants to get his central character off the stage, and so on. The character of Fyodor, in particular, is wholly unconvincing. In the first three acts he is the rampageous villain of melodrama, while in the fourth act he is shown as a man of irreproachable character, an astonishing transformation that is brought about, not as in an earlier version of the fourth act by the sudden death of his father, but by a bout of drinking and gambling to the effects of which, one would have thought, he should have become inured long ago. Tchekhov's attempt to reproduce 'life as it is,' in fact, made his play as unlike life as possible and this is emphasized by the double happy ending of the play.

The Wood Demon, performed in Moscow in December 1899, was a dismal failure. Only the convinced Tolstoians were impressed by it. In a letter to one of them, Prince Urussov, who urged Tchekhov to publish it, Tchekhov wrote: 'I can't publish *The Wood Demon*. I hate this play and I am trying to forget it. . . . It would be a serious blow to me if it were dragged into the light of day and revived.' Tchekhov did not include it in the collected edition of his works. It was published posthumously.

But it was undoubtedly *The Wood Demon* that drove Tchekhov to reconsider his position as a playwright and that was in the end instrumental in his perfecting a type of drama which enabled him to reveal the inner substance of his characters, to show them, that is to say, as they really are and not as they appear to be in real life. Such a play required a different kind of dramatic dialogue, and the fact that Tchekhov took infinite pains to develop it can be traced in the six versions of his monologue *On the Harmfulness of Tobacco*, covering a period from 1886 to 1902. The first version of this one-act play was written as a rather crude music-hall turn, while the last version, described by Tchekhov as 'an entirely new play,' depicted the inner tragedy of the henpecked and pathetically ignorant pedant lecturing on a subject he knows nothing about.

It took Tchekhov seven years to perfect his drama of indirect action, and his four dramatic masterpieces—*The Seagull*, written in 1896, *Uncle Vanya*, an adaptation of *The Wood Demon*, which Tchekhov rightly claimed to be an entirely new play, written in 1897, *The Three Sisters*, written in 1900–1, and *The Cherry Orchard*, written in 1903–4—show him to be not only one of the greatest playwrights of modern times, but also a dramatic innovator of great originality. The point to be always kept in mind about any of Tchekhov's four great plays is that their dramatic climax invariably occurs in the third act and that the fourth act is merely used to tie up the loose ends and to point the moral. The action in these plays moves to a tremendous crescendo till it reaches the third act when it literally explodes. Failure to observe this carefully built-up dramatic climax—the marvellous piling up and interweaving of the various themes of the play until they all converge in one focal point in the third act—leads to a total disintegration of the dramatic action and has resulted in the all-too-familiar fallacy that the distinguishing feature of a Tchekhov play is its lack of action. The opposite is true, though it is only by a careful study of Tchekhov's technique as a playwright that the difficulties inherent in the presentation of these plays of indirect action can be satisfactorily overcome.

Tchekhov began writing *The Seagull* in October 1895. The play was first published in December 1896. Its first production took place in Petersburg two months earlier and its complete failure has now become an historic example of how a great play can be ruined by people without imagination. In *The Seagull* the action flows logically and naturally out of the interplay of theme and character, which have become completely integrated. Indeed, so complete is this synthesis of theme and character that an illusion of real life is created upon the stage. Its main theme deals with one of the most important problems in art—what makes a creative artist, and its protagonists are the two young characters, Konstantin and Nina, each trying to achieve success in a different branch of art: the art of writing and the art of acting. Tchekhov called his play a comedy, a fact that has puzzled many producers and critics for almost sixty years, in fact, ever since the famous Russian producer Konstantin Stanislavsky was successful in producing it as a tragedy at the Moscow Art Theatre on 17th December 1898, and incurred Tchekhov's displeasure for doing

so. In both *The Seagull* and *The Cherry Orchard* life is presented in its tragic as well as its comic aspects and a supreme
artist like Tchekhov never allows his audiences to forget them,
but that is beside the point so far as his conception of comedy
is concerned. The seemingly unhappy ending of *The Seagull*,
Konstantin's suicide, has no tragic significance: Konstantin
shoots himself not because of his unhappy love affair but
because of his realization that he is a failure as an artist; Nina,
on the other hand, who is involved in a love affair which is
much more tragic than Konstantin's, is not a failure. 'You
have found your way,' Konstantin tells her in the fourth act.
'You know where you are going, but I am still lost in a maze
of images and dreams without knowing what it is all about or
who wants it. I have no faith and I don't know what my true
calling is.' To Tchekhov, who could contemplate death dis-
passionately and, as a doctor, almost clinically, it was not
Konstantin's suicide that mattered, but Nina's perseverance
on the road to success. The suicide of a failure, however much
it may bring tears to our eyes, is not a proper subject for
tragedy, since there is an element of the ludicrous in it. But
there is nothing ludicrous about Nina who realizes that in the
last analysis it is suffering that makes a great artist and who
has the strength to endure till her goal is attained.

In *The Cherry Orchard* the comic elements are, of course,
much more in evidence. Its main theme—the passing of the
old order—is symbolized in the sale of the cherry orchard which
is treated in the spirit of high comedy. In the first act Lopakhin, the rich self-made business man, the son of a serf, who
adores the owner of the cherry orchard, Mrs Ranevsky, as the
personification of goodness because she saved him as a child
from a beating by his brutal father, is determined to save her
in turn. His plan, however, fails to appeal to Mrs Ranevsky
and her aristocratic brother Gayev. In spite of this rebuff,
Lopakhin is still determined to save the cherry orchard for
its owner. In the second act, however, there is a significant
change in his attitude. He learns that Deriganov, another
rich business man—a character who never appears on the stage
but who, like all off-stage characters in a Tchekhov play, plays
an important part in the development of the plot—is also after
the cherry orchard. If, therefore, Mrs Ranevsky still refuses
to accept Lopakhin's plan and permits her estate to be sold at
a public auction to pay her creditors, she can no longer count on

Lopakhin's loyalty, and, in fact, this is what happens. That is why Tchekhov devotes so much time in the third act to Lopakhin's description of his battle with Deriganov and why, in the second act, his warning to Mrs Ranevsky assumes such an ominous significance. The same element of high comedy is characteristic of all the other themes in the play: the intricate love theme of Mrs Ranevsky herself, of Trofimov and Anya, Lopakhin and Varya and, as a supreme comic contrast, of Dunyasha, Yepikhodov, and Yasha. This is also true of the billiard theme which Tchekhov develops in such a masterly fashion in the first three acts. Every time it occurs it indicates the presence of a subconscious struggle in Gayev's mind. In the third act Tchekhov practically brings the billiard table on to the stage. When Gayev enters he is heartbroken by the sale of the cherry orchard. Then he hears the click of the billiard balls and he becomes transformed. He no longer weeps, Tchekhov remarks in his stage direction. He has, in fact, become completely reconciled to the loss of the cherry orchard, as is made abundantly clear in the fourth act.

But it is in the finale of the play (usually misinterpreted as tragic) that the element of high comedy reaches its highest point. Tchekhov gives it to the old butler Firs, a born serf who never wavers in his attitude to life and who is convinced that the liberation of the serfs was 'a calamity.' But when he is left alone locked up in the empty house, the scales fall from his eyes. He suddenly realizes that his ideas of the good old days were false and that his life had been wasted. He used to call everyone, including his liberal-minded master Gayev, a 'silly fool,' but now he sees for the first time in his life that it is he who has been a silly fool. That is the true significance of the final curtain and not the fact that a sick old man has been abandoned by his masters in the mansion in which he had spent all his life as their most devoted slave. The sound of the axe felling the cherry-trees is here merged with the dramatic realization of the born serf that the old order was wrong and that—whatever the younger generation may make of the new order—the past is dead.

1956.   DAVID MAGARSHACK.

CHRONOLOGICAL TABLE OF THE LIFE AND WORKS OF ANTON TCHEKHOV

The following table is intended to show the chief events of Tchekhov's life and the dates of publication of his principal works.

Date	Life	Date	Works
	Anton Tchekhov's pedigree is purely peasant. His grandfather, Yegor Tchekhov, was a serf in the Voronezh province, Central Russia. By persevering labour he managed to save 3,500 roubles, and with that sum in 1841, some twenty years before the abolition of serfdom in Russia, he bought the freedom of his family of eight, at the rate of 500 roubles per head, his daughter Alexandra being thrown into the gain. From the Voronezh province the family moved to the south.		
	Anton Tchekhov's father, Pavel Yegorovich, became a clerk in the city of Taganrog, and after his marriage to Eugenia Morozov, the daughter of a local cloth merchant, he opened his own grocery shop. The Tchekhov family consisted of five sons and one daughter: Alexander, Nicolay, *Anton*, Marie, Ivan, and Michael. (The only survivors at present are Marie and Michael Tchekhov.)		

Date	Life	Date	Works
1860 Jan. 17.	Anton born at Taganrog. Here is the copy of his birth certificate taken from the register of the Cathedral Church of the Assumption: 'January 17, 1860, born and January 27, baptized, boy Antonius. His parents: the Taganrog merchant of the third guild Pavel Yegorovich Tchekhov and his lawful wife Eugenia Yakovlevna, both of the Orthodox faith. Sponsors: Spiridon Fiodorov Titov, brother of a Taganrog merchant, and the spouse of Dmitri Kirikov Safianopoulo, Taganrog merchant of the third guild.'		
1867	Anton sent by his father to the Greek parish school of King Constantine's Chuch.		
1869	Anton enters first form of the Taganrog Grammar School.		
1876	Anton's father's business having completely failed, the family moves to Moscow and lives in poor circumstances. Anton remains at Taganrog to complete his studies at the Grammar School; and for three years has to support himself by teaching pupils.		
1879 July 15 Aug.	Anton passes his matriculation examination. Anton joins his family in Moscow, and enters the medical faculty of the Moscow University. Compelled to support his family and himself		

Date	Life	Date	Works
1879 Aug.	in the pursuit of his medical studies, Anton begins writing for humorous papers.		
		1880	Tchekhov's first story, *A Letter from a Don Squire Stepan Vladimirovich N. to his Learned Neighbour Doctor Friedrich,* was published in the humorous paper *Strekoza* [Dragon-fly]. During the first seven years of his literary activity Tchekhov contributed over four hundred stories, novels, sketches, feuilletons, pastiches, law reports to the following periodicals: *Strekoza, Budilnik, Zritel, Mirskoy Tolk, Sviet i Tieni, Moskva, Satirichesky Listok, Oskolki, Sputnik, Razvlechenie, Sverchok, Novosti Dnia,* and others. His contributions during that period appeared over the following pseudonyms: *A. Ch-te, Anche, A. Tchekhonté, Antosha Tchekhonté, Antonson, Baldastov, My Brother's Brother, A Doctor without Patients, A Quicktempered Man, A Man without a Spleen, Rover,* and *Ulysses.*
1884	Takes his degree of Doctor of Medicine. In the summer works as doctor in the Zemstvo Hospital at Voskressensk. In the winter, in Moscow, occurs his first haemorrhage.	1884	*Tales of Melpomene,* a collection of humorous stories, by Antosha Tchekhonté, published by the humorous paper *Oskolki,* Moscow.

Date	Life	Date	Works
1885	Spends his summer holidays in Babkino, and becomes acquainted with military life. Makes the acquaintance of Souvorin, the editor of the influential Petersburg daily, the *Novoye Vremya*, and afterwards the intimate correspondent to whom Tchekhov wrote his most interesting letters. (The Russian edition of Tchekhov's letters occupies six volumes. A selection from the letters was published by Cassell, in 1925.)	1885	*Motley Stories*, a collection of stories by Antosha Tchekhonté, Moscow.
1886	Invited to contribute to the *Novoye Vremya*, and thus enabled to begin more serious work.	1886	*The Swan Song*, a play in one act.
April	Has second attack of haemorrhage. Spends the summer in Babkino.		
1887	Makes a journey to the south of Russia, the impressions of which are described in *The Steppe*.	1887	*At Twilight*, a volume of collected stories, published by Souvorin, Petersburg. *Ivanov*, a play in four acts, produced by Korsh's Theatre in Moscow, and also in Petersburg (*Ivanov* was published only in 1889.)
1888	Spends the summer at Luka, in the Ukraine, with the Lintvariovs. Establishes friendship with Souvorin, Plescheyev, and Grigorovich. On his trip to the Crimea to meet Souvorin nearly drowned owing to the collision between his steamer *Dir* and another steamer.	1888	*The Steppe*, the story of a journey. *Lights* *The Birthday Party* *The Belles* *The Fit* ⎱ Stories. *The Bear*, a farce in one act.

Date	Life	Date	Works
1888	Awarded the Pushkin prize (500 roubles) by the Imperial Academy of Sciences, Petersburg.	1888	*Stories*, a volume of collected stories, published by Souvorin, Petersburg.
1889	Elected member of the Society of Lovers of Russian Literature.	1889	*The Wood Demon*, a comedy in four acts, produced by Solovzov's Theatre in Moscow. *A Tedious Story; from an Old Man's Journal. The Proposal.* A farce in one act.
1890	Makes a journey across Siberia to Saghalien Island.		*A Tragedian against his Will.* A farce in one act.
July	Arrives at Saghalien. Personally carries out a census of the convict settlement.		*Demons* (a story). *Across Siberia* (impressions). *Goussev* (a story).
1890	Returns home, via Singapore, India, Ceylon, Suez Canal.		
Dec. 23	'I cough, palpitations of the heart; I can't make out what it all means.'		
1891	Makes a journey to western Europe (Vienna, Venice, Florence, Rome, Naples, Paris, Nice, etc.).	1891	*Runaways in Saghalien* (impressions). *The Duel* (a long story). *Women* (a story).
1892	Goes to the Novgorod province to help the famine-stricken population; establishes an organization for supplying the impoverished peasants with horses and cattle. Buys a farm at Melikhovo village, in the Serpukhov district (for 13,000 roubles) and moves from Moscow to the country with all his family.	1892	*Ward No. 6 The Grasshopper The Wife In Exile Neighbours* } Stories

Date	Life	Date	Works
1892	Appointed honorary medical superintendent of his district in the fight against the cholera epidemic. ('I'm visiting all the villages and giving lectures . . .')		
1893 Oct.	'I cough, palpitations of the heart, indigestion, and headaches . . .'	1893	*The Chorus Girl* (a story). *The Story of an Unknown Man* (a story). *Saghalien Island.* Notes from a journey. First published in the October, November, and December numbers of the monthly review *Ruskaya Mysl*; and continued in the February, March, May, June, and July numbers of the same review in 1894.
1894 Feb. March	'My cough worries me, especially at dawn. There is nothing serious as yet.' Advised by the doctors to live in the Crimea for sake of his health. Advised by the doctors to go to the south of France.	1894	*The Black Monk* *Women's Kingdom* }Stories *The Story of the Head Gardener*
		1895 Mar. Oct., Nov.	*The House with the Mezzanine* ('I once had a sweetheart. Her name was Misiyús. It is of this that I am writing.') *The Seagull* ('I've finished the play; it is called *The Seagull*.') *Three Years* (long story). *Murder* *Ariadne* }Stories. *The Wife*
1896	Attacked by haemorrhage of the lungs.	1896	*The Seagull* produced by the Alexandrinsky Theatre in Petersburg.

Date	Life	Date	Works
		1896	Complete failure. ('I shall never forget last evening. Never again will I write plays or have them produced.') *The Seagull.* A comedy in four acts. Published in the December number of *Russkaya Mysl*.
1897	Works hard, in the Serpukhov district, on the general census of the population. Builds several schools, mostly at his own expense, in the villages of Melikhovo, Talezh, and Novosiolki. Attacked by a sudden violent haemorrhage of the lungs during a dinner with Souvorin at a Moscow restaurant. Removed to hospital. 'The doctors diagnose consumption and order a complete change of life.' Goes to the south of France for the winter.	1897	*My Life* (a long story). *Peasants* *In a Native Spot* } Stories. *In the Cart*
1898 Jan.	Manifests intense interest in the Dreyfus affair, and is disgusted by the anti-Dreyfus campaign carried on in the *Novoye Vremya*; hence a break with Souvorin. His father dies, and owing to the insistence of his doctors Tchekhov decides to settle in the Crimea with his family. Buys a plot of land and builds a house near Yalta.	1898	*The Seagull* produced by the Moscow ArtTheatre with tremendous success. 'My *Uncle Vanya* is being produced in the provinces and is a great success.' *A Man in a Case* *Yonych* *The Lodger* } Stories. *The Husband* *The Darling*

Date	Life	Date	Works
1899	Sells his Melikhovo farm, and moves with his family to the Crimea. Sells the copyright of his past and future work to the Petersburg publisher Marx for 75,000 roubles.	1899	*The Lady with a Toy Dog* *The New Bungalow* } Stories. *Uncle Vanya*, produced by the Moscow Art Theatre. *In the Ravine* (a story).
1900 March	Elected member of the Academy of Sciences, Petersburg. His state of health gets worse.	1900	*The Three Sisters* begun.
1901 May 25	Marries Olga Knipper, an actress of the Moscow Art Theatre.	1901	*The Three Sisters* produced by the Moscow Art Theatre. *Women* (a story).
1902	As a protest against the cancellation by the authorities of Maxim Gorky's election to the Academy of Sciences, Tchekhov resigns his membership.	1902	*The Bishop* (a story).
1903 Sept. Oct.	'I cough . . . feel rather weak.' Elected temporary president of the Society of Russian Literature.	1903	*The Cherry Orchard.* A comedy in four acts. *The Bride* (a story).
1904 May 27 June 3 July 2	'I've been ill since May 2nd; I have not been out of bed.' Goes to Badenweiler, a German health resort, accompanied by his wife. Dies at Badenweiler. Buried in the cemetery of the Novodevichiy Monastery in Moscow.	1904 Jan. 17	*The Cherry Orchard* produced by the Moscow Art Theatre.

CONTENTS

PLAYS

THE CHERRY ORCHARD

A COMEDY IN FOUR ACTS

*(Written in 1903 and first performed in Moscow on
17th January 1904.)*

CHARACTERS

MME RANEVSKY, LYUBOV ANDREYEVNA, the owner of the cherry
 orchard.
ANYA, her daughter, aged seventeen.
VARYA, her adopted daughter, aged twenty-two.
GAYEV, LEONID ANDREYEVITCH, brother of MME RANEVSKY.
LOPAKHIN, YERMOLAY ALEXEYEVITCH, a business man.
TROFIMOV, PIOTR SERGUEYEVITCH, university student.
SIMEONOV-PISCHIK, BORIS BORISOVITCH, a landowner.
CHARLOTTA IVANOVNA, a governess.
YEPIKHODOV, SEMYON PANTELEYEVITCH, a bailiff.
DOUNYASHA, a maid.
FEERS, a man-servant, aged eighty-seven.
YASHA, a young man-servant.
A Stranger.
The Station-master.
A Post Office Clerk.
Visitors; Servants.

The action takes place on the estate of Mme Ranevsky.

ACT I

*A room which is still called the nursery. One of the doors leads
into Anya's room. It is dawn : the sun will rise soon. It is
the month of May, the cherry trees are in blossom, but it is
cold in the garden, and there is a morning-frost. The windows
in the room are closed. Enter Dounyasha with a candle, and
Lopakhin with a book in his hand.*

Lopakhin. The train has come, thank God. What 's the time?
Dounyasha. Nearly two o'clock. [*Blowing out the candle.*] It 's
 daylight already.
Lopakhin. How many hours late was the train? A couple of

3

hours, at least. [*Yawning and stretching himself.*] I am a nice one; what a stupid thing to do. I purposely came here in order to go to meet them at the station, and then overslept . . . fell asleep sitting in the chair. . . . How annoying. . . . You should have woken me up.

Dounyasha. I thought you had gone. [*Listening.*] Now they 're coming, I think.

Lopakhin. [*Listening.*] No. . . . They have to get the luggage out, and one thing and another. . . . [*Pause.*] Lyubov Andrey-evna has been abroad five years, and I wonder what she 's like now. She 's a fine woman. Easy to get on with, simple. I remember when I was a boy about fifteen, my father—he used to keep a shop in the village here—punched my nose, and it began to bleed. . . . The two of us had come into the courtyard here on some errand, and he had a drop too much. Lyubov Andreyevna, I remember as if it were yesterday, she was so young and so slim, she took me to the washstand, in this very room, in the nursery. 'Don't cry, little mouzhik, it 'll be quite well in time for your wedding,' she said. . . . [*Pause.*] My father was a mouzhik, sure enough; and here am I, in a white waistcoat and brown shoes. . . . A silk purse out of a sow's ear. . . . With this difference, that I am rich, have plenty of money; but if you really think of it, I am just a mere mouzhik. . . . [*Turning the pages of the book.*] I was reading this book, and could not make anything of it. . . . I was reading, and dropped off to sleep.   [*Pause.*

Dounyasha. The dogs did not sleep all night long, they know their masters are coming.

Lopakhin. Dounyasha, why are you so——?

Dounyasha. My hands are trembling. I know I 'm going to faint.

Lopakhin. You 're much too sensitive, Dounyasha. You dress like a lady, and your hair is done in the fashion. It isn't right. One should not forget who one is.

Enter Yepikhodov with a bunch of flowers ; he wears a jacket and brightly polished top-boots that squeak noisily ; as he comes in he drops the flowers.

Yepikhodov. [*Picking up the flowers.*] The gardener has sent these; he says you are to put them in the dining-room.
                    [*Handing the flowers to Dounyasha.*

Lopakhin. And fetch me some cider.

Dounyasha. Certainly.   [*Goes out

Yepikhodov. There's this morning-frost, three degrees, and the cherries are all in blossom. I cannot approbate our climate. [*With a sigh.*] I cannot. Our climate never rises to the proper occasion. Now, Yermolay Alexeyevich, let me supplement, the day before yesterday I bought myself a pair of top-boots, but I venture to assure you, they squeak so that there's simply no possibility. What ought I to grease them with?

Lopakhin. Leave me alone. You're a nuisance.

Yepikhodov. Every day some misfortune happens to me. But I don't grumble any more. I've got used to it. I even smile.

Dounyasha comes in and gives the cider to Lopakhin.

I'd better go. [*Knocking against a chair, which he upsets.*] There . . . [*As though in triumph.*] There, you see! Pardon the expression, that's the kind of thing that is always occurring . . . it is simply extraordinary! [*Goes out.*

Dounyasha. I must tell you, Yermolay Alexeyevich, that Yepikhodov has proposed to me.

Lopakhin. Yes?

Dounyasha. I really don't know what to do. . . He's a quiet man, only at times when he starts talking you can't make anything of it. It is all very nice and full of feeling, but it does not make sense. I like him in a way. He's madly in love with me. He's an unlucky fellow; every day there's something or other. They all tease him here, and call him twenty-two miseries.

Lopakhin. [*Listening.*] I think they are coming now. . . .

Dounyasha. Yes, they are! Oh dear, what shall I do? . . . I'm all of a tremble.

Lopakhin. Yes, they are coming. Let's go and meet them. Will she know me, I wonder? I haven't seen her for five years.

Dounyasha. [*Agitated*] I know I shall faint. . . . I know I shall!
 [*Two carriages are heard driving up. Lopakhin and Dounyasha go out hastily. The stage is empty. In the adjoining rooms sounds begin to be heard. Feers, leaning on a stick, hastily passes across the stage—he has been to the station to meet Mme Ranevsky. He is dressed in ancient livery and a tall hat; he is muttering something to himself, but not a single word can be understood. The noise behind the scenes grows louder and louder. A voice: 'Come, let's go in there . . .' Enter Mme Ranevsky,*

Anya, and Charlotta Ivanovna with a pet dog on a lead, all in travelling clothes; Varya, in a coat and shawl. Gayev, Simeonov-Pischik, Lopakhin, Dounyasha with a hold-all and sunshade, servants with various articles of luggage—all pass across the room.

Anya. Let's come in here. Do you remember, mother, what room this is?

Mme Ranevsky. [*Happily, through tears.*] The nursery!

Varya. How cold, my hands are numb. Your rooms, mummy, the white and violet ones, have been left just the same.

Mme Ranevsky. Sweet, darling nursery. . . . I used to sleep here when I was a little child. . . . [*Crying.*] I'm behaving like a child even now. . . . [*Kissing her brother, Varya, and then her brother again.*] And Varya is just the same, like a nun. And there is Dounyasha. . . .   [*Kissing Dounyasha.*

Gayev. The train was two hours late. What? A nice state of things!

Charlotta. [*To Pischik.*] My dog eats nuts too.

Pischik. [*In surprise.*] You don't say so!

[*They all go out except Anya and Dounyasha.*

Dounyasha. We've missed you so much. . . .

[*Takes off Anya's coat and hat.*

Anya. I didn't sleep all the four nights of our journey. . . . And now I feel so chilly.

Dounyasha. You went away in Lent, there was snow then, and frost; but now! My dear! [*Laughing, kissing her.*] I've missed you so much, my darling, my pet. . . . I must tell you now, I can't wait a moment.

Anya. [*Dully.*] The same old thing again?

Dounyasha. Yepikhodov, the bailiff, proposed to me after Easter.

Anya. Always the same old story. . . . [*Arranging her hair.*] I've lost all my pins. . . .

[*She is very tired and can hardly stand.*

Dounyasha. I simply don't know what to do. He loves me—he loves me so much!

Anya. [*Looking through the door of her room, tenderly.*] My room, my windows, as though I had never been away. I am home! To-morrow morning I shall get up, and run into the orchard. Oh, if only I could fall asleep. I didn't sleep all through the journey. I was so worried and anxious.

Dounyasha. Piotr Sergueyevitch arrived the day before yesterday.

Anya. [*Joyfully.*] Petya!

Dounyasha. He sleeps in the bath-house; he lives there altogether. 'I'm afraid of being in the way,' he said. [*Looking at her watch.*] I ought to wake him, but Varvara Mikhailovna told me not to. 'Don't you wake him,' she said.

Enter Varya, with a bunch of keys at her waist.

Varya. Dounyasha, coffee, quick. . . . Mummy's asking for coffee.

Dounyasha. This very minute.   [*Going out.*

Varya. Thank God you are back. You're home again. . . . [*Fondling her.*] My little darling has come home! My beautiful one has come home!

Anya. I've been through so much!

Varya. I can imagine it!

Anya. I set off in Holy Week; it was cold then. Charlotta talking all through the journey and doing tricks. What made you plant Charlotta on me?

Varya. But surely you could not travel by yourself, my pet. At seventeen!

Anya. We arrive in Paris; it's cold there, snowing. My French is shocking. Mother lives on the fourth floor. I go to see her, and in her room there are Frenchmen, ladies, an old priest with a little book; the room full of smoke, cheerless. I suddenly felt sorry for mother, so sorry, I took her head in my arms and pressed it to me, and couldn't let it go. After that mother was so loving and cried——

Varya. [*Through tears.*] Don't, don't——

Anya. She had already sold her villa near Mentone, she had nothing left, nothing. Nor had I a penny left; we only just managed to get there. And mother does not realize! We would sit down to dinner at a railway station, and she would ask for the most expensive things, and tip the waiters a rouble each. Charlotta was just the same. Yasha, too, would order a good meal for himself—it was simply terrible. Mother has her own servant, Yasha; we brought him back with us——

Varya. I saw the rogue.

Anya. How are things here? Has the interest been paid?

Varya. Out of the question.

Anya. Oh, my God! my God!

Varya. In August the estate is to be sold by auction.

Anya. My God!——

Lopakhin. [*Looking in at the door and bleating.*] Ma-a-a——

          [*Goes out.*

Varya. [*Through tears.*] I should like to give him what for.

[*Shaking her fist.*

Anya. [*Embracing Varya, in a low voice.*] Varya, has he proposed to you? [*Varya gives a negative shake of her head.*] Surely he does love you. . . . Why don't you make the situation clear? What are you waiting for?

Varya. I don't think anything will come of it. He's too busy, he has other things to think of . . . and takes no notice of me. Let him go, it is hard on me to see him. . . . They all speak of our getting married, they all keep on congratulating me, but actually there's nothing; it's all like a dream. . . . [*In a different tone of voice.*] Your brooch looks like a little bee.

Anya. [*Sorrowfully.*] Mother bought it. [*Going into her room, speaking happily, like a child.*] And when I was in Paris, I went up in a balloon!

Varya. My own darling has come home! My beautiful one has come home!

[*Dounyasha has come back with the coffee pot and is making the coffee.*

Varya. [*Standing by the door.*] I am going about all day long, busy about the house, and dreaming all the while. If you married a rich man I should feel easier in my mind. I should go into the wilderness, and after that I should go on a pilgrimage to Kiev . . . to Moscow, and I should keep on going to holy places. . . . I should go on and on for ever. Pure grace!

Anya. The birds are singing. What's the time?

Varya. It must be after two. You must go to bed, my darling. [*Going into the room, to Anya.*] Pure grace!

Yasha enters, with a rug and a travelling bag.

Yasha. [*Walking down the stage, mincingly.*] May I pass through?

Dounyasha. One would hardly recognize you, Yasha. How you have changed abroad!

Yasha. H'm. . . . And who may you be?

Dounyasha. When you went abroad, I was only so high. [*Showing her height from the floor.*] I'm Dounyasha, the daughter of Fyodor Kozoyedov. You have forgotten me!

Yasha. H'm. . . . You are a peach!

[*After looking round, he embraces her; she screams and drops the saucer. Yasha goes out quickly.*

Varya. [*In the doorway, in a peevish voice.*] What's going on there?

Dounyasha. [*Through tears.*] I have broken the saucer——

Varya. That means good luck.

Anya. [*Coming out of her room.*] Mother ought to be told that Petya is here——

Varya. I gave orders not to wake him.

Anya. [*Pensively.*] Six years ago father died, a month later my little brother Grisha was drowned in the river here, such a charming boy of seven. Mother could not bear it; she went away, she went without looking back. . . . [*Shuddering.*] How well I can understand her, if she only knew! [*A pause.*] And Petya Trofimov was Grisha's tutor; he may bring it all back to her——

    Enter Feers ; he wears a jacket and white waistcoat.

Feers. [*Going to the coffee pot, anxiously.*] My lady will have her coffee here. . . . [*Putting on white gloves.*] Is the coffee ready? [*In a stern voice to Dounyasha.*] You! And where's the cream!

Dounyasha. O Lord! . . .
                         [*Goes out quickly.*

Feers. [*Fussing round the coffee-pot.*] Oh, you *nyedotyopa* ![1] [*Muttering to himself.*] They have come back from Paris. . . . The old master, too, once upon a time, used to go to Paris . . . by coach. . . .
                           [*Laughing.*

Varya. Feers, what is it you are saying?

Feers. Beg pardon! [*Joyfully.*] My lady has come home! At last! Now I can die. . . .
                       [*Weeping with joy.*

Enter Mme Ranevsky, Gayev, and Simeonov-Pischik. The latter wears a poddyovka [short-waisted full coat] of fine cloth, and wide trousers. Gayev, as he enters, makes movements with his arms and body as though he were playing billiards.

Mme Ranevsky. How does it go? Let me see if I can remember. . . . I pot the yellow! I double into the middle pocket!

Gayev. I go in, off! Once upon a time, sister, we used to sleep in this very room; and now I am fifty-one. Odd, isn't it?

Lopakhin. Yes, time is passing.

Gayev. Eh?

Lopakhin. Time, I say, is passing.

Gayev. There's a smell of cheap scent.

Anya. I am off to bed. Good night, mother. [*Kissing her mother.*

Mme Ranevsky. My own precious little child. [*Kissing her hands.*] You are glad to be back home? I don't feel myself yet.

Anya. Good night, uncle.

[1] *Nyedotyopa* — a duffer. A word coined by Anton Tchekhov that has become popular and is widely used.

Gayev. [*Kissing her face and hands.*] God bless you! How very like your mother you look! [*To his sister.*] Lyuba, at her age you were just like her.

[*Anya shakes hands with Lopakhin and Pischik, goes out, and shuts the door behind her.*

Mme Ranevsky. She's quite worn out.

Pischik. It's the long journey, for sure.

Varya. [*To Lopakhin and Pischik.*] Well, gentlemen, it's after two, time to be off.

Mme Ranevsky. You are just the same, Varya. [*Drawing her to herself and kissing her.*] Presently I'll drink my coffee, then we shall all be off. [*Feers puts a little cushion under her feet.*] Thank you, my friend. I've got used to coffee. I drink it day and night. Thank you, my old friend! [*Kissing Feers.*

Varya. I must see if all the things have come. [*Goes out.*

Mme Ranevsky. Is it really I who am sitting here? [*Laughing.*] I long to jump about and wave my arms. [*Covering her face with her hands.*] Perhaps it is a dream! I swear, I love my native land, I love it dearly; I could not see anything out of the train, I kept on crying. [*Through tears.*] Still, I must drink my coffee. Thank you, Feers. Thank you, my old friend! I am so glad that you are alive.

Feers. Only the day before yesterday . . .

Gayev. His hearing is not good.

Lopakhin. Soon, about five in the morning, I have to set off for Kharkov. How annoying! I wanted to have a good look at you, to have a nice talk. . . . You are just as magnificent as ever.

Pischik. [*Breathing heavily.*] Even more so . . . dressed in Parisian style. . . . Bang goes my wagon and all its four wheels!

Lopakhin. Your brother, Leonid Andreyevitch, says that I am a guttersnipe, that I am a *koulak*,[1] but it leaves me completely cold. Let him talk. Only I wish that you trusted me as you did, that your wonderful, bewitching eyes would look at me as they did. Good God! My father was a serf of your grandfather's, and of your father's, but you yourself, once upon a time, did such a great deal for me that I have forgotten all the rest, and I love you, as if you were my kith and kin . . . more than my kith and kin.

Mme Ranevsky. I can't sit quiet, I just can't. . . . [*Jumping up and walking about in great agitation.*] I shall not live through

---

[1] A money-grubbing peasant.

this happiness. Laugh at me, I am silly. . . . My own, my sweet bookcase. . . [*Kissing the bookcase.*] My dear little table——

Gayev. In your absence our old nurse died.

Mme Ranevsky. [*Sitting down and drinking her coffee.*] May she rest in peace. They wrote to me about it at the time.

Gayev. And Anastasy died. Squinting Petroushka has left my service, and is in the town now working for the police inspector.

[*Taking out of his pocket a box of sweets and sucking one.*

Pischik. My dear daughter Dashenka . . . sends you her compliments——

Lopakhin. I should love to say something very pleasant and cheerful to you. [*Glancing at his watch.*] I'll have to leave soon, and I have no time for a long talk . . . but, well, I'll say it in a few words. You know already that your cherry orchard is to be sold to pay your debts; the auction is fixed for August the twenty-second; but don't you worry, my dear friend, and sleep in peace. There's a way out. Here's my plan. Please listen! Your estate is only about thirty miles from the town, a new railway line is to run near by; and if the cherry orchard and the land along the river were to be divided up into plots for summer bungalows, and those plots let on lease for building bungalows, then you would have at the very least an income of 25,000 roubles a year.

Gayev. Pardon me, what rubbish!

Mme Ranevsky. I can't quite make you out, Yermolay Alexeyevitch!

Lopakhin. You will get twenty-five roubles a year at the lowest for a two-and-a-half-acre plot, and if you make it known now, then I bet you anything you like, by the autumn not a single vacant strip of land will be left; they'll be all snapped up. In a word, I congratulate you; you're saved. The situation is wonderful, there's a deep river. Only, of course, it ought to be tidied up, cleared up . . . for instance, let us say, you clear out all the old buildings; this very house, which is no longer good for anything; you cut down the old cherry orchard——

Mme Ranevsky. Cut it down? But, my dear man, you don't understand what you're talking about. If in the whole of our province there is anything of interest, even remarkable, it is our cherry orchard.

Lopakhin. What's remarkable about this orchard is that it is very big. There's a crop of cherries once in two years, and even that is of no use; no one buys it.

Gayev. Even in the *Encyclopaedia* our orchard is mentioned.

Lopakhin. [*Glancing at his watch.*] If we do not devise something or decide on something, then, on 22nd August, both the cherry orchard and the whole estate will be sold by auction. Do make up your mind! There is no other way out, I swear. None whatever.

Feers. In the old days, forty or fifty years ago, they used to dry the cherries, pickle them, preserve them, make jam, and sometimes——

Gayev. Keep quiet, Feers.

Feers. And sometimes cartloads of dried cherries would be sent to Moscow and to Kharkov. Lots and lots of money! And the dried cherries at that time were tender, juicy, delicious, sweet-smelling. . . . They knew a recipe then——

Mme Ranevsky. And where's the recipe now?

Feers. Forgotten. No one remembers it.

Pischik. [*To Mme Ranevsky.*] What's it like in Paris? How are things there? Did you eat frogs?

Mme Ranevsky. I ate crocodiles.

Pischik. You don't say so! . . .

Lopakhin. Up till now there used to be in the country only masters and peasants, and now there have also appeared bungalow-dwellers. All the towns, even the smallest ones, are now surrounded by bungalows. And it is safe to say that in about twenty years from now bungalow-dwellers will have multiplied enormously. Nowadays the bungalow-dweller is only sipping tea on his veranda, but it may quite possibly happen that he will cultivate his mere two-and-a-half-acre plot, and then your cherry orchard will be transformed into a happy, rich, fine——

Gayev. [*With indignation.*] What rubbish!

Enter Varya and Yasha

Varya. Yes, mummy, there are two telegrams for you. [*Picking the key out of the bunch and opening the ancient bookcase with a tinkling sound.*] Here they are.

Mme Ranevsky. It's from Paris. [*Tearing up the telegrams, without reading them.*] Paris is done with——

Gayev. Do you know, Lyuba, how old that bookcase is? A week ago I pulled out the bottom drawer, and lo! what do I see? There is a date on it. The case was made precisely a hundred

years ago. Well! Eh? We might as well celebrate its
jubilee. An inanimate object, and yet, come to think of it,
it is a bookcase.

Pischik. [*In surprise.*] A hundred years. . . . You don't say
so! . . .

Gayev. Yes. . . . An object. [*Feeling round the bookcase.*] Our
dear, greatly honoured bookcase! I salute thy existence,
which for over a hundred years now has been directed to
the illuminating ideals of goodness and justice. Thy silent
appeal to fruitful activity has not weakened throughout a
century, upholding [*Through tears.*] in the generations of our
family gallantry, belief in a brighter future, and fostering in
us the ideals of goodness and social consciousness.   [*A pause.*

Lopakhin. Just so. . . .

Mme Ranevsky. You're the same as ever, Lenya.

Gayev. [*A little abashed.*] I pot into the right pocket! into the
middle one!

Lopakhin. [*Consulting his watch.*] Well, I must be off.

Yasha. [*Handing medicine to Mme Ranevsky.*] Perhaps you will
take your pills now——

Pischik. You ought not to take any medicaments, my dearest
lady . . . there's neither harm nor benefit in them. . . .
Let me see them, please. . . . My honoured lady. [*Taking
the pills, dropping them into the palm of his hand, blowing on
them, putting them into his mouth, and washing them down with
some cider.*] There!

Mme Ranevsky. [*In alarm.*] You must be mad!

Pischik. I've taken them all.

Lopakhin. What an appetite!   [*All laugh.*

Feers. The gentleman paid us a visit here in Easter week, and
he ate a whole pailful of cucumbers——   [*Muttering.*

Mme Ranevsky. What's he saying?

Varya. He has been muttering like that for the last three years.
We've got accustomed to it.

Yasha. Senility——

*Charlotta Ivanovna, in a white dress; she is very thin, tightly
corseted, with a lorgnette at her belt; she crosses the stage.*

Lopakhin. Forgive me, Charlotta Ivanovna, I have not had the
chance yet of saying how do you do.
                            [*Attempting to kiss her hand.*

Charlotta. [*Taking away her hand.*] If you were allowed to kiss my hand, you would want to kiss my elbow next, and after that my shoulder——

Lopakhin. I have no luck to-day. [*All laugh.*] Charlotta Ivanovna, show us a trick!

Charlotta. No. I want to go to bed.   [*Goes out.*

Lopakhin. In three weeks I shall see you again. [*Kissing Mme Ranevsky's hand.*] Good-bye. I must go. [*To Gayev.*] *Au revoir.* [*He and Pischik embrace each other.*] *Au revoir.* [*Shakes hands with Varya, then with Feers and Yasha.*] I don't want to go. [*To Mme Ranevsky.*] When you make up your mind about the bungalows, and come to a decision, let me know, please; I'll arrange for a loan of about fifty thousand roubles. Do think of it seriously.

Varya. [*Angrily.*] Do go, do!

Lopakhin. I am going, I'm going . . .   [*Goes out.*

Gayev. The guttersnipe! Oh, forgive the expression. . . . Varya's going to marry him; he's Varya's own young man.

Varya. Don't say more than you need, uncle dear.

Mme Ranevsky. Why, Varya, I should be very glad. He's a good man.

Pischik. He is a man, I must truly say . . . a most worthy man. . . . And my dear Dashenka . . . also says . . . she says all sorts of things. [*Snores, but immediately awakes.*] However, my honoured lady, let me have . . . a loan of 240 roubles . . . to-morrow I must pay interest on a mortgage——

Varya. [*Frightened.*] We have no money, none at all!

Mme Ranevsky. Indeed, I have no money.

Pischik. You'll manage it. [*Laughing.*] I never lose hope. It happened many a time when I thought everything was finished and done for, that I was lost; and then unexpectedly a railway line was to pass across my land, and . . . they paid me. Something else is bound to turn up, if not to-day, then to-morrow. . . . My dear Dashenka may win 200,000 roubles . . . she has a State lottery ticket.

Mme Ranevsky. The coffee is finished, and we can go to bed.

Feers. [*Brushing Gayev down; admonishingly.*] You have put the wrong trousers on again. What am I to do with you?

Varya. [*In a low voice.*] Anya's asleep. [*Softly opening the window.*] The sun has already risen, it is no longer cold. Look, mummy, how marvellous the trees are! Heavens, and the air! The starlings chattering!

Gayev. [*Opening another window.*] The orchard is all white. You haven't forgotten it, Lyuba? That long avenue runs straight —straight as an arrow; it shines on moonlit nights. You do remember? You haven't forgotten?

Mme Ranevsky. [*Looking through the window into the garden.*] Oh, my childhood, my innocence! In this nursery I slept, I looked from here into the orchard, happiness awoke with me each morning and then the orchard was just as it is now; nothing has changed in it. [*Laughing with joy.*] All of it, all white. Oh, my orchard! After the dark rainy autumn and the cold winter, once more you are young, full of happiness, the angels of heaven have not deserted you. . . . If only I could cast the heavy load from my heart and from my shoulders, and if only I could forget my past!

Gayev. Just so, and the orchard will be sold to pay off our debts, odd as it may seem.

Mme Ranevsky. Look, our dead mother's walking in the orchard . . . in a white dress! [*Laughing with joy.*] It's she!

Gayev. Where?

Varya. Please don't, mummy!

Mme Ranevsky. There's no one there, I imagined it. On the right, by the turning to the arbour, a little white tree has bent down, and it looks like a woman.

Enter Trofimov, in a worn-out student's uniform, wearing glasses.

Mme Ranevsky. What a marvellous orchard! White masses of flowers, an azure sky——

Trofimov. Lyubov Andreyevna! [*She glances at him.*] I only want to say how do you do, and I shall be off. [*Kissing her hand ardently.*] I was told to wait until the morning, but my patience gave out—— [*Mme Ranevsky looks perplexed.*

Varya. [*Through tears.*] It is Petya Trofimov——

Trofimov. I'm Petya Trofimov, once tutor of your Grisha. . . . Am I so changed?

[*Mme Ranevsky embraces him and weeps quietly.*

Gayev. [*Embarrassed.*] There, there, Lyuba!

Varya. [*Weeping.*] Didn't I tell you, Petya, to wait till the morning?

Mme Ranevsky. My Grisha . . . my little boy. Grisha . . . my son——

Varya. What can we do, mummy, it was God's will.

Trofimov. [*Tenderly, through tears.*] There, there.

Mme Ranevsky. [*Weeping quietly.*] My boy gone, drowned. Why did it have to happen? Why, my friend? [*In a lower voice.*]

Anya's asleep in there, and I'm talking aloud . . . making a noise. . . . Well, Petya, why have you grown so homely? Why have you grown so old?

Trofimov. In the train a woman called me a peeled-off gent.

Mme Ranevsky. You were quite a boy then, a charming young undergraduate; and now your hair is no longer thick; and those glasses! Are you really still an undergraduate?

[*Going towards the door.*

Trofimov. I shall probably be an eternal undergraduate.

Mme Ranevsky. [*Kissing her brother, then Varya.*] Now, go to bed. . . . You, too, have grown old, Leonid.

Pischik. [*Following her.*] Well, it means bed-time now. . . . Oh, my gout! I'm staying with you. . . . Lyubov Andreyevna, my angel, I do need . . . early in the morning . . . 240 roubles——

Gayev. He goes on harping on it.

Pischik. Two hundred and forty roubles . . . the interest on the mortgage.

Mme Ranevsky. I haven't got any money, my dear man.

Pischik. I'll pay it back, my sweet lady . . . it's a trifling amount.

Mme Ranevsky. Well, all right, Leonid will let you have it. . . . Do give it to him, Leonid.

Gayev. You bet I won't.

Mme Ranevsky. But what can we do? . . . Do let him have it. . . . He's in need of it. . . . He'll pay it back.

[*Mme Ranevsky, Trofimov, Pischik, and Feers go out. Gayev, Varya, and Yasha remain.*

Gayev. My sister has not yet got out of the habit of throwing money away. [*To Yasha.*] Move away a bit, my good man, you smell of hens.

Yasha. [*With a grin.*] Leonid Andreyevitch, you are just the same as ever.

Gayev. Eh? [*To Varya.*] What was it he said?

Varya. [*To Yasha.*] Your mother has come up from the village; she has been waiting for you since yesterday, wanting to see you. . .

Yasha. She'd better leave me alone.

Varya. How shameful!

Yasha. Much do I care. She could come to-morrow just as well. [*Goes out.*

Varya. Mummy is just the same as ever, she has not altered a bit. If she could do what she liked she would give everything away.

Gayev. Just so. . . . [*A pause.*] If a great number of cures are recommended for some disease, that means that the disease is incurable. I am thinking, racking my brains. I have many expedients, very many indeed; but, essentially, it means that I have not got a single one. It would be nice to get a legacy from somebody; it would be nice to marry our Anya to a very rich man; it would be nice to go to Yaroslavl, and to try our luck with our aunt the countess. Our aunt is very, very rich.

Varya. [*Weeping.*] If God would only help.

Gayev. Don't whine. Our aunt is very rich, but she does not like us. In the first place, my sister married a barrister, and not a nobleman. [*Anya appears in the doorway.*] She did not marry a nobleman, and she behaved not too virtuously. She's good, kind, fine, I love her very much, but think of any extenuating circumstance you like, still, it must be admitted, she's immoral. You can feel it in her every movement.

Varya. [*In a whisper.*] Anya's standing in the doorway.

Gayev. Eh? [*A pause.*] Funny, something has got into my right eye . . . I can no longer see so well. And on Thursday, when I attended the assizes——

Anya enters.

Varya. Why aren't you asleep, Anya?

Anya. Sleep won't come. I cannot sleep.

Gayev. My little one! [*Kissing Anya's face and hands.*] My child! . . . [*Through tears.*] You aren't my niece, you are my angel, you are everything to me. Believe me, do. . . .

Anya. I believe you, uncle. Every one is fond of you, every one respects you . . . but, uncle dear, you should keep silent, just keep silent. What were you saying just now about my mother, your sister? What did you say it for?

Gayev. Just so, just so. . . . [*Covering his face with her hand.*] Indeed it is terrible! O God! Lord, help me! And the speech I made to the bookcase . . . so stupid! And it was only when I had finished that I realized it was stupid.

Varya. Really, uncle dear, you ought to keep silent. Keep silent and that's all.

Anya. If you would keep silent, you yourself would feel happier.

Gayev. I am silent. [*Kissing Anya's and Varya's hands.*] I am silent. But just a few words on a matter of business. On Thursday I attended the assizes; a party of us gathered together, we began to talk of one thing and another, all sorts of things, and I believe it might be possible to arrange a loan guaranteed by my friends' I O Us, so as to pay the interest on the mortgage at the bank.

Varya. If only God would help us!

Gayev. On Tuesday I'll go again, I'll talk it over again. . . . [*To Varya.*] Don't whine. . . . [*To Anya.*] Your mother will have a talk with Lopakhin; certainly, he won't refuse her. . . . And you, as soon as you have had a rest, you'll go to Yaroslavl to the countess, your granny. So we shall attack from three sides, and the business is as good as done. The interest will be found, I am convinced. [*Putting a sweet in his mouth.*] On my honour, I swear by anything you like, the estate shall not be sold. [*Agitatedly.*] I swear by my happiness! Here's my hand, call me a base, dishonest man, if I let it come up for auction. On my life, I swear to it!

Anya. [*A peaceful mood has returned to her, she is happy.*] What a good man you are, uncle, how clever you are! [*Embracing her uncle.*] I feel at ease now! I feel at ease! I am happy!

Enter Feers.

Feers. [*Admonishingly.*] Leonid Andreyevitch, for the love of God! Are you ever going to bed?

Gayev. Presently, presently. You may go, Feers. Well, so be it, I'll have to undress myself. Now, children, bye-bye. Particulars will follow to-morrow; and now you go to bed. [*Kissing Anya and Varya.*] I am a man of the eighties. That decade is not much in vogue nowadays, yet I can say, for my convictions I have suffered quite a lot in my life. It is not for nothing that the peasants love me. The peasants are a subject for profound study! One has to know from which side——

Anya. Again, uncle?

Varya. Uncle dear, keep silent!

Feers. [*Angrily.*] Leonid Andreyevitch!

Gayev. I'm coming, I'm coming. . . . You go to bed. From the two sides into the middle! I pot the white! . . .

[*Goes out ; Feers hobbling after him.*

Anya. I feel at ease now. I would rather not go to Yaroslavl, I don't like granny; still I feel at ease. Thanks to uncle.

[*Sitting down.*

Varya. It's time to sleep. I'm going. When you were away there was some fuss here. In the old servants' quarters, as you know, there live our old servants—Efimyoushka, Polya.

Evstigney, and also Karp, of course. They started letting all
sorts of rogues into their quarters for the night. I said
nothing. Then, suddenly, I learn that they have spread a
rumour that I had given orders for them to have no other
food but peas. You see, out of stinginess. . . . And Evstigney was at the bottom of it all. . . . Very well, then. If
it is like that, I say to myself, you just wait. I send for
Evstigney. . . . [*Yawning.*] He comes. . . . How dare you,
Evstigney, I say to him . . . you silly fool . . . [*Glancing
at Anya.*] Anya dear! . . . [*A pause.*] She's fallen asleep.
. . . [*Taking Anya by the arm.*] Come, let's go to bed. . . .
Come! . . . [*Leading her.*] My little angel has fallen asleep!
Come. . . .   [*Both go out.*

> [*From far away, beyond the orchard, is heard a shepherd's
> reed-pipe. Trofimov goes across the stage, and, seeing
> Varya and Anya, stops.*

Varya. Sh-h-h. . . . She's asleep, asleep. Come along, my
darling.

Anya. [*Softly, half asleep.*] I'm so tired . . . the bells are tinkling.
. . . Uncle . . . my own . . . mother and uncle——

Varya. Come along, my darling, come along. . . .
> [*They go into Anya's room.*

Trofimov. [*Deeply moved.*] My bright sun! My spring!

CURTAIN

ACT II

*A field. An old, crooked, tumble-down little chapel ; near it is
a well ; large stones, which once upon a time were evidently
tombstones ; and an old bench. The road can be seen leading
to Gayev's manor-house. On one side, on a slight rise, there
are poplars darkening : it is there that the cherry orchard
begins. In the distance a row of telegraph poles ; and far,
far away on the horizon there can just be discerned a big town,
visible only in very fine, clear weather. The sun will set soon.
Charlotta, Yasha, and Dounyasha are sitting on the bench ;
Yepikhodov is standing near by and playing the guitar ; all
the others are sitting, pensive. Charlotta wears a man's old
cap ; she has taken a gun from her shoulders and is fixing the
buckle on the strap.*

Charlotta. [*Pensively.*] I haven't got a proper passport, I do not know how old I am, and it seems to me all the time that I am as it were quite a young girl. When I was a little girl, my father and mother used to go to fairs and perform, very well, too. And I used to do *salto mortale* and all sorts of tricks. And when father and mother died, a German lady took me into her house and began to teach me. Very well. I grew up, then I became a governess. But where I come from and who I am, I do not know . . . nor who my parents were, maybe they were not properly married . . . I do not know. [*Taking a cucumber out of her pocket and eating it.*] I don't know anything. [*A pause.*] Sometimes I long to have a good talk, but haven't any one to talk to. . . . I have nobody.

Yepikhodov. [*Playing the guitar and singing.*] 'What's grand society to me, what do I care for friend and foe . . .' How delightful it is playing the mandoline!

Dounyasha. Yours is a guitar, not a mandoline.

[*Looking at herself in a little mirror and powdering her face.*

Yepikhodov. To a man madly in love, it is a mandoline. . . . [*Humming.*] 'Were out my heart warmed by the flame of mutual love . . .'

[*Yasha hums in accompaniment.*

Charlotta. How awful, the way these men sing. . . . Ugh! Like jackals.

Dounyasha. [*To Yasha.*] What good fortune to travel abroad!

Yasha. Yes, of course. I cannot but agree with you.

[*Yawning, then lighting a cigar.*

Yepikhodov. Quite clear. Abroad everything has already long ago been in full attainment.

Yasha. Just so.

Yepikhodov. I am a well-read man, I read various remarkable books, but I cannot possibly understand the direction of what I really wish—should I live or should I shoot myself, so to say—yet nevertheless I always have a revolver on me. . . . Here is is! [*Showing the revolver.*

Charlotta. I've finished it. Now I shall go. [*Putting on the gun.*] You, Yepikhodov, are a very clever man and very alarming. Women are sure to fall madly in love with you. Brrr! [*Going.*] These clever people are all so very stupid, there's no one I could have a talk with . . . I am all alone, alone. I have no one, and . . . and who I am, what I am for, no one can say. . . . [*Goes away unhurriedly.*

Yepikhodov. Properly speaking, without touching on other matters, I must express myself as regards myself, by the way, that fate treats me without pity, as a storm does a small vessel. If, let us suppose, I am mistaken, then why this morning when I awake, to take an instance, do I suddenly see there is on my chest a spider of terrifying size. . . . Like that. [*Showing with both hands.*] Or when I happen to get out some cider to have a drink, there, behold, there's in it something in the highest degree indecent, something like a black-beetle. [*A pause.*] Have you read the English author Buckle? [*A pause.*] I wish to trouble you, Avdotya Fyodorovna, with a few words.

Dounyasha. Go on.

Yepikhodov. I should wish to say it to you alone.   [*Sighing.*

Dounyasha. [*Embarrassed.*] All right . . . but won't you fetch me my jacket first? . . . It's by the cupboard. . . . It's a bit damp here——

Yepikhodov. Very well. . . . I will fetch it. . . . Now I know what to do with my revolver. . . .

[*Takes his guitar and goes away, playing softly.*

Yasha. Twenty-two miseries! He is a stupid chap, between ourselves.   [*Yawning.*

Dounyasha. God forbid that he should shoot himself. [*A pause.*] I have become so anxious. I keep on worrying all the time. I was a little girl when I was taken into our masters' service, and now I have got out of the ways of ordinary people, and my hands are perfectly white like a young lady's. I've become sensitive, so refined, ladylike, I'm scared of everything . . . just terrified. And if you, Yasha, deceive me, I don't know what's to become of my nerves.

Yasha. [*Kissing her.*] My peach! Of course, every girl must remember herself, but above all I hate a girl to be careless.

Dounyasha. I've fallen passionately in love with you, you are educated, you can talk about everything.   [*A pause.*

Yasha. [*Yawning.*] Just so. . . . My opinion is like this: if a girl is in love, that means that she is immoral. [*A pause.*] It is pleasant to smoke a cigar in the open air. . . . [*Listening.*] People are coming here. . . . It is the masters.

[*Dounyasha embraces him impulsively.*

Yasha. Go into the house, as though you had gone to the river to bathe, take that path, otherwise you will meet them, and they might suspect me of having had an assignation with you. I should hate that.

Dounyasha. [*With a little cough.*] Your cigar has given me a headache. . . .   [*Goes off.*

> *Yasha is left alone, sitting near the chapel. Enter Mme Ranevsky, Gayev, and Lopakhin.*

Lopakhin. You must decide once and for all—time won't stand still. The problem, surely, is quite a trifling one. Do you agree to let the land for building bungalows, or not? Answer one word: yes, or no? Only one word.

Mme Ranevsky. Who is smoking disgusting cigars here? . . .
                                                      [*Sitting down.*

Gayev. Now they have brought the railway line near us it is of some use. [*Sitting down.*] We took the train to town and had lunch. . . . I pot the yellow in the middle! I should like to go to the house first, to have just one game!——

Mme Ranevsky. You will have time enough.

Lopakhin. Only one word! [*Imploringly.*] Do give me an answer!

Gayev. [*Yawning.*] Eh?

Mme Ranevsky. [*Looking into her purse.*] Yesterday there was a lot of money in it, but to-day there's very little. My poor Varya, in order to economize, feeds us all on milk soup, the old servants in the kitchen are given nothing but peas, and I squander money just stupidly. . . . [*She drops her purse, and scatters gold coins.*] All fall down. . . .   [*She is vexed.*

Yasha. If I may, I 'll pick them up at once. [*Picking up the coins.*

Mme Ranevsky. Please do, Yasha. And why did I go to town for lunch? . . . Your nasty restaurant with its orchestra, the table-cloth smelling of soap. . . . Why drink so much, Lenya? Why eat such a lot? Why talk so much? To-day in the restaurant you talked too much again, and at random. About the significance of the seventies, about the decadent movement. And to whom? Talking to waiters about the decadent movement!

Lopakhin. Just so.

Gayev. [*Waving his hand.*] I am incorrigible, that is obvious. . . . [*Irritably, to Yasha.*] Why must you always be there in front of me? . . .

Yasha. [*Laughing.*] I cannot listen to your voice without laughing.

Gayev. [*To his sister.*] Either I, or he——

Mme Ranevsky. Go away, Yasha, get out. . . .

Yasha. [*Handing Mme Ranevsky her purse.*] I am going. [*With difficulty suppressing his laughter.*] At once. . . .   [*Goes off.*

Lopakhin. That rich man Deriganov intends to buy your estate. They say that he, in person, is coming to the sale.

Mme Ranevsky. Where did you hear that from?

Lopakhin. They are talking about it in town.

Gayev. Our aunt in Yaroslavl has promised to send us something, but when and how much she's going to send, we don't know.

Lopakhin. How much would she send? A hundred thousand? Two?

Mme Ranevsky. Come! . . . Ten or fifteen thousand, if that.

Lopakhin. Forgive me, but such scatter-brained people as you two are, so unbusinesslike, so strange, I have never met. You are told in plain Russian: Your estate is to be sold by auction, and you behave as though you don't understand it.

Mme Ranevsky. But what can we do? Tell us what to do.

Lopakhin. I tell you every day. Every day I keep on saying one and the same thing. Both the cherry orchard and the land must be leased for building bungalows, and this must be done immediately, as quickly as possible—an auction is hanging over you. Do realize it! If you definitely decide that there shall be bungalows, you will get any amount you like, and then you are saved.

Mme Ranevsky. Bungalows and bungalow-dwellers—it's so banal. Forgive me for saying so.

Gayev. I quite agree with you.

Lopakhin. I shall either burst into tears, or scream, or faint. There's nothing to be done! You have worn me out! [*To Gayev.*] You are an old woman!

Gayev. Eh?

Lopakhin. Old woman!   [*Making as if to go.*

Mme Ranevsky. [*Alarmed.*] No, don't go away; stay here, my good friend. I beg of you. Perhaps we shall devise some way out.

Lopakhin. What is there to devise?

Mme Ranevsky. Don't go away! I beg you. After all, with you here it's more cheerful. . . . [*A pause.*] I am waiting for something all the time, as though the house were going to fall down on our heads.

Gayev. [*Deep in thought.*] I double into the pocket! I pot into the middle! . . .

Mme Ranevsky. We stand condemned for our many sins. . . .

Lopakhin. Surely you have no sins. . . .

Gayev. [*Putting a sweet into his mouth.*] They say that I have spent all my fortune on sweets. . . .

Mme Ranevsky. Oh, my sins! . . . I have always squandered money without restraint, like a lunatic, and I married a man who made nothing but debts. My husband died of champagne—he drank terribly—and as bad luck would have it I fell in love with another man, had an affair with him, and precisely at that time—that was my first punishment, a knock-down blow—just here, in the river . . . my little boy was drowned; and I left for abroad, I left for good so as never to come back, never to see that river. . . . I shut my eyes, I ran, without thinking, and *he* followed me . . . ruthlessly, brutally. . . . I bought a villa near Mentone, for *he* had fallen ill there, and for three years I knew no rest day or night; the sick man wore me out, my soul withered. And last year, when the villa was sold to pay off the debts, I went to Paris, and there he fleeced me, threw me over, had an affair with another woman; I tried to poison myself . . . so stupid, so shameful. . . . And suddenly I felt a longing for Russia, for my native land, for my little daughter. . . . [*Wiping her tears*.] Lord, Lord, be merciful, forgive me my sins! Punish me no more. [*Getting a telegram out of her pocket*.] Got this from Paris to-day . . . asking forgiveness, imploring me to return. . . . [*Tearing up the telegram*.] I seem to hear music being played somewhere. [*Listening*.

Gayev. It is our famous Jewish orchestra. You remember, four violins, a flute, and double bass.

Mme Ranevsky. Does it still exist? We ought to have them here some time, and give a party.

Lopakhin. [*Listening*.] I cannot hear. . . . [*Humming softly*.] 'For ready cash a German will turn any Russian into a Frenchman.' [*Laughing*.] I saw such a funny play at the theatre yesterday.

Mme Ranevsky. And most likely there was nothing funny in it. It is not plays you should go to look at, but look at yourselves a little more often. How grey your lives are! what a lot of useless talk there is going on!

Lopakhin. That is true. I must say frankly, the way we live is stupid. . . . [*A pause*.] My father was a peasant, an idiot, he understood nothing, did not teach me anything, he only beat me, in his drunken fits, and always with a stick. Fundamentally, I am as big a blockhead and idiot as he was. I taught myself nothing, my handwriting is shocking, I write so that I am ashamed for people to see it, just like a pig.

Mme Ranevsky. You ought to marry, my friend.

Lopakhin. Yes . . . it's true.

Mme Ranevsky. Marry our Varya. She's a nice girl.

Lopakhin. Yes.

Mme Ranevsky. She's good and simple, she works all day long; but the chief thing is that she loves you. You, too, seem to have cared for her for a long time now.

Lopakhin. Well, I have no objection. . . . She's a good girl.
[*A pause.*

Gayev. I have been offered a post at the bank. Six thousand roubles a year. . . . What do you say?

Mme Ranevsky. No good! You are better off as you are. . . .

Enter Feers ; he has brought an overcoat.

Feers. [*To Gayev.*] Here it is, sir; put it on, it's damp.

Gayev. [*Putting on the overcoat.*] You are a nuisance, old man.

Feers. That's all right. . . . You went off in the morning without telling me.   [*Looking him over.*

Mme Ranevsky. How very old you have grown, Feers!

Feers. What did you say?

Lopakhin. They say you have grown very old!

Feers. I have lived a long time. They were arranging for me to get married when your father was not yet born. [*Laughing.*] And when the liberation of the serfs was proclaimed, I was head valet de chambre. So I did not take my freedom, I remained with my masters. . . . [*A pause.*] And I remember, one and all were glad, and what there was to be glad about they themselves did not know.

Lopakhin. Those were the good days. At any rate, they flogged soundly.

Feers. [*Not having heard.*] Rather! The peasants stuck to the masters, the masters stuck to the peasants, and now they are all divided; you can't make it out.

Gayev. Keep quiet for a minute, Feers. To-morrow I have to go to town. I have been promised an introduction to a general, who might lend us money against an I O U.

Lopakhin. Nothing will come of it. Nor will you succeed in paying the interest, you can rest assured.

Mme Ranevsky. He's imagining it. His generals don't exist.

Enter Trofimov, Anya, and Varya.

Gayev. Here are our young people.

Anya. Mother is sitting down.

Mme Ranevsky. [*Tenderly.*] Come along, come. . . . My precious

ones. . . . [*Embracing Anya and Varya.*] If the two of you
knew how I love you. Sit side by side, like this.

[*All sit down.*

Lopakhin. Our eternal undergraduate is always walking about
with young ladies.

Trofimov. Mind your own business.

Lopakhin. He'll be fifty soon, and still an undergraduate.

Trofimov. Stop your silly jokes.

Lopakhin. Why are you cross, you queer chap?

Trofimov. Don't bother me!

Lopakhin. [*Laughing.*] Allow me to ask you what's your idea
of me.

Trofimov. My idea of you, Yermolay Alexeyevitch, is this: you
are a rich man, and soon you will be a millionaire. Well, just
as, in the metabolic sense, there's need for a beast of prey
which devours everything that crosses its path, likewise you,
too, are needed.   [*All laugh.*

Varya. You had better tell us all about the planets, Petya.

Mme Ranevsky. No, do let us go on with our conversation of
yesterday.

Trofimov. What about?

Gayev. About the proud man.

Trofimov. Yesterday we talked a long time, but came to no
conclusion. In the proud man, in your sense, there's something mystical. Perhaps you are right in your own way; but,
to put the matter plainly, using no tricks, what damned pride
is there, or is there any sense in it, if man is physiologically
jerry-built; if man, the overwhelming majority, is coarse,
unintelligent, profoundly wretched? We ought to stop admiring ourselves. We ought only to work.

Gayev. All the same, one will die.

Trofimov. Who can tell? And what do you mean, one will die?
Perhaps man has a hundred senses, and at death only the five
familiar to us perish, and the other ninety-five go on living.

Mme Ranevsky. How clever you are, Petya!

Lopakhin. [*Ironically.*] Terrific!

Trofimov. Humanity goes forward, perfecting its powers. All
that it cannot achieve now will at some time become familiar,
comprehensible, only we must work, with all our strength; we
must help those who are seeking after the truth. With us, in
Russia, so far only a few are at work. The vast majority of
the intelligentsia whom I know are seeking after nothing,
doing nothing, and as yet incapable of work. They call them-

selves intelligentsia, but they 'thou' their servants, treat the peasants like cattle, they study badly, they read nothing seriously, do nothing at all, they only babble of the sciences, of art they understand little. All of them look serious, all of them have severe faces, all speak only of important matters, all theorize, and yet the great majority of us, ninety-nine out of a hundred, live like savages, on the least provocation a punch on the jaw, swearing; people eat disgustingly, sleep in filth, in stuffy rooms, there are bugs everywhere, stench, damp, moral untidiness. . . . And, apparently, all the fine talk people indulge in is only meant to hoodwink ourselves and others. Show me, where are the crèches that are so often and so much talked about, where are the libraries? The crèches and libraries exist only in our novels; in reality they don't exist at all. There's only dirt, banality, and barbarism. . . . I am afraid of too serious countenances and I do not like them; I am afraid of serious talks. Let us rather keep silent.

Lopakhin. Do you know, I get up soon after four in the morning, and I am at work from morning to night; well, I always have my own and other people's money to look after, and I see what the people around me are like. One has only to start doing something to realize how few honest, decent people there are. Sometimes, when I cannot sleep, I think: 'Lord, Thou gavest us huge forests, immeasurable lands, boundless horizons, and, living amidst it all, we ourselves ought truly to be giants. . . .'

Mme Ranevsky. You want giants. . . . They are all right in fairy-tales, but out of fairy-tales they are a horror.

[*Yepikhodov passes across the back of the stage, playing the guitar.*

Mme Ranevsky. [*Pensively.*] There goes Yepikhodov.

Anya. [*Pensively.*] There goes Yepikhodov.

Gayev. The sun has set.

Trofimov. Just so.

Gayev. [*In a low voice, as though declaiming.*] O wondrous Nature, thou shinest with everlasting radiance; thou art fair and unheeding; thou, whom men call mother, unitest in thyself life and death; thou givest life and destroyest——

Varya. [*Imploringly.*] Uncle dear!

Anya. Uncle, at it again!

Trofimov. You'd better double the yellow into the middle pocket.

Gayev. I am silent, I am.

> [*All sit pensive. Stillness. Only Feers's quiet muttering is heard. Suddenly there is heard a far-away sound, as though out of the sky, the sound of a snapped string, dying away, mournful.*

Mme Ranevsky. What is that?

Lopakhin. I don't know. Somewhere, far away in the shafts of a mine, a bucket has broken loose. But it must be very far away.

Gayev. Perhaps it is a bird. A heron.

Trofimov. Or a brown owl. . . .

Mme Ranevsky. [*With a shudder.*] I feel somehow uneasy.

> [*A pause.*

Feers. Before the troubles the same thing happened: an owl screeched, and the samovar hooted without stopping.

Gayev. Before what troubles?

Feers. Before the liberation. [*A pause.*

Mme Ranevsky. Well, good people, let us go, it's getting dark. [*To Anya.*] Tears in your eyes? . . . What's the matter, my dear little girl? [*Embracing her.*

Anya. There's nothing the matter, mother. Nothing at all.

Trofimov. Someone is coming.

> [*A stranger appears in a shabby white peaked cap and an overcoat ; he is tipsy.*

The Stranger. Pardon me. May I pass through here along to the railway station?

Gayev. You may. Go along that road.

The Stranger. I am most respectfully obliged to you. [*Emitting a cough.*] The weather is grand. . . . [*Reciting.*] 'Brother mine, my long-suffering brother. . . . All over the Volga, nothing but my brother's groans. . . .' [*To Varya.*] Mademoiselle! Spare some coppers to feed a famished Russian.

> [*Varya, frightened, shrieks.*

Lopakhin. [*Angrily.*] Even a beggar should know how to behave.

Mme Ranevsky. [*Rather frightened.*] Take this. Here. . . . [*Looking for a coin in her purse.*] No silver. . . . I can't help it, here's a gold coin for you. . . .

The Stranger. I am most respectfully obliged to you.

> [*He goes off. General laughter.*

Varya. [*Frightened.*] I'd better go—I'd better go. . . . Oh, mummy, the folks at home have nothing to eat, and you gave him a gold coin.

Mme Ranevsky. What can you do with me, silly creature that

I am? At home I'll hand you all I have. Yermolay
Alexeyevitch, you will give me one more loan! . . .

Lopakhin. At your service.

Mme Ranevsky. Come, good people, it's time. Oh, Varya, just
before you came we arranged about your betrothal; congratulations!

Varya. [*Through tears.*] Mother, this is not a thing to joke about.

Lopakhin. 'Ophelia, get thee to a nunnery. . . .'

Gayev. My hands are trembling: I haven't had a game of
billiards for a long time.

Lopakhin. 'Ophelia! nymph, in thy orisons be all my sins
remember'd!'

Mme Ranevsky. Come. It's almost time for supper.

Varya. That man frightened me. My heart is simply pounding.

Lopakhin. Let me remind you, my friends: on the twenty-second
of August the cherry orchard is to be sold. Think of it! . . .
Do think of it! . . .

[*All go off, except Trofimov and Anya.*

Anya. [*Laughing.*] Thanks to the stranger for having frightened
Varya; now we are by ourselves.

Trofimov. Varya is afraid of our suddenly falling in love with
each other; for days and days she would never leave us alone.
With her narrow outlook she cannot understand that we are
above love. To rid ourselves of the petty and the illusory
things that prevent men from being free and happy—that is
the purpose and meaning of our life. Forward! We are
progressing irresistibly towards the bright star that glows in
the distance! Forward! Don't lag behind, comrades!

Anya. [*Clapping her hands.*] How well you speak! [*A pause.*]
To-day it is marvellous here.

Trofimov. Yes, the weather is wonderful.

Anya. What have you done to me, Petya, that I no longer love
the cherry orchard as I used to? I loved it so dearly, it
seemed to me there was no finer place on earth than our
orchard.

Trofimov. The whole of Russia is our orchard. The land is
great and beautiful, there are many wonderful places in it.
[*A pause.*] Now think, Anya: your grandfather, your great-
grandfather, and all your ancestors were serf-owners, pro-
prietors of living souls. Don't you see that from every cherry
in the orchard, from every leaf, from every trunk, human beings
are looking at you; can't you hear their voices? . . . Oh, it
is dreadful, your orchard is terrible, and when of an evening

or at night I walk in it, the old bark on the trees glows dimly and the cherry trees seem to see in their sleep what happened a hundred, two hundred years ago, and sombre visions visit them. Why say more? We have lagged behind, we are at least two hundred years behind, we have not yet achieved anything at all, we have no definite attitude towards the past, we do nothing but theorize, complain of nostalgia, or drink vodka. Indeed, it is so obvious: in order to start to live in the present, we must first of all redeem our past, have done with it, and its redemption can be achieved only through suffering, only through tremendous, incessant labour. Do realize it, Anya.

Anya. The house in which we live is ours no longer, and I shall go away, I give you my word.

Trofimov. If you have the housekeeping keys throw them into the well, and go away. Be free as the wind!

Anya. [*Rapturously.*] How well you put it!

Trofimov. Believe me, Anya, do! I am not thirty yet, I am young, I am still an undergraduate, but I have already been through so much! When winter comes, I am hungry, ill, worried, poor, like a beggar—and the places fate drove me to, there's no spot I haven't been to! And yet my soul always, at any moment of the day or night, was full of inexplicable anticipations. I anticipate happiness, Anya, I experience it already.

Anya. [*Thoughtfully.*] The moon is rising.

[*Yepikhodov is heard playing on the guitar the same melancholy song. The moon is rising. Somewhere near the poplars Varya is looking for Anya and calling:* 'Anya! Where are you?']

Trofimov. Yes, the moon is rising. [*A pause.*] Happiness, it is here, it is coming nearer and nearer, I already hear its footsteps. And should we not see it, should we never come to know it, what matter! Others will experience it!

Varya's Voice. Anya! Where are you?

Trofimov. Varya, again! [*Angrily.*] Disgusting!

Anya. Shan't we go down to the river? It's nice there.

Trofimov. Yes, let us go. [*They go off*

Varya's Voice. Anya! Anya!

CURTAIN

ACT III

*The drawing-room, separated by an arch from the hall. The chan-
delier is lit. In the vestibule the Jewish orchestra, mentioned
in Act II, is playing. It is evening. In the hall they are
dancing a 'grand rond.' The voice of Simeonov-Pischik:
'Promenade à une paire!' They come into the drawing-
room: the first couple, Pischik and Charlotta Ivanovna; the
second, Trofimov and Mme Ranevsky; the third, Anya and
the Post Office Clerk; the fourth, Varya and the Station-master;
and so forth. Varya is crying quietly, and as she dances she
wipes her tears. In the last couple is Dounyasha. They
move about in the drawing-room, Pischik shouting: 'Grand
rond, balancez!' and 'Les cavaliers à genoux et remerciez
vos dames!'*

*Feers, in a tail-coat, brings in soda-water on a tray. Pischik
and Trofimov come into the drawing-room.*

Pischik. I am full-blooded. I've already had two strokes, and
I find dancing difficult; but, as the saying goes, if you get
into the pack, you can bark or not, but you must wag your
tail. I am as strong as a horse. My late father, funny
joker that he was, may he rest in peace, as regards our origin
put it like this: that the ancient breed of all the Simeonov-
Pischiks came from the very horse that Caligula made a
senator of. . . . [*Sitting down.*] But here's the rub: I have
no money! A hungry dog believes in nothing but meat. . . .
[*Letting out a snore, but waking instantly.*] And so it is in my
case. . . . I can speak of nothing but money. . . .

Trofimov. There is certainly something of the horse in your
figure.

Pischik. Well . . . a horse is a fine animal . . . one can get
money for a horse. . . .

[*There is heard the sound of billiards being played in the next
room. In the hall, under the arch, Varya appears.*

Trofimov. [*Teasing her.*] Madame Lopakhin! Madame Lopakhin!

Varya. [*Crossly.*] Peeled-off gent!

Trofimov. Yes, I am a peeled-off gent, and proud of it!

Varya. [*Reflecting bitterly.*] The musicians have been engaged,
but where's the money to pay them?   [*Goes off.*

Trofimov. [*To Pischik.*] Had the energy, which throughout all
your life you have spent in searching for money to pay the

interest on your mortgages—had that energy gone into something different, then, probably, at the end of it all, you might have moved the earth.

Pischik. Nietzsche . . . the philosopher . . . the greatest, most renowned, a man of astonishing wisdom, says in his works that one may, as it were, make counterfeit money.

Trofimov. Have you read Nietzsche?

Pischik. Not likely . . . my Dashenka told me. And I am at present in such a state that there's nothing left for me to do but make counterfeit money. . . . The day after to-morrow I have to pay 310 roubles. . . . I've already managed to find 130. . . . [*Feeling his pockets in alarm.*] The money's gone! I have lost the money! [*Through tears.*] Where can it be? . . . [*Joyfully.*] Here it is, under the lining. . . . I broke out in a sweat! . . .

Enter Mme Ranevsky and Charlotta Ivanovna.

Mme Ranevsky. [*Humming the tune of the Caucasian dance, the 'Lezguinka.'*] Why is Leonid so late? What can he be doing in town? Dounyasha, offer the musicians some tea.

Trofimov. Most likely the auction has not taken place.

Mme Ranevsky. The musicians came at the wrong moment, and the party was arranged at the wrong time, too. . . . Well, no matter. . . .   [*Sitting down and humming softly.*

Charlotta. [*Handing a pack of cards to Pischik.*] Here's a pack of cards. Think of a card.

Pischik. I've thought of one.

Charlotta. Now shuffle the cards. Very good. Hand them to me, my sweet Sir Pischik. Ein, zwei, drei! Now look for it—it's in your breast pocket.

Pischik. [*Getting the card out of his breast pocket.*] The eight of spades! It's perfectly true! [*In surprise.*] You don't say so!

Charlotta. [*Holding a pack of cards in the palm of her hand. To Trofimov.*] Say quickly which is the card on top?

Trofimov. Why? Well—the queen of spades!

Charlotta. It is the very one. [*To Pischik.*] Which card is on top?

Pischik. The ace of hearts!

Charlotta. The very one. . . . [*She strikes the palm of her hand, the pack of cards disappears.*] What beautiful weather we are having to-day! [*A mysterious feminine voice answers her, coming as though from under the floor :* 'Oh, yes, the weather is superb, madam!'] You are just my ideal. . . . [*The voice :* 'Madam, I fell for you at once, too.']

The Station-master. [*Applauding.*] Bravo, the lady ventrilo quist!

Pischik. [*In surprise.*] Think of it! Loveliest Charlotta Ivanovna. . . . I've quite fallen in love with you.

Charlotta. Fallen in love? [*Shrugging her shoulders.*] Can you love? Guter Mensch, aber schlechter Musikant.

Trofimov. [*Clapping Pischik on the shoulder.*] What a horse you are. . . .

Charlotta. Attention, please! One more trick! [*Taking a rug from the chair.*] Here's a fine rug, I wish to sell it. . . . [*Shaking it.*] Any one wishing to buy it?

Pischik. [*In surprise.*] You don't say so!

Charlotta. Ein, zwei, drei!

    [*She quickly lifts up the lowered rug; behind it stands Anya; she makes a curtsy, runs up to her mother, embraces her, and runs back into the hall, amid general excitement.*

Mme Ranevsky. [*Applauding.*] Bravo! Bravo! . . .

Charlotta. One more! Ein, zwei, drei!

    [*She lifts up the rug; behind it stands Varya, bowing.*

Pischik. [*In wonder.*] You don't say so! . . .

Charlotta. That's the end!

    [*She flings the rug at Pischik, makes a curtsy, and runs off into the hall.*

Pischik. [*Hastening after her.*] The rogue! What a rogue!

    [*Goes out.*

Mme Ranevsky. And Leonid has not come yet. What's he doing in town so long? I cannot make it out! Everything surely must be finished there, either the estate is sold, or the auction has not taken place at all—then why keep us in the dark so long?

Varya. [*Trying to comfort her.*] Dear uncle must have bought it, I am sure of it.

Trofimov. [*Derisively.*] Just so!

Varya. Granny sent him a power of attorney to buy the estate in her name with the transfer of the debts. It is her way of helping Anya. And I am sure God will help us and dear uncle will buy it.

Mme Ranevsky. Granny from Yaroslavl sent fifteen thousand to buy the estate in her name—us she does not trust—but that sum would not be enough even to pay the interest. [*Covering her face with her hands.*] To-day my fate is being decided, my fate. . . .

Trofimov. [*Teasing Varya.*] Madame Lopakhin!

Varya. [*Angrily.*] Eternal undergraduate! Twice sent down from the university!

Mme Ranevsky. Why are you cross, Varya? He's teasing you about Lopakhin—why, what of it? If you want to marry Lopakhin—he's a good, interesting man. If you don't want to—don't marry him: nobody forces you, my dear. . . .

Varya. I regard this matter seriously, mummy—I must say it straight out. He's a good man, I like him.

Mme Ranevsky. Marry him, then. What's the good of waiting? I can't understand!

Varya. But surely, mummy, I cannot propose to him myself. For two years now every one has been talking to me about him, every one talks, but he is silent, or laughs it off. I understand. He's getting richer and richer, he's absorbed in his work, he has no time to think of me. If I had some money, no matter how little, no matter if it were only a hundred roubles, I would leave everything, I would go far away. I would go into a convent.

Trofimov. Pure grace!

Varya. [*To Trofimov.*] A student should understand! [*In a gentle voice, tearfully.*] How homely you have grown, Petya, how old you have grown! [*To Mme Ranevsky, no longer crying.*] Only I cannot sit doing nothing, mummy. Every minute I must be up and doing.

Enter Yasha.

Yasha. [*Hardly able to suppress his laughter.*] Yepikhodov has smashed the billiard cue! . . . [*Goes out.*

Varya. What business has Yepikhodov to be there? Who allowed him to play billiards? I can't understand these people. [*Goes off.*

Mme Ranevsky. You mustn't tease her, Petya; you can see she's worried enough without that.

Trofimov. She's much too zealous, interfering in things that don't concern her. All through the summer she never left me and Anya alone, afraid of our falling in love. It is not her business, is it? And besides, I have not shown any sign of it, I am so far removed from such banality. We are above love!

Mme Ranevsky. And I, I take it, am beneath love. [*In great agitation.*] Why does not Leonid come? Just to know: has the estate been sold, or not? The disaster seems to me so utterly incredible that I simply don't know what to think,

I am losing my head. . . . I 'm quite capable just now of screaming and doing something silly. Save me, Petya. Say something, speak. . . .

Trofimov. Whether the estate has been sold to-day or not—does it really matter? It came to an end long ago; there 's no turning back, the path is obliterated. Be calm, my dear. One should not deceive oneself, one should at any rate once in one's life look straight into the eyes of truth.

Mme Ranevsky. What truth? You see where the truth is and where the untruth, and I am as if I had lost my sight, I see nothing. You solve all the important problems bravely; but tell me, my dear boy, is it not because you are young, because you have not yet had time to live through even a single one of your problems? You look bravely ahead, but is not this the reason: that you neither see nor expect anything terrible, that life is still hidden from your young eyes? You are braver, more honest, more profound than we are; but do try to understand, be a tiny bit magnanimous, do spare my feelings. I was born here; here lived my father and mother, and my grandfather. I love this house, without the cherry orchard I cannot imagine life; if selling it is so essential, then sell me, too, along with the orchard. . . . [*Embracing Trofimov, kissing him on the forehead.*] And my son was drowned here. . . . [*Weeping.*] Have pity on me, my good, kind friend.

Trofimov. You know that I sympathize with all my soul.

Mme Ranevsky. But you should say it differently, somehow differently. . . . [*Takes out her handkerchief; a telegram falls on the floor.*] To-day I feel such a heavy weight on my heart, you can't imagine. It 's too noisy for me here, my soul trembles at every sound, I am all trembling, and I dare not go into my room; alone, in the stillness, I am afraid. . . . Don't condemn me, Petya. . . . I love you as one of my own people. I would willingly let you marry Anya, I swear it; but, my dear, you must study, you must take your degree. You do nothing, fate tosses you from one place to another; that 's so queer. . . . Isn't it so? You agree? And something ought to be done about your beard to make it grow somehow. . . . [*Laughing.*] You are a funny fellow!

Trofimov. [*Picking up the telegram.*] I have no desire to look a dandy.

Mme Ranevsky. That telegram is from Paris. I get them every day. Yesterday and to-day. That wild man has fallen ill again; he's in a hole again. . . . He asks my forgiveness, imploring me to come to him, and truly I ought to go to Paris, to be near him. Your face looks stern, Petya, but what can I do, my dear, what can I do? He is ill, he is lonely, unhappy, and who is there to look after him, who will keep him from mistakes, who will give him his medicine at the right time? And what's the use of hiding or keeping silent? —I love him, that's clear. I do love him, I do. . . . It's a millstone round my neck, I am sinking with it to the very bottom; but I love that stone, and I cannot live without it. [*Pressing Trofimov's hand.*] Don't think hardly, Petya, don't say anything to me, say nothing. . . .

Trofimov. [*Through tears.*] Forgive my frankness, for the love of God; but he has fleeced you!

Mme Ranevsky. No, no, no, you must not say such things! . . .
[*Covering her ears.*

Trofimov. But he's a blackguard, you alone don't realize it! He's a pretty blackguard, a nonentity. . . .

Mme Ranevsky. [*In anger, but restraining herself.*] You're twenty-six or twenty-seven, but you're still a schoolboy in the second form.

Trofimov. All right!

Mme Ranevsky. You should be a man; at your age you should understand those who love. And you yourself should love . . . you should be falling in love! [*Angrily.*] Yes, you should! And there is no purity in you, you are just a prude, a ridiculous freak, a monster. . . .

Trofimov. [*In horror.*] What is she saying?

Mme Ranevsky. 'I am above love!' You are not above love, but simply, as our Feers puts it, a *nyedotyopa*. At your age not to have a mistress! . . .

Trofimov. [*In horror.*] It's terrible! What is she saying? [*Going quickly to the hall, clutching his head.*] It's terrible! . . . I can't, I am going for good. . . . [*Goes out, but returns immediately.*] All is over between us!
[*Goes into the vestibule.*

Mme Ranevsky. [*Shouting after him.*] Petya, wait! You funny boy, I said it all in fun! Petya!
[*In the vestibule someone can be heard running quickly up the staircase, and suddenly falling down with a crash. Anya and Varya cry out, but immediately laughter is heard.*

Mme Ranevsky. What has happened?

Anya comes running in.

Anya. [*Laughing.*] Petya has fallen down the staircase!

[*Runs away.*

Mme Ranevsky. What a funny boy Petya is!

[*The Station-master stops in the middle of the hall, and recites Alexey Tolstoy's poem, 'She who sinned.' They listen to him, but no sooner has he recited a few lines than the strains of a waltz are heard and the recital is broken off. All dance. Enter from the vestibule: Trofimov, Anya, Varya, and Mme Ranevsky.*

Mme Ranevsky. Now, Petya. . . . Now, pure soul. . . . I beg your forgiveness. . . . Come, let us dance. . . .

[*She dances with Petya.*

Anya and Varya dance. Feers enters and puts his stick by the side door. Yasha, too, comes in from the drawing-room, and watches the dancing.

Yasha. Well, grandpa!

Feers. I am a bit off colour. In the old days generals, barons, admirals danced at our parties, and now we invite the post office clerk and the station-master, and even they are none too willing to come. I have got weaker somehow. The old master, the grandfather, treated every one with sealing-wax for all complaints. I've been taking sealing-wax every day now these last twenty years, or perhaps more; maybe it is because of that that I am alive.

Yasha. I am sick of you, grandpapa! [*Yawning.*] I wish you would die and be done with it.

Feers. Eh? you . . . *nyedotyopa!*   [*Muttering.*

[*Trofimov and Mme Ranevsky dance in the hall, and then in the drawing-room.*

Mme Ranevsky. Merci. I'll sit down. . . . [*Sitting down.*] I'm tired.

Enter Anya.

Anya. [*In agitation.*] A stranger in the kitchen has just said that the cherry orchard was sold to-day.

Mme Ranevsky. To whom?

Anya. He did not say. He's gone.

[*She dances with Trofimov; they pass into the hall.*

Yasha. An old man just babbling. A stranger, too.

Feers. And Leonid Andreyevitch is still not here, he has not come yet. He has a light overcoat on, a between-seasons one; he may catch a cold. Ah, young people never stop to think.

Mme Ranevsky. I shall die. Yasha, go and ask to whom it was sold.

Yasha. But he's been gone a long time, the old chap.

[*Laughing.*

Mme Ranevsky. [*With some vexation.*] Well, what are you laughing at? What are you so pleased about?

Yasha. Yepikhodov is too ridiculous. A windbag. Twenty-two miseries!

Mme Ranevsky. Feers, if the estate were sold, where would you go?

Feers. I will go wherever you command me.

Mme Ranevsky. Why do you look like that? Aren't you well? You know, you ought to go to bed.

Feers. Just so. . . . [*With a smile.*] Me, go to bed—but without me who will hand things round, who will see to things? I am the only one in the whole house.

Yasha. [*To Mme Ranevsky.*] Lyubov Andreyevna! Allow me to ask you a favour, be so good! Should you go to Paris again, do take me with you, for pity's sake! It's quite impossible for me to stay here. . . . [*Looking round, in a low voice.*] What's the use of my talking? you know it yourself; it's an uncivilized country, the people are immoral, and the boredom! The food they give us in the kitchen is shocking, and added to it all there's that Feers walking about, muttering all sorts of unsuitable words. Do take me with you, be so good!

Enter Pischik.

Pischik. Allow me to request you . . . for a little waltz, fairest lady! . . . [*Mme Ranevsky goes with him.*] Enchantress, those 180 roubles which I need . . . you will give them to me. . . . You will. . . . [*Dancing, they pass into the hall.*

Yasha. [*Humming softly.*] 'My soul's agitation will you ever understand? . . .'

[*In the hall is seen a figure in a grey top-hat and check trousers, jumping about, waving its arms. Shouts of :* 'Bravo, Charlotta Ivanovna!'

Dounyasha. [*Stopping to powder her face.*] My young lady bids me dance—there are plenty of gentlemen, but few ladies—with so many dances my head feels dizzy, and my heart is thumping. Feers Nicolayevitch, the clerk from the post

office just said such a thing to me that it took my breath
away.   [*The music is getting softer.*

Feers. What did he say to you?

Dounyasha. 'You are like a flower,' says he.

Yasha. [*Yawning.*] What ignorance! . . .   [*Goes off.*

Dounyasha. Like a flower. . . . I am such a sensitive girl, I love
delicate words awfully. . . .

Feers. You are sure to get into trouble.

Enter Yepikhodov.

Yepikhodov. Avdotya Fyodorovna, you are not desirous of
seeing me . . . as if I were some insect. . . . [*With a sigh.*]
Oh, life!

Dounyasha. What do you want?

Yepikhodov. Without a doubt, perhaps, you are right. [*With
a sigh.*] But, of course, looking from one point of view, then,
may I be permitted to put it this way, pardon my frankness,
you have reduced me to such a state of mind. I know my
fate, every day some misfortune befalls me, but I have long
since got so accustomed to it that I look with a smile at my
lot. You gave me your word, and although I——

Dounyasha. I beg you, let us have a talk later on, now leave me
in peace. Now I am dreaming. . . . [*Playing with her fan.*

Yepikhodov. A misfortune befalls me every day, and I shall
permit myself the expression, I only smile, I even laugh.

Varya comes in from the hall.

Varya. You're still here, Semyon! What an inconsiderate
fellow you are! [*To Dounyasha.*] Get out of here, Dounyasha.
[*To Yepikhodov.*] Either you play billiards and smash the
cue, or else you walk about in the drawing-room as though you
were a guest.

Yepikhodov. Permit me to express myself to you, you have no
claim on me, you have none.

Varya. I'm making no claim on you, I only speak to you. You
wander about from one place to another, never doing your
work. We keep a bailiff—but what for, nobody knows.

Yepikhodov. [*In an offended tone.*] Whether I work, or wander
about, or eat, or play billiards, of that only those who understand and are my masters can judge.

Varya. You dare to speak like that to me! [*Flaring up.*] How
dare you? Then I understand nothing? Clear out of here!
This very minute!

Yepikhodov. [*Cowed.*] I beg you to express yourself in a delicate manner.

Varya. [*In a rage.*] Clear out, this very moment! Get out! [*He goes to the door, she follows.*] Twenty-two miseries! Get out! Get out of my sight! [*Yepikhodov has gone out ; but from outside the door his voice is heard :* 'I shall bring an action against you!'] Oh, you're coming back? [*Seizing the stick placed by Feers near the door.*] Come on then. . . . Come. . . . Come, I'll show you. . . . Ah, you are coming? Are you? Then take that. . . .
[*Brandishing the stick : at that very moment Lopakhin comes in.*

Lopakhin. Thanks awfully!

Varya. [*Angrily and derisively.*] I am sorry!

Lopakhin. Not at all. Thank you so much for the kind reception.

Varya. Not at all! [*Moving away, then looking round and asking gently.*] I haven't hurt you?

Lopakhin. No, it does not matter. There'll be a nice bump there.
[*Voices in the hall :* 'Lopakhin has come! Yermolay Alexeyevitch!'

Pischik. A sight for sore eyes. . . . [*He and Lopakhin kiss each other.*] There's an aroma of fine brandy about you, my dear, my good fellow. We, too, are making merry here.

Enter Mme Ranevsky.

Mme Ranevsky. Oh, it's you, Yermolay Alexeyevitch! Why so late? Where's Leonid?

Lopakhin. Leonid Andreyevitch arrived with me; he'll come in presently. . . .

Mme Ranevsky. [*In agitation.*] Well, what's the news? Did the sale take place? Do tell me!

Lopakhin. [*Embarrassed, afraid to show his joy.*] The auction was over by four o'clock . . . we were too late for the train, had to wait till half-past nine. [*Catching his breath.*] Ugh! My head feels a bit dizzy. . . .

Enter Gayev ; in his right hand he holds a few parcels ; with his left hand he is wiping away his tears.

Mme Ranevsky. Well, Lenya? Lenya, what's the news? [*Impatiently, through tears.*] Be quick, for the love of God!

Gayev. [*Giving her no reply, only waving his arms ; to Feers, weeping.*] Take it. . . . There are anchovies there, Crimean

herrings. . . . I haven't had anything to eat all day to-day.
. . . I have suffered so much! [*The door into the billiard-room
is open : the click of balls is heard, and Yasha's voice :* 'Seven
and eighteen!' *Gayev's expression changes, he stops weeping.*]
I am terribly tired. Feers, help me to change.

[*Going to his quarters through the hall, followed by Feers.*

Pischik. How did the auction go off? Do tell us!

Mme Ranevsky. Has the cherry orchard been sold?

Lopakhin. It has.

Mme Ranevsky. Who's bought it?

Lopakhin. I have bought it.

[*A pause. Mme Ranevsky is overcome ; she would have fallen
down, had she not been standing near the chair and the
table. Varya takes the keys from her belt, throws them on
the floor in the middle of the drawing-room, and goes out.*

Lopakhin. I have bought it! Wait a minute, please, my head is
all in a muddle, I cannot speak. . . . [*Laughing.*] We arrived
at the auction. Deriganov was already there. Leonid Andreyevitch had only fifteen thousand roubles, and Deriganov
bid thirty thousand, straight off on top of the debt on the
estate. I say to myself: 'That's how the matter stands,'
and I close with him, bidding forty. He, forty-five. I,
fifty-five. He, you see, advancing five thousand at a time;
myself, ten thousand. . . . And so it came to an end. Over
and above the debt I bid ninety thousand, and it was knocked
down to me. The cherry orchard is now mine! Mine!
[*Laughing aloud.*] O Lord, O God, the cherry orchard mine!
Tell me that I am drunk, out of my mind, that I am dreaming.
. . . [*Stamping his feet.*] Do not laugh at me! If my father
and grandfather could rise from their graves and see the whole
affair; how their Yermolay, beaten, uneducated Yermolay, who
in winter time used to run about barefoot—how that very
Yermolay bought an estate, the finest in the world! I have
bought the estate, on which my grandfather and father were
slaves, where they were not allowed even into the kitchen.
I must be fast asleep. I am only dreaming it, it only seems
like that. . . . All this is a figment of your imagination,
shrouded in the mist of uncertainty. . . . [*Picking up the keys,
with a gentle smile.*] She threw down the keys, she wanted to
show that she is no longer mistress here. . . . [*Jingling the
keys.*] Well, it can't be helped. [*The orchestra is heard tuning
up.*] Hallo, musicians, play, I want to hear you! Come, all
of you, and see how Yermolay Lopakhin will cut down the

cherry orchard, how the trees will fall to the ground! We will build plenty of bungalows, and our grandchildren and great-grandchildren shall have a new life. . . . Music! Play!

[*The orchestra plays. Mme Ranevsky has sunk down into a chair and is weeping bitterly.*

Lopakhin. [*Reproachfully.*] Why didn't you listen to me, why? My poor dear, there's no turning back. [*With tears.*] Oh, that all this might be over as quickly as possible, and that as quickly as possible our ugly, miserable life might be changed!

Pischik. [*Taking him by the arm, in a whisper.*] She's crying. Let us go into the hall, let her be by herself. . . . Come. . . .

[*Taking him by the arm and leading him into the hall.*

Lopakhin. Music, play clearly! Let everything be as I wish it! [*Ironically.*] Here comes the new squire, the proprietor of the cherry orchard! [*Accidentally knocks against the little table, and nearly upsets the candelabra.*] I can pay for everything!

[*Goes out with Pischik.*

There is no one left in the drawing-room and in the hall, except Mme Ranevsky, who sits huddled up and crying bitterly. The music plays softly. Enter quickly Anya and Trofimov. Anya comes up to her mother and drops down on her knees before her. Trofimov stands by the entrance to the hall.

Anya. Mother! Mother, you're crying! My dear, my good, my lovely mother, my beautiful one, I love you so . . . bless you. The cherry orchard is sold, it is no longer ours; it is so, it is true; but don't cry, mother, there is your life in front of you, there is your kind, pure soul. . . . Come with me, come, my dear, away from here, come! . . . We shall plant a new orchard, fairer than this; you shall see it, you shall realize, and joy, profound, calm joy, shall descend upon your soul, like the sun at the evening hour, and you shall smile, mother! Come, my dear! Come! . . .

CURTAIN

ACT IV

Décor as in Act I. No curtains on the windows, no pictures, only a few pieces of furniture left, stacked away in a corner, as though for sale. Emptiness can be felt. Near the back door and in the background of the stage are piled up trunks, travelling bags, and so on. On the left the door is open; from it are heard the voices of Anya and Varya. Lopakhin stands, waiting. Yasha is holding a tray with little glasses of champagne. In the vestibule Yepikhodov is roping up a box. Behind the scenes, in the distance, there is a hum of voices. It is the peasants who have come to bid farewell. Gayev's voice: 'Thanks, friends, thank you.'

Yasha. The simple folk have come to say good-bye. I am of this opinion, Yermolay Alexeyevitch: the peasants are kind-hearted, but understand little.

The hum is quieting down. Enter, through the vestibule, Mme Ranevsky and Gayev: she is not crying, but she is pale, her face is quivering, she cannot speak.

Gayev. You handed them over your purse, Lyuba. You must not do such things! You must not!

Mme Ranevsky. I could not restrain myself! I could not!

[*They go out.*

Lopakhin. [*In the doorway, after them.*] Please come in, I beg you! Let us have a glass for luck. I had not the sense to get it in town, and at the railway station I found only one bottle. Please! [*A pause.*] Why, my friends! You refuse? [*Coming away from the door.*] Had I known, I would not have bought it. Now I am not going to drink it either. [*Yasha cautiously places a tray on a chair.*] You, Yasha, at any rate will have one.

Yasha. To those who are going away! Your health! [*Drinking.*] This champagne is not the genuine article, I can assure you.

Lopakhin. Eight roubles a bottle. [*A pause.*] It's devilish cold here.

Yasha. They don't trouble to warm the place to-day, seeing that we are going away. [*Laughing.*

Lopakhin. Why are you laughing?

Yasha. From pleasure.

Lopakhin. It's October outside, yet it is sunny and still, as in summer. A good time for building. [*Glances at his watch, and calls out through the doorway.*] Don't forget, my friends, there's only forty-seven minutes left before the train! So that in twenty minutes you have to start for the station. Hurry a bit.

Trofimov, in an overcoat, enters from the yard.

Trofimov. I think it is time to start, the carriages are already at the door. What the devil, where are my galoshes? Gone astray. . . . [*In the doorway.*] Anya, I haven't got my galoshes! I can't find them!

Lopakhin. I have to go to Kharkov. I'm taking the same train as you are. I'll spend the winter in Kharkov. I've been hanging about all the time, and got sick and tired with no work to do. I cannot live without work, I don't know what to do with my hands here: they flap about in a strange way as though they belonged to someone else.

Trofimov. We are going soon, and you will start your useful activity again.

Lopakhin. Do have a glass!

Trofimov. I won't.

Lopakhin. You're going to Moscow, then?

Trofimov. Yes, I'm seeing them off to town, and to-morrow I'm going to Moscow.

Lopakhin. Just so . . . why, the professors haven't been giving their lectures, I suppose; they have been waiting all the time for you to come!

Trofimov. It isn't your business.

Lopakhin. How many years now have you been studying at the university?

Trofimov. Think out something new. That's stale and stupid. [*Looking for his galoshes.*] I say, it's quite likely we shall never meet again, so do allow me to give you this advice at parting: don't wave your arms! Do unlearn that habit—of waving. And this, too—to build bungalows, to expect that bungalow-dwellers will in time become masters on their own, to hope for that—that, too, is waving your arms. In spite of all, I am very fond of you. You have fine, sensitive fingers, like those of an artist; you have a fine, sensitive soul. . . .

Lopakhin. [*Embracing him.*] Good-bye, dear friend. Thank you for everything. If you are in need, please take some money from me for your journey.

Trofimov. What do I need money for?   I don't.

Lopakhin. But you haven't got any?

Trofimov. I have.   Thank you so much.   I received money for a translation.   Here it is, in my pocket. [*Uneasily.*] But the galoshes are gone!

Varya. [*From another room.*] There, take the filthy things!
[*Throwing on to the stage a pair of rubber galoshes.*

Trofimov. Why are you so cross, Varya?   H'm. . . . These are not my galoshes!

Lopakhin. In the spring I had three thousand acres sown with poppies, and now I have cleared forty thousand roubles.   And when the poppies were in bloom, what a beautiful sight it was!   Now then, I say I have cleared a profit of forty thousand, and therefore I offer you a loan, because I can afford it.   Why turn up your nose?   I am a peasant . . . straight-forward.

Trofimov. Your father was a peasant, mine a dispensing chemist, and from that fact nothing at all follows. [*Lopakhin takes out his pocket-book.*] No, no. . . . Even if you gave me two hundred thousand, I would not take it.   I am a free man.   And everything so highly prized, held so dear by you all, rich and poor alike, has not the slightest power over me—like a feather whirling in the air.   I can do without you all, I can pass you all by, I am strong and proud.   Mankind is marching towards the highest truth, towards the highest happiness attainable on earth, and I in the vanguard.

Lopakhin. Will you reach it?

Trofimov. I shall reach it. [*A pause.*] I shall reach it, or I shall show others the way to reach it.
[*In the distance is heard the sound of an axe striking on a tree.*

Lopakhin. Well, good-bye, my dear friend.   It's time to start. We show off in front of each other, and life passes by unheeding.   When I work, for a long spell, without rest, then my thoughts are clearer, and I begin to fancy that I too know what I live for.   But what multitudes of people in Russia, my friend, live without knowing what for.   Well, never mind, this is neither here nor there.   They say that Leonid Andreyevitch has taken a post in the bank, six thousand a year. . . . But he's sure to lose it, he's too lazy. . . .

Anya. [*In the doorway.*] Mother asks you not to cut down the trees until she has gone.

Trofimov. Really, not to have had enough tact——
[*Goes out through the vestibule.*

Lopakhin. At once, at once. . . . Those men. . . .

[*Follows him.*

Anya. Has Feers been sent off to the hospital?

Yasha. I told them in the morning. They must have sent him off.

Anya. [*To Yepikhodov, who is passing through the hall.*] Semyon Panteleyevitch, do find out, please, if Feers has been sent to the hospital.

Yasha. [*Injured.*] I told Yegov this morning. Why do you keep on asking?

Yepikhodov. Ancient Feers, in my final opinion, will not mend, he must join his ancestors. For my part I can only envy him. [*Putting the trunk on a hat-box and crushing it.*] What did I tell you!

Yasha. [*Mockingly.*] Twenty-two miseries!

Varya. [*Behind the door.*] Has Feers been sent off to the hospital?

Anya. He has.

Varya. Then why didn't they take the letter to the doctor?

Anya. It must be rushed off at once. . . .   [*Goes out.*

Varya. [*From the next room.*] Where's Yasha? Tell him his mother has come, she wants to say good-bye to him.

Yasha. [*Waving his hand.*] Try my patience, that's what they do.

[*All the time Dounyasha has been pottering about with the luggage ; now, when Yasha is alone, she goes up to him.*

Dounyasha. You might look at me just once, Yasha. You are going away . . . deserting me. . . .

[*Crying and throwing herself on his neck.*

Yasha. Why are you crying? [*Drinking champagne.*] In six days' time I shall be in Paris again. To-morrow we shall take the express, and off we go, out of sight. I can hardly believe it. Vive la France! I don't like the ways of this country, I cannot manage my life, so there! I have seen quite enough ignorance—that'll do for me. [*Drinking champagne.*] Why are you crying? Behave decently, and then you won't need to cry.

Dounyasha. [*Powdering her face, and looking into a pocket mirror.*] Send me a letter from Paris. I loved you, Yasha, I loved you so much! I am a sensitive creature, Yasha!

Yasha. People are coming.

[*Potters about with the trunks, humming softly.*

Enter Mme Ranevsky, Gayev, Anya, and Charlotta Ivanovna.

Gayev. It's time to start. There's very little time left. [*Looking at Yasha.*] Who is it smells of herring?

Mme Ranevsky. In about ten minutes we ought to be ready to take our seats in the carriages. . . . [*Glancing round the room.*] Good-bye, sweet house, dear grandfather-house. Winter will pass, spring will come, but you won't exist any longer, they 'll pull you down. The things these walls have seen! [*Ardently kissing her daughter.*] My treasure, you shine, your sweet eyes are like two diamonds. You are happy? Very?

Anya. Very! A new life is beginning, mother!

Gayev. [*Merrily.*] Indeed, everything is all right now. Up to the sale of the cherry orchard we were all agitated, we all suffered, but after that, when the question was finally settled, irrevocably, we all grew calm, even cheerful. I am a bank official now, a financier. . . . I pot the yellow . . . and you, Lyuba, say what you like, you look handsomer. No doubt about that.

Mme Ranevsky. Yes. My nerves are better, that 's true. [*Her hat and coat are handed to her.*] I sleep well. Carry out my things, Yasha. It 's time. [*To Anya.*] My little girl, soon we shall meet again. . . . I am going to Paris, I shall live there on the money which your Yaroslavl granny sent to buy the estate with—long live granny!—that money won't last very long, though.

Anya. You will come back, mother, soon, very soon . . . won't you? I shall study hard, pass my exam in the high school, and then I will work, I will help you. Mother, you and I will read all kinds of books. Won't we? [*Kissing her mother's hands.*] We shall read in the autumn evenings, we shall read many books, and before us will unfold a new, marvellous world. . . . [*Dreaming.*] Mother, do come back. . . .

Mme Ranevsky. I will, my golden one. [*Embracing her daughter.*

Enter Lopakhin. Charlotta is softly humming a song.

Gayev. Lucky Charlotta: she 's singing!

Charlotta. [*Picking up a bundle, which looks like a swaddled baby.*] My little baby, bye-bye. . . . [*The crying of a baby is heard :* 'Oo-ah, oo-ah, oo-ah! . . .'] Be quiet, my dear, my sweet little boy! ['Oo-ah, oo-ah!'] My heart aches for you! [*Throwing the bundle into its place.*] Will you be so good as to find me a post? I can't go on without a job.

Lopakhin. We shall find you one, Charlotta Ivanovna, don't you worry.

Gayev. Every one is deserting us; Varya is going away . . . we are suddenly no longer needed.

Charlotta. I have nowhere to go in town. I must go away. . [*Humming.*] I don't care. . . .

Enter Pischik.

Lopakhin. Here comes the nature's riddle.

Pischik. [*Panting.*] Ooh, let me get my breath! . . . I'm worn out. . . . My dear good people. . . . Give me some water. . . .

Gayev. I suppose you have come for money? I'd better remove myself. [*Goes out.*

Pischik. I haven't been to see you for such a long time . . . my fairest lady. [*To Lopakhin.*] You here . . . so pleased to see you . . . man of tremendous understanding . . . take . . . accept . . . [*Handing money to Lopakhin.*] Four hundred roubles. . . . I owe you now 840 only. . . .

Lopakhin. [*Puzzled, shrugging his shoulders.*] It's like a dream. . . . Where did you get it from?

Pischik. Wait. . . . It is hot. . . . Most extraordinary event. Englishmen arrived at my place and found in the earth a sort of white clay . . . [*To Mme Ranevsky.*] and four hundred to you . . . my fair, my wonderful lady. . . . [*Handing her the money.*] The rest will follow later. [*Drinking water.*] Only just now a young man was saying in the train that a certain great philosopher counsels jumping from the housetops. . . . 'Jump!' he says, and therein consists the whole problem. [*In amazement.*] You don't say so! Some water, please.

Lopakhin. Who are those Englishmen?

Pischik. I leased them the plot of land with the clay for twenty-four years. . . . And now, excuse me, I have no time. . . . I must rush off. . . . I must now go and see Znoykov . . . Kardamanov. . . . I owe money to every one. . . . [*Drinking.*] Keep well and happy. . . . I'll call on Thursday.

Mme Ranevsky. We are going to town immediately, and to-morrow I am leaving for abroad. . . .

Pischik. Why? [*Alarmed.*] Why go to town? Oh, I say, there's no furniture . . . only trunks. . . . Never mind. . . . [*Through tears.*] Never you mind. . . . They are men of the highest intellect . . . those English. . . . Never mind. . . . God will help you. . . . Never mind. . . . Everything in this world comes to an end. . . . [*Kissing Mme Ranevsky's hand.*] And when the news reaches you that my end has come, recall to your mind that same . . . horse, and say: 'There once lived So-and-so . . . Simeonov-Pischik . . . may his soul rest in peace. . . .' Superb weather. . .

Just so. . . . [*Goes out, greatly perturbed, but immediately returns, and says in the doorway :*] My Dashenka asked to be remembered to you! [*Goes out.*

Mme Ranevsky. Now we are ready to start. I am going away with two worries. The first is about Feers's illness. [*Glancing at her watch.*] We have still another five minutes.

Anya. Mother, Feers has already been sent off to the hospital. Yasha sent him off this morning.

Mme Ranevsky. My second worry is about Varya. She's used to getting up early, and to working, and now, with no work to do, she's like a fish out of water. She has got thin, pale, she cries all the time, poor thing. . . . [*A pause.*] You know it very well, Yermolay Alexeyevitch; I had an idea . . . that she would marry you, everything pointed to your getting married. [*She says something in a whisper to Anya ; the latter motions to Charlotta, and both go out.*] She loves you, you are fond of her, and I wonder, I wonder why you behave as though you were trying to avoid each other. I can't understand it!

Lopakhin. I myself can't understand it either, to tell the truth. It seems all so strange. . . . If there's still time, I am willing even now. . . . Let's have done with it—and *basta*; but, without you, I feel, I shan't propose to her.

Mme Ranevsky. But that's excellent. Surely it needs only a minute. I'll call her at once.

Lopakhin. And to fit the occasion there's the champagne. . . . [*Glancing at the glasses.*] They are empty; someone has already drunk them. [*Yasha coughs.*] That's what you call lapping it up!

Mme Ranevsky. [*Vivaciously.*] Splendid! We'll leave you. Yasha, *allez!* I'll call her. [*Through the door.*] Varya, leave everything, come here! Come! [*She and Yasha go out.*

Lopakhin. [*Looking at his watch.*] Just so. . . . [*A pause.*

Behind the door there is audible suppressed laughter, whispering, and finally Varya comes in.

Varya. [*Looking at the luggage for a long while.*] Strange, I cannot find it anywhere. . . .

Lopakhin. What are you looking for?

Varya. I did the packing myself and I cannot remember where I put it. [*A pause.*

Lopakhin. What are you going to do with yourself now, Varvara Mikhailovna?

Varya. Me? I shall go to the Razgulins. . . . I've arranged to go there to look after their household . . . a kind of housekeeper.

Lopakhin. Their place is in Yashnevo? It's about seventy versts from here. [*A pause.*] Now, life has come to an end in this house.

Varya. [*Examining the luggage.*] Where can it be? . . . Oh, perhaps I packed it away in the trunk. . . . Yes, life in this house has come to an end . . . it will be no more. . . .

Lopakhin. And I am going to Kharkov now . . . by the next train. Plenty of work. And Yepikhodov will stay on here. . . . I have taken him on.

Varya. Well!

Lopakhin. Last year about this time it was already snowing, if you remember, and now it is still and sunny. Only it's cold . . . three degrees of frost, I should say.

Varya. I haven't looked. [*A pause.*] Anyhow our thermometer is broken. . . .   [*A pause.*

[*A voice from the yard through the door:* 'Yermolay Alexeyevitch!'

Lopakhin. [*As though he had been waiting for the call for a long time.*] Coming this minute!   [*Goes out hastily.*

Varya sits on the floor, laying her head on a bundle of clothes, and weeps softly. The door opens, and Mme Ranevsky comes in cautiously.

Mme Ranevsky. Well? [*A pause.*] We must be going.

Varya. [*No longer crying, she has wiped her eyes.*] Yes, it is time, mummy. I shall manage to get to the Razgulins to-day, so long as we are not late for the train. . . .

Mme Ranevsky. [*Through the door.*] Anya, put your things on!

Enter Anya, then Gayev, and Charlotta Ivanovna. Gayev has a warm coat on and a muffler. Servants, coachmen come in. Yepikhodov is busy with the luggage.

Mme Ranevsky. And now on our road!

Anya. [*Joyfully.*] On our road!

Gayev. My friends, my kind, dear friends! Leaving this house for ever, can I pass over in silence, can I restrain myself from expressing at parting those feelings which fill now my whole being——

Anya. [*Imploringly.*] Uncle!

Varya. Uncle dear, please don't

Gayev. [*Dejectedly.*] I double the yellow into the middle pocket!
. . . I am silent. . . .

        Enter Trofimov, then Lopakhin.

Trofimov. Come, my friends, it is time to start.

Lopakhin. Yepikhodov, my overcoat!

Mme Ranevsky. I must stay one more minute. It is just as
though I had never before seen what the walls in this house
are like, what the ceilings are like, and now I look at them so
eagerly, with so tender a love——

Gayev. I remember, when I was six, it was a Whit-Sunday,
sitting at that window, watching my father going to church——

Mme Ranevsky. Have they taken all the things?

Lopakhin. All of them, I think. [*To Yepikhodov, as he puts on
his overcoat.*] You, Yepikhodov, mind that everything is in
proper order.

Yepikhodov. [*Speaking in a hoarse voice.*] Rest assured, Yer
molay Alexeyevitch!

Lopakhin. What's the matter with your voice?

Yepikhodov. I've just drunk some water, and I swallowed
something.

Yasha. [*With contempt.*] What ignorance. . . .

Mme Ranevsky. When we go, not a soul will remain here. . . .

Lopakhin. Until the spring.

Varya. [*Pulls a parasol out of a bundle ; it looks as if she were
going to hit someone , Lopakhin pretends to be frightened.*] Why
why . . . I never thought of such a thing.

Trofimov. Let us take our seats in the carriages. . . . It is time!
The train will be in soon!

Varya. Petya, there they are, your galoshes, by the trunk
there. . . . [*With tears.*] How dirty they are, how old. . . .

Trofimov. [*Putting on his galoshes.*] Do let us go!

Gayev. [*Deeply moved, afraid of bursting into tears.*] The train
. . . the station. . . . I pot the middle, I double the white
into the pocket. . . .

Mme Ranevsky. Come, let us go!

Lopakhin. Is every one here? Is there no one there? [*Locking
the side-door on the left.*] There are things stacked away here,
it must be locked. Let us go!

Anya. Farewell, house! Farewell, the old life!

Trofimov. Hail, the new life! . . .   [*Goes out with Anya.*
   [*Varya, casting a glance round the room, unhurriedly goes out.*
    Yasha and Charlotta Ivanovna go out with the pet dog.

Lopakhin. Till the spring, then.   Come on. . . . *Au revoir !* . . .

                                                           [Goes out.

    [Mme Ranevsky and Gayev are left alone.   Just as though they had been waiting for this, they fling themselves on each other's necks, and sob discreetly, softly, afraid of being overheard.

Gayev. [*In despair.*] My sister, my sister. . . .

Mme Ranevsky. Oh, my lovely, my sweet, my beautiful orchard! . . . My life, my youth, my happiness, good-bye! . . . Good-bye.

Anya's voice. [*Happily, defiantly.*] Mother! . . .

Trofimov's voice. [*Happily, excitedly.*] Coo-ee! . . . Coo-ee!

Mme Ranevsky. I want to look for the last time at the walls, at the windows. . . . Mother loved to walk about in this room. . . .

Gayev. My sister, my sister! . . .

Anya's voice. Mother! . . .

Trofimov's voice. Coo-ee! . . .

Mme Ranevsky. We are coming! . . .   *[They go out.*

    [The stage is empty.   The doors are heard all being locked, and then the carriages driving away.   It grows quiet.   In the stillness is audible the dull thud of an axe on a tree, a forlorn and melancholy sound.   Footsteps are heard.   Through the door on the right appears Feers.   He is dressed as usual in a jacket and white waistcoat, with slippers on his feet.   He is ill.

Feers. [*Going to the door, trying the handle.*] It is locked.   They have gone. . . . [*Sitting down on the sofa.*] They have forgotten me. . . . No matter. . . . I'll sit down here for a while. . . . And I am sure Leonid Andreyevitch has not put on his fur coat, he's gone off in his coat. . . . [*With an anxious sigh.*] I ought to have seen to it.   Young people never stop to think. [*He mutters something which cannot be understood.*] Life has gone by as though I hadn't lived. . . . [*Lying down.*] I'll lie down. . . . You have no more strength left; there's nothing left, nothing. . . . Oh, you *nyedotyopa.* . . .

                                [He lies without motion.

    [*There is a far-off sound, as though out of the sky, the sound of a snapped string, dying away, mournful.   A stillness falls, and there is heard only, far away in the orchard, the thud of axes striking on the trees.*

CURTAIN

THE SEAGULL

A COMEDY IN FOUR ACTS

CHARACTERS

IRENE NICOLAYEVNA ARKADIN (her married name MME TRYE-
PLYEV), an actress.

KONSTANTIN GAVRILOVICH TRYEPLYEV, her son, a young man.

PETER NICOLAYEVICH SORIN, her brother.

NINA MIKHAILOVNA ZARYECHNY, a young girl, the daughter of
a rich landowner.

ILYA AFANASYEVICH SHAMRAYEV, a retired lieutenant, Sorin's
steward.

PAULINE ANDREYEVNA, his wife.

MASHA (MARIE ILYINISHNA), his daughter.

BORIS ALEXEYEVICH TREEGORIN, a novelist.

YEVGUENIY SERGUEYEVICH DORN, a doctor.

SEMYON SEMYONOVICH MYEDVYEDENKO, a schoolmaster.

YAKOV, a labourer.

A Cook.

A Housemaid.

The action takes place in Sorin's country house and on his
estate.

Between the third and fourth Acts an interval of two years
elapses.

ACT I

*Part of the park on Sorin's estate. The wide avenue, leading away
from the spectators into the depth of the park towards the lake,
is blocked by a stage platform, hastily erected for a private performance, so that the lake cannot be seen at all. To the left
and to the right of the platform are bushes. A few chairs, a
little table.*

*The sun has just set. On the platform, behind the curtain, Yakov
and other labourers are at work ; sounds of coughing and ham-
mering are heard. Masha and Myedvyedenko come in on the
left, returning from a walk.*

Myedvyendenko. Why do you always wear black?

Masha. I'm in mourning for my life. I am unhappy.

Myedvyedenko. Why? [*Meditatively.*] I can't understand. . . . You're healthy; your father, although not rich, is quite well off. Mine is a much harder life than yours. All told, I get twenty-three roubles a month, from which something will have to go to a pension fund, and yet I don't wear mourning.
[*They sit down.*

Masha. It isn't a question of money. Even a poor man can be happy.

Myedvyedenko. That is so in theory, but in practice it's like this: mother, and two sisters and a little brother and myself—on a salary of twenty-three roubles all told. We need to eat and drink surely? We need tea and sugar? Tobacco? A stiff proposition, isn't it?

Masha. [*Glancing at the platform.*] The performance is going to begin soon.

Myedvyedenko. Yes. Nina Zaryechny is to be the actress and the play is by Konstantin Gavrilovich. They are in love, and to-day their souls will be fused in an attempt to create a harmonious artistic image. But your soul and mine have no common points of contact. I love you, and from anguish I can't sit at home; every day I walk six miles here and six miles back, and only meet with indifference from you. It's understandable. I'm without means, I have a large family to support. . . . Who would want to marry a man who can scarcely feed himself?

Masha. Nonsense! [*Sniffing at her snuff-box.*] Your love touches me, but I can't return it, that's all. [*Holding out the snuff-box to him.*] Help yourself.

Myedvyedenko. I'd rather not. [*A pause.*

Masha. It's sultry. We shall have a storm to-night. You're always philosophizing or talking about money. According to you, there's no greater misfortune than poverty; and, to my mind, it's a thousand times easier to go in rags and to beg than—— Still, you won't understand that. . . .

Sorin and Tryeplyev come in on the right.

Sorin. [*Leaning on his walking-stick.*] In the country, my dear fellow, I don't feel quite the thing, and clearly enough I shall never get used to it here. Last night I went to bed at ten o'clock and woke up this morning at nine with a feeling as though, with the long sleep, my brain had got glued to my skull, and all that. [*Laughing.*] And after lunch I unexpectedly dropped off again, and now I am all an ache, as though I were in a nightmare, and that's the long and short of it. . . .

Tryeplyev. You really ought to live in town. [*Noticing Masha and Myedvyedenko.*] When we start, they will call you, but now you mustn't be here. Do please go away.

Sorin. [*To Masha.*] Marie Ilyinishna, be so kind as to ask your father to tell them to unchain the dog; it keeps on howling. My sister could not sleep the whole night again.

Masha. You'd better speak to father yourself. I shan't. Please don't ask me. [*To Myedvyedenko.*] Come along!

Myedvyedenko. [*To Tryeplyev.*] So you will send someone to let us know when you start? [*Both then go out.*

Sorin. That means the dog will be howling all night long again. What a rum thing, I've never lived in the country in the way I should have liked to. I used to take a month's leave and come here for a rest, and all that; but they would plague me with all sorts of nonsense so much that on the very first day I longed to rush back. [*Laughing.*] I was always glad to get away from here. . . . Well, now I'm retired I have nowhere else to go, and that's the long and short of it. Like it or not, I've got to stay here. . . .

Yakov. [*To Tryeplyev.*] We are going to have a bathe, sir.

Tryeplyev. Right, only you must all be back in your places in ten minutes. [*Looking at his watch.*] It'll soon begin now.

Yakov. All right, sir. [*Goes out.*

Tryeplyev. [*Taking a quick glance at the stage.*] Here's the theatre. The curtain, then the first coulisse, then the second and beyond that—empty space. No scenery at all. The back gives straight on the lake and the horizon. We shall raise the curtain precisely at half-past eight, when the moon will have risen.

Sorin. Excellent.

Tryeplyev. If Nina is late, then, of course, the whole effect will be lost. It's time she was here. Her father and stepmother keep watch on her, and it's as difficult for her to get out of the house as out of prison. [*Adjusting his uncle's tie.*] Your hair and beard are untidy. You ought to have your hair cut, or what?

Sorin. [*Combing his beard.*] It's the tragedy of my life. Even in my youth I looked as though I were always having a drunken bout, and all that. Women never loved me. [*Sitting down.*] Why is my sister out of humour?

Tryeplyev. Why? She's bored. [*Sitting down beside him.*] She's jealous. She's already against me, and against the performance, and against the play, because it's not she who's acting in it, but Nina. She doesn't know anything about my play, but she hates it already.

Sorin. [*Laughing.*] Really, you fancy things. . . .

Tryeplyev. She's vexed already that Nina will be a success, and not she on this little stage here. [*Looking at his watch.*] My mother is a psychological puzzle. She has undoubted talent, she's intelligent, capable of crying over a book, she can reel off the whole of Nyekrassov by heart; as a nurse she's an angel; but you try to say a word in praise of Duse in her presence! Oho, oho! She's the only one to be praised, to be written about, discussed, people have to be carried away by her extraordinary acting in *La Dame aux Camélias* or in *The Fumes of Life*; but since here, in the country, this opiate is missing, she feels bored and irritable, and we are all her enemies, we all are to blame. Also, she's superstitious, she's afraid of three candles, of the number thirteen. She's close-fisted. She keeps seventy thousand roubles at an Odessa bank—I know it for a fact. But you try to ask her for a loan, and she'll start weeping.

Sorin. You fancy your mother doesn't like your play, and you're already upset and all that. Be calm, your mother adores you.

Tryeplyev. [*Plucking the petals off a flower.*] Loves me—loves me not, loves me—loves me not, loves me—loves me not. [*Laughing.*] See, mother doesn't love me. Rather not. She longs to live, to love, to wear light-coloured blouses, and I am twenty-five already, and perpetually remind her that she's no longer young. If I'm not there, she's only thirty-two; but in my presence she's forty-three, and she hates me for that. She knows, too, that I don't recognize the theatre. She loves the theatre, she thinks that she serves mankind, sacred art; but to my mind the present-day theatre is nothing but routine, superstition. When the curtain rises, and lit by artificial light, in a room with three walls, these great geniuses, the priests of sacred art, show how people eat, drink, love, walk, wear their jackets; when out of banal scenes and phrases they try to fish a moral—a tiny little moral, easily comprehensible, useful for everyday needs; when in a thousand variations one and the same thing is offered me, one and the same, one and the same—I run and run, as Maupassant ran from the Eiffel Tower, which weighed on his brain with its vulgarity.

Sorin. You can't dispense with the theatre.

Tryeplyev. It's new forms we need. It's new forms we need, and if they aren't there, then we'd better have nothing. [*Looking at his watch.*] I love mother, I love her dearly; but she leads a nonsensical life, she's always taken up with that novelist, her name is always being dragged into the newspapers, and that wearies me. At moments the mere egotism of an ordinary mortal speaks in me, and I'm sorry that I have a famous actress for my mother, and it seems to me that were she an ordinary woman I should be happier. Uncle, can there be a more desperate and stupid situation? There would be guests sitting with her, all celebrities, actors and authors, and among them all I was the only nonentity: and they endured me only because I was her son. Who am I? What am I? I had to leave the university in my third year for reasons, as they say, for which the editor takes no responsibility. I have no talents, not a penny of my own, and, according to my passport, I'm a mere burgher of the city of Kiev. My father was a burgher of Kiev, though he, too, was a famous actor. Well now, when all those actors and authors in her drawing-room used to afford me their gracious attention, it seemed to me that they were measuring my insignificance with their glances—I divined their thoughts and suffered humiliation.

Sorin. By the way, tell me, please, what sort of man is that novelist? I can't make him out. He's always silent.

Tryeplyev. He's an intelligent man, simple, rather melancholy, you know. Quite decent. He's still a good way off forty, but he's already famous and has had his fill of life. . . . As regards his writings, well . . . how shall I put it to you? Pretty, talented . . . but . . . after Tolstoy or Zola you wouldn't care to read Treegorin.

Sorin. Well I, my dear fellow, I am fond of authors. Once upon a time I passionately longed for two things: I longed to marry and longed to become an author; but I achieved neither object. Just so. It's pleasant to be even a minor author, that's the long and short of it.

Tryeplyev. [*Listening.*] I hear footsteps. . . . [*Embracing his uncle.*] Without her I can't live . . . Even the sound of her footsteps fascinates me. . . . I'm madly happy. [*Rushing to meet Nina Zaryechny as she enters.*] Enchantress, my dream. . . .

Nina. [*Agitated.*] I am not late? . . . Surely, I am not. . . .

Tryeplyev. [*Kissing her hands.*] No, no, no. . . .

Nina. All day long I have felt restless and afraid. I feared father wouldn't let me come. . . . But he 's just gone away with stepmother. The sky was red, the moon was rising, and I hurried on my horse, I hurried him on. . . . [*Laughing.*] But I 'm happy. [*Shaking Sorin's hand warmly.*

Sorin. [*Laughing.*] The dear little eyes seem red with tears. . . . Oh, oh! They mustn't!

Nina. Never mind. . . . See, I 'm out of breath. In half an hour I shall have to leave, we must hurry up. No, no, please don't keep me back. Father doesn't know I 'm here.

Tryeplyev. Indeed, it 's time to start. We must call the others.

Sorin. I 'll call them and all that. At once. [*Going to the right and singing.*] 'To France two grenadiers . . .' [*Looking back.*] Once when I began singing like that a certain junior crown-prosecutor said to me: 'Your Excellency has a strong voice.' . . . Then he thought for a while and added: 'But . . . an unpleasant one.' [*Laughs and goes off.*

Nina. Father and his wife don't allow me to come here. They say you are Bohemians here . . . they 're afraid of my becoming an actress. . . . But, like a seagull, I am drawn to this lake. . . . I have lost my heart to you. [*Looking round.*

Tryeplyev. We are alone.

Nina. I fancy someone is here. . . .

Tryeplyev. There 's no one. [*They kiss.*

Nina. What tree is this?

Tryeplyev. An elm.

Nina. Why is it so dark?

Tryeplyev. It 's already evening, all objects are growing dark. Don't go away early, I implore you.

Nina. I must.

Tryeplyev. Suppose I come over to your place, Nina? All night long I will stand in your garden and look up at your window.

Nina. You mustn't; the watchman will see you. Trésor hasn't yet got used to you and he will bark.

Tryeplyev. I love you!

Nina. Sh-h! . . .

Tryeplyev. [*Hearing footsteps.*] Who's there? Is it you, Yakov?

Yakov. [*Behind the platform.*] Yes, sir.

Tryeplyev. All of you take your places. It 's time. The moon is getting up.

Yakov. Yes, sir.

Tryeplyev. Have you got the spirits? Have you the sulphur? When the red eyes appear there must be a smell of sulphur. [*To Nina.*] Come, everything is ready there. You are nervous?

Nina. Yes, very nervous. Your mother I don't mind, I'm not afraid of her; but you have Treegorin here. . . . To act in his presence frightens me and makes me shy. . . . A famous writer. Is he young?

Tryeplyev. Yes.

Nina. How wonderful his stories are!

Tryeplyev. [*Coldly.*] I don't know. I haven't read them.

Nina. Your play is hard to act. There are no living characters in it.

Tryeplyev. Living characters! Life must be presented not as it is, nor as it ought to be, but as it appears in our dreams.

Nina. In your play there's little action, mere recitation. And a play, I think, ought to deal with love. . . .

[*Both go off behind the platform.*

Enter Pauline Andreyevna and Dorn.

Pauline Andreyevna. It's getting damp. Go back and put on your galoshes.

Dorn. I'm hot.

Pauline Andreyevna. You don't take care of yourself. It's obstinacy. You're a doctor, and know quite well that the damp air is bad for you; but you wish to make me miserable, you deliberately sat out the whole of last evening on the terrace. . . .

Dorn. [*Humming.*] 'Say not youth is wasted.'

Pauline Andreyevna. You were so much engrossed in conversation with Irene Nicolayevna . . . you didn't mind the cold. Confess, you're attracted by her. . . .

Dorn. I'm fifty-five.

Pauline Andreyevna. Nonsense, that's not old for a man. You're remarkably well preserved and are still attractive to women.

Dorn. What are you driving at?

Pauline Andreyevna. Before an actress you are all ready to knee down. Every one of you!

Dorn. [*Humming.*] 'Again I'm here before thee.' . . . If actors and actresses are liked in society, and are regarded differently from tradesmen, for instance, that's only as it should be. It's idealism.

Pauline Andreyevna. Women have always fallen in love with you and hung round your neck. Is that also idealism?

Dorn. [*Shrugging his shoulders.*] Why? In women's relations to me there has been a great deal that is fine. It was the excellent doctor in me that they mainly loved. Ten or fifteen years ago, you remember, I was the only good *accoucheur* in the whole province. Besides, I've always been an honourable man.

Pauline Andreyevna. [*Seizing his arm.*] My dear!

Dorn. Quiet! People are coming.

Enter Mme Arkadin arm-in-arm with Sorin and Treegorin, Shamrayev, Myedvyedenko, and Masha.

Shamrayev. In 1873 at Poltava, during the fair, she acted amazingly. A sheer delight! She acted wonderfully! You don't happen to know where Chadin, Paul Semyonovich, the comic actor, is now? In the role of Rasplyuev he was inimitable, better than Sadovsky, I swear, my honoured lady. Where is he now?

Mme Arkadin. You keep on asking about antediluvians. How can I tell? [*Sits down.*

Shamrayev. [*Drawing his breath.*] Old Paul Chadin! There are no more actors like him. The stage has degenerated, Irene Nicolayevna! There used to be mighty oaks, and now we see mere stumps.

Dorn. There are not a great many outstanding talents now, that's true, but the average actor has much improved.

Shamrayev. I can't agree with you. Though that's a matter of taste. *De gustibus aut bene, aut nihil.*
[*Tryeplyev comes out from behind the platform.*

Mme Arkadin. [*To her son.*] My darling son, when is it to begin?

Tryeplyev. In a minute. Patience, please.

Mme Arkadin. [*Reciting from 'Hamlet.'*] 'O Hamlet, speak no more:
    Thou turn'st mine eyes into my very soul;
    And there I see such black and grained spots,
    As will not leave their tint.'

Tryeplyev. [*Reciting from 'Hamlet.'*] 'Nay, but to live
    In the rank sweat of an enseamed bed;
    Stew'd in corruption; honeying, and making love
    Over the nasty sty. . . .'
[*From behind the platform comes the sound of a horn.*

Tryeplyev. Now it begins! I beg your attention! [*A pause.*]
I begin. [*Knocking with a little stick and speaking in a loud

voice.] O you ancient honourable shades that nightly haunt this lake, lull us to sleep, and may we see in a dream what is going to be two hundred thousand years from now!

Sorin. Two hundred thousand years from now there will be nothing.

Tryeplyev. Then let us have that nothing presented to us.

Mme Arkadin. Let us. We are asleep.

[*The curtain rises, revealing a view of the lake ; the moon is above the horizon, and its reflection is seen in the water ; on a large stone sits Nina Zaryechny, all in white.*

Nina. Men, lions, eagles, and partridges, horned deer, geese, spiders, dumb fishes that used to dwell in the water, star-fishes and such as could not be seen by the eye—in a word, all lives, all lives, all lives, having accomplished the sad cycle, have been extinguished. . . . It is thousands of years since a single living thing was seen on the earth, and this poor moon lights its lantern in vain. On the meadow no longer do the cranes awaken with a cry, and the cockchafers are no longer heard in the lime groves. Cold, cold, cold! Void, void, void! Terrible, terrible, terrible! [*A pause.*] The bodies of living things have turned to dust, and the eternal matter has converted them into stones, water, clouds, and all their souls have become fused into one. The common universal soul—that is I . . . I. . . . In me is the soul of Alexander the Great, and of Caesar, and of Shakespeare, and of Napoleon, and of the tiniest leech. In me the consciousnesses of men have become fused with the instincts of animals, and I remember everything, everything, everything, and each life I am living through again in myself.   [*Marsh lights appear.*

Mme Arkadin. [*Quietly.*] That's something in the decadent style.

Tryeplyev. [*Imploringly and with reproach.*] Mamma!

Nina. I am lonely. Once in a hundred years I open my lips to speak, and in this void my voice rings dolefully, and no one hears me. . . . Nor do you, you pale lights, heed me. . . . Towards morning you are begotten of the putrescent marsh and you wander before the dawn, but without thought, without will, without the throb of life. Afraid lest life should arise in you, the father of eternal matter, the devil, produces every instant in you, as in stones and in water, an interchange of atoms, and you are changing ceaselessly. In the universe only the spirit remains permanent and unaltered. [*A pause.*] Like a prisoner, thrown into a hollow, deep well, I know not where I am and what is awaiting me. Only it is not hidden from me that in the stubborn, fierce fight with the devil, the principle of material forces, I am destined to conquer, and after that matter and spirit will be fused in a consummate harmony and there will begin the kingdom of universal will. But this will only arise when, little by little, through a long, long succession of millenniums, the moon, and bright Sirius, and the earth have turned to dust. . . . And until then— terror, terror. . . . [*A pause. Over the lake appear two red spots.*] Lo, there approaches my mighty adversary, the devil. I see his terrible, flaming eyes. . . .

Mme Arkadin. It smells of sulphur. Is that necessary?

Tryeplyev. Yes.

Mme Arkadin. [*Laughing.*] Yes, that's a good effect.

Tryeplyev. Mamma!

Nina. He is weary without man. . . .

Pauline Andreyevna. [*To Dorn.*] You've taken off your hat. Put it on, or you'll catch cold.

Mme Arkadin. The doctor has taken his hat off to the devil, the father of eternal matter. . . .

Tryeplyev. [*Flaring up, in a loud voice.*] The piece is over! Stop! Curtain!

Mme Arkadin. But why are you cross?

Tryeplyev. Stop! Curtain! Drop the curtain. [*With a stamp of his foot.*] Curtain! [*The curtain falls.*] I'm sorry! I overlooked the fact that only a few of the elect can write plays and act on the stage. I've infringed a monopoly! To me . . . I . . .

[*Tries to say something, but with a wave of the hand goes out to the left.*]

Mme Arkadin. What's the matter with him?

Sorin. Irene, my dear, you shouldn't treat young ambition like that.

Mme Arkadin. But what did I say to him?

Sorin. You hurt him.

Mme Arkadin. He warned us himself it was a joke, and I treated his play as a joke.

Sorin. Still——

Mme Arkadin. Now it appears he has written a great work! Just think of it! So he arranged this performance and smoked us with sulphur not as a joke, but as a protest. . . . He meant to give us a lesson on how plays should be written and how they should be acted. In the end, it gets tedious. Say what you will, these continual outbursts against me, these incessant pin-pricks, would tire out any one! A capricious, selfish boy.

Sorin. He meant to give you pleasure.

Mme Arkadin. You think so? Yet he did not choose some ordinary piece, but forced us to listen to this decadent raving. For a joke I am ready to listen even to raving, but here are pretensions to new forms, to a new era in art. To my mind, there are no new forms here at all, but just bad temper.

Treegorin. Every one writes in accordance with his desires and capacity.

Mme Arkadin. Let him write in accordance with his desires and capacity, only let him leave us in peace.

Dorn. Jupiter, thou art angry——

Mme Arkadin. I'm not Jupiter, I am a woman. [*Lighting a cigarette.*] I'm not angry, I'm only vexed that a young man should spend his time so stupidly. I didn't want to hurt him.

Myedvyedenko. There are no sufficient grounds for separating spirit from matter; for it may well be that spirit itself is a combination of material atoms. [*Vivaciously, to Treegorin.*] If only, you know, someone would describe the life of us teachers in a play, and then have it acted on the stage. It's a hard, hard life!

Mme Arkadin. That's right, but let us have no more talk either of plays or of atoms. It's such a glorious evening! Hearken! someone's singing? [*Listening.*] How fine!

Pauline Andreyevna. It's over there on the other side.

Mme Arkadin. [*To Treegorin.*] Sit down beside me. Ten or fifteen years ago, here, on the lake, music and singing used to be heard continually, nearly every night. Surrounding the lake here are six estates, and I remember the laughter, noise, shooting, and love-making. . . . The *jeune premier* and idol of all these six estates was then—let me introduce him [*With a turn of her head to Dorn.*]—Doctor Yevgueniy Sergueyevich. He's still charming, but then he was irresistible. However, my conscience begins to prick me. Why did I hurt my poor boy? I'm uneasy. [*Aloud.*] Kostya! Son! Kostya!

Masha. I'll go and look for him.

Mme Arkadin. Please do, my dear.

Masha. [*Going to the left.*] A-ou! Konstantin Gavrilovich! . . . A-ou! [*Goes off.*

Nina. [*Coming out from behind the platform.*] Evidently there's to be no continuation, so I may come out. How do you do?
[*Kissing Mme Arkadin and Pauline Andreyevna.*

Sorin. Bravo! Bravo!

Mme Arkadin. Bravo! Bravo! We admired you. With such an appearance, such a wonderful voice, you should not sit in the country, it's a sin. You must possess talent. I say! You must go on the stage!

Nina. Oh, it is my dream! [*With a sigh.*] But it is never to be realized.

Mme Arkadin. Who can tell? Let me introduce: Treegorin, Boris Alexeyevich.

Nina. Oh, I am so glad. . . . [*Blushing.*] I 'm always reading you. . . .

Mme Arkadin. [*Making room for her beside her.*] Don't be shy, my dear. He's a celebrity, but he has a simple heart. See, he's blushing.

Dorn. I suppose the curtain may be raised now; it's rather eerie.

Shamrayev. [*Aloud.*] Yakov, pull up the curtain, lad!

[*The curtain goes up.*

Nina. [*To Treegorin.*] Isn't it a strange play?

Treegorin. I could not make it out. Still, I looked on with pleasure. You acted so sincerely. And the scenery was superb. [*A pause.*] I suppose there must be a lot of fish in this lake?

Nina. Yes.

Treegorin. I love fishing. There's nothing I enjoy more than sitting, at twilight, on the bank and watching the float.

Nina. But I believe that to one who has experienced the joy of creative work, all other joys cease to exist.

Mme Arkadin. [*Laughing.*] You mustn't speak to him like that. When kind things are said to him he doesn't know where to turn.

Shamrayev. I remember once in Moscow at the opera the famous Silva took the bottom C. And at that moment, as though on purpose, a bass, one of our cathedral choristers, was sitting in the gallery; and all of a sudden—you can imagine our extreme amazement—we heard from the gallery: 'Bravo, Silva!' a whole octave lower . . . like this: [*In a deep tiny bass.*] 'Bravo, Silva!' . . . The whole theatre was struck dumb.

[*A pause.*

Dorn. The angel of silence is hovering round.

Nina. It's time I went. Good-bye.

Mme Arkadin. Where to? Where to so early? We shan't let you go.

Nina. Father's waiting for me.

Mme Arkadin. How bad of him! . . . [*Kissing one another.*]
   Well, it can't be helped. It's a pity, it's a pity to let you go.

Nina. If you knew how very painful it is for me to have to go
   away.

Mme Arkadin. Someone ought to see you home, my darling.

Nina. [*In fright.*] Oh, no, no!

Sorin. [*To her, beseechingly.*] Do stay!

Nina. I can't, Peter Nicolayevich.

Sorin. Do stay one hour and all that. Do, really——

Nina. [*After some reflection, through tears.*] It is impossible!
                                    [*Shakes his hand and hurries off.*

Mme Arkadin. What an unfortunate girl. They say her late
   mother bequeathed to her husband all her huge fortune,
   everything to the last penny, and now this little girl is left
   with nothing, for her father has already made over everything
   to his second wife. It is revolting.

Dorn. Yes, her dad, to do him full justice, is a thorough beast.

Sorin. [*Rubbing his chilled hands.*] Well, let's all go in; it's
   getting damp. My legs ache.

Mme Arkadin. Your legs seem to be made of wood, they hardly
   move. Well, let's go in, poor old thing.   [*Taking his arm.*

Shamrayev. [*Offering his wife his arm.*] Madame?

Sorin. I hear the dog howling again. [*To Shamrayev.*] Do please,
   Ilya Afanasyevich, tell them to take the dog off the chain.

Shamrayev. Can't be done, Peter Nicolayevich, I am afraid of
   thieves getting into the barn. There's the millet there. [*To
   Myedvyedenko, who is walking beside him.*] Yes, a whole octave
   lower: 'Bravo, Silva!' And he not a singer, a mere choir
   boy.

Myedvyedenko. And what pay does a chorister get?
                                    [*All go off, except Dorn.*

Dorn. [*Alone.*] I don't know, perhaps I understand nothing or
   have gone out of my mind; but I liked the play. There's a
   something in it. When the girl spoke of loneliness, and then
   when the eyes of the devil appeared, my hands trembled with
   agitation. It's fresh, naïve. . . . There he comes, I think.
   I mean to say a lot of nice things to him.

Tryeplyev. [*Entering.*] Is there no one here?

Dorn. I'm here.

Tryeplyev. Mashenka is looking for me all over the park.
   Unbearable creature.

Dorn. Konstantin Gavrilovich, I liked your play immensely. It
   isn't an ordinary play. I haven't heard it to the end, but the

impression it has made on me is strong. You are a man of talent, you must go on.

[*Tryeplyev warmly presses his hand and embraces him impulsively.*

Dorn. Oh, how nervous! Tears in your eyes. . . . I meant to say. You've taken a subject from the province of abstract ideas. And so it should be, for a work of art must needs express some great idea. Only that is beautiful which is serious. How pale you are!

Tryeplyev. So you say—go on!

Dorn. Certainly. . . . But present only what's important and eternal. You know, I've had a pretty varied experience and I've enjoyed it; I'm content; but if I were to experience the exaltation of spirit which artists experience in moments of creation, I think I should despise my material vesture and all that is peculiar to it, and I should soar to heights far away from the earth.

Tryeplyev. I'm sorry, where's Nina?

Dorn. And also this. In a work there must be a clear, definite idea. You must know your purpose in writing, otherwise, if you pursue that picturesque path without a definite objective, you will lose your way and your talent will destroy you.

Tryeplyev. [*Impatiently.*] Where's Nina?

Dorn. She has ridden home.

Tryeplyev. [*In despair.*] What shall I do? I want to see her. . . . I must see her. . . . I'll ride over. . . .

Enter Masha.

Dorn. [*To Tryeplyev.*] Be calm, my friend!

Tryeplyev. No, I will go. I must go.

Masha. Go into the house, Konstantin Gavrilovich. Your mother's waiting for you. She's uneasy.

Tryeplyev. Tell her that I have gone. And I beg all of you to leave me alone! Leave me alone! Don't follow me about!

Dorn. Come now, come, come, old man . . . you mustn't. . . . It isn't right!

Tryeplyev. [*Through tears.*] Good-bye, doctor. Thank you. . . .
[*Goes off.*

Dorn. [*With a sigh.*] Oh, youth, youth!

Masha. When there's nothing else to say, people say: 'Youth, youth!' . . .
[*Snuffs tobacco.*

Dorn. [*Taking the snuff-box from her and throwing it into the bushes.*] It's odious! [*A pause.*] I fancy I hear music in the house. We'd better go in.

Masha. Wait awhile.

Dorn. Why?

Masha. I want to tell you once more. I want to speak. . . [*In agitation.*] I don't love my father . . . but my heart goes out to you. Somehow I feel with all my soul that you're near to me. . . . Do help me. Do help me, or I shall do something stupid, I shall make a mess of my life, I'll spoil it all. . . . I can't go on any longer. . . .

Dorn. Help you in what way?

Masha. I suffer. Nobody, nobody knows my sufferings! [*Laying her head on his breast; in a gentle voice.*] I love Konstantin.

Dorn. How nervous you all are! How nervous you all are! And what an amount of love! . . . Oh, you enchanted lake! [*Tenderly.*] But what is it I can do for you, my child? What? What?

CURTAIN

ACT II

A croquet lawn. Far back on the right is the house with a large terrace; on the left is seen the lake, in which the sun is reflected, and glistening. Flower beds. Time: midday. Hot. By the side of the lawn, in the shade of an old lime tree, Mme Arkadin, Dorn, and Masha sit on a bench. An open book is lying on Dorn's knees.

Mme Arkadin. [*To Masha.*] Now let's stand up. [*Both get up.*] Let's stand side by side. You're twenty-two, and I'm nearly twice your age. Yegueniy Sergueyevich, which of us looks the younger?

Dorn. You, certainly.

Mme Arkadin. See. . . . And why? Because I work, I feel, I'm always doing something, and you keep on sitting always in the same place, you are not alive. . . . Also I make it a rule—not to peep into the future. I never think either of old age, or of death. What is to be, must be.

Masha. And I feel as though I had been born ages ago; I'm dragging on my life like an endless train. . . . And often I've no desire whatever to go on. [*Sitting down.*] Of course, it's all rubbish. One should give oneself a shake and cast all that off.

Dorn. [*Humming in a low voice.*] 'Tell her, my flowers . . .'

Mme Arkadin. Again, I'm as correct as an Englishman. I, my dear, keep myself up to the mark, as they say, and I'm always dressed and have my hair done *comme il faut.* I shouldn't dream of walking out of the house, even as far as the garden here, in a blouse, or with my hair not done. Never. I keep my looks because I have never been a sloven, I never let myself get slack, as some do. . . . [*With arms akimbo, she makes a few steps on the lawn.*] There you are—as lively as a chick. I could act a girl of fifteen.

Dorn. Well, nevertheless and in spite of it, I'm going to read on. [*Taking the book.*] We stopped at the corn-chandler and the rats——

Mme Arkadin. And the rats. Read on. [*Sitting down.*] But, let me, I will read. It's my turn. [*Taking the book and searching in it.*] And the rats. . . . Here it is. . . . [*Reading.*] 'And, evidently, for society people to pamper novelists and to win them over is as dangerous as for a corn-chandler to breed rats in his store-rooms. And yet they are run after. So that when a woman has chosen a writer whom she wishes to captivate, she besieges him with compliments, flattery, and favours.' . . . Well, it may perhaps be so with the French, but with us there's nothing like that, no programme at all. With us, before a woman sets out to captivate a writer, she has already fallen in love with him up to the ears, you may be sure. No need to go far, take even myself and Treegorin.

Sorin walks up, leaning on his stick, side by side with Nina; Myedvyedenko follows them, wheeling a chair.

Sorin. [*In the tone in which one speaks to children.*] Yes. We've good news! We are happy to-day, and that's the long and short of it. [*To Mme Arkadin.*] We have good news! Father and stepmother have gone to Tver, and we're free now for three whole days.

Nina. [*Sitting down beside Mme Arkadin and embracing her.*] I'm so happy! Now I belong to you.

Sorin. [*Sitting down in the chair.*] She's a pretty little thing to-day.

Mme Arkadin. Smartly dressed, attractive. . . . Now you're a clever girl. [*Kissing Nina.*] But take care not to be praised too much, just to escape the evil eye. Where's Boris Alexeyevich?

Nina. He's in the bathing tent, fishing.

Mme Arkadin. How does he manage not to get sick of it?

[Wishes to go on reading.

Nina. What are you reading?

Mme Arkadin. Maupassant's *Sur l'eau*, darling. [*Reading a few lines to herself.*] Now, what follows isn't interesting nor true. [*Shutting the book.*] My mind feels uneasy. Tell me what's the matter with my son? Why is he so weary and gloomy? He spends whole days on the lake and I hardly ever see him at all.

Masha. He's depressed. [*To Nina, timidly.*] I beg you, read a passage out of his play.

Nina. [*Shrugging her shoulders.*] Do you want me to? Is it so interesting?

Masha. [*Restraining her delight.*] When he himself reads something, his eyes glow and his face turns pale. He has a beautiful, sad voice, and the manner of a poet.

[Sorin is heard snoring.

Dorn. Good night!

Mme Arkadin. Petrusha!

Sorin. Eh?

Mme Arkadin. You're asleep?

Sorin. Not a bit. [*A pause.*

Mme Arkadin. You won't take medical advice, and that's wrong, brother.

Sorin. I should be glad to take it, but the doctor here won't give me any.

Dorn. To take advice at sixty!

Sorin. Even at sixty one wants to live.

Dorn. [*With annoyance.*] Ah! well, take valerian drops.

Mme Arkadin. I think it might do him good to go to some watering place.

Dorn. Well? It might. Or it might not.

Mme Arkadin. How's one to make you out!

Dorn. There's nothing to make out. It's all clear. [*A pause.*

Myedvyedenko. Peter Nicolayevich ought to give up smoking.

Sorin. Nonsense.

Dorn. No, it isn't nonsense. Wine and tobacco rob your personality. After a cigar or a glass of vodka you are no longer Peter Nicolayevich, but Peter Nicolayevich plus someone else; your 'I' dissolves in you, and you already take yourself for a third person—'he.'

Sorin. [*Laughing.*] It's all very well for you to talk. You've enjoyed yourself in your lifetime, but I? I served in the law courts for twenty-eight years, but I haven't yet lived, I haven't yet experienced anything, and that's the long and short of it; and quite naturally I very much want to live. You're satiated and indifferent, and that's why you have an inclination to philosophize, but as for me, I want to live, and therefore I have sherry at dinner and smoke cigars, and all that. That's all.

Dorn. One should take life seriously; to undergo medical treatment at sixty, and be sorry that one hasn't enjoyed one-self sufficiently in one's youth, is, pardon me, childish.

Masha. [*Getting up.*] It must be lunch-time now. [*Walking with an indolent, careless step.*] I feel stiff in my leg. . . .

[*Goes off.*

Dorn. Off to gulp a couple of glasses before lunch.

Sorin. The poor thing has no personal happiness.

Dorn. Rot. Rot, Your Excellency.

Sorin. You reason like a satiated man.

Mme Arkadin. Ah, can there be anything more boring than this sweet country boredom? Hot, still, no one doing anything, all philosophizing. . . . It's nice to be with you, friends, it's pleasant to listen to you, but sitting in one's room at a hotel and learning a part—oh, that's ever so much better!

Nina. [*Ecstatically.*] How fine! I do understand you.

Sorin. Of course, it's better in town. One sits in one's study, the butler lets no one in unannounced, the telephone . . . traffic in the street, and all that. . . .

Dorn. [*Humming.*] 'Tell her, my flowers . . .'

Enter Shamrayev, and after him Pauline Andreyevna.

Shamrayev. Here they are! Good day! [*Kissing Mme Arkadin's hand and then Nina's.*] Very glad to see you so well. [*To Mme Arkadin.*] My wife says that you intend driving to town to-day with her. Is that so?

Mme Arkadin. Yes, we do.

Shamrayev. H'm. . . . That's splendid, but how will you get there, honoured lady? To-day we are carting the rye, all the labourers are at work. And which horses are you going to take, may I ask?

Mme Arkadin. Which horses? How do I know which?

Sorin. But we have carriage-horses.

Shamrayev. [*Excited.*] Carriage-horses? But where am I to get the collars? Where shall I get the collars? It is surprising! It is inconceivable! My honoured lady! Excuse me, I adore your talent, I 'm ready to give ten years of my life for you, but I can't let you have any horses.

Mme Arkadin. But suppose I must go? How strange!

Shamrayev. My honoured lady! You do not know what the management of an estate involves.

Mme Arkadin. [*Flaring up.*] The old story over again! In that case I 'm going back to Moscow this very day. Tell them to hire horses for me in the village, or I 'll walk to the station.

Shamrayev. [*Flaring up.*] In that case I resign my post! Find another steward! [*Goes off.*

Mme Arkadin. Every summer it is like that, every summer I am insulted here! I 'll never set foot in this place again!

[*Goes off to the left where the bathing-tent is supposed to be ; after a minute she is seen passing to the house ; after her follows Treegorin with fishing-rods and a pail.*

Sorin. [*Flaring up.*] It is impertinence! It 's the devil knows what! I 'm sick of it all, and that 's the long and short of it. Let all the horses be brought up here this minute!

Nina. [*To Pauline Andreyevna.*] Refuse Irene Nicolayevna, the famous actress! Isn't any wish of hers, even her caprice, more important than the whole estate? It 's simply incredible!

Pauline Andreyevna. [*In despair.*] What can I do? Put yourself in my place: what can I do?

Sorin. [*To Nina.*] Come, let us go to my sister. . . . We will all implore her not to go away. Isn't that so? [*Glancing in the direction in which Shamrayev has gone off.*] An intolerable man! A despot!

Nina. [*Not letting him get up.*] Don't get up. . . . We will take you there. . . . [*She and Mydevyedenko wheel the Bath chair.*] Oh, how awful it is! . . .

Sorin. Yes, yes, it is awful. . . . But he won't resign. I 'll talk to him directly.

[*They go off ; only Dorn and Pauline Andreyevna remain.*

Dorn. People are tiresome. As a matter of fact, your husband ought to be kicked out of here neck and crop. And yet it 's sure to end in that old woman, Peter Nicolayevich, and his sister begging his pardon. You 'll see!

Pauline Andreyevna. He has even sent the carriage-horses into the fields. And that sort of misunderstanding occurs every day. If only you knew how it all worries me! I 'm falling ill; you see, I 'm trembling. . . . I can't endure his rudeness

[*Beseechingly.*] Yevgueniy, my dear, my beloved, take me away. . . . Our time is passing, we are no longer young, and if even at the end of our life we could only avoid concealment and falsehood. [*A pause.*

Dorn. I'm fifty-five; it's too late to change one's life.

Pauline Andreyevna. I know you refuse me because, besides myself, there are other women who are attached to you. You can't take them all away. I understand. Forgive me, I'm boring you.

[*Nina appears near the house ; she plucks flowers.*

Dorn. No, it's all right.

Pauline Andreyevna. I suffer from jealousy. Of course, you're a doctor, you can't avoid women. I understand. . . .

Dorn. [*To Nina, who is coming up to them.*] How are matters there?

Nina. Irene Nicolayevna is crying, and Peter Nicolayevich has got an attack of asthma.

Dorn. [*Getting up.*] I'll go and give them both valerian drops. . . .

Nina. [*Giving him the flowers.*] Please!

Dorn. Merci bien! [*Goes towards the house.*

Pauline Andreyevna. [*Going with him.*] What lovely flowers! [*Near the house, in a dull voice*]. Give me those flowers! Give me those flowers!

[*On receiving the flowers she tears them and flings them aside ; both go into the house.*

Nina. [*Alone.*] How strange to see a famous actress cry, and for such a trifling reason, too! And isn't it strange—a famous writer, beloved by the public, all the papers writing about him, his photographs on sale, translated into foreign languages— and he spends the whole day fishing and is delighted at having caught two chub? I thought that famous people were proud, and inaccessible, that they despised the crowd, and by means of their fame, of the lustre of their names, they, as it were, avenged themselves on the crowd which exalts birth and wealth above everything else. But they cry, fish, play cards, laugh, and get angry, like all the rest.

Tryeplyev. [*Coming in, hatless, with a gun and a shot seagull.*] You are here alone?

Nina. Alone. [*Tryeplyev lays the seagull at her feet.*] What does that mean?

Tryeplyev. I had the baseness to kill this seagull to-day. I lay it at your feet.

Nina. What's the matter with you?

[*Picking up the seagull and gazing at it.*

Tryeplyev. [*After a pause.*] Soon I shall kill myself in the same way.

Nina. I don't recognize you.

Tryeplyev. Yes, but only after I've ceased to recognize you. You've changed towards me, your look is cold, my presence embarrasses you.

Nina. Lately you've become irritable, you express yourself quite incomprehensibly, in symbols. And this seagull here is also evidently a symbol, but, pardon me, I don't understand. [*Placing the seagull on the seat.*] I'm too simple to understand you.

Tryeplyev. It started that evening, my play turned out such a stupid failure. Women don't forgive failure. I've burnt everything, everything, to the last scrap. If you only knew how unhappy I am! Your coldness is terrible, incredible, exactly as if I were to wake up and see that this lake had suddenly dried up, or disappeared into the earth. You've just said that you're too simple to understand me. Oh, what is there to understand! My play was not liked, you despise my inspiration, you already consider me mediocre, worthless, like so many others . . . [*Stamping his foot.*] How well I understand it, how I understand it! A nail seems to be boring into my brain, damn it, and my imbecility which is sucking my blood, sucking it like a snake . . . [*On noticing Treegorin, who walks and reads a book.*] Here comes a real genius, marching, like Hamlet, and he too with a book. [*Scoffingly.*] 'Words, words, words.' . . . That sun has not yet come up to you, and you're smiling, your look has softened under its rays. I won't be in your way. [*Walks away hurriedly.*

Treegorin. [*Making notes in his note-book.*] 'Takes snuff and drinks vodka. . . . Always in black. The schoolmaster is in love with her. . . .'

Nina. How do you do, Boris Alexeyevich?

Treegorin. How do you do? Circumstances have taken such a sudden turn that, I think, we're going away to-day. We are hardly likely ever to meet again. And it's a pity. I don't often meet young girls, girls who are young and interesting, and I've already forgotten, and can't picture to myself clearly, what girls feel like at eighteen or nineteen, and therefore in my novels and stories young girls are usually untrue to life. I should just like to be in your place even for one hour, so as to learn how you think, and generally what sort of creature you are.

Nina. And I should like to be in your place.

Treegorin. What for?

Nina. In order to learn how a famous gifted writer feels. What fame feels like. How does your fame affect you?

Treegorin. How? Nohow, I should think. I never thought of it. [*After some reflection.*] One of two things: either you exaggerate my fame, or else it doesn't affect me at all.

Nina. And if you read about yourself in the papers?

Treegorin. When I am praised, it's pleasant, and when I'm abused, I feel out of humour for two days afterwards.

Nina. It's a wonderful world! If only you knew how I envy you! How different people's destinies are. Some just manage to drag on a tedious, obscure existence, all alike, all unhappy; while to others, for instance, to you—who are one of a million—there has been given a life—interesting, glorious, full of significance. . . . You're happy. . . .

Treegorin. I? [*Shrugging his shoulders.*] H'm. . . . Now you speak of fame, of happiness, of a glorious, interesting life, and to me all these nice words, pardon me, are just like Turkish delight, which I never eat. You're very young and very kind.

Nina. Yours is a grand life!

Treegorin. What is there particularly fine in it? [*Looking at his watch.*] I must go at once and write. Excuse me, I'm busy. . . . [*Laughing.*] You've trodden on my favourite corn, as they say, and I'm beginning to get upset and a bit cross. Still, let's talk. Let's talk of my grand, glorious life. . . . Well, where shall we start? [*After some reflection.*] There are haunting ideas which compel a man to go on day and night thinking, for instance, of the moon; and I, too, have my moon. Day and night I am overwhelmed by one besetting idea: I must write, I must write, I must . . . I have scarcely finished one long story when I must at once somehow write another, then a third, after the third a fourth. . . . I write ceaselessly, as though travelling post haste, and I can't do otherwise. Where's the splendour and glory in that, I ask you? Oh, what a crazy life! Here I am now with you, I'm excited, yet every instant I remember that an unfinished story is waiting for me. I see a cloud, resembling a piano. And I think I must mention in a story that a cloud floated by which resembled a piano. I catch a whiff of heliotrope. Immediately I register it in my mind: a cloying odour, a widow's flower, to be mentioned in a description of a summer evening. I catch you and myself up at every phrase, at every word, and I hasten to lock up at once all those phrases and words in my literary warehouse: it may come in useful! When I finish work, I run to the theatre or go fishing; there I ought to find rest and forget myself, but no, already a heavy cannon-ball is tossing in my head—a new subject—and I'm already impelled to the desk, and must hasten again to write, and write. And so it is always without end, and I have no rest from myself, and I feel that I'm devouring my own life, that for the honey, which I'm giving to someone in the void, I strip the pollen from my best flowers, pluck those very flowers and trample on their roots. Am I not mad? Do my friends and acquaintances behave to me as they do to a sane person? 'What are you writing now? What surprise have you in store for us?' Ever the same, ever the same, and it seems to me that the attention of acquaintances, their praises, admiration—that all this is deception—I'm deceived by them as a sick person is deceived, and at times I fear that they will suddenly steal up to me from behind, seize me and carry me off, like Gogol's Popryschin, to a lunatic asylum. And in those years, the youthful, the best years, when I was beginning, my authorship was one continuous torture. A beginner, particularly when he has no luck, seems to himself clumsy, awkward, superfluous. His nerves on edge, worn to pieces, he's irresistibly drawn to people who have to do with literature and art—and he is ignored, unnoticed by every one, afraid to look straight and boldly into people's eyes, just like an inveterate gambler who has no money. I hadn't seen my reader, but somehow in my imagination he seemed unfriendly, distrustful. I feared the public, it frightened me, and when I had to produce my new play, it seemed to me all the while that all the dark people were hostile to me, and the fair coldly indifferent. Oh, how awful! What torture it was!

Nina. But surely inspiration and the process of creation in itself gives you high and happy moments?

Treegorin. Yes. When I write, it is pleasant. And reading the proofs is also pleasant, but . . . no sooner has the thing come out, than I can't endure it, and realize at once that it isn't it, that it's a mistake, that it oughtn't to have been written at all, and I'm vexed, and feel quite sick inside me. . . . [*Laughing.*] And the public reads it. 'Yes, charming, clever, Charming, but a long way off Tolstoy.' Or: 'It's a fine thing, but Turgenev's *Fathers and Children* is better.' And so until I drop into my grave, it'll always be charming and clever, charming and clever—nothing more; and after I am dead, acquaintances, passing by my tomb, will say: 'Here lies Treegorin. A fine writer, but he didn't write as well as Turgenev.'

Nina. Forgive me, I refuse to understand you. You're simply spoilt by success.

Treegorin. Success? I've never liked myself. I don't love myself as a writer. The worst of it all is that I'm in a sort of daze and I don't understand what I'm writing. . . . I love this water here, the trees, the sky, I feel Nature, she awakens a passion in me, an irresistible desire to write. But I'm not only a painter of landscapes, I'm a citizen as well, I love my country, the people, I realize that if I'm a writer I must write of the people, of their sufferings, of their future, that I must speak of science, of the rights of man and so on, and so on, and I speak about it all, I'm in a hurry, I'm beset on all sides, and people get angry with me; I rush here and there, like a fox baited by hounds, I see that life and science keep on advancing further and further, and I am lagging behind all the time, like a peasant, too late for the train, and, at last I feel that I can compose landscapes only, and in all the rest I'm false and false to the marrow of my bones.

Nina. You've worked too hard and you have neither the time nor the desire to realize your significance. You may be dissatisfied with yourself, but to others you're great and glorious! If I were such a writer as you, I should give all my life to the crowd, but I should be conscious that their happiness consisted only in always rising up to my level, and they would harness themselves to my chariot.

Treegorin. Chariot, why . . . Me an Agamemnon? [*Both smile.*

Nina. For the happiness of being an authoress or actress, I would endure the indifference of those near to me, poverty, disappointment, I would live in a garret and eat black bread only—I would suffer from self-dissatisfaction, from the consciousness of my imperfections, but then in return I should demand fame . . . genuine, resounding fame. . . . [*Covering her face with her hands.*] My head feels dizzy! Ough! . . .

Mme Arkadin's voice. [*From the house.*] Boris Alexeyevich!

Treegorin. I'm summoned. . . . It must be to pack. Yet I've no desire to go away. [*Looking at the lake.*] The beauty of it all! . . . Wonderful!

Nina. Do you see the house and orchard on the other side?

Treegorin. Yes.

Nina. It 's my late mother's manor. I was born there. All my life I 've spent round this lake and I know every islet in it.

Treegorin. It is beautiful here! [*Noticing the seagull.*] And what 's this?

Nina. A seagull. Konstantin Gavrilych killed it.

Treegorin. Beautiful bird. Really I don't want to go away. Do try and persuade Irene Nicolayevna to stay. [*Makes a note in his note-book.*]

Nina. What are you writing?

Treegorin. I 'm just making a note. . . . A subject flashed across my mind. . . . [*Putting away his note-book.*] A subject for a short story: on the banks of a lake, a young girl, like you, has lived from her childhood; she loves the lake, like a seagull, and she 's happy and free, like a seagull. But by chance a man comes, sees her, and wantonly destroys her, like this seagull here. [*A pause.*

Mme Arkadin appears at the window.

Mme Arkadin. Boris Alexeyevich, where are you?

Treegorin. This minute! [*Goes and looks back at Nina: when near the window says to Mme Arkadin.*] Well?

Mme Arkadin. We 're staying on.

[*Treegorin goes into the house.*

Nina. [*Advancing to the footlights; after some meditation.*] It is a dream!

CURTAIN

ACT III

The dining-room in Sorin's house. Doors on the right and on the left. A sideboard. A cupboard for medicines. A table in the middle of the room. A trunk and hat-boxes; there are visible preparations for departure. Treegorin is having an early lunch; Masha is standing by the table.

Masha. I 'm telling you all this because you are a writer. You may make use of it. Upon my conscience, if he had wounded himself seriously, I wouldn't live a single minute. Still I 'm plucky. I 've made up my mind: I 'll tear out this love from my heart, I 'll tear it out by the roots.

Treegorin. How?

Masha. I 'm going to get married. To Myedvyedenko.

Treegorin. The schoolmaster, isn't he?

Masha. Yes.

Treegorin. I don't see where the need for it is.

Masha. To love hopelessly, to wait for whole years for something. . . . But after I 'm married, I shall no longer think of love, new cares will drown all the past. Still, don't you know, a change. Shall we have another?

Treegorin. Won't that be too much?

Masha. Why? [*Pouring out two glasses.*] Don't look at me like that. Women drink more often than you suppose. The minority drink openly, like myself, and the majority do it on the sly. That 's it. And it 's always vodka or cognac. [*Clinking glasses.*] Here 's to you! You 're a simple soul, I 'm sorry we have to part.   [*Both drink.*

Treegorin. I myself don't want to leave.

Masha. Get her to stay on.

Treegorin. No, this time she won't stay. Her son is behaving extremely tactlessly. First he attempts to shoot himself, and now, they say, he 's going to challenge me to a duel. And why? He only snorts and preaches new forms. . . . But surely there 's room both for the new and for the old—what's the sense in shoving?

Masha. Well, and jealousy too. Still it isn't my business.

> [*A pause. Yakov passes from the right to the left with a trunk; enter Nina who stands by the window.*

Masha. My schoolmaster isn't too brainy, but he 's a good man and poor, and loves me very much. I 'm sorry for him. And I 'm sorry also for his old mother. Well, let me wish you all that 's best. And think of me kindly. [*Firmly grasping his hand.*] I 'm very grateful to you for your friendship. Do send me your books, but with your autograph, please. Only you mustn't write 'to deeply respected,' but just like this: 'to Marie, a nobody, who 's living in this world for no known reason.' Good-bye!   [*Goes out.*

Nina. [*Holding out her clenched fist to Treegorin.*] Odd or even?

Treegorin. Even.

Nina. [*With a sigh.*] No. There 's only one pea in my hand. I 've wished: shall I go on the stage or not? I wish someone would advise me.

Treegorin. One can't advise in such a matter.   [*A pause.*

Nina. We 're parting and . . . may perhaps never meet again. I beg you to accept from me as a souvenir this little medallion. I had your initials engraved . . . and on the other side is the title of your book, *Days and Nights.*

Treegorin. How exquisite! [*Kissing the medallion.*] A delightful present!

Nina. Remember me sometimes.

Treegorin. I will remember you. I shall remember you as you were on that fine day—do you recollect?—a week ago, when you had a light dress on . . . and we had a talk then . . . and a white seagull was lying on the bench.

Nina. [*Thoughtfully.*] Yes, a seagull. . . . [*A pause.*] We can't speak now, someone's coming here. . . . Before you leave, give me two minutes, I implore you. . . .

> [*Goes out on the left; at the same time enter on the right Mme Arkadin, Sorin in a dinner jacket with a star; then Yakov, busy packing.*

Mme Arkadin. You'd better stay at home, old thing. With your rheumatism, you oughtn't to drive about paying visits. [*To Treegorin.*] Who was it that just went out? Nina?

Treegorin. Yes.

Mme Arkadin. Sorry to have disturbed you. [*Sitting down.*] I think I've packed everything. I'm dead tired.

Treegorin. [*Reading on the medallion.*] 'Days and Nights, page 121, lines 11 and 12.'

Yakov. [*Clearing the table.*] Shall I pack the fishing rods, too, sir?

Treegorin. Yes, I shall want them. The books you may give away.

Yakov. Yes, sir.

Treegorin. [*Speaking to himself.*] Page 121, lines 11 and 12. What is there in those lines? [*To Mme Arkadin.*] Are there any copies of my books in the house?

Mme Arkadin. Yes, in my brother's study, in the corner bookcase.

Treegorin. Page 121. . . .   [*Goes out.*

Mme Arkadin. Indeed, Peter dear, you'd better stay at home. . . .

Sorin. You're going away, I shall be miserable here without you.

Mme Arkadin. And what is there in town?

Sorin. Nothing particular. Still, [*laughing*] there'll be the laying of the foundation of the Zemstvo House, and all that. . . . I want to get out of this minnow-like sort of life, if only for an hour or two; for I've got too stale, just like an old cigarette-holder. I've ordered the horses to be here at one o'clock, so we'll set off at the same time.

Mme Arkadin. [*After a pause.*] Now, keep alive here, don't get bored, don't catch cold. Look after my son. Take good care of him. Advise him. [*A pause.*] I'm going away now, and so shan't know why Konstantin attempted to shoot himself. It seems to me that the chief reason was jealousy, and the sooner I get Treegorin away from here, the better.

Sorin. How shall I put it to you? There were other reasons, too. It 's quite clear—here is a young man, intelligent, living in the country, in a remote place, without money, without a position, without a future. No occupation. He 's ashamed and afraid of his inactivity. I 'm extremely fond of him, and he 's attached to me, too; but still, and that 's the long and short of it, he fancies that he 's not needed in the house, that he 's a dependant, a hanger-on. It 's quite clear— *amour-propre.* . . .

Mme Arkadin. What can I do for him? [*Pondering.*] Perhaps he ought to get some job. . . .

Sorin. [*Whistling a tune, then hesitatingly.*] It seems to me that the very best thing would be if you . . . gave him some money. First of all he ought to be dressed like a man and all that. Look, he 's been wearing the same old little jacket for three years, he walks about with no overcoat on. . . . [*Laughing.*] And it would not be bad for the young fellow to have some fun. . . . He ought perhaps to go abroad. . . . It doesn't cost much, does it now?

Mme Arkadin. Still . . . Well, I might perhaps let him have a suit, but as for going abroad . . . No; at present I can't even let him have a suit. [*Resolutely.*] I have no money! [*Sorin laughs.*] I have none!

Sorin. [*Whistling a tune.*] Just so. Forgive me, my dear, don't be cross. I believe you. . . . You 're a magnanimous, noble woman.

Mme Arkadin. [*Through tears.*] I have no money!

Sorin. If I had any money myself, it 's quite clear, I would give him some, but I have nothing, not a sixpence. [*Laughing.*] The whole of my pension goes to the steward, who takes it away and spends it on farming, on cattle-breeding, on bees, and my money is all wasted. The bees die, the cows die, I 'm never allowed to use the horses. . . .

Mme Arkadin. Yes, I have money, but I 'm an actress; the dresses alone have quite ruined me.

Sorin. You 're kind, you 're a darling. . . . I respect you . . . I do. . . . But I 'm again not at all . . . [*Staggering.*] My head is dizzy. [*Clutching at the table.*] I 'm ill and all that.

Mme Arkadin. [*Alarmed.*] Peter dear! [*Trying to support him.*] Peter, my dear. . . . [*Calling.*] Help! Help!

Enter Tryeplyev with a bandage on his head, and Myedvyedenko.

Mme Arkadin. He feels faint!

Sorin. It's all right, it's all right. . . . [*Smiling and drinking some water.*] It's gone already . . . and all that. . . .

Tryeplyev. [*To his mother.*] Don't be alarmed, mamma, it isn't dangerous. It comes on uncle quite often now. [*To his uncle.*] You ought to lie down, uncle.

Sorin. Yes, I will for a moment. . . . Still, I'll go to town. . . . I'll lie down for a while and then go . . . it's quite clear. . . .
                                    [*Goes out, leaning on his stick.*

Medvyedenko. [*Supporting him by the arm.*] There's a riddle: in the morning it walks on four legs, at noon on two, and in the evening on three. . . .

Sorin. [*Laughing.*] Precisely. And at night on its back. Thank you, I can walk by myself. . . .

Myedvyedenko. Why stand on ceremony? . . .   [*Both go out.*

Mme Arkadin. How he frightened me!

Tryeplyev. It's bad for him to live in the country. He gets melancholy. If you, mamma, were suddenly to become generous and make him a loan of fifteen hundred roubles, he might manage to live in town for a whole year.

Mme Arkadin. I haven't any money. I'm an actress, not a banker.   [*A pause.*

Tryeplyev. Mamma, change my bandage. You do it so nicely.

Mme Arkadin. [*Taking some iodine and bandages out of the medicine cupboard.*] And the doctor's late.

Tryeplyev. He promised to be here at ten, and it's now midday.

Mme Arkadin. Sit down! [*Taking the bandage off his head.*] You look as if you were wearing a turban. Yesterday a stranger who came into the kitchen asked what nationality you were. It has almost completely healed. Only a tiny bit left. [*Kissing his head.*] When I'm gone you won't try click-click again?

Tryeplyev. No, mamma. That was a moment of mad despair, when I could not control myself. It won't happen again. [*Kissing her hand.*] You have golden hands. I remember, long ago, when you were still engaged at the State theatres—I was tiny then—there was a row in our courtyard and a lodger, a washerwoman, was soundly beaten. . . . Do you remember? She was picked up unconscious . . . you kept on going to her, taking medicines to her, bathing her children in a tub. Don't you remember it?

Mme Arkadin. No.   [*Putting on a new bandage.*

Tryeplyev. At that time two ballet dancers lived in the same house as we did. They used to come to have coffee with you. . . .

Mme Arkadin. That I remember.

Tryeplyev. They were so very devout. [*A pause.*] Lately, these last days, I love you as tenderly and devotedly as in my childhood. I have no one left now, except you. Only why, why do you submit to the influence of that man?

Mme Arkadin. You don't understand him, Konstantin. He's a most noble character. . . .

Tryeplyev. Yet when they told him that I intended to challenge him to a duel, his nobility did not prevent him acting the coward. He's going away. Poor runaway!

Mme Arkadin. What nonsense! I myself am asking him to go away from here.

Trypleyev. Most noble character! Here we are almost quarrelling on his account, and he's now somewhere in the drawing-room or in the garden laughing at us . . . educating Nina, trying to convince her once for all that he's a genius.

Mme Arkadin. You delight in saying unpleasant things to me. I respect that man, and I ask you not to speak ill of him in my presence.

Tryeplyev. Well, I don't respect him. You wish that I, too, should regard him as a genius; but, forgive me, I can't lie, his writings make me sick.

Mme Arkadin. That's envy. To people without talent, and with only pretensions, there's nothing else left but to abuse real talent. Poor comfort, I must say!

Tryeplyev. [*Ironically.*] Real talent! [*Angrily.*] I have more talent than all of you, if it comes to that! [*Tearing the bandage off his head.*] You routineers have seized the lead in art and you consider as valid and genuine only what you yourselves are doing, and the rest you keep down and strangle! I don't acknowledge you! I don't acknowledge either you or him!

Mme Arkadin. Decadent! . . .

Tryeplyev. Go back to your beloved theatre and act there in your miserable, worthless plays!

Mme Arkadin. I've never acted in such plays. Leave me alone! You can't even write a miserable farce. You Kiev burgher! Beggar!

Tryeplyev. Skinflint.

Mme Arkadin. Gutter-snipe.

[*Tryeplyev sits down and weeps quietly.*

Mme Arkadin. You nonentity! [*Pacing in agitation.*] Don't cry. You mustn't. . . . [*Crying.*] Please don't. . . . [*Kissing him on his forehead, cheeks, and head.*] My dear child, forgive me. . . . Forgive your sinful wretched mother.

Tryeplyev. [*Embracing her.*] If only you knew! I've lost everything! She does not love me, I can no longer write . . . all my hopes are blasted. . . .

Mme Arkadin. Don't despair. Everything will come right. He's going away now, and she'll love you again. [*Wiping his tears away.*] Enough. We're friends again.

Tryeplyev. [*Kissing her hands.*] Yes, mother.

Mme Arkadin. [*Tenderly.*] Make it up with him too. No need for a duel . . . is there now?

Tryeplyev. Right. . . . Only, mamma, don't insist on my meeting him. It hurts me . . . it 's more than I can bear. . . . [*Enter Treegorin.*] Now . . . I 'll be off. . . . [*Hurriedly putting away the medicines and bandages into the cupboard.*] The doctor will see to the bandage now. . . .

Treegorin. [*Searching in a book.*] Page 121 . . . lines 11 and 12. . . . Here we are. . . . [*Reading.*] 'If ever you need my life, come and take it.'

[*Tryeplyev picks up the bandage from the floor and goes out.*

Mme Arkadin. [*Looking at her watch.*] The horses will be here directly.

Treegorin. [*To himself.*] 'If ever you need my life, come and take it.'

Mme Arkadin. I suppose you have all your things packed?

Treegorin. [*Impatiently.*] Yes, yes. . . . [*Pondering.*] In this appeal from a pure soul why do I seem to hear a note of sadness and why has my heart so painfully contracted? . . . 'If ever you need my life, come and take it.' [*To Mme Arkadin.*] Let 's stay one more day!

[*Mme Arkadin shakes her head in refusal.*

Treegorin. Please let us stay!

Mme Arkadin. My dear, I know what detains you here. But get control of yourself. You 've got a little intoxicated; sober down.

Treegorin. You, too, be sober, be sensible, reasonable, I implore you, regard it all as a true friend should. . . . [*Pressing her hand.*] You 're capable of sacrifices. . . . Be my friend, set me free. . . .

Mme Arkadin. [*In violent agitation.*] Are you so deeply infatuated?

Treegorin. I 'm drawn to her! Perhaps this is just what I need.

Mme Arkadin. The love of a country girl? Oh, how little you know yourself!

Treegorin. Sometimes people sleep-walk, so though I 'm talking to you now, I am asleep and see her in my dream. . . . Sweet, wonderful dreams have taken hold of me. . . . Set me free. . . .

Mme Arkadin. [*Trembling.*] No, no. . . . I 'm an ordinary woman, you shouldn't talk like that to me. . . . Don't torment me, Boris . . . I 'm terrified. . . .

Treegorin. If you cared, you could be extraordinary. Love—young, beautiful, poetic, which carries one off into a world of dreams—such love alone can give happiness on earth! I haven't yet experienced such love. . . . In my youth there was no time; I haunted editorial offices, I struggled with poverty. . . . Now here it is, that love. It has come at last, it lures me. . . . What 's the sense of running away from it?

Mme Arkadin. [*In anger.*] You 've gone mad!

Treegorin. Then let me be so.

Mme Arkadin. To-day you 've all conspired to torment me!
[*Cries.*

Treegorin. [*Clutching his head.*] She doesn't understand! She doesn't want to understand!

Mme Arkadin. Am I so old and so ugly that you can talk to me, in this easy way, of other women? [*Embracing and kissing him.*] Oh, you 've gone crazy! My beautiful, my wonderful . . . the last page of my life! [*Kneeling down.*] My joy, my pride, my bliss. . . . [*Embracing his knees.*] If you desert me even for one hour, I shan't survive it, I shall go out of my mind, my amazing, my exquisite, my king. . . .

Treegorin. Someone may come in. [*Helps her to get up.*

Mme Arkadin. Let them, I 'm not ashamed of my love for you [*Kissing his hands.*] My treasure, my reckless boy, you want to do mad things, but I won't have it, I won't let you. . . . [*Laughing.*] You 're mine . . . you 're mine. . . . And this forehead is mine, and these eyes mine, and this lovely silky hair is also mine. . . . You 're all mine. You 're so gifted, you 've such understanding, you 're the best of all modern writers, you 're the only hope of Russia. . . . You have so much sincerity, simplicity, freshness, healthy humour. . . . You can with one stroke present the most characteristic feature of a person or a landscape, your people are all alive.

Oh, one can't read you without ecstasy! You think this is incense? Flattery? Now, look into my eyes. . . . look. . . . Do I look a liar? Now you see, I alone can appreciate you; I alone am telling you the truth, my darling, my wonderful. . . . You are coming with me? Yes? You won't desert me? . . .

Treegorin. I have no will. . . . I've never had a will of my own . . . lethargic, limp, always yielding; can this indeed be attractive to a woman? Take me, carry me off, only don't let me stray one step from you. . . .

Mme Arkadin. [*To herself.*] Now he's mine. [*In a free and easy tone, as if nothing was the matter.*] Though, if you like, you can stay on. I'll go by myself, and you can come later, in a week's time. Indeed, why hurry?

Treegorin. No, we will go together.

Mme Arkadin. Just as you like. If you say so then we'll go together. . . .
[*A pause.*
[*Treegorin makes a note in his note-book.*

Mme Arkadin. What's that for?

Treegorin. This morning I heard a nice expression: 'The maiden copse.' It'll come in useful. [*Stretching himself.*] So we're leaving then? Trains again, stations, refreshment-buffets, steaks, conversations. . . .

Shamrayev. [*Entering.*] I have the honour regretfully to announce that the horses are waiting. It's time, honoured lady, to start for the station; the train arrives at five past two. So you will do me the favour, Irene Nicolayevna, you won't forget to make that little inquiry about where Suzdaltsev the actor is now. Is he alive? Is he well? Once upon a time we used to drink together. . . . In *The Lyons Mail* he acted inimitably . . . in those days. I remember, at Elisavetgrad, that Izmayilov, the tragic actor—he, too, was a remarkable personality—played with him. . . . You need not be in a hurry, honoured lady, you can stop another five minutes. Once, in a melodrama, they acted the parts of conspirators, and when, suddenly taken by surprise, they should have said: 'We are caught in a trap,' Izmayilov said: 'We are caught in a nap.' [*Giggling.*] A nap! . . .

[*While he is talking, Yakov is busy with the trunks: the maid brings Mme Arkadin her hat, cloak, sunshade, gloves; all help Mme Arkadin to put on her things. The cook looks in from the door on the left, then hesitatingly walks in. Enter Pauline Andreyevna, then Sorin and Myedvydenko.*

Pauline Andreyevna. [*With a little basket.*] Here are plums for the journey. . . . Very sweet ones. You may like to taste them. . . .

Mme Arkadin. It 's very kind of you, Pauline Andreyevna.

Pauline Andreyevna. Good-bye, my dear. If you found anything amiss, please forgive it. [*Crying.*]

Mme Arkadin. [*Embracing her.*] Everything was perfect, everything was right. Only you mustn't cry now.

Pauline Andreyevna. Our time is passing away.

Mme Arkadin. We can't help that!

Sorin. [*In an overcoat with a cape, with his hat on, and a stick, comes in by the left door; crossing the room.*] Sister, it 's time, or you may miss the train, and that 's the long and short of it. I 'm going to my carriage. [*Goes out.*

Myedvyedenko. And I shall walk to the station . . . to see you off. I 'll do it in a jiffy. . . . [*Goes out.*

Mme Arkadin. Good-bye, my dears. . . . If we are all alive and well, we 'll meet again next summer. . . . [*The maid, Yakov, and the cook kiss her hand.*] Don't forget me. [*Handing a rouble to the cook.*] There 's a rouble between the three of you.

The Cook. We thank you very much, my lady. Happy journey to you! We are pleased to serve you.

Yakov. God grant you a good journey!

Shamrayev. A letter from you would delight us! Good-bye, Boris Alexeyevich!

Mme Arkadin. Where 's Konstantin? Tell him I 'm starting. We must say good-bye to one another. Well, remember me kindly. [*To Yakov.*] I gave the cook a rouble. It 's for the three of you.

> [*All go out to the right. The stage is empty. Behind the scenes is heard the usual noise made when people are going away. The maid returns to take the basket of plums from the table and goes out again.*

Treegorin. [*Returning.*] I 've forgotten my stick. I believe it 's there, on the terrace. [*Goes out and at the door on the left meets Nina, who is coming in.*] It 's you? We 're starting. . . .

Nina. I felt we should meet again. [*Excitedly.*] Boris Alexeyevich, I 've made an irrevocable decision, the die is cast, I 'm going on the stage. To-morrow I shall no longer be here, I 'm leaving my father, I 'm leaving everything, I 'm beginning a new life. . . . I 'm going, as you are . . . to Moscow. We shall meet there.

Treegorin. [*Looking round.*] Stop at the Slavyansky Bazar. . . .

Let me know as soon as you arrive. . . . Molchanovka, Grokholsky's house. . . . I 'm in a hurry. . . .

Nina. One minute. . . .

Treegorin. [*In an undertone.*] You 're so lovely. . . . Oh, the happiness to think that we shall soon meet again! [*She leans on his breast.*] I shall see again these wonderful eyes, this inexpressibly beautiful, tender smile . . . these gentle features, this expression of angelic purity. . . . My dear. . . . [*A prolonged kiss.*]

CURTAIN

BETWEEN ACT III AND ACT IV AN INTERVAL OF
TWO YEARS ELAPSES

ACT IV

One of the drawing-rooms in Sorin's house, turned by Konstantin Tryeplyev into his study. Doors on the right and on the left leading into the inner apartments. Opposite is a glass door to the terrace. Besides the usual furniture of a drawing-room, there is in the right corner a writing-table; near the left door stands a Turkish divan; there is a book-case full of books, and books on the window seats and on the chairs. Time: evening. One shaded lamp alight. The room is in semi-darkness. Outside the trees are rustling and the wind is howling in the chimneys. The night-watchman is knocking.

Enter Myedvyedenko and Masha.

Masha. [*Calling.*] Konstantin Gavrilych! Konstantin Gavrilych! [*Looking round.*] No one here. The old man keeps on asking every minute: 'Where 's Kostya, where 's Kostya?' . . . He can't live without him. . . .

Myedvyedenko. He 's afraid of being alone. [*Listening.*] What awful weather! And this is the second day of it.

Masha. [*Turning up the lamp*]. There are waves on the lake. Huge waves.

Myedvyedenko. It 's dark in the garden. They ought to be told to pull down that theatre in the garden. It stands there bare and ugly like a skeleton, and the curtain keeps on flapping in the wind. Last night when I was passing by I fancied someone was crying there.

Masha. What an idea. . . . [*A pause.*

Myedvyedenko. Come, Masha, let's go home.

Masha. [*Shaking her head in refusal.*] I shall stay here for the night.

Myedvyedenko. [*Imploringly.*] Do come, Masha! Our dear baby must be hungry.

Masha. Nonsense! Matryona will feed him. [*A pause.*

Myedvydenko. What a pity! This is the third night he will have been without his mother.

Masha. You 've become tiresome. Formerly at any rate you used to philosophize, but now 'baby—home, baby—home,' is all I hear from you.

Myedvyedenko. Do come, Masha.

Masha. Go by yourself.

Myedvyedenko. Your father won't let me have a horse.

Masha. He will. You ask him, he will.

Myedvyedenko. I 'll try. So you 'll be back to-morrow then?

Masha. [*Taking snuff.*] To-morrow, yes. Nuisance. . . .

Enter Tryeplyev and Pauline Andreyevna; Tryeplyev has brought pillows and a blanket, and Pauline Andreyevna sheets; they place them on the Turkish divan; then Tryeplyev goes to his table and sits down.

Masha. What 's it for, mother?

Pauline Andreyevna. Peter Nicolayevich asked to have his bed made up in Kostya's room.

Masha. Let me, I 'll do it. . . . [*Making the bed.*

Pauline Andreyevna. [*With a sigh.*] Old and young are alike. . . . [*Coming up to the writing-table and resting her elbow, glancing at a manuscript; a pause.*

Myedvyedenko. I 'm going then. Good-bye, Masha. [*Kissing his wife's hand.*] Good-bye, mother. [*About to kiss his mother-in-law's hand.*]

Pauline Andreyevna. [*Annoyed.*] Well, go, and God bless you! [*Tryeplyev silently shakes his hand; Myedvyedenko goes out.*

Pauline Andreyevna. [*Glancing at the manuscript.*] No one thought or dreamt that you, Kostya, would turn into a regular author. And now, God be thanked, they have begun sending you money from the magazines. [*Passing her hand over his hair.*] And you 've grown handsome. . . . Darling Kostya, dear, be more affectionate to my dear Mashenka! . . .

Masha. [*Making the bed.*] Leave him alone, mother.

Pauline Andreyevna. [*To Tryeplyev.*] She 's a glorious creature.

[*A pause.*] A woman, Kostya, needs nothing, only give her an affectionate look. I know it from my own experience.

[*Tryeplyev gets up from the table and goes out without speaking.*

Masha. Now you 've made him angry. You shouldn't have worried him!

Pauline Andreyevna. I do feel for you, Mashenka dear.

Masha. There 's no need!

Pauline Andreyevna. My heart is aching for you. Indeed I see it all, understand it all.

Masha. It 's all nonsense. Hopeless love—that 's in novels only. Nonsense. But I must keep a tight rein on myself, I mustn't wait for something to happen, sitting by the sea and waiting for fine weather. . . . Once love has stolen into the heart, it has to be driven clean out. They 've promised now to transfer my husband to another district. As soon as we get there—I shall forget it all. . . . I 'll tear it out from my heart by the roots.

[*A melancholy waltz is being played two rooms off.*

Paulina Andreyevena. Kostya 's playing. That means he 's depressed.

Masha. [*Noiselessly dances two or three steps.*] The chief thing, mother, is that I shouldn't be able to see him. If they grant Semyon that transfer, then believe me, in one month I shall forget it all. It 's all nonsense.

[*The door on the left opens; Dorn and Myedvyedenko wheel in Sorin in a chair.*

Myedvyedenko. We 're six of us now in my house. And flour is seventy copecks a pood.

Dorn. That 's a stiff proposition, isn't it?

Myedvyedenko. It 's all right for you to laugh. You 've got pots of money.

Dorn. Money? After thirty years' practice, my friend, trouble-some practice, when I couldn't call my time my own either by day or by night, I 've managed to save only two thousand roubles, and those I 've spent during my recent visit abroad. I 've nothing.

Masha. [*To her husband.*] You haven't gone?

Myedvyedenko. [*Guiltily.*] Why? They won't let me have a horse!

Masha. [*With bitter annoyance, in an undertone.*] I wish I might never set eyes on you again!

[*The chair halts in the left half of the room; Pauline An-dreyevna, Masha and Dorn sit down near it. Myedvye-denko, grieved, goes aside.*]

Dorn. I say, what a lot of changes you 've made here! The drawing-room turned into a study!

Masha. It 's more convenient for Konstantin Gavrilych to work here. He can walk out into the garden, at any moment, to think there.

[*The watchman knocks.*

Sorin. Where 's my sister?

Dorn. She has driven to the station to meet Treegorin. She 'll be back directly.

Sorin. If you found it necessary to summon my sister here, it means then that I must be dangerously ill. [*After a silence.*] That 's a rum thing—I 'm dangerously ill, and yet I 'm given no medicines at all.

Dorn. And what would you like? Valerian drops? Soda? Quinine?

Sorin. There, he 's philosophizing again! Oh, what an infliction! [*With a nod of the head towards the divan.*] Is that made for me?

Pauline Andreyevna. It is for you, Peter Nicolayevich.

Sorin. Thank you.

Dorn. [*Humming a tune.*] 'The moon is afloat in the midnight sky.' . . .

Sorin. I mean to give Kostya a subject for a novel. It should be called: *The Man who wanted—L'Homme qui a voulu.* In my young days long ago I wanted to become an author—and didn't; I wanted to speak eloquently—and spoke disgustingly . . . [*Mimicking himself.*] 'and all, and all that, and that 's the long and short of it' . . . and in summing up a case I used to go on spinning it out and out, until I got into a regular sweat; I wanted to marry—and didn't; I always wanted to live in town—and now I 'm finishing my life in the country, and all that.

Dorn. You wanted to become a State Councillor—and became one.

Sorin. That I didn't aspire to. It came of itself.

Dorn. To express discontent with life at sixty-two, you must agree, isn't generous.

Sorin. What an obstinate fellow! Do understand, I want to live!

Dorn. That 's levity. By the laws of nature every life must have an end.

Sorin. You argue like a satiated man. You 're satiated and therefore indifferent to life, all is the same to you. But dying will frighten even you.

Dorn. Fear of death is animal fear. One has to suppress it. Only those who believe in eternal life, and are terrified by their sins, are consciously afraid of death. But you, firstly, aren't a believer, and secondly, what are your sins? You 've served in the law courts for twenty-five years—and that 's all.

Sorin. [*Laughing.*] Twenty-eight. . . .

Enter Tryeplyev and sits down on a stool at Sorin's feet; Masha never takes her eyes off him all the time.

Dorn. We 're in Konstantin Gavrilovich's way.

Tryeplyev. No, it 's all right. [*A pause.*

Myedvyedenko. May I ask, doctor, what town you liked best abroad?

Dorn. Genoa.

Myedvyedenko. Why Genoa?

Dorn. The crowd in the streets there is magnificent. When in the evening you walk out of your hotel, the whole street is teeming with people. You move in the crowd without any purpose, to and fro, in a curved line, you live with the crowd, you are psychically fused with it, and begin to believe that one universal soul is indeed a possibility like the one which once was acted by Nina Zaryechny in your play. Apropos, where 's Nina Zaryechny now? Where and how is she?

Tryeplyev. I expect she 's all right.

Dorn. I was told she had adopted a singular sort of life. What 's it all about?

Tryeplyev. It 's a long story, doctor.

Dorn. Cut it short then. [*A pause*

Tryeplyev. She ran away from home and had an affair with Treegorin. You know that?

Dorn. I do.

Tryeplyev. She had a child. The child died. Treegorin lost his love for her and returned to his old attachments, as might have been expected. I should say that he had never given up the old ones, but from sheer lack of character, he contrived to keep on with both loves. As far as I could make out from what I 've learnt, Nina's personal life turned out a complete failure.

Dorn. And her acting?

Tryeplyev. Worse still, it appears. She started at a little theatre in a summer resort near Moscow, then she went away to the provinces. At that time I didn't lose sight of her, and for a time, wherever she went, I was there too. She always took big parts, but acted crudely, without taste, ranting, with angular gestures. There were moments when a cry or a death scene of hers showed talent, but those were but moments.

Dorn. That means she must have some talent after all?

Tryeplyev. It was hard to say. I should think she had. I saw her, but she didn't want to see me, and the servants wouldn't admit me to her room. I understood her mood and didn't insist on meeting her. [*A pause.*] What more shall I tell you? Later on, when I was back home, I received letters from her. Understanding, warm, interesting letters; she didn't complain, but I felt that she was utterly unhappy; every line betrayed sick, overstrung nerves. And her imagination was somewhat deranged too. She signed herself 'The Seagull.' In Pushkin's *Mermaid* the miller says he's a raven, so in her letters, too, she went on always repeating that she was a seagull. Now she's here.

Dorn. What do you mean, here?

Tryeplyev. In the town, staying at an inn. She has been occupying a room there for the last five days. I drove over to see her, and Marie Ilyinishna went over there, but she refused to see any one. Semyon Semyonovich declares that yesterday after dinner he saw her in a field, two miles from here.

Myedvyedenko. Yes, I did. She was walking in the direction of the town. I greeted her and asked her why she didn't call on us. She said she would.

Tryeplyev. She won't come. [*A pause.*] Her father and step-mother don't want to know her. They have set watchmen all over the place so as to prevent her from even coming near the manor. [*He and the doctor move to the writing-table.*] How easy it is, doctor, to be philosophical on paper, and how hard it is in actual life!

Sorin. She was an excellent girl.

Dorn. What's that you say?

Sorin. I say she was an excellent girl. The State Councillor Sorin was even in love with her for a time.

Dorn. The old rip!

[*Shamrayev's laughter is heard.*

Pauline Andreyevna. I believe they're back from the station.

Tryeplyev. Yes, I hear mother.

Enter Mme Arkadin and Treegorin, followed by Shamrayev

Shamrayev. We're all growing old and wearing away, under the influence of the elements, while you, honoured lady, go on being young. . . . Light blouses, sprightliness . . . gracefulness. . . .

Mme Arkadin. Again you want to give me the evil eye, you tiresome man!

Treegorin. [*To Sorin.*] How do you do, Peter Nicolayevich! Still seedy? It isn't right! [*Noticing Masha, joyfully.*] Marie Ilyinishna!

Masha. You recognized me? [*Grips his hand.*

Treegorin. Are you married?

Masha. Long ago.

Treegorin. Are you happy? [*Greets Dorn and Myedvyedenko, then goes hesitatingly up to Tryeplyev.*] Irene Nicolayevna has told me that you have forgotten what happened and are no longer angry with me.

[*Tryeplyev holds out his hand to him.*

Mme Arkadin. [*To her son.*] Boris Alexeyevich has brought a magazine with a new story of yours in it.

Tryeplyev. [*Taking the magazine; to Treegorin.*] Thank you, it's very kind of you. [*They sit down.*

Treegorin. I'm bringing you greetings from your admirers. . . . In Petersburg and in Moscow there's a general interest in you and people are asking me about you. They ask: 'What's he like? how old is he? is he dark or fair?' For some reason they believe that you are no longer young. And no one knows your real name since you publish under a pseudonym. As mysterious as the Man in the Iron Mask.

Tryeplyev. Stopping for some time?

Treegorin. No, I think I shall be off to Moscow to-morrow. I must. I'm in a hurry to finish a novel, and also I've promised to send in something to an annual. In a word, the same old story.

[*While they are talking Mme Arkadin and Pauline Andreyevna place a card-table in the middle of the room and unfold it; Shamrayev lights candles, places chairs. A lotto box is brought out of the cupboard.*

Treegorin. The weather has given me an unkind reception. A cutting wind. To-morrow morning, if it calms down, I'll go to the lake to fish. And I must, too, have a look at the garden and that place there—do you remember?—where your play was acted. I've got a theme ready in my head, I have only to refresh my mind with the place where the scene is laid.

Masha. [*To her father.*] Papa, let my husband have a horse! He must get home.

Shamrayev. [*Teasingly.*] Horse . . . home. . . . [*Sternly.*] You saw yourself: the horses have just come from the station. I can't keep on driving horses.

Masha. But there are other horses. . . . [*Seeing that her father keeps silent, she waves her hand.*] I should have known better than to ask you. . . .

Myedvyedenko. Really, Masha, I'll walk.

Pauline Andreyevna. [*With a sigh.*] Walk in such weather. . . . [*Sitting down to the card-table.*] Won't you all sit down.

Myedvyedenko. It's only six miles. . . . Good-bye. . . . [*Kissing his wife's hand.*] Good-bye, mother. [*Masha's mother reluctantly holds out her hand for him to kiss.*] I wouldn't trouble any one but for the dear baby. . . . [*Bowing to the company.*] Good-bye.

[*Goes out, with an apologetic gait.*

Shamrayev. He'll get there all right. He's not a General.

Pauline Andreyevna. [*Tapping on the table.*] Come, sit down. Don't let us waste time, for we shall soon be called to supper.

[*Shamrayev, Masha, and Dorn sit down at the table.*

Mme Arkadin. [*To Treegorin.*] When the long autumn evenings come on, they play lotto here. Just have a look: it's the old lotto with which mother used to play with us when we were children. Won't you have a game with us before supper? [*Sitting down with Treegorin to the table.*] It's a tedious game, but if you get used to it, it's all right.

[*Dealing three cards to every one.*

Tryeplyev. [*Turning the pages of the magazine.*] He's read his own story, but mine he hasn't even cut.

[*He places the magazine on the writing-table, and walks towards the left door; passing by his mother he kisses her on the head.*

Mme Arkadin. And you, Kostya?

Tryeplyev. Excuse me, I'd rather not. . . . I'll go for a stroll.

[*Goes out.*

Mme Arkadin. The stake is ten copecks. Put it down for me, doctor.

Dorn. Certainly.

Masha. Has every one put down? I start. . . . Twenty-two!

Mme Arkadin. Right.

Masha. Three! . . .

Dorn. Yes.

Masha. Have you put three? Eight! Eighty-one! Ten!

Shamrayev. Don't be in a hurry.

Mme Arkadin. What a reception they gave me in Kharkov! Heavens! I still feel dizzy with it all!

Masha. Thirty-four!

[*A melancholy waltz is played behind the scenes.*

Mme Arkadin. The students gave me an ovation. . . . Three baskets of flowers, two wreaths, and this. . . .
[*Taking the brooch off her breast and throwing it on the table.*
Shamrayev. Yes, that is the genuine article. . . .
Masha. Fifty!
Dorn. Is it exactly fifty?
Mme Arkadin. I wore a wonderful dress. . . . Whatever else I can't do, I know how to dress. . . .
Pauline Andreyevna. Kostya's playing. He's depressed, poor fellow.
Shamrayev. The newspapers abuse him very much.
Masha. Seventy-seven!
Mme Arkadin. Why take any notice of them?
Treegorin. He has no luck. He's trying to strike an original note but he hasn't succeeded yet. There's something strange and vague in what he writes, at times even a kind of raving. Not one living character.
Masha. Eleven!
Mme Arkadin. [*Turning her head towards Sorin.*] Peter dear, do you feel bored? [*A pause.*] He's asleep.
Dorn. The State Councillor asleep.
Masha. Seven! Ninety!
Treegorin. If I lived on such a manor, by a lake, should I write? I should conquer that passion of mine, and should do nothing else but fish.
Masha. Twenty-eight!
Treegorin. The joy of catching a pike or a perch!
Dorn. I do believe in Konstantin Gavrilych. He has something to say. He has! He thinks in images, his stories are full of colour, vivid, and I feel them strongly. The only pity is that he has no definite aims. Produces impressions and that's all, but impressions alone won't carry you very far. Irene Nicolayevna, you are glad that your son is a writer?
Mme Arkadin. Imagine, I've not read him yet. Never had the time.
Masha. Twenty-six!
[*Tryeplyev comes in quietly and goes to his table.*
Shamrayev. [*To Treegorin.*] We have got something here, Boris Alexeyevich, which belongs to you.
Treegorin. What's that?
Shamrayev. Konstantin Gavrilych once shot a seagull and you asked me to have it stuffed for you.
Treegorin. I don't remember. [*Thinking.*] I don't remember.

Masha. Sixty-six! One!

Tryeplyev. [*Throwing the window open; listening.*] How dark! I can't understand why I feel so uneasy.

Mme Arkadin. Kostya, shut the window, it 'll cause a draught.

Masha. Eighty-eight!

Treegorin. The game 's mine!

Mme Arkadin. [*Happily.*] Bravo, bravo!

Shamrayev. Bravo!

Mme Arkadin. That man has luck always, and in everything. [*Getting up.*] And now let 's go and have something to eat. Our celebrity had no lunch to-day. After supper we will continue. [*To her son.*] Kostya, leave your manuscripts alone, come and have something to eat.

Tryeplev. I don't want anything, mother. I 've had all I want.

Mme Arkadin. As you please. [*Waking Sorin.*] Peter dear, supper! [*Taking Shamrayev's arm.*] I 'll tell you of my reception in Kharkov. . . .

> [*Pauline Andreyevna puts out the candles on the table; then she and Dorn wheel Sorin in his chair. All go out by the left door; only Tryeplyev is left on the stage, at his writing table.*

Tryeplyev. [*Settling himself to write; running through what he has written already.*] I 've talked so much about new forms, and now I feel that I myself am gradually slipping into routine. [*Reading.*] 'The poster on the fence announced. . . . The pale face, framed by dark hair. . . .' Announced . . . framed. . . . It 's banal. [*Striking the words out.*] I 'll begin with the hero awakened by the noise of the rain, and away with all the rest. The description of the moonlit evening is long and laboured. Treegorin has worked out certain methods for himself, it 's easy for him. . . . He says, the neck of a broken bottle glistens on the dam, and the shadow of the mill-wheel is growing blacker—there 's a moonlight night all complete; while I describe the tremulous light, the gentle gleaming of the stars, and the distant sounds of the piano, dying away in the still, scented air. . . . It is tormenting. [*A pause.*] Yes, I 'm growing more and more convinced that it isn't a question either of old or new forms, but of what a man writes, without thinking of any forms; he writes because it pours freely forth from his soul. [*Someone taps at the window next to the table.*] What is it? [*Looking out of the window.*] I can't see anything. . . . [*Opening the glass door and looking out into the garden.*] Someone ran down the steps. [*Calling.*] Who 's there? [*He goes out; is heard walking quickly along the terrace; in half a minute returns with Nina Zaryechny.*] Nina! Nina!

[*Nina lays her head on his breast and sobs quietly.*

Tryeplyev. [*Moved.*] Nina! Nina! It's you . . . you. . . . It's as though I had a presentiment, all day long my soul has been in terrible anguish. [*Taking off her hat and cloak.*] Oh, my darling, my precious, she has come! Don't cry, don't!

Nina. There's someone here.

Tryeplyev. There's no one.

Nina. Lock the doors or someone may come in.

Tryeplyev. No one will come in.

Nina. I know, Irene Nicolayevna's here. Lock the doors. . . .

Tryeplyev. [*Locking the door on the right, going to that on the left.*] There's no lock to this door. I'll bar it with a chair. [*Putting a chair against the door.*] Don't be afraid, nobody will come in.

Nina. [*Looking fixedly into his face.*] Let me have a good look at you. [*Looking round.*] It's warm here, nice. . . . This used to be a drawing-room. Have I changed very much?

Tryeplyev. Yes. . . . You've become thin and your eyes have grown bigger. Nina, it's strange, my seeing you. Why did you not let me come to you? Why didn't you come before now? I know, you have been staying here almost a week. . . . Every day, several times a day I went to see you, I stood under your window, like a beggar.

Nina. I was afraid that you hated me. Every night I dream that you look at me and don't recognize me. If only you knew! Ever since I arrived here I keep on walking here . . . by the lake. Many a time I have been near your house and dared not come in. Come, let's sit down. [*They sit down.*] Let's sit down and let's talk, talk. It's so nice here, warm, cosy. Listen to the noise of the wind. There's a passage in Turgenev which says: 'Happy is he who on such a night sits under the shelter of a roof, who has a warm corner.' I'm a seagull. . . . No, it isn't that. [*Rubbing her forehead.*] What was I saying? . . . Yes, Turgenev. . . . 'May the Lord comfort all homeless wanderers.' . . . Don't mind me.

[*Sobbing.*

Tryeplyev. Nina . . . Nina!

Nina. It's all right, I feel relieved. . . . It's two years since I've cried. Late last night I went into the garden to see if our theatre was still there. And it's still standing there. For the first time for two years I burst into tears, and I felt better, my heart felt lighter. See, I am not crying. [*Taking his hand.*] And so you 've become a writer. . . . You—a writer, I—an actress. . . . We, too, have got into the swim of things. . . . My life used to be pure joy, like a child's—I would wake in the morning and sing; I loved you, I dreamed of fame— and now? To-morrow, early in the morning I go to Yeletz, third class . . . with peasants; and in Yeletz your cultured tradesmen will be pressing their attentions on me. Life is brutal!

Tryeplyev. Why go to Yeletz?

Nina. I 've got an engagement for the whole winter. My time's up.

Tryeplyev. Nina, I used to curse you and hate you. I tore up your letters and photographs, but every minute I was aware that my soul was attached to you for ever. To cease to love you isn't in my power, Nina. Ever since I lost you and began to get my work published, my life has been unbearable—I suffer. . . . My youth suddenly left me as though cut off, and I seem already to have lived ninety years on earth. I called you, I kissed the earth on which you walked; wherever I looked I seemed to see your face, the caressing smile, which beamed on me in the best days of my life. . . .

Nina. [*Confused.*] Why does he say these things, why does he say them?

Tryeplyev. I am lonely, warmed by no affection, I am as cold as if I lived in a cave, and whatever I write, it 's all dry, harsh, gloomy. Stay here, Nina, I implore you, allow me to go with you.

[*Nina quickly puts on her hat and cloak.*

Tryeplyev. Nina, why? For the love of God, Nina. . . .

[*Looks at her as she puts on her things ; a pause.*

Nina. The horses are waiting outside the gates. Don't see me off, I 'll walk there by myself. . . . [*Through tears.*] Give me some water. . . .

Tryeplyev. [*Waiting till she has drunk the water.*] Where are you going now?

Nina. To town. [*A pause.*] Irene Nicolayevna is here?

Tryeplyev. Yes. . . . Uncle was taken very ill on Thursday, we wired for her to come.

Nina. Why do you say that you kissed the earth on which I walked? I deserve to be killed. [*Leaning over the table.*] I am so tired! If only I could rest awhile. . . . Rest! [*Lifting her head.*] I 'm—a seagull. . . . Not that. I 'm an actress.

Yes, just so! [*Hearing Mme Arkadin and Treegorin laugh, she listens, then runs to the door on the left and looks through the keyhole.*] And he, too, is here. . . . [*Going back to Tryeplyev.*] Just so. . . . Why. . . . Yes. . . . He didn't believe in the theatre, he laughed all the time at my dreams, and little by little I also ceased believing and lost heart. . . . And then the anxieties of love, jealousy, the constant fear for the little one. . . . I became petty, insignificant, I played badly. . . . I didn't know what to do with my arms, I didn't know how to stand on the stage, I had no control over my voice. You don't understand the state when one feels one is acting horribly. I'm—a seagull. No, not that. . . . You remember, you shot a seagull? 'By chance a man comes, sees her, and wantonly destroys her. . . . A subject for a short story.' . . . No, not that. . . . [*Rubbing her forehead.*] What was I saying? . . . I was speaking of the stage. . . . I'm no longer what I was. I'm now a real actress, I act with joy, with rapture, the stage intoxicates me, and I feel glorious. And now, since I have been here, I walk about, I walk all the time and think, I think and feel how every day my soul is growing in strength. . . . I do know now, I understand, Kostya, that in our business—whatever it is, acting or writing—the chief thing isn't fame, isn't glory, not what I had dreamt of, but the capacity for taking pains. Bear your cross and have faith. I have faith, and it does not pain me so much, and when I think of my vocation, I'm not afraid of life.

Tryeplyev. [*Sadly.*] You've found your path, you know where you're going, but I'm still tossed about in a chaos of reveries and images, without knowing why or wherefore. I have no faith and don't know in what my vocation consists.

Nina. [*Listening.*] Sh-h. . . . I'll go away. Good-bye. When I become a great actress, come and have a look at me. Do you promise? And now. . . . [*Presses his hand.*] It is late. I can hardly stand on my feet. . . . I'm exhausted, hungry.

Tryeplyev. Do stay, I'll bring you some supper. . . .

Nina. No, no. . . . Don't see me off, I'll go by myself. . . . The horses are close by. . . . So she has brought him with her? Well, it makes no difference. When you see Treegorin, you mustn't tell him anything. . . . I love him! I love him even more intensely than before. . . . A subject for a short story. . . . I love him, I love him passionately, I love him desperately. . . . How good it was in the old days, Kostya! You remember? What a clear, warm, joyous, pure life, what feelings—feelings like delicate, exquisite flowers. . . . You remember? . . . [*Reciting.*] 'Men, lions, eagles, and partridges, horned deer, geese, spiders, dumb fishes that used to dwell in the water, starfishes, and such as could not be seen by the eye—in a word, all lives, all lives, all lives, having accomplished the sad cycle, have been extinguished. It is thousands of years since a single living thing was seen on the earth, and this poor moon lights its lantern in vain. On the meadow no longer do the cranes awaken with a cry, and the cockchafers are no longer heard in the lime groves.' . . .

> [*She embraces Tryeplyev impetuously and runs out by the glass door.*

Tryeplyev. [*After a pause.*] It won't do for someone to come across her in the garden and then tell mother. It may upset mother. . . .

> [*During two minutes he silently tears up all his manuscripts and throws them under the table; then unlocks the door on the right, and goes out.*

Dorn. [*Trying to open the door on the left.*] Strange. . . . The door seems to be locked on the inside. . . . [*Entering and putting the chair in its place.*] An obstacle race.

Enter Mme Arkadin and Pauline Andreyevna, followed by Yakov, carrying bottles, and by Masha, then Shamrayev and Treegorin.

Mme Arkadin. Put the claret and the beer for Boris Alexeyevich on the table, here. We'll play and drink. Come take your seats all.

Pauline Andreyevna. [*To Yakov.*] And bring in the tea directly.

> [*Lighting the candles and sitting down at the card-table.*

Shamrayev. [*Leading Treegorin to the cupboard.*] Here's the article I mentioned a while ago. [*Taking the stuffed seagull out of the cupboard.*] Your order.

Treegorin. [*Looking at the seagull.*] I don't remember. [*After some reflection.*] I don't remember.

> [*On the right behind the scenes a shot is heard; every one starts.*

Mme Arkadin. [*Frightened.*] What is it?

Dorn. Never mind. Something in my medicine box must have burst. Don't worry. [*Goes out by the right door and returns in half a minute.*] That's it. A bottle of ether has burst. [*Humming.*] 'Again before thee I stand enchanted.'

Mme Arkadin [*Sitting down to the table.*] Oh, it gave me such a fright. It reminded me of how . . . [*Covering her face with her hands.*] I nearly fainted. . . .

Dorn. [*Turning over the pages of the magazine, to Treegorin.*] There was an article published here some two months ago . . . a letter from America, and I meant to ask you, by the way . . . [*Putting his arm round Treegorin's shoulder and leading him to the footlights.*] . . . As I am very much interested in that problem . . . [*In a lower voice, in an undertone.*] Get Irene Nicolayevna away from here, anywhere. . . . The fact is, Konstantin Gavrilovich has shot himself. . . .

CURTAIN

THE WOOD DEMON

A COMEDY IN FOUR ACTS

A PREFATORY NOTE

THE original plan and programme of *The Wood Demon* is contained in the following letter of 18th October 1888, written by Anton Tchekhov to A. S. Souvorin:[1]

'I have received the beginning of the play. Thank you. Blagosvietlov will go in whole, just as he is. You have done him admirably; from his very first words he is boring and irritating, and if the public has five consecutive minutes of him, it will get just the impression we want. The spectator will say to himself, "Oh, *do* shut up!" Blagosvietlov must have a double effect on the audience—of an intelligent man with the gout and a grievance, and of a tedious piece of music which has been playing for hours. I think you 'll see how far you 've succeeded with him when I 've sketched out the first act and sent it to you.

'Of Anouchin I shall leave only the name and "all that." His conversation needs greasing. He is a soft, oily, amorous nature, and his talk is soft and oily, too. You 've made him abrupt, not genial enough. This godfather must exude old age and indolence. His listening to Blagosvietlov is pure indolence; rather than argue he 'd infinitely prefer to have a snooze, or to hear stories about Petersburg and the Tsar and literature and science, or to feed in pleasant company.

'I 'll remind you of the plan of our play.

'(1) Alexander Platonich Blagosvietlov, a member of the Privy Council, with the Order of the White Eagle and a pension of four hundred a year. The son of a clergyman and educated as a priest. He has got to his position by his own personal efforts. Not a blemish on his past. Suffers from gout, rheumatism, insomnia, and noises in the ears. His property came with his wife. Has a positive mind. He can't stand mystics, dreamers, cranks, poets, or fanatics. He doesn't believe in God, and looks at the whole world from a business point of view. Work, work, work—all the rest is nonsense or humbug.

'(2) Boris, his son, a young student, very sensitive and honest,

[1] This letter and other extracts are taken from *The Life and Letters of Anton Tchekhov*, published by Cassell, 1925.

but utterly ignorant of life. Once he imagined himself to be a Social Revolutionary and arranged to dress like a peasant, but he looked like a Turk. Plays the piano admirably, sings with feeling, writes plays in secret, is always falling in love, spends a lot of money, and invariably talks nonsense. He does very little work.

' (3) Blagosvietlov's daughter. But don't call her Sasha, please. Since *Ivanov* I'm tired of that name. If the son is Boris, let the daughter be Nastya. (We'll erect an everlasting monument to Boris and Nastya.[1]) Nastya is twenty-two or twenty-four. She is well educated and can think. She's tired of Petersburg, and of the country, too. She's never been in love. Indolent, fond of philosophizing, lies on the sofa to read a book. Wants to marry, but only for the sake of a change and so as not to be left an old maid. Says she could only fall in love with an interesting man. She'd be pleased to marry Pushkin or Edison, but she'd marry an ordinary decent man merely out of boredom. Still, she'll respect her husband and love her children. When she has met and listened to the Wood Demon, she surrenders herself wholly to passion, to the uttermost lengths—hysterics and silly, senseless giggling. The powder, made damp by the Petersburg marshes, dries in the sun and explodes with terrific force. . . . I've thought out an extraordinary declaration of love for her.

'(4) Anouchin, an old man. He thinks himself the happiest man in the world. His sons have made their careers, his daughters are married, and he's as free as the wind. He has never been to a doctor, never had a lawsuit, never been decorated, forgets to wind up his watch, and is friends with everybody. He eats well, sleeps well, drinks plenty of wine, with no aftereffect, doesn't grumble at his age, can't think about death. Once upon a time he used to feel depressed and grumble, to have a bad appetite and be interested in politics, but he was saved by a single incident. One day, about ten years ago, at a meeting of the District Council he had to make a general apology to everybody present. After which he immediately felt jolly, regained his appetite, and, being of a subjective nature and social to the marrow of his bones, came to the conclusion that absolute sincerity and something like a public repentance is a remedy for all diseases. He recommends the remedy to everybody, Blagosvietlov included.

'(5) Victor Petrovich Korovin, a young squire of thirty to thirty-three, the Wood Demon. A poet, a landscape painter,

---

[1] Souvorin's two children were called Boris and Nastya.

extraordinarily responsive to nature. Once, while he was still a schoolboy, he planted a little birch tree. When it grew green and began to shake in the wind, when it began to whisper and give a little shade, his soul filled with pride. He had helped God to create a new birch tree! Through his act there was one more tree on the earth! This was the beginning of his own peculiar creativeness. He embodies his idea, not on canvas or paper, but in the earth; not in lifeless paint, but in living organisms. . . . The tree is beautiful; but that's not everything; it has its own right to live, it is as necessary as water, the sun, or the stars. Life on earth is inconceivable without trees. Forests condition the climate, the climate influences the character of man, etc. There can be neither civilization nor happiness if the forests fall under the axe, if the climate is rough and hard and the people, too, are rough and hard. . . . The prospect is terrible! He pleases Nastya not with his idea, which is alien to her, but with his talent, his passion, the wide range of his thought. . . . It pleases her that he has swung his mind over the whole of Russia and across ten centuries of the future. When he comes running up to her father, sobbing and with tears, and implores him not to sell his forest to be cut down, she laughs for ecstasy and happiness: at last she has met the man. She never believed in him before, when she saw him in her dreams or read of him in books.

'(6) Galakhov, of the same age as the Wood Demon, but already a Privy Councillor, a rich man, with a high position in a Government department. A bureaucrat to his marrow, he cannot possibly get rid of the bureaucrat in himself, for it is inherited from his grandfathers and is in his flesh and blood. He desires to live from the heart, but he cannot. He tries to appreciate nature and music, but he does not. He's an honest and sincere man, who realizes that the Wood Demon is superior to him, and frankly admits it. He wants to marry for love, thinks he is in love, tunes himself up to a lyrical key, but nothing comes of it. He likes Nastya as a beautiful, intelligent girl, as a good wife—and nothing more.

'(7) Vassily Gavrilovich Volkov, a brother of Blagosvietlov's late wife. He manages Blagosvietlov's estate. (He ran through his own long ago.) He is sorry that he hasn't embezzled. He didn't expect his Petersburg relatives would be so unappreciative of his virtues. He thinks he is not understood; they don't want to understand him, and he's sorry that he hasn't embezzled. He drinks Vichy and grumbles. His deportment is very dignified. He is emphatic that he is not afraid of Generals. He shouts.

'(8) Lyuba, his daughter. Her mind is set on things of the earth. Chickens, ducks, knives, forks, the cattleyard, the prize given by the *Neeva* newspaper, which would be put in a frame if she got it, entertaining guests, dinners, suppers, tea— that's her sphere. She takes it as a personal insult if any one wants to pour out tea instead of her, and says to herself, "Ah! I'm no longer needed in this house." She doesn't like people who spend a great deal of money and do no definite work. She worships Galakhov for his positiveness. She must come in agitated from the garden and call shrilly, "How was it Mary and Akulina dared to leave the young turkeys out all night in the dew?" or something like that. She is always strict. With people and ducks as well. Really domestic women are never overpleased with what they've done. On the contrary, they try to make out that their life is slavery. "There's no time, God forgive me, for a moment's rest. Every one sits around with their arms folded." Only she, poor dear, has to wear herself to the bone. She lectures Nastya and Boris for their idleness, and she's afraid of Blagosvietlov.

'(9) Semyon, a peasant, the Wood Demon's assistant steward.

'(10) Feodossyi, a pilgrim, an old man of eighty, but not yet grey. A soldier under Nicholas I, served in the Caucasus, and speaks the native languages. A congenital optimist. He loves anecdote and jolly conversations, bows to the ground in front of every one, kisses their shoulder, and insists on kissing women. A lay brother of the Mount Athos Monastery. During his life he has collected 300,000 roubles, and sent off every farthing of it to the monastery. He himself lives by begging. He'll call a man a fool and a scoundrel without any regard to his rank or position.

'That's the whole programme. Not later than Christmas you will receive my material for the first Act. I shan't touch Blagosvietlov. He and Galakhov belong to you; I renounce them. Most of Nastya is yours, too. I can't cope with her by myself. Boris isn't difficult to manage. Up to Act IV the Wood Demon is mine, but in Act IV, until his conversation with Blagosvietlov, he is yours. In that conversation I'll have to see that the general tone of the character is kept—a tone that you won't catch.

'In Act II (the guests) you begin again.

'Feodossyi is an episodic character, who, I think, will be

needed. I don't want the Wood Demon to be left alone on the stage; I want Blagosvietlov to feel that he is surrounded by a lot of cranks. I 've left out of the plan Mademoiselle Emily, an old Frenchwoman, also in raptures over the Wood Demon. We must show how Wood Demons affect women. Emily is a nice old woman, a governess, who has not yet lost her electricity. When she gets excited she mixes up French and Russian. She's a patient nurse to Blagosvietlov. She 's yours. I 'll leave blanks for her in Scene I.'

. . . . . .

Michael Tchekhov, in his biography of his brother, gives the following account of *The Wood Demon*:

'Wishing now [1] to write something of more significance than farce, Anton welcomed the idea which came to him of *The Wood Demon*. He proposed to Souvorin that they should collaborate in writing the play; but the suggestion that they should work together did not materialize, and Anton wrote the play himself. In the season following the production of *Ivanov*, Solovzov, the actor, left Korsh's Theatre, and, together with Mlle Abramov, decided to start his own theatre in Moscow. The prospects were not bright. They had no plays with a punch in them. There was only the Christmas season, on which any hopes could be built; and to get full houses it was necessary to have a "striking" play written by a playwright of some reputation. Solovzov turned to Anton:

'"Give us a hand, Anton Pavlovich, help me out, give me a play."

'To Christmas week it only wanted ten or twelve days. Solovzov held out alluring terms—a thousand roubles. Anton sat down to write the play, the idea of which he had already thought out. He would write one act each day, and I would make two copies. Solovzov would come and take away the copies and send them by messenger to the censor in Petersburg. The work was an awful grind; Anton wrote, Solovzov sat near by urging on, I copied. Thus the play was ready in time. It was performed several times, and the author made a thousand roubles, yet Solovzov's productions went up the chimney.

[1] Anton Tchekhov's first play *Ivanov*, written by him in 1887, at the age of twenty-seven, was produced the following year in Moscow and in Petersburg, and became an immediate success. Very soon after Tchekhov wrote his vaudevilles *The Bear* and *The Proposal* (originally published in the *Novoye Vremya* as feuilletons), which also were instant successes, and have ever since remained favourites on the Russian stage.

'Anton felt dissatisfied with the play. *The Wood Demon* was written in a hurry, and Solovzov's production was bad. Because she was the lessee of the theatre, Mlle M. N. G. took the part of the young heroine, though she was an extremely stout woman. To see the *jeune premier*, the actor Roschin-Insarov, making a declaration of love to her was positively incongruous; he called her beautiful, yet could not get round her to embrace her. Then the glow of the forest fire was such that it aroused laughter. Anton took off *The Wood Demon*, kept it for a long time in his drawer and would not allow its performance. Several years later, in 1898, he re-wrote the play, gave it a totally different construction, and a new name, *Uncle Vanya*.'

.　　　.　　　.　　　.　　　.

In his letter to Souvorin of 30th September 1889, Anton Tchekhov says:

'I am writing a big comedy-novel, and have already fired a salvo of two and a half acts. Fancy! After the story [1] a comedy is very easy to write. I introduce in the comedy nice, healthy people, half-sympathetic; the end is a happy one. The general tone throughout is lyrical. It is called *The Wood Demon*.'

.　　　.　　　.　　　.　　　.

It will not be out of place here to quote the letter written to Anton Tchekhov by his friend Prince A. I. Urusov, and bearing on *The Wood Demon*.

'*27th January* 1899, Moscow.

'I have read your *Uncle Vanya* carefully, and with grief am bound to say that, in my opinion, you have spoilt *The Wood Demon*. You have cut all the meat off it, reduced it to a conspectus and defaced it. You had a superb comical villain. [The writer evidently refers to the character of Fyodor.] He has vanished now, yet he is needed for the inner symmetry of the play; and this too, though you are particularly good at describing that peculiar type of young idler, of luxuriant and bright plumage. To the play he was invaluable as introducing a humorous note. The second and, in my opinion, the still graver sin is the change in the development of the play. The suicide in Act III, and the night-scene by the river, at the mill, with the tea-table in Act IV, and the wife's return to the professor—all

---

[1] The story here referred to is Tchekhov's *A Tedious Story*, originally published in the *Severny Vestni*, No. 11, 1889.

these were more novel, more daring, more interesting, than the present end [in *Uncle Vanya*]. When I related to the French the contents of *The Wood Demon* they were struck just by this: the hero is killed, and life goes on. The actors with whom I talked are also of the same opinion. Of course, *Uncle Vanya* too is good, better than anything that is being written nowadays, but your *Wood Demon* was better; and it would be well if you allowed it to be produced. And what an agitation we are having here about *The Seagull*. Had we waited a little while longer, we could have got another two hundred signatures. It is funny to see the faces of the playwrights! I hope you have seen my article in the *Courier*, and were not cross with me.

'The depth of the poetic atmosphere of *The Seagull* is amazing. The acting superb. Don't believe that Mlle Roxanov is not good: she carries the first three acts surprisingly well, thoughtfully and minutely; in Act IV she is a shade less impressive, yet very fine. As to Olga Knipper, well, there's no better actress in Moscow for that part. Only Mme Savina might perhaps compete with her. "Sorin"-Kaluzhsky is better each time. I have seen the play four times.

Your fanatic,

URUSOV.'

THE WOOD DEMON

A Comedy in Four Acts

CHARACTERS

ALEXANDER VLADIMIROVICH SEREBRYAKOV, a retired professor.
ELENA ANDREYEVNA, his wife, aged twenty-seven.
SOPHIE ALEXANDROVNA (Sonya), the professor's daughter, by his first marriage, aged twenty.
MARIE VASSILIEVNA VOYNITSKY, widow of a privy councillor, the mother of the professor's first wife.
GEORGE PETROVICH VOYNITSKY, her son.
LEONID STEPANOVICH ZHELTOUKHIN, a wealthy young man, who has studied technology at the university.
YULIA STEPANOVNA (Julie), his sister, aged eighteen.
IVAN IVANOVICH ORLOVSKY, a landowner.
FYODOR IVANOVICH ORLOVSKY, his son.
MIKHAIL LVOVICH KHROUSCHOV (the Wood Demon), a landowner, who holds the degree of doctor of medicine.
ILYA ILYICH DYADIN.
VASSILI, Zheltoukhin's man-servant.
SEMYON, a labourer employed at Dyadin's flour mill.

ACT I

The garden of Zheltoukhin's estate. The manor house with a terrace; in front of the house, on a platform, there are two tables; the large table is set for lunch; on the smaller table are placed zakouski [hors-d'œuvres]. Time: A little after two o'clock.

SCENE I

Zheltoukhin and Julie come out of the house

Julie. You 'd better put on your grey suit. This one does not become you.

Zheltoukhin. It doesn't matter. Nonsense.

Julie. Lennie dear, why are you so dull? How can you be like that on your birthday? You are naughty! . . .

[*Laying her head on his chest.*

Zheltoukhin. No sentiment, please!

Julie. [*Through tears.*] Lennie!

Zheltoukhin. Instead of all these sour kisses, all these loving glances, and little shoes as watch-stands, which are no damned use to me, you 'd better do what I ask you to do! Why didn't you write to the Serebryakovs?

Julie. Lennie, but I did write!

Zheltoukhin. Whom did you write to?

Julie. I wrote to Sonya. I asked her to come to-day without fail, without fail at one o'clock. Honestly, I wrote to her!

Zheltoukhin. And yet it is past two now, and they 're not here. Still, no matter! I don't care! I must give it all up, nothing is to come of it. . . . Only humiliations, and a rotten feeling, and nothing else. . . . She doesn't take the slightest interest in me. I 'm not good-looking, I 'm uninteresting, there 's nothing romantic about me, and if she were to marry me, it could only be out of calculation . . . for the sake of money!

Julie. Not good-looking! . . . You 've a wrong opinion of yourself.

Zheltoukhin. Oh, yes, as if I were blind! My beard grows from there, from the neck, not as beards should grow. . . . My moustache, damn it . . . and my nose . . .

Julie. Why do you press your cheek?

Zheltoukhin. It aches again under the eye.

Julie. It is a tiny bit swollen. Let me kiss it, and it will go.

Zheltoukhin. That 's silly!

Enter Orlovsky and Voynitsky.

SCENE II

The same, Orlovsky and Voynitsky

Orlovsky. Ducky, when are we going to have our lunch? It 's past two!

Julie. Godpa dear, the Serebryakovs haven't come yet!

Orlovsky. How long have we to wait then? I want to eat, my sweet. George, too, wants his lunch.

Zheltoukhin. [*To Voynitsky.*] Are your people coming?

Voynitsky. When I left, Elena Andreyevna was dressing.

Zheltoukhin. They 're coming for certain then?

Voynitsky. You can never be certain. Our general may suddenly imagine he has got an attack of the gout, or some other caprice—and then they will stop at home.

Zheltoukhin. In that case let's start. What's the use of waiting? [*Shouting.*] Ilya Ilyich! Serguey Nikodimych!

Enter Dyadin and two or three guests.

Scene III

The same, Dyadin and the guests

Zheltoukhin. Please help yourselves. Please. [*They all stand round the table on which the zakouski are placed.*] The Serebryakovs haven't come. Fyodor Ivanych isn't here; the Wood Demon, too, has not arrived . . . people have forgotten us!

Julie. Godpa, will you have a drop of vodka?

Orlovsky. The tiniest drop. Just so. . . . That'll do.

Dyadin. [*Adjusting the napkin round his neck.*] How superbly you manage everything, Yulia Stepanovna! Whether I drive across your fields, or walk under the shade of your orchard, or contemplate this table—everywhere I see the mighty power of your bewitching little hand. Your health!

Julie. There are all sorts of worries, Ilya Ilyich! Last night, for instance, our Nazarka forgot to shut the young turkeys into the shed, and they spent the night in the garden in the dew, and this morning five young ones gave up the ghost.

Dyadin. Such a thing oughtn't to happen. A turkey is a delicate bird.

Voynitsky. [*To Dyadin.*] Waffle, cut me a slice of ham!

Dyadin. With particular pleasure. It is a superb ham. One of the wonders of the Arabian nights. [*Cutting.*] I'm cutting it, Georgie, according to all the rules of art. Beethoven and Shakespeare could not do it better. Only the knife is a bit blunt. [*Sharpening the knife on another knife.*]

Zheltoukhin. [*Shuddering.*] Br-r-r! . . . Stop it, Waffle! I can't bear it!

Orlovsky. Tell us, George Petrovich, about your people. How are you all getting on at home?

Voynitsky. We aren't getting on at all.

Orlovsky. Any news?

Voynitsky. None. Everything is as it used to be. Just the same now as it was last year. I, as usual, talk a great deal and do very little. My old jackdaw of a mater keeps on jabbering about the emancipation of women: with one eye she's looking into the grave, and with the other she's searching in her clever little books for the dawn of a new life!

Orlovsky. And how's Alexander?

Voynitsky. The professor has, unfortunately, not yet been devoured by moths. As usual, he sits in his study from morning to night. 'Straining his wits, knitting his brows, he composes ode after ode, but no heed is paid either to him or to them.' Poor paper! Sonya, as usual, reads clever books and keeps a very clever diary.

Orlovsky. My dear old chap, my dear fellow. . . .

Voynitsky. With my sense of observation I ought to write a novel. The plot is begging to be written. A retired professor, an old hard-tack, a learned owl. . . . Gout, rheumatism, megrims, liver, and all sorts of tricks. . . . He's as jealous as Othello. He is forced to live on the estate of his first wife, for he can't afford to live in town. Always grumbling about his misfortunes, although he's extraordinarily happy!

Orlovsky. Well, now!

Voynitsky. Of course! Only think what luck! I shan't dwell on the fact that he, the son of a simple sexton, who went to a church school, managed to secure learned degrees and a chair at the university; that he's now an Excellency, the son-in-law of a senator, etc. All that is of no consequence. But do consider just this. The man has for precisely twenty-five years been lecturing and writing on art, without understanding art in the very least. Precisely for twenty-five years he has been chewing other men's ideas on realism, tendencies, and various other nonsense. For twenty-five years he has been lecturing and writing on what to sensible people has been ever so long familiar, and what to fools is of no interest; that is, for twenty-five years he has been pouring water into a sieve. And along with that — what success! What popularity! Wherefore? Why? By what right?

Orlovsky. [*Laughing aloud.*] It's envy, envy!

Voynitsky. Just so, envy! And what success with women! No Don Juan has known such complete success! His first wife, my sister—a charming, gentle creature, as pure as this blue sky, noble, generous, who had more admirers than he had students—she loved him as ardently as only pure angels are capable of loving just such pure and beautiful angels as themselves. My mother—his mother-in-law—adores him to this very day, and he still inspires her with sacred awe. His second wife, a beautiful, clever woman—you've seen her—married him when he was already old, she gave him her youth, her beauty, her freedom, her brilliance. . . . What for? Why?

And she so gifted, such an artist! How wonderfully she plays the piano!

Orlovsky. Altogether they are a gifted family. A rare family.

Zheltoukhin. Yes, Sophie Alexandrovna, for instance, has a most remarkable voice. A wonderful soprano! I have never heard anything like it even in Petersburg. But, you know, she rather strains her upper notes. It's a great pity. Give me the upper notes! Give me the upper notes! Ah, if she had those notes, I stake my life, she would be wonderful, do you know. . . . I'm sorry, gentlemen, I must have a word with Julie. . . . [*Taking Julie aside.*] Send a messenger on horseback to them. Send them a note to say that if they can't come now, at any rate, let them come to dinner. . . . [*In a lower voice.*] But don't be stupid, don't disgrace me, and write correctly. . . . 'Drive' is spelt i-v-e. . . . [*Aloud and tenderly.*] Please, my dear!

Julie. Certainly.   [*Goes out.*

Dyadin. They say that the professor's spouse, Elena Alexandrovna, whom I have not the honour to know, is distinguished not only by spiritual beauty, but by beauty of countenance as well.

Orlovsky. Just so, she's a wonderful woman.

Zheltoukhin. She's faithful to her professor?

Voynitsky. Unfortunately, she is.

Zheltoukhin. Why unfortunately?

Voynitsky. Because this faithfulness is wrong from beginning to end. There's a great deal of rhetoric, but no logic in it at all. To be unfaithful to an old husband, whom you can't bear— that's considered immoral; but to try to suppress one's poor youth and a living feeling—that is not immoral. Damn it all, where's the logic of it?

Dyadin. [*In a tearful voice.*] Georgie dear, I don't like you to speak like this. Indeed, please, don't. . . . It makes me tremble. . . . Gentlemen, I possess no talent, no flowers of eloquence, but allow me to speak out without elegant phrases, as my conscience prompts me. . . . Gentlemen, one who is unfaithful to a wife or to a husband, is a false person, a person who may be unfaithful even to his country!

Voynitsky. Turn the tap off!

Dyadin. But allow me, Georgie! . . . Ivan Ivanych, Lennie, and all of you my dear friends, do take into consideration the vicissitudes of my fate. It is not a secret nor is it enveloped in the darkness of obscurity that my wife, on the day after our wedding, ran away from me with the man she loved, on account of my unattractive appearance.

Voynitsky. And she did quite right.

Dyadin. But listen, gentlemen! After that incident I did not violate my duty. I love her to this very day and am faithful to her, I help her in every possible way I can, and I have bequeathed my property to the children, whom she has borne to the man she loved. I have not violated my duty, and am proud of it. Yes, I am proud! I was deprived of happiness, but my pride remains. And she? Her youth has gone, her beauty, under the influence of the laws of nature, has faded away, her lover is dead—may he rest in peace. And what's left to her? [*Sitting down.*] I speak seriously to you, and you laugh. . . .

Orlovsky. You're a kind-hearted man, you're a great spirit, but your speech is too long and you wave your hands. . . .

[*Fyodor Ivanovich comes out of the house. He is dressed in a poddiovka (sleeveless overcoat worn by Russian peasants) made of the finest cloth; high boots; his chest covered with orders, medals, and a solid gold chain with trinkets; has expensive rings on his fingers.*

SCENE IV

The same and Fyodor

Fyodor. How do you do, old chaps?

Orlovsky. [*Joyously.*] Fyodor, my boy, darling sonny!

Fyodor. [*To Zheltoukhin.*] I congratulate you on your birthday . . . be a big boy. . . . [*Greeting the whole company.*] Pater! Waffle, how d' ye do? I wish you all a good appetite!

Zheltoukhin. Where have you been wandering? You should not come so late.

Fyodor. It's hot! I must gulp some vodka.

Orlovsky. [*With an admiring look at him.*] My dear fellow, what a fine beard he has! . . . Friends, he's a beauty! Look at him: isn't he a beauty?

Fyodor. Congratulations to the new-born! [*Drinking.*] Aren't the Serebryakovs here?

Zheltoukhin. They've not come.

Fyodor. H'm! . . . And where's Julie?

Zheltoukhin. I don't know why she's got stuck there. It's time to bring in the birthday pie. I'll call her instantly.

[*Goes out.*

Orlovsky. And our Lennie, our new-born, isn't in the right humour to-day. So sulky!

Voynitsky. He's a beast!

Orlovsky. His nerves must be upset, he can't help it. . . .

Voynitsky. He loves himself too much, hence his nerves. If you were to say in his presence that this herring here is good, he would at once feel hurt because it was not he who was praised. Here he comes.

Enter Julie and Zheltoukhin.

SCENE V

The same, Zheltoukhin and Julie

Julie. How do you do, Fyodor dear? [*They kiss one another.* Do have something, dear. [*To Orlovsky.*] Look, godpa, what a present I am giving Lennie.
                [*Showing a little shoe to serve as a watch-stand.*

Orlovsky. My ducky, my dear little girl, what a fine shoe! What a fine thing!

Julie. The gold wire-ribbon alone cost eight and a half roubles. Look at the borders: tiny little pearls, tiny little pearls, tiny little pearls. And here are the letters: 'Leonid Zheltoukhin.' Here's embroidered in silk: 'A present to him I love.' . . .

Dyadin. Do let me have a look! That is fascinating!

Fyodor. That'll do . . . that's enough! Julie, tell them to fetch champagne!

Julie. Fyodor dear, that's for the evening!

Fyodor. Why, why evening? Tell them to bring it at once, or I'll go away. 'Pon my word, I'll go away. Where do you keep it? I'll go and fetch it myself.

Julie. Fyodor dear, in a well-ordered house, you're always a nuisance. [*To Vassili.*] Vassili, here's the key! The champagne is in the pantry, you know, in the corner, just by the bag of raisins, in a basket. Only be careful, don't break anything!

Fyodor. Vassili, three bottles!

Julie. You'll never make a good housekeeper, Fyodor. . . . [*Serving out the pie to the company.*] Have some more, please, gentlemen. . . . Dinner won't be yet, not till six. . . . Nothing will come of you, Fyodor dear. . . . You're a lost creature!

Fyodor. Now, you've started preaching.

Voynitsky. I think someone has driven up. . . . Do you hear?

Zheltoukhin. Yes. . . . It's the Serebryakovs. . . . At last!

[*Vassili announces the Serebryakovs.*

Julie. [*Crying out*]. Sonechka!   [*Runs out.*

Voynitsky. [*Singing.*] 'Let's go to meet them, let's go.' . .

[*Goes out.*

Fyodor. How overjoyed they are!

Zheltoukhin. How very little tact some people possess! He lives with the professor's wife and cannot conceal it.

Fyodor. Who does?

Zheltoukhin. George, of course. He praised her so much just now, before you came, that it was even indecent.

Fyodor. How do you know that he lives with her?

Zheltoukhin. As if I were blind! . . . Besides, the whole district is talking about it.

Fyodor. Nonsense. Nobody has yet lived with her up to now but soon I shall live with her. . . . Do you see? I!

SCENE VI

The same, Serebryakov, Marie Vassilievna, Voynitsky, with Elena Andreyevna on his arm, Sonya and Julie

Julie. [*Kissing Sonya.*] My dear! Darling!

Orlovsky. [*Going to meet them.*] How do you do, Alexander, how are you, old boy? [*Embracing one another.*] You are well? Quite well?

Serebryakov. And how are you, my dear friend? You look fine! I am very glad to see you. How long have you been back?

Orlovsky. I returned on Friday. [*To Marie Vassilievna.*] Marie Vassilievna! How are you, Your Excellency?

[*Kissing her hand.*

Marie Vassilievna. My dear! . . .   [*Kissing him on the head.*

Sonya. Dearest godpa!

Orlovsky. Sonechka, my darling! [*Kissing her.*] My own darling, my little canary bird! . . .

Sonya. As usual, your face is radiant, kindly, sweet! . . .

Orlovsky. And you've grown taller, and handsomer, and shapelier, my sweet! . . .

Sonya. How are you getting on? Are you well?

Orlovsky. Tremendously well!

Sonya. That's right, godpa! [*To Fyodor.*] I failed to notice the elephant. [*They embrace.*] Sunburnt, hairy . . . a real spider!

Julie. Darling!

Orlovsky. [*To Serebryakov.*] How are you getting on, old boy?

Serebryakov. So-so. . . . And you?

Orlovsky. What can be the matter with me? I live! I gave my estate to my son, my daughters are married to good men, and now there's no freer man than myself. I'm enjoying myself!

Dyadin. [*To Serebryakov.*] It pleased Your Excellency to arrive a little late. The temperature of the pie has considerably gone down. Allow me to introduce myself, Ilya Ilyich Dyadin, or Waffle, as some very wittily call me on account of my pock-marked countenance.

Serebryakov. Glad to make your acquaintance.

Dyadin. Madame! Mademoiselle! [*Bowing to Elena and to Sonya.*] Here are all my friends, Your Excellency. Once upon a time I had a considerable fortune, but for domestic reasons, or, as people in intellectual centres put it, for reasons for which the editor accepts no responsibility, I had to give up my share to my own brother, who, on a certain unfortunate occasion, found himself short of seventy thousand roubles of Government money. My profession consists in the exploitation of the stormy elements. I make the stormy waves turn the wheels of a flour mill, which I rent from my friend, the Wood Demon.

Voynitsky. Waffle, turn the tap off!

Dyadin. I always bow down with reverence [*bowing down to the ground*] before the luminaries of science, who adorn our country's horizon. Forgive me the audacity with which I crave to pay a visit to Your Excellency and to delight my soul in a conversation about the ultimate deductions of science.

Serebryakov. Pray, do come. I shall be pleased.

Sonya. Do tell us, godpa, where did you spend the winter? Where did you disappear to?

Orlovsky. I was in Gmunden, my sweet, I was also in Paris, in Nice; I was in London. . . .

Sonya. Splendid! What a happy man!

Orlovsky. Come with me in the autumn. Won't you?

Sonya. [*Singing.*] 'Tempt me not without need' . . .

Fyodor. Don't sing at lunch, or your husband's wife will be a silly.

Dyadin. It would be interesting now just to have a glance at this table *à vol d'oiseau.* What a fascinating bouquet! A combination of grace, beauty, profound learning, popu——

Fyodor. What fascinating language! Damn you! You speak

as though someone were at work on your back with a plane. . . .   [*Laughter.*

Orlovsky. [*To Sonya.*] And you, my darling, you are not yet married. . . .

Voynitsky. Good heavens, whom could she marry? Humboldt is dead, Edison is in America, Schopenhauer is also dead. . . . The other day I found her diary on her table: this size! I opened it and read: 'No, I shall never fall in love. . . . Love is the egotistical attraction of my ego to an object of the opposite sex.' . . . And I wonder what is not there? Transcendental, culminating point of the integrating principle . . . ugh! And where have you got to know all this?

Sonya. Whoever else may be ironical, you ought not to be, Uncle George.

Voynitsky. Why are you cross?

Sonya. If you say another word, one of us will have to go home. You or I. . . .

rlovsky. [*Laughing aloud.*] What a character!

Voynitsky. Yes, a character indeed, I must say. . . . [*To Sonya.*] Give me your little paw! Please do! [*Kissing her hand.*] Peace and goodwill. . . . I won't do it again.

Scene VII

The same and Khrouschov (the Wood Demon)

Khrouschov. [*Coming out of the house.*] Why am I not a painter? What a wonderful group!

Orlovsky. [*Joyously.*] My dear godson!

Khrouschov. My congratulations to the new-born. How do you do, Julie? How fine you look to-day! Godpa! [*Kissing Orlovsky.*] Sophie Alexandrovna! . . .
                [*Greeting the rest of the company.*

Zheltoukhin. How can you be so late! Where have you been?

Khrouschov. At a patient's.

Julie. The pie has gone cold.

Khrouschov. It doesn't matter, Julie, I'll eat it cold. Where shall I sit?

Sonya. Sit down here. . . .   [*Pointing to a seat beside her.*

Khrouschov. The weather is wonderful, and I have a ravenous appetite. . . . Yes, I'll have some vodka. . . . [*Drinking.*] To the new-born! I'll have this little pie. . . . Julie, give it a kiss, it'll taste better. . . . [*She kisses it.*] *Merci!* How are you, godpa? I haven't seen you for a long time.

Orlovsky. Yes, it is a long time. I've been abroad.

Khrouschov. I heard about it . . . and envied you. And how are you, Fyodor?

Fyodor. All right, your prayers support us, like pillars. . . .

Khrouschov. How are your affairs?

Fyodor. I must not grumble. I am having a good time. Only, my dear fellow, there's a lot of running to and fro. Sickening! From here to the Caucasus, from the Caucasus back here—continuously on the move, until I'm dazed. You know, I've got two estates there!

Khrouschov. I know.

Fyodor. I am engaged in colonization and in catching tarantulas and scorpions. Business is going all right, but as regards 'my surging passions, keep still!'—all is as it used to be.

Khrouschov. You're in love, of course?

Fyodor. On which account, Wood Demon, we must have a drink. [*Drinking.*] . . . Gentlemen, never fall in love with married women! My word, it's better to be wounded in the shoulder and shot through the leg, like your obedient servant, than to love a married woman. . . . It's such a misfortune! . . .

Sonya. Is it hopeless?

Fyodor. Hopeless indeed! Hopeless! . . . In this world there's nothing hopeless. Hopeless, unhappy love, oh, ach!—all this is just nonsense! One has only to will. . . . If I will that my gun should not miss fire, it won't. If I will a woman to love me, she shall love me. Just so, Sonya, old chap! If I pick out a woman, I think it's easier for her to jump to the moon than to get away from me.

Sonya. What a terrific fellow!

Fyodor. She won't get away from me! I hardly have time to say three words to her before she's already in my power. . . . Yes. . . . I have only to say to her: 'My lady, whenever you look at the window you must remember me. I will it.' And she remembers me a thousand times a day. Moreover, I bombard her every day with letters. . . .

Elena Andreyevna. Letters surely aren't a safe method; she may receive them, but she may not read them.

Fyodor. You think so? H'm! . . . I have been living in this world for thirty-five years, and somehow I haven't yet come across such phenomenal women as would have the courage not to open a letter.

Orlovsky. [*Looking admiringly at him.*] See! My dear son, my beautiful son! I, too, was like that. Precisely, to a degree!

Only that I was not in the war; but I drank and threw money about—terrible!

Fyodor. Misha, I do love her, seriously, hellishly. . . . Were she only to agree, I would just give her everything and all. . . . I would carry her to the Caucasus, to the mountains, we should live like singing birds. . . . I should guard her, Elena Andreyevna, like a faithful dog, and she would be to me as 𝜤ur marshal of nobility sings: 'Thou wilt be the queen of the universe, thou my dearest.' Oh, she does not know how very happy she could be!

Khrouschov. And who's that lucky woman?

Fyodor. If you know too much, you'll age quickly. . . . But enough about that. Now, let's sing from a different opera. I remember, it's about ten years ago—Lennie was still at school then—we were celebrating his birthday as we are now. I rode home—Sonya on my right arm, and Julie on my left, and both held on to my beard. Now, let's drink the health of the friends of my youth, of Sonya and Julie!

Dyadin. [*Laughing aloud.*] That is fascinating! That is fascinating!

Fyodor. Once, it was after the war, I was having drinks with a Turkish pasha in Trebizond. . . . All at once he asks me——

Dyadin. [*Interrupting.*] Let's drink a toast to friendly relations. *Vivat* friendship! Here's luck!

Fyodor. Stop, stop, stop! Sonya, I claim attention! I am having a bet, damn it! I am putting three hundred roubles on the table! Let's go after lunch to play croquet, and I bet that in one round I shall get through all the hoops and back.

Sonya. I accept the bet; only I haven't got three hundred roubles.

Fyodor. If you lose, you are to sing to me forty times.

Sonya. Agreed.

Dyadin. That is fascinating! That is fascinating!

Elena Andreyevna. [*Looking at the sky.*] What bird is that?

Zheltoukhin. It is a hawk.

Fyodor. Friends, let's drink the hawk's health!

[*Sonya laughs aloud.*

Orlovsky. Now, she has started! What's the matter?

[*Khrouschov laughs aloud.*

Orlovsky. Why are you laughing?

Marie Vassilievna. Sophie! It is not right!

Khrouschov. Oh, I am so sorry! . . . I'll stop presently, presently. . . .

Orlovsky. This is laughing without reason.

Voynitsky. Those two, you 've only to lift up your finger, and they burst out laughing. Sonya! [*Lifting his finger.*] Look now! . . .

Khrouschov. Stop it! [*Looking at his watch.*] Well, I have eaten and drunk, and now I must be off. It 's time I went.

Sonya. Where to?

Khrouschov. To a patient. I 'm as tired of my medical practice as of an unloved wife, or a long winter. . . .

Serebryakov. But, look here, medicine is your profession, your work, so to say. . . .

Voynitsky. [*Ironically.*] He has another profession. He digs peat on his estate.

Serebryakov. What?

Voynitsky. Peat! A mining engineer has calculated with absolute certainty that there is peat on his land worth seven hundred and twenty thousand roubles. It isn't a joke.

Khrouschov. I don't dig peat for the sake of money.

Voynitsky. Why do you dig it then?

Khrouschov. In order that you should not cut down forests.

Voynitsky. Why not cut them? To hear you, one might think that forests only existed for the courtships of youths and maidens.

Khrouschov. I never said anything of the sort.

Voynitsky. What I have had the honour of hearing you say up to now in defence of forests is all antiquated, not serious, and tendentious. Pray forgive me. I say this not without grounds, I know almost by heart all your arguments in defence. . . . For instance. . . . [*Raising the tone of his voice and gesticulating, as though imitating Khrouschov.*] You men are destroying the forests, but they adorn the earth, they teach man to understand beauty and inspire him with a sense of majesty. Forests soften harsh climates. Where the climate is milder, there man exerts less effort in his struggle with nature, and therefore man there is gentler and kindlier. In countries with a mild climate people are handsome, alert, easily excited, their speech is elegant, their movements graceful. Arts and science flourish there, their philosophy is not gloomy, their relations to women are full of fine courtesy. And so on and so on. . . . All this is fine, but so unconvincing that you must allow me to go on burning wood in the fireplaces and building wooden barns.

Khrouschov. Cut forests, when it is a matter of urgency, you may, but it is time to stop destroying them. Every Russian forest is cracking under the axe, millions of trees are perishing, the abodes of beasts and birds are being ravaged, rivers are becoming shallow and drying up, wonderful landscapes are disappearing without leaving a trace; and all this because lazy man has not got the sense to stoop to pick up fuel from the ground. One must be a barbarian [*pointing to the trees*] to burn that beauty in the fireplace, to destroy what we cannot create. Understanding and creative power have been granted to man to multiply what has been given him, but hitherto he has not created, he has only destroyed. The forests grow less and less, the rivers dry up, wild birds disappear, the climate is spoilt, and every day the earth grows poorer and uglier. You look at me ironically, and all I am saying seems to you antiquated and not serious, but when I pass by woods belonging to the peasants, woods which I have saved from being cut down, or when I hear the rustling of the young forest, which I have planted with my own hands, I realize that the climate is to a certain extent also in my power; and if a thousand years hence man is to be happy, I too shall have had a share in it. When I plant a little birch tree and then see how it is growing green and shaking in the wind, my soul is filled with pride from the realization that, thanks to me, there is one more life added on earth——

Fyodor. [*Interrupting*.] Your health, Wood Demon!

Voynitsky. All this is very fine, but if you looked at the matter, not from a novelette point of view, but from a scientific point of view, then——

Sonya. Uncle George, your tongue is covered with rust. Do keep quiet!

Khrouschov. Indeed, George Petrovich, let's not discuss it. Please.

Voynitsky. As you like!

Marie Vassilievna. Ah!

Sonya. Granny, what's the matter?

Marie Vassilievna. [*To Serebryakov*.] I had forgotten to tell you, Alexander. . . . I'm losing my memory. . . . I had a letter to-day from Kharkov, from Paul Alexeyevich. . . . He asks to be remembered to you. . . .

Serebryakov. Thank you, I am very glad.

Marie Vassilievna. He sent me his new pamphlet and asked me to show it to you.

Serebryakov. It is interesting?

Marie Vassilievna. It is interesting, but somewhat odd. He refutes what he himself was defending seven years ago. It is very, very typical of our time. Never have people betrayed their convictions with such levity as they do now. It is terrible!

Voynitsky. There's nothing terrible. Won't you have some fish, *maman?*

Marie Vassilievna. But I want to speak!

Voynitsky. We have been talking for the last fifty years about tendencies and schools; it's time we stopped.

Marie Vassilievna. It does not please you for some reason when I speak. Excuse me, George, but this last year you have changed so much that I can't make you out at all. You used to be a man of definite conviction, an enlightened personality. . . .

Voynitsky. Oh, yes! I was an 'enlightened personality' from which no one got any light. Permit me to get up. I was an 'enlightened personality.' A more venomous joke couldn't have been uttered! Now I am forty-seven. Up till last year I was deliberately trying, like you, to fog my eyes with all sorts of abstractions and scholasticism, in order not to see real life; and I thought that I was doing the right thing. . . . But now, if only you knew what a great fool I seem to myself for having so stupidly let slip the time when I might have had everything, everything which my old age denies me now!

Serebryakov. Look here, George, you seem to blame your former convictions for something——

Sonya. Enough, papa! It's dull!

Serebryakov. Look here! You, as it were, blame your former convictions for something. But it is not they, it's yourself who is at fault. You forgot that convictions without deeds are dead. You ought to have been at work.

Voynitsky. Work? Not every one is capable of being a writing *perpetuum mobile.*

Serebryakov. What do you mean to convey by that?

Voynitsky. Nothing. Let's stop the conversation. We aren't at home.

Marie Vassilievna. I am completely losing my memory. . . . I forgot to remind you, Alexander, to take your drops before lunch; I brought them with me, but forgot to remind you.

Serebryakov. You need not.

Marie Vassilievna. But you are ill, Alexander! You're very ill!

Serebryakov. Why make a fuss about it? Old, ill, old, ill . . . that's the only thing I hear! [*To Zheltoukhin.*] Leonid Stepanovich, allow me to get up and to go into the house. It is rather hot here and the mosquitoes are biting.

Zheltoukhin. Please do. We've finished lunch.

Serebryakov. Thank you.

> [*Goes into the house; Marie Vassilievna follows him.*

Julie. [*To her brother.*] Go to the professor! It's awkward!

Zheltoukhin. [*To her.*] Damn him! [*Goes out.*

Dyadin. Yulia Stepanovna, allow me to thank you from the bottom of my soul. [*Kissing her hand.*

Julie. Don't mention it, Ilya Ilyich! You've eaten so little. . . . [*The company get up and thank her.*] Don't mention it! You've all eaten so little!

Fyodor. What are we going to do now? Let's now go to the croquet lawn and settle our bet . . . and then?

Julie. And then we shall have dinner.

Fyodor. And then?

Khrouschov. And then you all come to me. In the evening we'll arrange a fishing party on the lake.

Fyodor. Splendid!

Dyadin. That is fascinating!

Sonya. Well, it is settled then. It means we are going now to the croquet lawn to settle our bet. . . . Then Julie will give us an early dinner, and about seven we'll drive over to the Wood—— I mean to M. Khrouschov. Splendid! Come, Julie, let's get the balls. [*Goes with Julie into the house.*

Fyodor. Vassili, carry the wine to the lawn! We will drink the health of the conquerors. Now, pater, come and let's have a noble game.

Orlovsky. Wait awhile, my own, I must sit with the professor for a few minutes, for it's a bit awkward. One must keep up appearances. You play my ball for a while, I'll come presently. . . . [*Goes into the house.*

Dyadin. I am going to listen to the most learned Alexander Vladimirovich. In anticipation of the high delight, which——

Voynitsky. You're a bore, Waffle! Go away!

Dyadin. I am going. [*Goes into the house.*

Fyodor. [*Walking into the garden, singing.*] 'Thou wilt be the queen of the universe, thou my dearest.' . . . [*Goes out.*

Khrouschov. I'll leave quietly. [*To Voynitsky.*] George Petrovich, I earnestly ask you, let us never talk either of forests, or of medicine. I don't know why, but when you start discussing these matters, I have a feeling all day afterwards as if I had eaten my dinner out of rusty pots. Allow me! [*Goes out.*

Scene VIII

Elena Andreyevna and Voynitsky

Voynitsky. The narrow-minded fellow! Every one is permitted to say stupid things, but I dislike it when it is done with pathos.

Elena Andreyevna. You have again behaved impossibly, George! Why need you have argued with Marie Vassilievna and Alexander, and spoken about *perpetuum mobile?* How petty it is!

Voynitsky. But if I hate him?

Elena Andreyevna. There's nothing to hate Alexander for; he's like all the rest. . . .

[*Sonya and Julie pass into the garden with croquet balls and mallets.*

Voynitsky. If you could see the expression on your face, your movements! . . . You're too lazy to live! Oh, what laziness!

Elena Andreyevna. Oh, lazy, boring! [*After a pause.*] Every one scoffs at my husband before my eyes, without minding my presence. Every one looks at me with compassion: 'Poor woman, she has an old husband!' All, even very kind people, would like me to leave Alexander. . . . That sympathy, all those compassionate glances and sighs of pity come simply to this. As the Wood Demon has just said, all of you nonsensically destroy forests, and soon none will be left on the earth. Just as nonsensically do you all destroy man, and soon, thanks to you, there will remain on earth neither faithfulness, nor purity, nor the capacity for self-sacrifice. Why can't you look unconcernedly at a faithful wife, if she's not yours? The Wood Demon is right. There's lurking in all of you a demon of destruction. You spare neither forests, nor birds, nor women, nor one another.

Voynitsky. I don't love this philosophy!

Elena Andreyevna. Tell that Fyodor that his impudence bores me. It's loathsome in the end. To look into my eyes and to speak aloud in the presence of all about his love for a married woman—how wonderfully witty!

Voices in the garden. Bravo! Bravo!

Elena Andreyevna. But how nice the Wood Demon is! He often comes to us, but I 'm shy and have never talked to him, as I should have liked to; I did not make a friend of him. He may think that I am ill-natured or proud. George, probably you and I are such good friends, because we both are dull and boring people! Bores! Don't look at me like that, I don't like it.

Voynitsky. But how else can I look at you, if I love you? You are my happiness, my life, my youth! . . . I know that the chances of your returning my love are *nil*, but I want nothing more, only allow me to look at you, to hear your voice. . . .

Scene IX

The same and Serebryakov

Serebryakov. [*At the window.*] Elena dear, where are you?
Elena Andreyevna. I 'm here.
Serebryakov. Come and sit with us awhile, dear. . . .
    [*Disappears. Elena Andreyevna goes into the house.*
Voynitsky. [*Following her.*] Allow me to speak of my love, don't drive me away, and this alone will be my greatest happiness.

CURTAIN

ACT II

The dining-room of the Serebryakovs' house. A sideboard, a dinner table in the middle of the room. Time: after one o'clock at night. From the garden comes the sound of the night watchman's knocks.

Scene I

Serebryakov (sitting in a chair in front of the window and dozing) and Elena Andreyevna (sitting near by and also dozing)

Serebryakov. [*Awaking.*] Who 's there! Is it you, Sonya?
Elena Andreyevna. It 's me. . . .
Serebryakov. You, Lena dear? . . . The pain is excruciating!
Elena Andreyevna. Your rug is on the floor. . . . (*Wrapping it round his legs.*) I 'll shut the window, Alexander.

Serebryakov. No, don't, I'm hot. . . . I had just fallen into a doze and dreamed that my left leg did not belong to me. . . . I awoke with excruciating pain. No, it's not gout. I think it is rheumatism. What's the time now?

Elena Andreyevna. Twenty past one. [*A pause.*

Serebryakov. Have a look in the morning, in the library, for Batyushkov. I believe we've got his books.

Elena Andreyevna. What?

Serebryakov. Have a look for Batyushkov. I remember we had his works. But why am I breathing with such difficulty?

Elena Andreyevna. You're tired. It's the second night now you haven't slept.

Serebryakov. They say that Turgenev's gout has developed into angina pectoris. I am afraid that this will happen in my case, too. Cursed, loathsome old age! Curse it! Since I've grown old I've become disgusting to myself. And to all of you I must present a disgusting spectacle.

Elena Andreyevna. You speak of your old age in such a tone as if we all were to blame for your growing old.

Serebryakov. You are the first to be disgusted by me.

Elena Andreyevna. How stupid of you!

[*Moving away and sitting down at some distance.*

Serebryakov. Of course, you're right. I'm not a fool and quite understand. You're young, healthy, handsome, you're eager for life; and I am an old man, almost a corpse. Well? Don't I realize it all? And, of course, it is foolish of me to be still alive. But wait a little while, I'll free you all soon.

Elena Andreyevna. Alexander, it's crushing me! If I deserve any reward for the sleepless nights, I ask only this from you: be quiet! For the love of Christ, be quiet! I ask for nothing else.

Serebryakov. It comes to this then, that, thanks to me, all of you have become crushed, and are bored and wasting your youth; and I am the only one who is enjoying life and is content. Just so, of course!

Elena Andreyevna. Be quiet! You've worn me out!

Serebryakov. I have worn out every one. Of course!

Elena Andreyevna. [*Crying.*] It's unbearable! Tell me what you want from me.

Serebryakov. Nothing.

Elena Andreyevna. Be quiet, then, I beg.

Serebryakov. Isn't it curious, if George or that old idiot Marie

Vassilievna starts speaking, it seems all right; everybody listens to them. But if I say a single word, everybody begins to feel distressed. Even my voice is disgusting. Well, let us suppose I am disgusting, I am an egotist, I am a despot; but indeed haven't I, even in my old age, a certain right to egotism? Haven't I indeed deserved it? My life has been hard. I and Orlovsky were undergraduates together. Ask him. He had a good time and went about with gipsy women; he was my benefactor; and I at that time lived in a cheap, dirty room. I worked day and night, like an ox. I starved and worried because I lived at someone else's expense. Then I went to Heidelberg University, but I saw nothing of Heidelberg; I went to Paris, but I saw nothing of Paris—all the time I sat within four walls and worked. And since I became professor, and all through my life, I have served science, as they say, with faith and truth, as I am still serving her. Indeed, for all this, I ask you, have I not the right to a peaceful old age, to some consideration from people?

Elena Andreyevna. Nobody disputes your right. [*The window is rattling in the wind.*] The wind is getting up; I'll shut the window. [*Shutting it.*] It's going to rain presently. . . . Nobody disputes your rights.

[*A pause. Outside the night watchman knocks and sings a song.*

Serebryakov. To work all one's life long for science, to get accustomed to one's study, to one's audience, to respected colleagues, and then all of a sudden, without rhyme or reason, to find oneself in this sepulchre, to have to see stupid people, day in and day out to hear trivial conversations! I want to live, I love success, I love popularity, noise; but here I am—in exile. Every minute pining for the past, watching the successes of others, afraid of death! . . . I cannot! I haven't the strength! And here some people won't even forgive me my old age!

Elena Andreyevna. Wait awhile, have patience: in five or six years' time I too shall be old.

Enter Sonya.

SCENE II

The same and Sonya

Sonya. I wonder why the doctor has not come yet. I told Stepan, if the Zemstvo doctor was out, to drive over and fetch the Wood Demon.

Serebryakov. Of what use is your Wood Demon to me? He understands as much about medicine as I do about astronomy.

Sonya. You don't want us to call in the whole medical faculty to treat your gout?

Serebryakov. I am not even going to talk to that crazy fellow.

Sonya. Just as you please. [*Sitting down.*] I don't mind.

Serebryakov. What's the time now?

Elena Andreyevna. Not yet two.

Serebryakov. It's stifling here. . . . Sonya, give me the medicine on the table.

Sonya. Certainly.   [*Handing him the medicine.*

Serebryakov. [*Irritably.*] Ah, not this one. It's no use asking for anything!

Sonya. Please, don't be capricious! Some may like it, but pray spare me. I don't like it.

Serebryakov. That girl has an impossible character. Why are you cross?

Sonya. And why do you speak in such a mournful tone! Any one might think that you are actually unhappy. Yet there are very few people as happy as you are.

Serebryakov. Just so, of course! I am very, very happy.

Sonya. Certainly, you're happy. . . . And if you have gout, you know perfectly well that the attack will pass by the morning. Why grieve then? Why make a fuss?

Enter Voynitsky in a dressing-gown, with a candle.

SCENE III

The same and Voynitsky

Voynitsky. There's a storm coming on. [*A flash of lightning.*] I say! Elena and Sonya, go to bed; I'll take your place here.

Serebryakov. [*Frightened.*] No, no, don't leave me with him! No, he'll talk my head off.

Voynitsky. But they need a rest! They've not slept for two nights.

Serebryakov. Let them go to bed, but you too must go away. Thank you. I implore you to go. In the name of our past friendship, don't refuse me. We will have a talk some other time.

Voynitsky. Our past friendship! . . . This, I must say, is news to me.

Elena Andreyevna. Be quiet, George!

Serebryakov. My dear, don't leave me with him! He'll talk my head off.

Voynitsky. It is getting ridiculous.

Khrouschov's voice. [*Behind the scenes.*] They're in the dining-room? Here? Please attend to my horse!

Voynitsky. The doctor has come.

Enter Khrouschov.

SCENE IV
The same and Khrouschov

Khrouschov. What weather! The rain ran after me, but I just managed to escape it. How do you do? [*Greeting them.*

Serebryakov. I'm sorry we troubled you. I did not want it at all.

Khrousehov. Never mind, it's perfectly all right! But what's the matter with you, Alexander Vladimirovich? Aren't we ashamed of being seedy? Oh, we mustn't! What's wrong?

Serebryakov. Why do doctors always speak to patients in a condescending tone?

Khrouschov. [*Laughing.*] Well, you shouldn't be so observant. . . . [*In a gentle voice.*] Won't you lie down on your bed? You aren't comfortable here. In bed you'll be warmer and more restful. Come . . . I will examine you there . . . and everything will be all right.

Elena Andreyevna. Do as the doctor says, Alexander. Do go.

Khrouschov. If you find it hard to walk, we will move you there in your chair.

Serebryakov. I can manage. . . . I'll walk. . . . [*Getting up.*] Only they should not have troubled you. [*Khrouschov and Sonya support him under the arms.*] Besides, I don't very much believe in . . . pharmacy. Why are you supporting me? . . . I can walk by myself.

[*Goes out with Khrouschov and Sonya.*

SCENE V
Elena Andreyevna and Voynitsky

Elena Andreyevna. I'm worn out by him. I can hardly stand.

Voynitsky. You're worn out by him, and I'm worn out by myself. I've not slept for three nights.

Elena Andreyevna. There's something wrong about this house. Your mother hates everything, except her little books and the professor. The professor is irritable; he doesn't trust me; he's afraid of you. Sonya is cross with her father and does not speak to me; you hate my husband and openly despise your mother; my boring self, I too am irritated, and to-day I was twenty times on the point of crying. In a word, it's a war of all against all. What's the sense of that war, what's it for?

Voynitsky. Don't let us philosophize!

Elena Andreyevna. There's something wrong about this house. You, George, are well-educated, intelligent, and it seems that you ought to understand that the world perishes not because of murderers and thieves, but from hidden hatred, from hostility among good people, from all those petty squabbles, unseen by those who call our house a haven of intellectuals. Do help me to reconcile every one! Alone I cannot do it!

Voynitsky. You first reconcile me to myself! My dear! . . .
[*Clinging to her hand.*

Elena Andreyevna. You must not! [*Withdrawing her hand.*] Go away!

Voynitsky. The rain will pass presently, and everything in nature will be refreshed and breathe freely. I alone shall not be refreshed by the storm. Day and night I am haunted and oppressed by the idea that my life has been wasted irretrievably. I have no past, it was all stupidly thrown away on trifles; and the present is terrible in its absurdity. Here's my life and love: what shall I do with them, what use can I make of them? My feelings are wasted, like a sunbeam that falls into a ditch, and I myself am wasted. . . .

Elena Andreyevna. When you speak to me of your love, I grow stupid and don't know what to say. Forgive me, I can't say anything to you. [*Making as if to go.*] Good night!

Voynitsky. [*Barring her way.*] If only you knew how I suffer from the thought that side by side with me in this house another life is being wasted—your own! What are you waiting for? What cursed philosophy stands in your way? Understand, the highest morality does not consist in putting fetters on your youth and in trying to suppress your thirst for life. . . .

Elena Andreyevna. [*Looking fixedly at him.*] George, you're drunk!

Voynitsky. Maybe, maybe! . . .

Elena Andreyevna. Is Fyodor Ivanovich stopping here with you?

Voynitsky. He's stopping the night with me. Maybe, maybe. . . . Anything may be!

Elena Andreyevna. And you've been drinking together to-day? Why did you do it?

Voynitsky. At any rate, it resembles life. . . . Don't take it away from me, Elena!

Elena Andreyevna. Formerly you never used to drink, and you never talked so much, as you do now. Go to bed! You bore me. And tell your Fyodor Ivanovich that if he does not stop worrying me I will take steps to stop him! Go!

Voynitsky. [*Clinging to her hand.*] My dear! . . . Dearest!

Enter Khrouschov.

SCENE VI
The same and Khrouschov

Khrouschov. Elena Andreyevna, Alexander Vladimirovich is asking for you.

Elena Andreyevna. [*Tearing away her hand from Voynitsky.*] In a moment! [*Goes out.*

Khrouschov. [*To Voynitsky.*] Nothing is sacred to you! You and the dear lady who has just gone out ought to remember that her husband was once the husband of your own sister, and that there is a young girl living under the same roof! The whole district is speaking of the affair. What a disgrace! [*Goes out to the patient.*

Voynitsky. [*Alone.*] She's gone. . . . [*After a pause.*] Ten years ago I used to meet her at the house of my dead sister. She was seventeen then, and I thirty-seven. Why didn't I fall in love with her then and propose to her? It was all so possible! She would now be my wife. . . . Yes. . . . We two would now be awakened by the storm. Frightened of the thunder, she would cling to me, and I should keep her in my embrace and whisper: 'Don't be afraid, I am here with you.' Oh, wonderful thoughts! How fine! I laugh even. . . . But, my God, my ideas are getting mixed. . . . Why am I old? Why does she not understand me? Her rhetoric, her lazy morality, her absurd lazy ideas of the world's ruin—all this is profoundly hateful to me. . . . [*A pause.*] Why am I so wrongly made? How much I envy that gay dog Fyodor, or that silly Wood Demon! They're direct, sincere, silly. . . . They're free from this cursed, poisonous irony. . . .

Enter Fyodor Ivanovich, wrapped in a blanket.

SCENE VII
Voynitsky and Fyodor Ivanovich

Fyodor. [*In the doorway.*] Are you by yourself? No ladies present? [*Entering.*] I was awakened by the storm. Glorious rain. What's the time?

Voynitsky. The time be damned!

Fyodor. I fancy I heard the voice of Elena Andreyevna.

Voynitsky. She was here just now.

Fyodor. Magnificent woman! [*Examining the medicines on the table.*] What's this? Peppermint lozenges? [*Tasting.*] Yes, a magnificent woman! . . . Is the professor ill, or what?

Voynitsky. He's ill.

Fyodor. I can't understand such an existence. They say that the ancient Greeks used to throw their weak and ailing children into the abyss from Mont Blanc. Such as he ought to be thrown down too!

Voynitsky. [*Irritably.*] Not Mont Blanc, but the Tarpeian rock. What crass ignorance!

Fyodor. Well, if it's a rock, let it be a rock. . . . As if it damned well mattered! Why are you so gloomy now? Are you sorry for the professor, are you?

Voynitsky. Let me alone. [*A pause.*

Fyodor. Or perhaps you are in love with Mme Professor? Eh? Why, that's right. . . . Sigh for her. . . . Only listen: if in the rumours, which are circulating in the district, there's a hundredth part of truth, and if I find it out, then don't ask for mercy, I'll throw you down from the Tarpeian rock.

Voynitsky. She's my friend!

Fyodor. Already?

Voynitsky. What do you mean by 'already'?

Fyodor. A woman can be a man's friend only on this condition: first she's his acquaintance, then his mistress, and only then his friend.

Voynitsky. What a coarse philosophy!

Fyodor. On which account let's have a drink. Come, I think I've still got a bottle of Chartreuse. We'll drink. And when the dawn comes, we will drive over to my place. Agreed? [*Seeing Sonya enter.*] Oh, heavens, excuse my not having a tie on! [*Runs out.*

Scene VIII

Voynitsky and Sonya

Sonya. And you, Uncle George, have been drinking champagne again with Fyodor and driving about with him in a troika. The bright birds singing together! Well, Fyodor is a downright born rake; but you, what makes you behave like that? At your time of life it does not at all become you.

Voynitsky. Time of life has nothing to do with it. If there's no real life, one lives by illusions. Anyhow, it's better than nothing.

Sonya. The hay hasn't been gathered in; Guerasim said to-day that the rain would rot it away; and you are busy with illusions. [*Frightened.*] Uncle, there are tears in your eyes!

Voynitsky. Tears? Not a bit . . . nonsense! . . . You just looked at me as your dead mother used to look. My dear! . . . [*Eagerly kissing her hands and face.*] My sister . . . my sweet sister! . . . Where is she now? If she knew! Oh, if she only knew!

Sonya. What? If she knew what, uncle?

Voynitsky. It is hard, bad. . . . [*Enter Khrouschov.*] No matter. . . . I'll tell you afterwards. . . . I'll go. . . . [*Goes out.*

Scene IX

Sonya and Khrouschov

Khrouschov. Your father refuses to listen to anything. I tell him it's gout, and he says it's rheumatism; I ask him to lie down, and he sits up. [*Taking his hat.*] Nerves!

Sonya. He's spoilt. Put away your hat. Wait till the rain stops. Won't you have something to eat?

Khrouschov. I think I will.

Sonya. I love to have something to eat at night. I believe there must be something in the sideboard. . . . [*Rummaging there.*] He does not need a doctor. What he needs is to have round him a dozen ladies gazing into his eyes and sighing, 'Professor, professor!' Here's some cheese. . . .

Khrouschov. You ought not to speak of your father like that. I agree, he's a difficult person; but if you compare him with the others, all these Uncle Georges and Orlovskys aren't worth his little finger.

Sonya. Here's a bottle of something. . . . I'm not speaking of my father, but I'm sick of great men with their Chinese ceremonies. . . . [*They sit down.*] What a downpour! [*A flash.*] Oh!

Khrouschov. The storm is passing away, it's only on the borders of the estate. . . .

Sonya. [*Pouring out.*] Here you are!

Khrouschov. May you live to be a hundred! [*Drinking.*

Sonya. You are cross because we have troubled you in the night?

Khrouschov. On the contrary. If you had not called me in, I

should be sleeping now, and to see you in the flesh is much
more pleasant than to see you in a dream.

Sonya. Why, then, do you look so cross?

Khrouschov. Because I am cross. There's nobody about here,
so I can speak frankly. With what pleasure, Sophie Alexandrovna, would I carry you away from here this very minute!
I can't breathe this air here, and it seems to me that it is
poisoning you. Your father, completely absorbed in his gout
and in his books, and refusing to take notice of anything else;
that Uncle George; finally your stepmother——

Sonya. What about my stepmother?

Khrouschov. One can't speak of everything. . . . One can't! My
dear, there's a great deal which I don't understand in people.
In a human being everything should be beautiful: the face,
the clothes, the soul, the thoughts. . . . Often I see a beautiful
face and clothes, so beautiful that my head gets giddy with
rapture; but as for the soul and thoughts, my God! In a
beautiful outside there's sometimes hidden such a black soul
that no whitening can rub it off. . . . Forgive me, I'm
agitated. . . . Indeed, you are infinitely dear to me. . . .

Sonya. [*Dropping a knife.*] I've dropped it. . . .

Khrouschov. [*Picking it up.*] That's all right. . . . [*After a
pause.*] One happens sometimes to walk on a dark night in a
forest, and when one sees a light gleaming far away in the
distance, one's soul is filled with such joy that one cares
nothing for the fatigue, for the darkness, or for the prickly
branches stinging one's face. . . . I work from morning till
late at night; winter and summer I know no rest, I fight with
those who do not understand me, at times I suffer intolerably.
. . . But at last I've found my little light. . . . I shan't
boast that I love you above all on earth. Love to me is not
everything in life . . . love is my reward. My dear, my
glorious, there is no higher reward to one who works, struggles,
suffers——

Sonya. [*In agitation.*] I'm sorry. . . . One question, Mikhail
Lvovich!

Khrouschov. What? Ask it quickly. . . .

Sonya. You see . . . You often come to our house, and I
sometimes go with my people to yours. Do own that you
can't forgive yourself for it. . . .

Khrouschov. What do you mean?

Sonya. I mean, I want to say that your democratic sentiment is
offended by your being close friends with us. I have studied

at the Institute, Elena Andreyevna is an aristocrat, we dress fashionably; and you are a democrat. . . .

Khrouschov. Why . . . why . . . let's not speak about that! It isn't the time!

Sonya. You yourself dig peat, plant trees . . . it's somewhat strange. . . . To be brief, in a word, you're a socialist. . . .

Khrouschov. Democrat, socialist! . . . Sophie Alexandrovna, how can you speak of it seriously and even with a tremble in your voice!

Sonya. Yes, yes, seriously, a thousand times seriously.

Khrouschov. But you can't, you can't. . . .

Sonya. I assure you, I swear, that if, for instance, I had a sister and you fell in love with her and proposed to her, you would never forgive yourself, and you would be ashamed to show yourself to your Zemstvo men and women doctors. You would feel ashamed of having married an aristocratic girl, a 'muslined young lady,' who has never learnt to do any useful work, and who dresses fashionably. I know it quite well. . . . I see in your eyes that it's true! In a word, to be brief, these forests of yours, this peat of yours, your embroidered blouse—all this is an affectation, play-acting, a falsehood and nothing else!

Khrouschov. Why, my child, why have you insulted me? . . . Yet, I am a fool. It serves me right. I shouldn't have intruded where I was not welcome! Good-bye.

[*Going to the door.*

Sonya. Forgive me. . . . I was blunt, I apologize.

Khrouschov. [*Returning.*] If you knew how oppressive and stifling it is here! A set of persons who approach every one sideways, look at a man askance, and try to make him out a socialist, a psychopath, a phrase-monger, anything you like, save a human being. 'Oh, he's a psychopath!' and they're satisfied. 'He's a phrase-monger,' and they're delighted as though they had discovered America. And when people don't understand me and don't know what label to stick on my forehead, they don't blame themselves for this, but me, and say, 'He's a queer fellow, odd!' You're not twenty yet, but you are already old and sober-minded, like your father and Uncle George; and I shouldn't in the least be surprised if you were to call me in to cure you of gout. One can't live like that! Whoever I am, look straight into my eyes, candidly, without reservations, without programmes, and above all try to see me as a human being; otherwise in your relations with people there will never be any peace. Good-bye! And remember my words: with such cunning, suspicious eyes as yours, you will never love! . . .

Sonya. It is untrue!

Khrouschov. It is true!

Sonya. It's untrue! Just to spite you . . . I do love you! I love, and it pains me, it pains me! Leave me alone! Go away, I implore . . . don't come to our house . . . don't come. . . .

Khrouschov. Allow me then! [*Goes out.*

Sonya. [*Alone.*] He got angry. God forbid I should have a temper like his! [*After a pause.*] He speaks admirably, but who can guarantee that it is not phrase-mongering? He constantly thinks of forests, he plants trees. . . . It is all very well, but it is quite possible that all this is psychopathic. . . . [*Covering her face with her hands.*] I cannot make out anything! [*Crying.*] He has studied medicine, and yet his deepest interests lie outside medicine. . . . It's all strange, strange. . . . Lord, help me to think it all out!

Enter Elena Andreyevna.

Scene X

Sonya and Elena Andreyevna

Elena Andreyevna. [*Opening the windows.*] The storm's over! The air is so wonderfully fresh! [*After a pause.*] Where's the Wood Demon?

Sonya. He's gone.

Elena Andreyevna. Sophie!

Sonya. Well?

Elena Andreyevna. How long are you going to be cross with me? We've done no wrong to one another. Why be enemies? It's time we stopped. . . .

Sonya. I myself had wished . . . [*Embracing her.*] Dear!

Elena Andreyevna. Splendid! . . . [*Both are agitated.*

Sonya. Has papa gone to bed?

Elena Andreyevna. No, he's sitting in the drawing-room. . . . You and I don't speak to one another for a month on end—God knows why. It's time at last to stop it. . . . [*Looking at the table.*] What's all this?

Sonya. The Wood Demon had something to eat.

Elena Andreyevna. And there's wine, too. . . . Let's drink to our friendship.

Sonya. Let's.

Elena Andreyevna. From the same glass. . . . [*Pouring out wine.*] It's much better like that. From now on we say 'thou' to one another. Thou!

Sonya. Thou! [*They drink and embrace.*] I have long wished to make peace, but I felt shy. . . .   [*Crying.*

Elena Andreyevna. Why are you crying then?

Sonya. For no reason, just so.

Elena Andreyevna. You must not, you must not. . . . [*Crying.*] You queer creature, I too have started crying! [*After a pause.*] You are cross with me because you seem to think that I married your father from calculation. If you believe me, I swear that I married him for love. It was the scholar and famous man in him by whom I was infatuated. My love was not real love, it was artificial; but indeed it seemed to me that it was real. I am not to blame. And you, from the very day of our marriage, have punished me with your cunning, suspicious eyes. . . .

Sonya. Come, peace, peace! Let us forget. This is the second time to-day that I've heard that I have cunning, suspicious eyes.

Elena Andreyevna. One must not look at life so cunningly. It does not suit you at all. One must trust, otherwise life's impossible.

Sonya. 'A frighted crow fears the bush.' I have so often been disillusioned.

Elena Andreyevna. In whom? Your father is a good, honest man, a worker. To-day you reproved him for being happy. If he indeed was happy—absorbed in his work, he did not notice his happiness. I have done no deliberate wrong either to your father or to you. Uncle George is a very nice, honest, but unhappy, dissatisfied man. . . . [*After a pause.*] Whom, then, do you not trust?

Sonya. Tell me truly, as a friend. . . . Are you happy?

Elena Andreyevna. No.

Sonya. I knew it. One more question. Tell me frankly, would you like your husband to be young?

Elena Andreyevna. What a little girl you are! Certainly, I should! [*Laughing.*] Well, ask some more questions—do ask. . . .

Sonya. Do you like the Wood Demon?

Elena Andreyevna. Yes, very much.

Sonya. [*Laughing.*] I have a silly expression on my face . . .

have I? He's gone, and I still seem to hear his voice, his steps, and as I look at the dark window I seem to see his face there. . . . Let me tell you everything. . . . But I can't speak aloud, I'm ashamed. Come to my room, I'll tell you there. Do I seem silly to you? Tell me. . . . He's a nice man?

Elena Andreyevna. Very, very nice. . . .

Sonya. His forests, peat—they seem strange to me. . . . I can't make it all out.

Elena Andreyevna. But forests are not the point! My darling, you see, it is talent that matters! You know what talent is? Courage, a free spirit, soaring to the heights . . . he plants a little tree or digs up a hundredweight of peat—and already he visualizes what's to happen in a thousand years, he already dreams of the happiness of mankind. Such men as he are valuable, and should be loved. God bless you. You both are pure, courageous, honest. He's rather untamed, but you are sensible, clear-headed. . . . You will complete one another splendidly. . . . [*Getting up.*] And I, I am tiresome, I am an episodic character. . . . In my music, in my husband's house, and in all your love-makings—in everything I have only been an episodic character. Indeed, Sonya, if you come to think of it, I am, probably, very, very unhappy! [*Pacing the room in agitation.*] There's no happiness for me in this world! No! . . . Why do you laugh?

Sonya. [*Laughing and covering her face.*] I am so happy! So very happy!

Elena Andreyevna. [*Wringing her hands.*] Indeed, how unhappy I am!

Sonya. I am happy . . . happy.

Elena Andreyevna. I want music. . . . I should like to play now. . . .

Sonya. Do play. [*Embracing her.*] I can't sleep. . . . Do play.

Elena Andreyevna. I will. Your father hasn't gone to bed. When he's not well, music irritates him. Go and ask him. If he does not object, I'll play . . . go and ask him.

Sonya. I shall be back in a moment.

[*Goes out. The night watchman knocks in the garden.*

Elena Andreyevna. I haven't played for a long time. I shall play, and cry like a fool. . . . [*Going to the window.*] Is it you knocking there, Yefim?

The Watchman's Voice. Ye-s!

Elena Andreyevna. Stop knocking. The master is not well.

The Watchman's Voice. I'm going! [*Whistling.*] Nigger! Jack! [*After a pause.*] Nigger!

Sonya. [*Returning.*] No!

CURTAIN

ACT III

The drawing-room of the Serebryakovs' house. Three doors: one to the right, one to the left, and one in the middle. Time: afternoon. Behind the scene Elena Andreyevna is heard playing Lensky's aria, before the duel, from the opera 'Evgueny Oneyguin.'

SCENE I

Orlovsky, Voynitsky, and Fyodor Ivanovich (the latter dressed in Circassian attire with a papakha (a fur cap) in his hand)

Voynitsky. [*Listening to the music.*] It's Elena Andreyevna playing . . . my favourite aria. . . . [*The music coming to an end.*] Yes . . . it's a fine piece. . . . It seems never to have been so boring here as it is now. . . .

Fyodor. You've never tasted real boredom, my dear fellow. When I was a volunteer in Serbia, there I experienced the real thing! Hot, stuffy, dirty, head simply splitting after a drinking bout. . . . Once I remember sitting in a dirty little shed. . . . Captain Kashkinazi was there, too. . . . Every subject of conversation long exhausted, no place to go to, nothing to do, no desire to drink—just sickening, you see, sickening to the point of putting one's head in a noose! We sat, in a frenzy, gazing at one another. . . . He gazes at me, I at him; he at me, I at him. . . . We gaze and don't know why we're doing it. . . . An hour passes, you know, then another hour, and still we keep on gazing. Suddenly he jumps up for no reason, draws his sabre and goes for me. . . . Hey presto! . . . I, of course, instantly draw my sabre—for he'll kill me!—and it started: chic-chac, chic-chac, chic-chac, . . . with the greatest difficulty we were at last separated. I got off all right, but to this very day Captain Kashkinazi walks about with a scar on his face. See how desperately bored one may get! . . .

Orlovsky. Yes, such things do happen.

Enter Sonya.

SCENE II

The same and Sonya

Sonya. [*Aside.*] I don't know what to do with myself! . . .
[*Walking about and laughing.*

Orlovsky. Puss, darling, where are you going? Do sit with us a while.

Sonya. Fedya, come here. . . . [*Taking Fyodor aside.*] Come here. . . .

Fyodor. What do you want? Why such a radiant face?

Sonya. Give me your word that you will do what I ask you!

Fyodor. Well?

Sonya. Drive over to the . . . Wood Demon.

Fyodor. What for?

Sonya. Just so . . . just drive over to him . . . ask him why he has kept away so long . . . a fortnight now.

Fyodor. Blushing! Shame! Here, Sonya's in love!

All. Shame! Shame!

Sonya. [*Covers her face and runs away.*]

Fyodor. She's flitting about, like a shadow, from room to room, and doesn't know what to do with herself. She's in love with the Wood Demon.

Orlovsky. She's a glorious little girl. . . . I love her. I longed, Fyodor dear, that you should marry her, you won't easily find a better bride. But well, probably God wills it so. . . . And what a pleasure and delight mine would be! I should come over to you, you with your young wife, your family hearth, the samovar chirping away on the table. . . .

Fyodor. I'm unskilled in these matters. If the crazy notion of marriage ever came into my head, I should in any case marry Julie. She, at any rate, is little, and of all evils one should always choose the least. And then, too, she's a good house-keeper. . . . [*Clapping his forehead.*] That's an idea!

Orlovsky. What is it?

Fyodor. Let's have champagne!

Voynitsky. It's too early, and also it's hot . . . you wait awhile. . . .

Orlovsky. [*Admiringly*.] My sonny, my beauty! . . . He wants champagne, the dear soul! . . .

Enter Elena Andreyevna.

SCENE III

The same and Elena Andreyevna

Elena Andreyevna. [*Walks across the stage*.]

Voynitsky. Look at her: she walks and sways from sheer indolence! Fine! Very fine!

Elena Andreyevna. Stop it, George! It's boring enough without your buzzing.

Voynitsky. [*Barring her way*.] A talent, an artist! Well, do you look like an artist? Apathetic, indolent, sluggish. . . . So much virtue that, pardon me, it's even unpleasant to look at. . . .

Elena Andreyevna. Don't look then . . . let me go. . . .

Voynitsky. Why are you pining away? [*In a lively tone*.] My dear, my lovely one, be a good girl! There's mermaid's blood flowing in your veins, why not be a mermaid?

Elena Andreyevna. Let me alone!

Voynitsky. Let yourself go, if only once in your life, fall in love quickly up to your very eyes with a merman! . . .

Fyodor. And then flop headlong into the water with him and leave the Herr Professor and all of us waving our hands!

Voynitsky. Mermaid, eh? Love while you may!

Elena Andreyevna. And why do you go on teaching me? As if I don't know, without your telling me, how I should live if I had my will! Like a care-free bird I should fly away, from all of you, from your sleepy faces, from your boring, wearisome conversations. I should forget your very existence in the world, and no one would dare then teach me. But I haven't my own will. I'm cowardly, shy, and it seems to me all along that, if I were to be unfaithful, all wives would follow my example and leave their husbands; that God would punish me, and my conscience torment me; otherwise I would show you what a free life is like! [*Goes out.*

Orlovsky. Dear soul, the beauty! . . .

Voynitsky. I believe I shall soon begin to despise this woman! She's shy like a little girl, and philosophizes like an old deacon, adorned with virtues! Curdled milk!

Orlovsky. Stop, stop! . . . Where's the professor now?

Voynitsky. In his study. Writing away.

Orlovsky. He called me here by letter on some business. Do you happen to know what the business is?

Voynitsky. He can't have any business. He writes rubbish, grumbles and is jealous, that's all.

Zheltoukhin and Julie enter by the door on the right.

Scene IV

The same, Zheltoukhin and Julie

Zheltoukhin. How do you do, all?   [*Greeting them.*

Julie. How do you do, godpa dear? [*Kissing him.*] How do you do, Fedya? [*Kissing him.*] How do you do, George Petrovich? [*Kissing him.*

Zheltoukhin. Alexander Vladimirovich is at home?

Orlovsky. Yes. He's in his study.

Zheltoukhin. I must go to him. He wrote asking to see me on a matter of business. . . .   [*Goes out.*

Julie. George Petrovich, did you receive the barley yesterday, for which you asked in your note?

Voynitsky. Thanks, I did. How much is it? We also had something from you in the spring. I don't remember what . . . we must settle our accounts. I can't bear messing up things and postponing settlements.

Julie. In the spring you had eight quarters of corn, two heifers, a calf, and also butter for your farm hands.

Voynitsky. How much does it all come to?

Julie. How can I say? I can't say straight away without a counting-board, George Petrovich.

Voynitsky. I'll fetch you a counting-board, if you must have one. . . .   [*Goes out and returns with a counting-board.*

Orlovsky. Ducky, is your brother quite well?

Julie. Thank God he is. Godpa dear, where did you buy that nice tie?

Orlovsky. In town, at Kirpichov's.

Julie. How pretty! I'll buy one like it for Lennie.

Voynitsky. Here's the counting-board.

       [*Julie sits down and raps the beads on the counting-board.*

Orlovsky. What a splendid manager God has given Lennie! A wee thing, hardly visible, and see how she works away! See!

Fyodor. Yes, and he's only lounging about, smoothing his cheek. Idler!

Julie. Now, you have confused my reckoning.

Voynitsky. Come, let's go to some other room. Into the hall. It's so dull here. . . . [*Yawning.*

Orlovsky. Well, let's go into the hall. . . . I don't mind. . . .
[*They go out by the left door.*

Julie. [*Alone: after a pause.*] Fedya dressed as a Circassian! . . . That's what happens when parents fail to give the right direction. There's no handsomer man in the whole district, clever, rich, and yet no earthly good. . . . Hopeless! . . .
[*Raps on the counting-board.*

Enter Sonya.

SCENE V

Julie and Sonya

Sonya. You're here, Julie dear? I didn't know. . . .

Julie. [*Kissing her.*] My dear!

Sonya. What are you doing? Counting? What an admirable manager you are—the mere sight of you makes me envious! Julie dear, why don't you marry?

Julie. You see . . . One or two men have been suggested to me, but I have refused. A real suitor would not want to marry me! [*Sighing.*] No!

Sonya. But why?

Julie. I am an uneducated girl. I was taken from the high school in my second year.

Sonya. But why did they take you away, Julie dear?

Julie. For incapacity.
[*Sonya laughs.*

Julie. Why do you laugh, Sonya?

Sonya. There's something queer going on in my head. . . . Julie dear, I am so happy to-day, so happy, that I feel even bored by my happiness. . . . I don't know what to do with myself. . . . Now let's talk of something, come. . . . Have you ever been in love? [*Julie nods her head.*] Yes? Is he interesting? [*Julie whispers in her ear.*] Who? Fyodor?

Julie. [*Nodding her head.*] And you?

Sonya. I, too . . . only not with Fyodor. [*Laughing.*] Go on, tell me more. . . .

Julie. I have wanted to have a talk with you for a long time, Sonechka.

Sonya. Please do.

Julie. I want to make things clear. . . . You see . . . Truly I've always been well disposed towards you. . . . I have many girl friends, but you are the very best of them all. If you were to say to me, Julie, give me ten horses, or, say, two hundred sheep, I would do it with pleasure. . . . To you I should grudge nothing. . . .

Sonya. Why are you blushing, Julie?

Julie. I'm rather shy of . . . I . . . I am sincerely well disposed towards you. You are the very best of them all . . . not proud. . . . What a pretty print you are wearing!

Sonya. We'll talk of the print later. . . . Go on. . . .

Julie. [*Getting up.*] I don't know how it's done among clever people. . . . Allow me to propose to you. . . . Make me happy. . . . I mean . . . I mean . . . I mean . . . marry Lennie.   [*Covering her face.*

Sonya. [*Getting up.*] We'd better not talk about it, Julie dear. . . . No, we'd better not. . . .

Enter Elena Andreyevna.

Scene VI

The same and Elena Andreyevna

Elena Andreyevna. There's simply no place to sit in. The two Orlovskys and George are lounging about all over the house, and whatever room I go into, they're there. It's simply exasperating. What do they want here? Why don't they go somewhere else?

Julie. [*Through tears.*] How do you do, Elena Andreyevna?   [*About to kiss her.*

Elena Andreyevna. How do you do, Julie dear? Forgive me, I don't like continual kissing. Sonya, what's your father doing? [*A pause.*] Sonya, why don't you answer me? I ask you: what's your father doing? [*A pause.*] Sonya, why don't you answer me?

Sonya. You want to know? Come here. . . . [*Taking her aside.*] Well, I'll tell you. . . . My heart feels too pure to-day to allow me to talk to you and go on dissembling. Here, take this! [*Handing her a letter.*] I found it in the garden. Julie, come, let's go!   [*Goes out with Julie by the left door.*

Scene VII

Elena Andreyevna, and then Fyodor Ivanovich

Elena Andreyevna. [*Alone.*] What? A letter from George to me! But how am I to blame? Oh, how harsh and cruel of her! . . . Her heart feels so pure to-day that she can't talk to me. . . . My God, what an insult! My head is dizzy. . . . I shall drop! . . .

Fyodor. [*Coming out by the left door and crossing the stage.*] Why do you always start when you see me? [*A pause.*] H'm! . . . [*Taking the letter from her hands and tearing it to pieces.*] You must stop all this. You must think of me only.

[*A pause.*

Elena Andreyevna. What does that mean?

Fyodor. It means that if I once pick out someone, it 's no use her trying to escape from my hands.

Elena Andreyevna. No, it only means that you are an impudent fool.

Fyodor. This evening at half-past seven you will be by the little bridge behind the garden and wait for me. . . . Well? . . . I 've nothing more to say to you. . . . And so, my angel, until half-past seven! [*Tries to take her arm. She gives him a slap on the face.*] Forcibly expressed! . . .

Elena Andreyevna. Off you go!

Fyodor. At your service. . . . [*Walking away and returning.*] I am touched. . . . Let 's reason it out peacefully. . . . You see. . . . I 've experienced everything in this world; I have even tasted gold-fish soup once or twice. . . . But I' ve never yet gone up in a balloon, nor ever once carried off learned professors' wives. . . .

Elena Andreyevna. Go!

Fyodor. In a minute. . . . I 've experienced everything. . . . And because of that, there 's so much impudence in me that I simply don't know what to do with myself. I mean, I am saying all this to you with this object, that if you ever happen to need a friend or a faithful dog, just turn to me. . . . I am touched. . . .

Elena Andreyevna. I want no dogs. . . . Go!

Fyodor. At your service. [*With feeling.*] Nevertheless and in spite of all, I am touched. . . . Certainly, I am touched. . . . Yes. . . . [*Irresolutely goes out.*

Elena Andreyevna. [*Alone.*] My head aches. . . . Every night I dream bad dreams and have a presentiment of something terrible. . . . Yet how horrid! The young people were born here and grew up together, they 'thou' one another, always kiss one another; they ought to live in peace and harmony; but soon, I think, they will all have devoured one another. . . . The forests are being saved by the Wood Demon, but there's no one to save human beings.

[*She goes towards the left door, but on noticing Zheltoukhin and Julie coming in by that door, she goes out by the middle door.*

Scene VIII

Zheltoukhin and Julie

Julie. How unlucky we are, you, Lennie, and I, ah, how unlucky!

Zheltoukhin. But who authorized you to speak to her? You self-appointed match-maker, you minx! You've spoilt the whole business for me! She'll think that I can't speak for myself, and . . . how very common! I've told you a thousand times that the whole affair must be let alone. Nothing but humiliation and all these hints, vileness, meanness. . . . The old fellow must have guessed that I'm in love with her, and is already exploiting my feelings! He wants me to buy this estate from him.

Julie. And how much does he ask for it?

Zheltoukhin. Sh-h! . . . They're coming. . . .

Enter by the left door Serebryakov, Orlovsky, and Marie Vassilievna; the latter reading a pamphlet as she comes in.

Scene IX

The same, Serebryakov, Orlovsky, and Marie Vassilievna

Orlovsky. I too, old boy, am not quite fit. The last two days my head and my whole body have been aching. . . .

Serebryakov. Where are the others? I don't like this house. It is a labyrinth. Twenty-six huge rooms. They all disperse and you can never find any one. [*Ringing.*] Ask George Petrovich and Elena Andreyevna to come here.

Zheltoukhin. Julie, you have nothing to do: go and find George and Elena Andreyevna. [*Julie goes out.*

Serebryakov. One can reconcile oneself to one's ailments, however hard it may be, but what I can't stand is this present mood of mine. I have a feeling as though I were already dead, or had fallen off the earth on to a strange planet.

Orlovsky. It depends on how you look at it. . . .

Marie Vassilievna. [*Reading.*] Give me a pencil. . . . There's a contradiction again! I must mark it.

Orlovsky. Here you are, Your Excellency!

[*Handing her a pencil and kissing her hand.*

Enter Voynitsky

Scene X

The same, Voynitsky, and then Elena Andreyevna

Voynitsky. You wanted me?

Serebryakov. Yes, George.

Voynitsky. What is it you want?

Serebryakov. Now . . . why are you cross? [*A pause.*] If I am in the wrong, excuse me, please. . . .

Voynitsky. Drop that tone. . . . Let's come to business. . . . What is it you want?

Enter Elena Andreyevna

Serebryakov. Here's Lenochka, too. . . . Sit down, ladies and gentlemen. [*A pause.*] I have summoned you here, gentlemen, to announce that the inspector-general is about to arrive. . . . But no more joking. It is a serious matter. I have invited you here, gentlemen, in order to ask your help and advice, and knowing your unfailing kindness, I hope you will grant me them. I am a scholar, a bookish man, and I have always been a stranger to practical life. Dispense with the advice of well-informed people I cannot, and I beg you, Ivan Ivanych, and you, Leonid Stepanych, and you, George. . . . The point of the matter is *manet omnes una nox*, that is, we are all in God's hands. I am old, ill, and therefore I consider it opportune to settle my financial affairs in so far as they concern my family. My life is over, I am not thinking of myself; but I have a young wife, and a young daughter. To continue living in the country is impossible for them.

Elena Andreyevna. It's all the same to me.

Serebryakov. We are not made for the country. But to live in town on the income we receive from this estate is impossible. The day before yesterday I sold part of a wood for timber for four thousand roubles; but that is an extraordinary measure, of which one cannot avail oneself every year. Such measures have to be taken as will guarantee us a constant, more or less fixed amount of income. I 've thought out such a measure, and I have the honour to submit it for your consideration. Without entering into details, I will submit it in its general lines. Our estate yields us an average interest of two per cent. I propose to sell the estate. If we invest the money thus realized in interest-bearing securities, we shall get from four to five per cent. I think there might even be left a surplus of a few thousand roubles, which would allow us to buy a small bungalow in Finland. . . .

Voynitsky. Wait a moment, I fancy my hearing is playing me false. . . . Repeat what you 've just said. . . .

Serebryakov. To invest the money in interest-bearing securities and to buy a bungalow in Finland. . . .

Voynitsky. Not Finland. . . . You said something else. . . .

Serebryakov. I propose to sell the estate.

Voynitsky. Yes, that 's it. . . . You 'll sell the estate. . . . Admirable—a grand idea! . . . And what 's to happen to me and mother?

Serebryakov. We will consider all this in its turn. . . . Not everything at once. . . .

Voynitsky. Wait a moment. . . . Evidently, up till now I had not a grain of common sense. Up till now I was stupid enough to think that the estate belonged to Sonya. My late father bought this estate and settled it on my sister. Up till now I was naïve, I understood the law in no Turkish fashion, and I thought that the estate devolved from my sister to Sonya.

Serebryakov. Yes, the estate belongs to Sonya. Who disputes it? Without Sonya's consent I shan't undertake to sell it. Besides, I 'm doing it for Sonya's benefit.

Voynitsky. Inconceivable! Inconceivable! Either I 've gone out of my mind, or . . . or . . .

Marie Vassilievna. George, don't contradict the professor! He knows better than we do what 's right and what's wrong.

Voynitsky. Give me some water. . . . [*Drinking.*] Go on with it! Go on!

Serebryakov. I can't understand why you are so agitated, George! I don't say that my plan is ideal. If all of you find it unsound, I shan't insist.

Enter Dyadin, wearing a frock-coat, white gloves, and a broad-brimmed top-hat.

Scene XI

The same and Dyadin

Dyadin. I have the honour to salute you. I apologize for venturing to enter without being announced. I am guilty, but I claim your indulgence, as there was not a single domestic in the hall.

Serebryakov. [*Perplexed.*] Glad to see you. . . . Come in. . . .

Dyadin. [*Bowing ceremoniously.*] Your Excellency! Mesdames! My intrusion on your domains has a double object. I 've come, firstly, to pay a visit and to testify to my reverential respect; secondly, to invite you all to take advantage of this beautiful weather to make an expedition to my province. I dwell at the water mill, which I rent from our common friend the Wood Demon. It is a cosy, poetical corner of the earth, where in the night you can hear naiads splashing, and in the daytime. . . .

Voynitsky. Wait a while, Waffle, we are talking business. . . . Wait awhile! . . . [*To Serebryakov.*] Now ask him. . . . The estate was bought from his uncle.

Serebryakov. Oh, why should I ask him? What for?

Voynitsky. The estate was then bought for ninety-five thousand roubles. My father paid down only seventy thousand, with a debt on the estate of twenty-five thousand. Now listen. . . . The estate could not have been bought had I not renounced my share of the inheritance in favour of my sister, whom I loved. Moreover, I worked for ten years like an ox, and cleared off the whole debt.

Serebryakov. What do you want then, my dear man?

Voynitsky. The estate is clear of debt and is in good order, thanks only to my personal exertions. And now, when I 'm getting old, you want to bundle me out neck and crop!

Serebryakov. I can't understand what you 're driving at!

Voynitsky. For twenty-five years I have managed this estate. I have worked, and have sent you money regularly, like a most conscientious bailiff, and all those years you have never once even thanked me! All those years, when I was young, and even now, I have received from you an annual wage of five hundred roubles—a beggarly wage!—and it has never once occurred to you to increase it even by one rouble!

Screbryakov. George, how could I know? I 'm not a practical man and understand nothing of such matters. You could have increased it as much as you liked!

Voynitsky. Why didn't I steal, is that it? Why don't you all despise me because I didn't steal? That would be just, and now I should not be a pauper.

Marie Vassilievna. [*Sternly.*] George!

Dyadin. [*In agitation.*] George dear, don't . . . don't. . . . I am trembling. . . . Why spoil friendly relations? [*Embracing him.*] Please don't! . . .

Voynitsky. For twenty-five years, like a mole, I have sat with her, with mother here, within these four walls. . . . All our thoughts and feelings have belonged to you alone. By day we spoke of you, of your works, we were proud of your fame, uttered your name with reverence; and the evenings we wasted reading reviews and books, which I now profoundly despise!

Dyadin. Don't, Georgie dear, don't! . . . Please! . . .

Serebryakov. I don't understand what you want!

Voynitsky. You were to us a being of a higher order, and your articles we knew by heart. . . . But now my eyes are opened. I see everything! You write on art, but understand nothing about art! All your works, which I loved, aren't worth a brass farthing!

Serebryakov. Gentlemen! Why don't you restrain him? I shall leave the room!

Elena Andreyevna. George, I demand that you keep silent! Do you hear?

Voynitsky. I shall not keep silent! [*Barring Serebryakov's way.*] Wait, I've not finished yet! You have ruined my life! I have not lived! I have not lived! Thanks to you, I wasted, ruined the best years of my life! You're my worst enemy!

Dyadin. I can't bear it! . . . I can't! . . . I'll go into another room! . . .

[*Goes out in violent agitation by the door on the right.*

Serebryakov. What do you want from me? And what right have you to talk to me in this tone? You nonentity! If the estate is yours, take it. I don't want it!

Zheltoukhin. [*Aside.*] Now the fat's in the fire! . . . I'll go!

[*Goes out.*

Elena Andreyevna. If you say any more, I shall leave this hell this very minute! [*Crying out.*] I can't bear it any longer!

Voynitsky. A life wasted! I have talent, I'm intelligent, courageous. . . . If I had lived normally I might have been a Schopenhauer, a Dostoevsky. . . . My mind's wandering! I am going mad! . . . Mother, I am in despair! Mother!

Marie Vassilievna. Obey the professor!

Voynitsky. Mother! What shall I do? Oh, don't say a word! I know myself what I must do! [*To Serebryakov.*] You shall remember me!

    [*Goes out by the middle door; Marie Vassilievna follows after him.*

Serebryakov. Gentlemen! What does all this signify? Rid me of that lunatic!

Orlovsky. He'll be all right, all right, Alexander; let him calm down. Don't upset yourself so much.

Serebryakov. I won't live under the same roof with him! He lives here. [*Pointing to the middle door.*] Almost beside me. . . . Let him go and live in the village, or in one of the wings; otherwise I shall go away from here. Remain with him I will not. . . .

Elena Andreyevna. [*To her husband.*] If anything like this happens again, I shall leave the house!

Serebryakov. Oh, don't frighten me, please!

Elena Andreyevna. I'm not frightening you, but all of you seem to have agreed to turn my life into a hell. . . . I'll leave the house! . . .

Serebryakov. Every one knows quite well that you are young, and I am old, and that you're conferring a great favour by living here. . . .

Elena Andreyevna. Go on! . . . Go on! . . .

Orlovsky. Why, why, why! . . . My dear friends! . . .

    Enter Khrouschov hurriedly.

Scene XII

The same and Khrouschov.

Khrouschov. [*In agitation.*] I'm very glad to find you in, Alexander Vladimirovich. . . . Excuse me for coming unseasonably and for being in your way. . . . But this isn't the point. How do you do?

Serebryakov. What is it you want?

Khrouschov. Excuse me, I'm agitated . . . it's because I rode so quickly. . . . Alexander Vladimirovich, I hear that you have just sold your wood to Kouznezov for timber. If it is true, not mere gossip, then I beg you, don't do it.

Elena Andreyevna. Mikhail Lvovich, my husband isn't in the mood now to talk business. Won't you come with me into the garden?

Khrouschov. But I must speak at once!

Elena Andreyevna. As you please. . . . I can do no more. . . .

[*Goes out.*

Khrouschov. Permit me to drive over to Kouznezov and tell him that you 've changed your mind. . . . Yes? Will you allow me? To fell a thousand trees, to destroy them for the sake of two or three thousand roubles, for women's rags, whims, luxury. . . . To destroy them so that posterity should curse our savagery! If you, a scholar, a famous man, dare perpetrate such a cruelty, what may not others do who stand so much below you! How very terrible!

Orlovsky. Misha, talk about it later!

Serebryakov. Come, let 's go, Ivan Ivanych; this will never end.

Khrouschov. [*Barring Serebryakov's way.*] In that case, look here, professor. . . . In three months' time I shall have the money and buy it myself.

Orlovsky. Excuse me, Misha, this is rather strange. . . . Why, you, let us say, are a man of ideas . . . we thank you most humbly for it, we bow to the ground before you. [*Bowing.*] But why such a rumpus?

Khrouschov. [*Flaring up.*] You universal godfather! There are too many good-natured men on earth, and this always seemed suspicious to me! They 're good-natured because they 're indifferent!

Orlovsky. Why, you 've come here to quarrel, my boy. It is not right! An idea is an idea, but, look here, old chap, this thing too is needed. [*Pointing to his heart.*] Without this thing, my dear fellow, all your forests and peat-beds are not worth a brass farthing. . . . Don't take offence, but you 're still green—ugh! how very green!

Serebryakov. [*Sharply.*] Next time, please don't trouble to come in unannounced, and please spare me your psychopathic pranks! You were all bent on trying my patience, and you 've succeeded. . . . Please leave me alone! All these forests of yours, peat-beds of yours, I consider sheer raving and psychopathy—there, you have my opinion! Come, Ivan Ivanych! [*Goes out.*

Orlovsky. [*Following after him.*] Alexander my boy, that 's too much! . . . Why be so harsh? [*Goes out.*

Khrouschov. [*Alone, after a pause.*] Raving, psychopathy! . . . According to the famous scholar and professor I am mad. . . . I bow to the authority of Your Excellency and

I'm going home immediately to shave my head. . . . No!
It is the earth, which still endures you, that is mad!

[*Goes hurriedly towards the right door; Sonya, who has stood
listening outside all through the last scene, comes in by
the left door.*

Scene XIII

Khrouschov and Sonya

Sonya. [*Running after him.*] Stop! . . . I heard everything.
. . . Speak! . . . Speak quickly . . . or I shan't bear it
any longer and shall start speaking myself!

Khrouschov. Sophie Alexandrovna, I have already said all I
wanted to say. I implored your father to spare the wood. I
was right, but he insulted me, and called me a madman.
. . . I, mad!

Sonya. Please, please! . . .

Khrouschov. No, mad are not those who beneath their learning
hide their cruel, stony heart, and pass off their soullessness for
profound wisdom! Mad are not those who marry old men in
order to deceive them openly, in order to obtain fashionable,
elegant dresses with the money got from the felling of forests!

Sonya. Listen to me, listen! . . . [*Grasping his hands.*] Let me
say . . .

Khrouschov. Let us finish it. Let there be an end. I am a
stranger to you, I know already your opinion of me, and
I've nothing more to do here. Good-bye. I am sorry that
after our brief friendship, which was so dear to me, I shall
only retain the memory of your father's gout and of your
arguments about my democratic sentiments. . . . But it is
not I who am to blame for it. . . . No. . . .

[*Weeping and covering her face, Sonya hurries out by the
left door.*

Khrouschov. I had the imprudence to fall in love here, it shall
be a lesson to me! Out of this dungeon!

[*Goes to the right door; Elena Andreyevna comes in by the
left door.*

Scene XIV

Khrouschov and Elena Andreyevna

Elena Andreyevna. You are here! One moment. . . . Ivan
Ivanych has just told me that my husband was harsh with

you. . . . You must forgive him, he's cross to-day and did not understand you. . . . As for myself, my soul is with you, Mikhail Lvovich! Believe in the sincerity of my respect, I sympathize with you, I am moved; and allow me with a pure heart to offer you my friendship!   [*Holding out both hands.*

Khrouschov. [*With aversion.*] Get away from me! . . . I despise your friendship!   [*Goes out.*

Elena Andreyevna. [*Alone, groaning.*] Why, why?

[*A shot is heard behind the scenes.*

Scene XV

Elena Andreyevna, Marie Vassilievna, and then Sonya, Serebryakov, Orlovsky, and Zheltoukhin

Marie Vassilievna comes out by the middle door, staggers, cries out and falls unconscious to the ground. Sonya comes in and runs to the middle door.

Serebryakov, Orlovsky, and Zheltoukhin. What's the matter?

[*Sonya is heard crying out; she returns and cries:* 'Uncle George has shot himself!' *She, Orlovsky, Serebryakov, and Zheltoukhin run out through the middle door.*

Elena Andreyevna. [*Groaning.*] Why, why?

Dyadin appears at the door on the right.

Scene XVI

Elena Andreyevna, Marie Vassilievna, and Dyadin

Dyadin. [*In the doorway.*] What's the matter?

Elena Andreyevna. [*To him.*] Take me away from here! Throw me into a deep pit, kill me, but I can't remain here any longer! Quick, I implore you!

[*Goes out with Dyadin.*

CURTAIN

ACT IV

The forest and the house by the mill which Dyadin rents from Khrouschov.

Scene I

Elena Andreyevna and Dyadin sitting on a bench under the window

Elena Andreyevna. Ilya Ilyich dear, to-morrow you 'll drive over again to the post office.

Dyadin. Most certainly.

Elena Andreyevna. I shall wait another three days. If I get no answer to my letter from my brother, I 'll borrow some money from you and go to Moscow. I can't stay for ever at your mill.

Dyadin. Just so! . . . [*A pause.*] I dare not give you advice, my deeply respected lady, but all your letters, telegrams, and my daily journeys to the post office—all these, pardon me, are labour lost. Whatever answer your brother may send you, all the same you will go back to your husband.

Elena Andreyevna. I shan't go back. . . . One must be logical, Ilya Ilyich. I do not love my husband. The young people, of whom I was fond, were unjust to me all along. Why should I go back there? You will say—duty. . . . I too know this perfectly well, but, I say again, one must be logical.

[*A pause.*

Dyadin. Yes! . . . The greatest Russian poet, Lomonosov, ran away from the Archangel province to seek his fortune in Moscow. This was certainly noble of him. . . . But why did *you* run away? Your happiness, if we fairly consider the matter, is nowhere to be found. . . . It was appointed that the canary should sit in its cage and look on at the happiness of others; well, it must sit there all its life long.

Elena Andreyevna. Perhaps I 'm not a canary, but a free sparrow!

Dyadin. O-oh! A bird is judged by its flight, my deeply respected lady. . . . During these last two weeks any other lady would have managed to be in ten towns, and would have thrown dust in everybody's eyes; but you have only ventured to run as far as the mill, and even this has worn your soul out. . . . No, no! You 'll stay here a short time longer, your heart will be softened, and you 'll return to your husband. [*Listening.*] Someone 's coming in a carriage.   [*Getting up.*]

Elena Andreyevna. I 'll go in.

Dyadin. I dare not trouble you any more with my presence. . . . I 'll go to the mill to have a little nap. . . . I rose this morning before Aurora.

Elena Andreyevna. After you 've had your nap, come and we 'll have tea together.   [*Goes into the house.*

Dyadin. [*Alone.*] If I lived in an intellectual centre, they could draw a caricature of me for a magazine, with a very funny satirical inscription. Gracious! I, at my time of life and with an unattractive appearance, to have carried off a famous professor's young wife! That is fascinating! [*Goes away.*

Scene II

Semyon carrying buckets and Julie coming in

Julie. Good day, Semyon! God assist you! Is Ilya Ilyich at home?

Semyon. Yes. He 's gone to the mill.

Julie. Will you go and call him.

Semyon. Yes.   [*Goes away.*

Julie. [*Alone.*] He must be asleep! . . . [*Sitting down on the bench under the window and sighing deeply.*] Some sleep, others lounge about, and I all day long am running about, running about. . . . God won't end my life. [*With a still deeper sigh.*] Good God, that there can be such foolish people as that Waffle! As I drove by his barn a black pig came out of the door. . . . It 'll serve him right if the pigs tear the sacks which aren't his. . . .

Enter Dyadin.

Scene III

Julie and Dyadin

Dyadin. [*Putting on his coat.*] It is you, Yulia Stepanovna! Excuse my *déshabillé*. . . . I wanted to rest awhile in the embraces of Morpheus.

Julie. How do you do?

Dyadin. Excuse me for not asking you in. . . . The rooms aren't tidied, etc. Perhaps you will come with me to the mill? . . .

Julie. I shall be all right here. This is what I 've come for,

Ilya Ilyich. Lennie and the professor, to amuse themselves, wish to have a picnic here at the mill, to have tea. . . .

Dyadin. I 'm delighted!

Julie. I came in advance. . . . They 'll be here presently. Please order a table to be brought out here, and of course the samovar. . . . Tell Semyon to get the provision baskets out of the carriage.

Dyadin. Certainly. [A pause.] Well? How are you all getting on?

Julie. Badly, Ilya Ilyich. . . . Believe me, all this worry has made me ill. You know, the professor and Sonechka are living with us now!

Dyadin. Yes, I know.

Julie. After George laid hands on himself, they could not stay in the house. . . . They 're afraid. In the daytime they don't mind it so much, but when night falls, they all gather in one room and sit there until dawn. They are afraid of George's appearing in the darkness. . . .

Dyadin. Superstitions! . . . And do they mention Elena Andreyevna?

Julie. Of course they do. [A pause.] Vanished!

Dyadin. Yes, it 's a subject worthy of Aivasovsky's brush. . . . Just gone and vanished!

Julie. And now nobody knows where she is. . . . Perhaps she has run away, or perhaps, in despair . . .

Dyadin. God is merciful, Yulia Stepanovna! All will be well.

Enter Khrouschov with a portfolio and drawing-case.

Scene IV

The same and Khrouschov

Khrouschov. Hi! Is there anybody here? Semyon!

Dyadin. Have a look round.

Khrouschov. Oh! . . . How do you do, Julie?

Julie. How do you do, Mikhail Lvovich?

Khrouschov. I 've come again to you, Ilya Ilyich, to work here. I can't sit at home. Tell them to place my table under this tree, as they did yesterday, and to have two lamps ready. It 'll soon be dark. . . .

Dyadin. At your service, your worship. [Goes out.

Khrouschov. How are you getting on, Julie?

Julie. So-so. . . . [A pause.

Khrouschov. The Serebryakovs are staying with you?

Julie. Yes.

Khrouschov. H'm! . . . And what's your Lennie doing?

Julie. He sits at home. . . . All the time with Sonechka. . . .

Khrouschov. Of course! [*A pause.*] Why doesn't he marry her?

Julie. Well? [*Sighs.*] God bless him! He's well educated, a
nobleman; she, too, is of a good family. . . . I have always
wished it for her. . . .

Khrouschov. She's a fool! . . .

Julie. Now, you mustn't say that.

Khrouschov. And your Lennie is a bright one, too. All your
people are a picked lot! A palace of wisdom!

Julie. Probably you've had no lunch to-day.

Khrouschov. What makes you think so?

Julie. You're so very cross.

Enter Dyadin and Semyon carrying a table.

Scene V

The same, Dyadin and Semyon

Dyadin. You've an eye, Misha, for the right place. You've
chosen an exquisite spot to work in. It's an oasis! A pure
oasis! Imagine that you are surrounded with palm trees,
Julie here—a gentle hind, you—a lion, I—a tiger! . . .

Khrouschov. You're a good fellow, a gentle soul, Ilya Ilyich,
but your manners! Treacly words, shuffling feet, hunched
shoulders! . . . If a stranger were to see you, he'd think that
you weren't a man, but the devil knows what! . . . It is
annoying! . . .

Dyadin. I think this must be my destiny. . . . Fatal predestination.

Khrouschov. At it again . . . fatal predestination! Stop it all.
[*Fixing a chart on the table.*] I'm going to stay the night with
you here.

Dyadin. I'm extremely glad. . . . Now, Misha, you are cross,
while in my soul there's inexpressible joy! As though a bird
were sitting in my heart and singing a song.

Khrouschov. Rejoice then. [*A pause.*] There's a bird in your
heart, but there's a frog in mine. Twenty thousand scandals!
Shimansky has sold his forest for timber. That's one! Elena
Andreyevna has run away from her husband, and nobody
knows now where she is. That's two! I feel that every day
I'm getting more foolish, petty, and stupid. . . . That's
three! I meant to tell you yesterday, but I lacked the

courage. You may congratulate me. George left a diary. That diary got first into Orlovsky's hands; I went over and read it a dozen times....

Julie. Our people have also read it.

Khrouschov. George's affair with Elena Andreyevna, with which the whole district rang, turns out to be an abominable, dirty slander. . . . I believed that slander and slandered along with the rest; I hated, despised, insulted. . . .

Dyadin. That's certainly wrong.

Khrouschov. The first person whose word I took was your brother, Julie dear. Yes, I too am a fine fellow! I believed your brother, whom I don't respect; and disbelieved the woman, who before my very eyes was sacrificing herself. I more readily believe evil than good, and see no further than my nose. And this means that I am as stupid as the rest.

Dyadin. [*To Julie*] Come, let's go to the mill, my dear. Let the cross baby work here, and we will go for a walk. . . . Work away, Misha, old chap! [*Goes out with Julie.*

Khrouschov. [*Alone; mixing the colours in a saucer.*] One night I saw him leaning his face against her hand. In his diary, that night is described in full; he tells how I came there, what I said to him. He quotes my words and calls me a fool and narrow-minded. [*A pause.*] . . . It's too thick! . . . It should be thinner. . . . And then he blames Sonya for having fallen in love with me. . . . She never loved me. . . . Now, there's a blot. . . . [*Scraping the paper with a knife.*] If even I admit that there's some truth in it, yet I must not think of it. . . . It began foolishly, and ended foolishly. . . . [*Semyon and the labourers bring in a large table.*] What's this? What's it for?

Semyon. Ilya Ilyich told us to bring it in. Company is coming from the Zheltoukhin estate to have tea here.

Khrouschov. All right. No work for me now. . . . I'll pack up my things and go home.

Enter Zheltoukhin with Sonya on his arm.

Scene VI

Khrouschov, Zheltoukhin and Sonya

Zheltoukhin. [*Singing.*] 'Unwillingly to these shores am I drawn by an unknown power.'

Khrouschov. Who's there? Eh?

[*Hastily packing his case of instruments.*

Zheltoukhin. One more question, dear Sophie. . . . Do you remember that day you lunched at our house, my birthday?
Do own that you laughed then at my appearance.

Sonya. Leonid Stepanych, how can you say such a thing? I
laughed for no reason.

Zheltoukhin. [*Noticing Khrouschov.*] Oh, you too are here! How
do you do?

Khrouschov. How do you do?

Zheltoukhin. You're working away! Splendid! . . . Where's
Waffle?

Khrouschov. There. . . .

Zheltoukhin. Where's there?

Khrouschov. I think I speak quite clearly. . . . There, at the
mill.

Zheltoukhin. I'd better ask him to come here. [*Walking away
and singing.*] 'Unwillingly to these shores . . .' [*Goes out.*

Sonya. How do you do? . . .

Khrouschov. How do you do?

Sonya. What are you drawing?

Khrouschov. Oh! . . . nothing interesting.

Sonya. Is it a plan?

Khrouschov. No, it's a map showing the forests of our district.
[*After a pause.*] I've mapped them out. The green colour
indicates the places where there were forests during the time
of our grandfathers and before them; the bright green, where
forests have been cut down during the last twenty-five years;
and the blue, where there are forests still left intact. . . . Yes.
. . . [*A pause.*] Well, and how are you? Are you happy?

Sonya. This is not the time, Mikhail Lvovich, to think of
happiness.

Khrouschov. What else is there to think of?

Sonya. Our sorrow came only because we thought too much of
happiness. . . .

Khrouschov. [*After a pause.*] So!

Sonya. There's no evil without some good in it. Sorrow has
taught me this, that one must forget one's own happiness and
think only of the happiness of others. One's whole life should
consist of sacrifices. . . .

Khrouschov. [*After a pause.*] Yes. . . . Marie Vassilievna's son
shot himself, and she goes on searching for contradictions in
her little books. A great misfortune befell yourself, and
you're pampering your self-love: you are trying to distort
your life and you think this a sacrifice. . . . No one has a

heart. . . . Neither you nor I. . . . Quite the wrong things are being done, and everything goes to waste. . . . I'll go away presently and won't be in your way and Zheltoukhin's. . . . Why are you crying? I did not at all mean to make you cry.

Sonya. Never mind, never mind. . . . [*Wiping away her tears.*

Enter Julie, Dyadin, and Zheltoukhin.

Scene VII

The same, Julie, Dyadin, Zheltoukhin, and then Serebryakov and Orlovsky

Serebryakov's Voice. Hallo! Where are you all?

Sonya. [*Crying out.*] We're here, papa!

Dyadin. They're bringing the samovar! That is fascinating!
[*He and Julie arrange things on the table.*

Enter Serebryakov and Orlovsky.

Sonya. Here, papa!

Serebryakov. I see, I see! . . .

Zheltoukhin. [*Aloud.*] Gentlemen, I declare the sitting open! Waffle, uncork the liqueur.

Khrouschov. [*To Serebryakov.*] Professor, let us forget what has occurred between us! [*Holding out his hands.*] I beg you to forgive me. . . .

Serebryakov. I thank you. I am very glad. You too must forgive me. When the next day after that incident I tried to think over all that had taken place and recalled our conversation, I felt very upset. . . . Let us be friends.
[*Taking his arm and going to the table.*

Orlovsky. You should have done this long ago, dear soul. A bad peace is better than a good quarrel.

Dyadin. Your Excellency, I am delighted that it pleased you to honour my oasis. Inexpressibly delighted!

Serebryakov. Thank you, my dear sir. Indeed, it is a fine place. A real oasis!

Orlovsky. And do you, Alexander, love nature?

Serebryakov. Very much. [*A pause.*] Gentlemen, let us not keep silent, let us talk. In our position that is the best thing to do. One must look misfortune straight and boldly in the face. I am more cheerful than any of you, and for this reason, that I am the most unhappy.

Julie. I shan't add any sugar; have your tea with jam.

Dyadin. [*Bustling about among the company.*] How glad, how very glad I am!

Serebryakov. Latterly, Mikhail Lvovich, I have gone through such a great deal and thought over things so much that I believe I could write a treatise, for the edification of posterity, on how to live. Live an age and learn an age, but it is misfortunes that teach us.

Dyadin. He who remembers the evil past, should lose an eye. God is merciful; all will end well.   [*Sonya starts.*

Zheltoukhin. What made you start?

Sonya. I heard a cry.

Dyadin. It's the peasants on the river catching crayfish. [*Pause.*

Zheltoukhin. Didn't we agree to spend the evening as if nothing had happened? . . . And yet . . . there's some kind of tension. . . .

Dyadin. Your Excellency, I cherish towards science feelings not only of reverence, but even of blood relationship. My brother's wife's brother—you may perhaps have heard his name, Konstantin Gavrilych Novossyolov—was a master of foreign literature.

Serebryakov. I didn't know him personally, but I know the name.   [*A pause.*

Julie. To-morrow it will be exactly fifteen days since George died.

Khrouschov. Julie dear, don't let us talk about it.

Serebryakov. Courage! Courage!   [*A pause.*

Zheltoukhin. There is still some kind of tension. . . .

Serebryakov. Nature abhors a vacuum. She has deprived me of two intimate relations and, in order to fill up the gap, she has soon given me new friends. I drink your health, Leonid Stepanovich!

Zheltoukhin. I thank you, dear Alexander Vladimirovich! Allow me in my turn to drink to your fruitful scientific activity.

'Sow the seeds of wisdom, of goodness, of eternity!
'Sow the seeds! The Russian folk will give you their hearty gratitude!'

Serebryakov. I value the compliment you pay me. I wish from my heart that the time may soon come when our friendly relations shall have grown into more intimate ones.

Enter Fyodor.

Scene VIII

The same and Fyodor

Fyodor. That's where you are! A picnic!

Orlovsky. My sonny . . . my beauty!

Fyodor. How do you do? [*Embracing Sonya and Julie.*

Orlovsky. I've not seen you for a fortnight. Where have you been? What have you seen?

Fyodor. I just drove over to Lennie's; there I was told that you were here; and I came here.

Orlovsky. Where have you been wandering?

Fyodor. Three nights without sleep. . . . Yesterday, dad, I lost five thousand at cards. I drank, played cards, went to town five times. . . . Fairly crazy!

Orlovsky. That's a brave fellow. You must be a little drunk still!

Fyodor. Not a bit. Julie, tea, please! Only with lemon, as sour as you like. . . . And George, eh! Without rhyme or reason to put a bullet in his head! And with a French revolver, too! As if he couldn't have got an honest English one!

Khrouschov. Hold your tongue, you beast!

Fyodor. Beast, but a pedigree one! [*Stroking his beard.*] The beard alone, what isn't it worth! . . . Here I am, a beast, and a fool, and a knave, yet I have only to will—and the finest girl would marry me. Sonya, marry me! [*To Khrouschov.*] Oh, I'm so sorry. . . . Pardon! . . .

Khrouschov. Stop playing the fool.

Julie. You're a lost soul, Fedenka! In the whole district there is no such drunkard and spendthrift as you. The mere sight of you is heartbreaking. You are a caution!

Fyodor. Now you've started whining! Come here, sit beside me. . . . That's right. I'll come and stay with you for a fortnight. . . . I must have a rest. [*Kissing her.*

Julie. You ought to be ashamed of yourself. You should be a comfort to your father in his old age, but you only disgrace him. Yours is a stupid life and nothing else.

Fyodor. I am giving up drink! *Basta!* [*Pouring out some liqueur.*

Julie. Don't drink then, don't drink!

Fyodor. One glass I may. [*Drinking.*] Wood Demon, I make you a present of a pair of horses and a gun. I'm going to stay at Julie's. . . . I'll stay there about a fortnight.

Khrouschov. It would do you more good to be sent to a disci-
plinary battalion.

Julie. Drink, drink some tea!

Dyadin. Have some rusks, old chap.

Orlovsky. [*To Serebryakov.*] Up to the age of forty, Alexander
old boy, I led the same life as my Fyodor here. One day, my
dear soul, I began counting how many women I had made
unhappy in my life. I counted, counted, arrived at seventy,
and gave it up. Well, as soon as I reached the age of forty,
suddenly, Alexander old boy, something came over me. Sick
at heart I could find no peace; in a word, my soul was at odds
with itself, and there I was. I tried all sorts of things—I read
books, worked, travelled—all of no avail. Once, my dear
soul, I went to pay a visit to my late friend, the Most Serene
Dmitri Pavlovich. We sat down to lunch. After lunch, so
as to keep awake, we started shooting at a target in the courtyard. There were numbers and numbers of people present.
And our Waffle was there, too.

Dyadin. I was there, yes . . . I remember. . . .

Orlovsky. Lord, my anguish then! . . . I could endure it no
longer. Suddenly tears gushed from my eyes, I staggered,
and suddenly cried out at the top of my voice across the whole
yard with all my power: 'My friends, my good people, forgive
me, for the love of Christ!' And that very moment I felt my
heart to have become pure, gentle, warm; and since that time,
my dear soul, there is no happier man than I in the whole
district. You too ought to do the same.

Serebryakov. What?

> [*A glow appears in the sky.*

Orlovsky. Do just as I did. Capitulate. Surrender.

Serebyakov. That's an example of our native philosophy. You
advise me to ask forgiveness. For what? Let others ask
forgiveness of me!

Sonya. Papa, but it is *we* who are to blame!

Serebryakov. Yes? Gentlemen, evidently at the present moment you all have in view my attitude towards my wife. Am
I, in your opinion, am I to blame? It is ridiculous even.
She has violated her duty, she left me at a difficult moment
in life. . . .

Khrouschov. Alexander Vladimirovich, please listen to me. . . .
For twenty-five years you have been a professor and served
science; I plant forests and practise medicine—but for what
purpose and for whom is it all, if we do not spare those for

whom we are working? We say that we are serving humanity, and at the same time we are inhumanly destroying one another. For instance, did you or I do anything to save George? Where's your wife, whom every one of us insulted? Where's your peace, where's your daughter's peace? All is ruined, destroyed, all is going to waste. All of you call me Wood Demon, but not in me alone, in all of you sits a demon, all of you wander in a dark forest and grope your way. Of understanding, knowledge and heart we have just enough to spoil our own and other people's lives. . . .

Elena Andreyevna comes out of the house and sits down on the bench under the window.

Scene IX

The same and Elena Andreyevna

Khrouschov. I considered myself a man of ideas, a humane man, and at the same time I did not forgive people their slightest mistakes. I believed slanders, I gossiped along with others; and when, for instance, your wife trustfully offered me her friendship, I fired off at her from the height of my loftiness: 'Get away from me! I despise your friendship!' That's what I am like. There sits a demon in me, I am petty, without talent, blind; but you too, professor, are no eagle! And yet the whole district, all the women see in me a hero, an advanced man, and you are famous all over Russia. And if such as I are seriously taken as heroes, and if such as you are seriously famous, it means only that for lack of better men Jack is a nobleman, that there are no real heroes, no talents, no men who might lead us out of this dark forest, who might repair what we are spoiling; that there are no real eagles who might by right enjoy honourable fame. . . .

Serebryakov. Sorry! . . . I came here not in order to carry on a polemic with you and to defend my title to fame. . . .

Zheltoukhin. Now, Misha, let's stop this talk.

Khrouschov. I'll finish presently and leave you. Yes, I am petty, but, professor, you too are no eagle. George was petty, who could not devise anything cleverer than to put a bullet in his head. All are petty! And as to the women . . .

Elena Andreyevna. [*Interrupting.*] As to the women, neither are they any bigger. [*Advancing towards the table.*] Elena Andrey-evna left her husband, and do you think she will turn her freedom to any good use? Don't worry. . . . She will come

back. . . . [*Sitting down at the table.*] She has already come
back. . . .   [*General consternation.*

Dyadin. [*Laughing aloud.*] That is fascinating! Suspend sen-
tence, gentlemen, and let me say a word. Your Excellency,
it is I who carried off your wife, as once upon a time a certain
Paris carried off the fair Helen. I! Although there are no
pock-marked Parises, yet there are more things in heaven and
earth, Horatio, than are dreamt of in your philosophy!

Khrouschov. I can't make it out. . . . It is you, Elena
Andreyevna?

Elena Andreyevna. The last fortnight I've stayed here with
Ilya Ilyich. . . . Why do you all look at me so? Well, how
do you do? . . . I sat by the window and heard everything.
[*Embracing Sonya.*] Let's be friends! How are you, my dear
girl? . . . Peace and goodwill!

Dyadin. [*Rubbing his hands.*] That is fascinating!

Elena Andreyevna. [*To Khrouschov.*] Mikhail Lvovich! [*Holding
out her hand.*] He who remembers the evil past, should lose an
eye. How do you do, Fyodor Ivanych? . . . Julie dear! . . .

Orlovsky. Darling, our glorious Mme Professor, our beauty . . .
she has come back, she has returned again to us! . . .

Elena Andreyevna. I missed you all so much. How do you do,
Alexander? [*Holds out her hand to her husband; the latter
turns his face away.*] Alexander!

Serebryakov. You have violated your duty.

Elena Andreyevna. Alexander!

Serebryakov. I shan't deny I am very glad to see you and am
ready to talk to you, but not here, at home. . . .
                         [*Moving away from the table.*

Orlovsky. Alexander!   [*A pause.*

Elena Andreyevna. So! . . . It means, Alexander, our problem
is solved quite plainly: in no way at all. Well, so it must be!
I am an episodic character, mine is a canary's happiness, a
woman's happiness. . . . To stick all my life long at home, to
eat, to drink, to sleep, and every day to hear you talk of your
gout, of your rights, of your merits. . . . Why have you all
dropped your heads, as if ashamed? Let's drink the liqueur
—let us. Come!

Dyadin. Everything will turn out well, and get better; everything will be right and safe.

Fyodor. [*Coming up to Serebryakov, in agitation.*] Alexander
Vladimirovich, I am touched. . . . I pray you, be kind to her,
show your wife some tenderness, say one kind word to her,

and on the word of an honourable man, all my life long I will be your true friend, I'll make you a present of my best troika.

Serebryakov. Thank you, but excuse me, I don't understand you. . . .

Fyodor. H'm! . . . you don't understand! . . . Once I was coming back from the hunt and saw a tawny owl sitting on a tree. . . . I bang a pellet at him! He sits. . . . I bang at him a number nine . . . he sits. . . . Nothing moves him. He sits and only blinks his eyes.

Serebryakov. What does this refer to?

Fyodor. To the tawny owl.   [*Returning to the table.*

Orlovsky. [*Listening.*] I say, friends . . . quiet . . . I think the church bells are ringing a fire alarm somewhere.

Fyodor. [*Noticing the glow.*] O-o-oh! Look at the sky! What a glow!

Orlovsky. Dear souls, and we're sitting here and missing it all!

Dyadin. Grand!

Fyodor. O-oh! What an illumination! It must be near Alexeyevsk.

Khrouschov. No, Alexeyevsk is more to the right. . . . It must be Novo-Petrovsk.

Julie. How terrible! I'm afraid of a fire.

Khrouschov. It's Novo-Petrovsk for certain.

Dyadin. [*Shouting.*] Semyon, run to the dyke and have a look where the fire is. You might see it from there.

Semyon. [*Shouting.*] It is the Telibeyev forest burning.

Dyadin. What?

Semyon. The Telibeyev forest.

Dyadin. Forest! . . . [*A long pause.*]

Khrouschov. I must go there . . . to the fire. . . . Good-bye! . . . Forgive me, I was harsh, it is because I never felt so depressed as to-day. My soul is in anguish. . . . But all this is no matter. . . . One must be a man and stand firmly on one's feet. I shall not shoot myself, nor throw myself under the wheels of the mill. . . . I may not be a hero, but I will become one! I will grow the wings of an eagle, and neither this glow nor the devil himself shall frighten me! Let forests burn—I will plant new ones! Let me not be loved by one, I will love another!   [*Rushes off.*

Elena Andreyevna. What a splendid man!

Orlovsky. Yes. . . . 'Let me not be loved by one, I will love another.' How is this to be understood?

Sonya. Take me away from here . . . I want to go home. . . .

Serebryakov. Yes, it's time to go. It's dreadfully damp here. My rug and overcoat are somewhere about. . . .

Zheltoukhin. The rug is in the carriage, and here's the overcoat.
[Handing it to him.

Sonya. [*In violent agitation.*] Take me away from here. . . . Take me away. . . .

Zheltoukhin. At your service. . . .

Sonya. No, I will go with godpa. Take me with you, godpa! . . .

Orlovsky. Certainly, my dear soul, come with me.
[Handing her her things.

Zheltoukhin [*Aside.*] Curse it! . . . Nothing but humiliation and meanness!

[*Fyodor and Julie pack the tea things and serviettes into the basket.*]

Serebyakov. The heel of my left foot is aching. . . . It must be rheumatism. . . . Again I shan't sleep all night.

Elena Andreyevna. [*Buttoning up her husband's coat.*] Ilya Ilyich dear, please fetch my hat and cloak from the house.

Dyadin. I will.
[*Goes into the house and comes back with her hat and cloak.*

Orlovsky. You are frightened at the glow, my dear! Don't be afraid, it's growing smaller. The fire is being put out. . . .

Julie. There's half a jar of medlar jam left. . . . Well, let Ilya Ilyich have it. . . . [*To her brother.*] Lennie dear, take the basket.

Elena Andreyevna. I'm ready! . . . [*To her husband.*] Well, take me, you statue of the commander, and go to blazes with me in your twenty-six dismal rooms! That's all I'm good for!

Serebryakov. Statue of the commander! . . . I should laugh at this simile, but the pain in my foot prevents me! . . . [*To the whole company.*] Good-bye, friends! I thank you for the entertainment and for your pleasant company. . . . A superb evening, splendid tea—everything perfect; but, excuse me, there's one thing I can't approve of here—your native philosophy and views on life. One must work, gentlemen! Your way is impossible! One must do things. . . . Yes, one must work. . . . Good-bye! [*Walks off with his wife.*

Fyodor. Come, Julie! [*To his father.*] Good-bye, pater!
[*Walks off with Julie.*

Zheltoukhin. [*With the basket, following them.*] A heavy basket, damn it . . . I can't stand these picnics. . . . [*Shouting behind the scene to his coachman.*] Alexey, drive up!

Scene X

Orlovsky, Sonya, and Dyadin

Orlovsky. [*To Sonya.*] Well, why are you sitting down? Come, my ducky! . . .   [*Goes out with Sonya.*

Dyadin. [*Aside.*] No one said good-bye to me! . . . That is fascinating!   [*Puts out the candles.*

Orlovsky. [*To Sonya.*] What's the matter?

Sonya. I can't go away, dear godpa. . . . I can't! I'm in despair, godpa. . . . I'm in despair! It's so unbearably difficult!

Orlovsky. [*Alarmed.*] What's wrong? My ducky, my beauty! . . .

Sonya. Let's remain here. . . . Let's stay here a little while.

Orlovsky. One moment it's 'take me away,' the other moment 'let's stay'! . . . I can't make you out. . . .

Sonya. Here to-day I have lost my happiness. . . . It's unbearable! . . . Oh, godpa dear, why am I still alive? [*Embracing him.*] Oh, if you knew, if you knew!

Orlovsky. I'll give you some water. . . . Let's sit down. . . . Come!

Dyadin. What's wrong? Sophie Alexandrovna dear . . . you mustn't, I am all of a tremble! . . . [*Tearfully.*] I can't bear to see it! . . . My dear child! . . .

Sonya. Ilya Ilyich, drive me over to the fire! I implore you!

Orlovsky. What do you want with the fire? What will you do there?

Sonya. I implore you, drive me over to the fire, or I'll walk there. I'm in despair. . . . Godpa, it's hard, unbearably hard! Drive me over to the fire.

Enter Khrouschov hurriedly.

Scene XI

The same and Khrouschov

Khrouschov. [*Shouting.*] Ilya Ilyich!

Dyadin. Here! What is it you want?

Khrouschov. I can't walk, let me have your horse.

Sonya. [*Recognizing Khrouschov, and crying out joyfully.*] Mikhail Lvovich! [*To Orlovsky.*] Go away, godpa dear, I have something to say to him. [*To Khrouschov.*] Mikhail Lvovich, you said that you would love another. . . . [*To Orlovsky.*]

Go away, godpa! . . . [*To Khrouschov.*] I am another now
. . . I only want the truth. . . . Nothing, nothing but the
truth! I love you, I love you, I love . . .

Orlovsky. Now I see!   [*Laughing.*

Dyadin. That is fascinating!

Sonya. [*To Orlovsky.*] Go away, godpa dear! [*To Khrouschov.*]
Yes, yes, only the truth and nothing else! . . . Speak then,
speak! . . . I 've said everything. . . .

Khrouschov. [*Embracing her.*] My darling!

Sonya. Don't go, godpa dear! . . . When you told me of your
love, I panted for joy, but I was fettered by prejudices. I
was prevented from giving you a true answer just as father
is prevented from smiling on Elena. Now I am free! . . .

Orlovsky. [*Laughing aloud.*] Singing in tune at last! Scrambled
out on to the bank! I have the honour to congratulate you.
[*Bowing low.*] Ah, you naughty, naughty children!

Dyadin. [*Embracing Khrouschov.*] Misha, my dear boy, how
glad you make me! Misha, dear boy!

Orlovsky. [*Embracing and kissing Sonya.*] My darling, my little
canary! . . . My dear little goddaughter! [*Sonya laughs
aloud.*] Now you 've started!

Khrouschov. I can hardly grasp it all! . . . Let me have a word
with her. Don't get in our way. . . . Pray, go away! . . .

Enter Fyodor and Julie.

SCENE XII

The same, Fyodor, and Julie

Julie. But it 's all a fib, Fyodor dear! You 're fibbing!

Orlovsky. Sh-h! Quiet, boys! My rascal is coming here. Let
us hide ourselves, quick! Do!

[*Orlovsky, Dyadin, Khrouschov, and Sonya hide themselves.*

Fyodor. I left my whip and gloves here.

Julie. But it 's all a fib!

Fyodor. Well, let it be a fib! . . . What of it? I don't want
to go to your house yet. . . . Let 's walk for a while, and
then we will go. . . .

Julie. You are a nuisance! [*Clapping her hands.*] Now, isn't
that Waffle a silly! The table is not yet cleared! Someone
might have stolen the samovar. . . . Oh, Waffle, Waffle—an
old man, and yet he has less sense than a baby!

Dyadin. [*Aside.*] Thanks!

Julie. As we came up I heard someone laughing. . . .

Fyodor. It's the peasant women bathing! . . . [*Picking up a glove.*] Here's someone's glove. . . . Sonya's. . . . To-day Sonya behaved as though she were bitten by a fly. She's in love with the Wood Demon. She's in love with him up to her eyes, and he, the blockhead, does not see it!

Julie. [*Angrily.*] Where are we going then?

Fyodor. To the dyke. . . . Let's go for a walk. . . . There's no finer spot in the whole district. . . . Beautiful!

Orlovsky. [*Aside.*] My sonny, my beauty, his fine beard! . . .

Julie. I just heard a voice.

Fyodor. [*Reciting.*] 'Here are wonders, the Wood Demon loiters, the mermaid sits on the branches.' . . . Yes, old chap!
[*Clapping her on the shoulder.*

Julie. I'm not a chap.

Fyodor. Let us reason it out peacefully. Listen, Julie dear! I've gone through fire and water. . . . I am already thirty-five, and have no status except that of lieutenant in the Serbian army and non-com. in the Russian reserve. I'm dangling between the sky and the earth. . . . I must change my mode of life, and you see . . . do you understand, I've now a fancy in my head that if I were to marry, a huge change will happen in my life! . . . Do marry me, do! I ask for no one better. . . .

Julie. [*Confused.*] H'm! . . . You see . . . you first reform, Fyodor dear.

Fyodor. Well, don't bargain like a gipsy! Speak straight out!

Julie. I'm shy! . . . [*Looking round.*] Stop, someone might come in or overhear us! . . . I believe Waffle is looking through the window.

Fyodor. There's no one.

Julie. [*Falling on his neck.*] Fedenka!
[*Sonya laughs aloud; Orlovsky, Dyadin, and Khrouschov laugh, clap their hands and shout:* 'Bravo! Bravo!']

Fyodor. Ugh! How you frightened us! Where did you come from?

Sonya. Julie dear, I congratulate you! And you may congratulate me! . . .
[*Laughter, kisses, noise.*

Dyadin. That is fascinating! That is fascinating!

CURTAIN

TATYANA RIEPIN

A DRAMA IN ONE ACT

In the preface to Anton Tchekhov's unpublished play, *Tatyana Riepin*, Michael Tchekhov says:

'Anton Tchekhov's one-act play was written by him in 1889, and dedicated to Souvorin, who instructed his printing house to have only *two* copies of the play printed. One of them Souvorin sent to Tchekhov, the other he kept for himself. For thirty-four years the play lay among Anton's papers, zealously guarded by our sister Marie. Souvorin's copy seems to have been lost; yet should it ever be found, it cannot contain the explanatory notes, which are here made by one who knew Anton Tchekhov intimately and who also knows the origin of the play.

'That is why our sister Marie has given me permission to publish our brother's play, in the hope that the reader will regard it as a mere pastime; for neither Anton Tchekhov nor Souvorin regarded it in any other light.'

After giving a detailed account of Tchekhov's career as a playwright, Michael Tchekhov describes the mutual help and advice which Anton Tchekhov and Souvorin gave one another at the time when Tchekhov had his *Ivanov*, and Souvorin his *Tatyana Riepin*, produced. And he goes on to say:

'The plot in Souvorin's play *Tatyana Riepin* is not at all complicated. I should rather say that there is no plot in it.

'In the middle of the eighties of the last century there lived a well known provincial actress called Mlle Kadmin. I do not know her life-story very well, but this fact is known about her, that, having been betrayed by her lover, she decided to poison herself. She was to act in the historic play *Vassilissa Melentievna*, in which play the wife of Ivan the Terrible is poisoned. Before the poisoning scene, Mlle Kadmin swallowed some poison. If I remember right, this happened at a theatre in Kharkov. When the poisoning scene in the play began to be enacted, the poison taken by Mlle Kadmin began to work on her system. She died on the stage, in terrible agonies, but in the knowledge that among the audience in the theatre was her faithless lover. That was her revenge. Not suspecting the truth, the spectators were overwhelmed by Mlle Kadmin's acting, until at last the performers on the stage as well as the audience realized what had actually happened. The unusual death of Mlle Kadmin was discussed everywhere at that time; people talked of her as of a real heroine, and those who knew her well spoke of her as of an unusual woman. Although Anton did not know Mlle Kadmin personally, yet I have heard from various people that he was interested in her. She seemed to him a real woman and, judging by her photograph which we had in our house, she must have been beautiful. In one of his letters to Souvorin, Anton writes: "I am sick of the golden mean, I am idling, and I am grumbling that there are no more original, wild women. . . . In a word, 'he, the tumultuous, is looking for a storm. . . .' And every one keeps on saying to me with one voice: 'Now, old fellow, you would have liked Mlle Kadmin!' And gradually I am studying her; and, as I listen to what is being said about her, I realize that she was indeed an extraordinary character."

'It was that very same Mlle Kadmin whom Souvorin presented as the heroine in his play *Tatyana Riepin*. In his play, the provincial actress Tatyana Riepin is madly in love with Sobinin, a beau and 'lady-killer.' But Sobinin becomes infatuated with Mme Olenin, a local belle, and he proposes marriage to her. Tatyana Riepin cannot survive such unfaithfulness, she takes poison and dies in terrible agony. That is the whole plot of Souvorin's play. I remember the famous actress M. P. Yermolov acting the part of Tatyana Riepin in Moscow, and depicting her agonies through poisoning. The whole audience was so agitated and the ladies went into such hysterics that, through their crying, the performers could hardly be heard. Among the *dramatis personae* of Souvorin's play are Kotelnikov and Patronikov, two local landowners; Sonnenstein, a financier; Adashev, a journalist; Mme Kokoshkin, a great lady, a patroness of the theatre and admirer of talent; and several other episodic characters, who, as always in the provinces, gather around the newly arrived theatrical celebrity. But none of these characters has any direct influence on the action or plot of Souvorin's piece. There is no need to go into fuller details. I only want to draw the attention of the reader to the fact that the play ends with Tatyana Riepin's death. As to the further development of events, that is, whether Sobinin eventually marries the local belle, or not; and if he does marry her, what his state of mind is when he learns of the death of the woman he has deserted—all this is left unexplained in Souvorin's play, nor are any hints dropped. . . .

'Very soon after the production of Souvorin's *Tatyana Riepin* in Moscow, it so happened that Anton needed a French dictionary. Souvorin had bookshops in Petersburg, in Moscow, and in the provinces, where Anton used to buy books on credit or on deferred payment. But now after his labours with the production of Souvorin's play in Moscow, he asked for a dictionary as a present, promising Souvorin to let him have a present in exchange. And Anton's present took the form of a manuscript continuation of Souvorin's *Tatyana Riepin*.

'Anton was a great connoisseur of church literature. He knew the Bible perfectly, he knew it from his early childhood; he was also very fond both of the directness and of the florid unusual words of the hymns, many of which he knew by heart. He also had a small library of church ritual and service books, part of which is still to be found in Anton's house in Yalta. And thinking what present he could make to Souvorin, he took down from his shelf a missal, opened it at the marriage service, and "for his own amusement," without intending it for the critics or for the public, he wrote a one-act play in continuation of Souvorin's *Tatyana Riepin*. . . .

'In Anton's *Tatyana Riepin* the action takes place in church. At that time the idea was quite unusual, and of course perfectly inadmissible from the point of view of the censor. Sobinin marries Mme Olenin and the marriage takes place in the church. All the *dramatis personae* of Souvorin's play are present in Anton's play, but only as guests, having nothing to do with the action. The whole interest of Anton's play centres in the marriage ceremony, for which purpose he introduces the following new characters:

Father Ivan, the archpriest of the cathedral, a man of seventy.

Father Nicolay ⎱ young priests.
Father Alexey ⎰

A Deacon.
An Acolyte.
A Verger.
A Lady in Black.
The Crown Prosecutor.
Actors and Actresses.
Two Choirs—the cathedral choir and the archbishop's.

'The marriage ritual is fully adhered to in the play, with the reading of the New Testament and all the other particulars.

'Anton entitled his one-act play *Tatyana Riepin,* and sent the MS., for fun, to Souvorin, accompanying it with the following letter:

'"I am sending you, my dear Alexey Sergueyevich, the very cheap and useless present which I promised you. If I am to have a tedious time over your dictionary, then you can have a tedious time over my present. I wrote it in one sitting, and therefore it turned out cheaper than cheap. For making use of your title you can bring an action against me. Don't show it to *anybody,* and when you have read it throw it into the fire. You can throw it there without reading it. I allow you anything. After reading it you may even exclaim 'Damn!'"

'But Souvorin did not throw the manuscript away. A month passed and no word from him came to Anton. It was rather puzzling. Then Anton had a letter from Souvorin to say that he had ordered two copies of Anton's *Tatyana Riepin* to be printed, one for the author and the other for himself, and that he had already sent him the proofs. At last the printed copy arrived. Anton was delighted; the paper and get-up was fine. "Thank you," Anton wrote to Souvorin on 14th May 1889, "I received my *Tatyana.* The paper is very good. I struck out my name in the proof and can't understand why it is still there. I also struck out, that is, corrected, many misprints, which also remain. It is all nonsense, though. To make the illusion greater, Leipzig, not Petersburg, should have been printed on the cover."'

CHARACTERS

MME VERA OLENIN, the bride.
PETER SOBININ, the bridegroom.
KOTELNIKOV ⎫
VOLGUIN, a young officer ⎰ the bridegroom's best men.
THE STUDENT ⎫
THE CROWN PROSECUTOR ⎰ the bride's best men.
MATVEYEV, actor.
MME KOKOSHKIN.
M. KOKOSHKIN
SONNENSTEIN.
A Young Lady.
A Lady in Black.
Actors and Actresses.
FATHER IVAN, the archpriest of the cathedral, a man of seventy.
FATHER NICOLAY ⎫
FATHER ALEXEY ⎰ young priests.
A Deacon.
An Acolyte.
KOUZMA, the verger.

Time : a little after six o'clock in the evening. The cathedral church. All the lamps and lights are burning. The holy gates in front of the altar are open. Two choirs—that of the archbishop and that of the cathedral—are engaged. The church is packed with people. It is close and stifling. A marriage ceremony is taking place. Sobinin is being married to Mme Olenin. Sobinin's best men are Kotelnikov and Volguin ; Mme Olenin's are her brother, a student, and the Crown Prosecutor. The whole local intelligentsia are present. Smart dresses. The officiating clergy are : Father Ivan, in a faded surplice ; Father Nicolay, young and shaggy ; Father Alexey, in dark coloured glasses ; behind them, to the right of Father Ivan, stands the tall, thin Deacon, with a book in his hands. Among the crowd is the local theatrical company headed by Matveyev.

Father Ivan. [*Reading.*] Remember, O God, also their parents who have brought them up: for the blessings of parents establish the foundations of houses. Remember, O Lord, thy servants the paranymphs, who have come together here to this joy. Remember, O Lord, our God, Thy servant Peter and Thy handmaid Vera, and bless them. Grant unto them fruit of the womb, good offspring, and concord in soul and body; exalt them as the cedars of Lebanon, as a fruitful vine. Vouchsafe to them abundance, that having all sufficiency they may excel in every good work and in everything well-pleasing unto Thee; that they may see their sons' sons, as young olive plants round about their table; and that having been well-pleasing in Thy sight, they may shine as the stars in heaven, in Thee our Lord. To Thee be all glory, might, honour, and worship, now and for ever, world without end.

The Archbishop's Choir. [*Singing.*] Amen!

Patronikov. It is stuffy. What's the order you wear round your neck, Monsieur Sonnenstein?

Sonnenstein. Belgian. Why are there so many people here? Who has let them in? Ugh! Russian vapour baths.

Patronikov. It's the scoundrelly police.

The Deacon. Let us supplicate the Lord!

The Cathedral Choir. [*Singing.*] Lord have mercy!

Father Nicolay. [*Reading.*] O holy God, who didst form a man out of earth and of his rib didst raise up woman and join her to him as a helpmeet, for so it pleased Thy Majesty that man should not be alone upon the earth, do Thou Thyself now, O Lord, send forth Thy hand from Thy holy dwelling place and join together Thy servant Peter to Thy handmaid Vera, for by Thee woman is joined unto man. Conjoin them in the same mind, unite them in one flesh, grant them the fruit of the womb, and the joy of good children. For Thine is the might, and Thine is the kingdom, and the power, and the glory, Father, Son, and Holy Ghost, now and for ever, world without end.

The Cathedral Choir. [*Singing.*] Amen!

The Young Lady. [*To Sonnenstein.*] The crowns will presently be put on the heads of the bride and of the bridegroom. Look, look!

Father Ivan. [*Taking the crown from the altar and turning his face to Sobinin.*] The servant of God, Peter, is betrothed to the handmaid of God, Vera, in the name of the Father, and of the Son, and of the Holy Ghost. Amen.

　　　　　　　　[*He hands the crown over to Kotelnikov.*]

In the Crowd. The best man is just as tall as the bridegroom. He's not interesting. Who is he?

It is Kotelnikov. The other best man, the officer, is also quite uninteresting.

Gentlemen, let the lady pass, please!

I am afraid, madam, you won't be able to get through!

Father Ivan. [*Turns to Mme Olenin.*] The handmaid of God, Vera, is betrothed to the servant of God, Peter, in the name of the Father, and of the Son, and of the Holy Ghost. Amen.

[*He hands the crown to the Student.*

Kotelnikov. The crowns are heavy. My hand feels numb.

Volguin. It's all right; I'll take my turn presently. Who smells here of patchouli, I should like to know!

The Crown Prosecutor. It is Kotelnikov.

Kotelnikov. You lie.

Volguin. Sh-h-h!

Father Ivan. O Lord our God, with glory and honour crown them! O Lord our God, with glory and honour crown them! O Lord our God, with glory and honour crown them!

Mme Kokoshkin. [*To her husband.*] How very lovely Vera looks now! I do admire her. And she isn't at all nervous.

M. Kokoshkin. She's used to it. She's going through it for the second time!

Mme Kokoshkin. Yes, just so. [*Sighing.*] From all my heart I wish her joy! . . . She has a kind heart.

The Acolyte. [*Coming into the middle of the church.*] Thou didst set upon their heads crowns of precious stones. Life they asked of Thee, and Thou gavest it to them.

The Archbishop's Choir. [*Singing.*] Thou didst set upon their heads . . .

Patronikov. I wish I could smoke now.

The Acolyte. The words of Paul the Apostle.

The Deacon. Let us hear the words.

The Acoloyte. [*In a drawling octave.*] Brethren, giving thanks always for all things unto God and the Father in the name of our Lord Jesus Christ; submitting yourselves one to another in the fear of God. Wives, submit yourselves unto your husbands, as unto the Lord. For the husband is the head of the wife, even as Christ is the head of the Church: and He is the saviour of the body. Therefore as the Church is subject unto Christ, so let the wives be to their husbands in everything. . . .

Sobinin. [*To Kotelnikov.*] You are crushing my head with the crown.

Kotelnikov. No, I 'm not.   I 'm holding the crown seven inches above your head.

Sobinin. I tell you, you 're crushing my head.

The Acolyte. Husbands, love your wives, even as Christ also loved the Church, and gave Himself for it; that He might sanctify and cleanse it with the washing of water by the Word, that He might present it to Himself a glorious Church, not having spot or wrinkle, or any such thing; but that it should be holy and without blemish . . .

Volguin. He has a fine bass . . . [*To Kotelnikov.*] Do you want me to take my turn now?

Kotelnikov. I 'm not tired yet.

The Acolyte. So ought men to love their wives as their own bodies.   He that loveth his wife loveth himself.   For no man ever hated his own flesh; but nourisheth and cherisheth it, even as the Lord the Church: for we are members of His body, of His flesh and of His bones.   For this cause shall a man leave his father and mother . . .

Sobinin. [*To Kotelnikov.*] Keep the crown higher.   You crush me.

Kotelnikov. What nonsense!

The Acolyte. And shall be joined unto his wife, and they two shall be one flesh.

M. Kokoshkin. The governor-general is here.

Mme Kokoshkin. Where do you see him?

M. Kokoshkin. There, standing near the right aisle with M. Altoukhov.   Incognito.

Mme Kokoshkin. I see, I see him now.   He 's speaking to little Marie Hansen.   He 's crazy about her.

The Acolyte. This is a great mystery: but I speak concerning Christ and the Church.   Nevertheless, let every one of you in particular so love his wife even as himself; and let the wife fear her husband.

The Cathedral Choir. [*Singing.*] Alleluia, Alleluia, Alleluia. . . .

In the Crowd. Do you hear, Natalie Sergueyevna?   The wife is to fear her husband.

Let me alone.   [*Laughter.*

Sh-h-h! be quiet there!

The Acolyte. Let us hear the Holy Gospel.

Father Ivan. Peace be to all!

The Cathedral Choir. [*Singing.*] And to thy spirit.

In the Crowd. They are reading the Gospel, the New Testament. . . . How very long it all is!   It 's time they finished.

I can't breathe. I must go away.

You won't get through. Wait a bit, it 'll soon be over.

Father Ivan. The lesson from the Holy Gospel of John.

The Acolyte. Let us hear the lesson.

Father Ivan. [*After taking off his surplice.*] At that time there was a marriage in Cana of Galilee; and the mother of Jesus was there; and both Jesus was called, and His disciples, to the marriage. And when they wanted wine, the mother of Jesus saith unto Him: They have no wine. Jesus saith unto her: Woman, what have I to do with thee? Mine hour is not yet come. . . .

Sobinin. [*To Kotelnikov.*] Is it going to end soon?

Kotelnikov. I don't know. I 'm not an expert in these matters. But it 'll probably soon be over.

Volguin. You still have to go in a circle round the altar.

Father Ivan. His mother saith unto the servants: Whatsoever He saith unto you, do it. And there were set there six water-pots of stone, after the manner of the purifying of the Jews, containing two or three firkins apiece. Jesus saith unto them: Fill the waterpots with water. And they filled them to the brim. And He saith unto them: Draw out now, and bear unto the governor of the feast. . . .   [*A groan is heard.*

Volguin. Qu'est-ce que c'est? Is someone being crushed?

In the Crowd. Sh-h-h! Quiet!   [*A groan.*

Father Ivan. And they bare it. When the ruler of the feast had tasted the water that was made wine, and knew not whence it was (but the servants which drew the water knew), the governor of the feast called the bridegroom, and saith unto him . . .

Sobinin. [*To Kotelnikov.*] Who was groaning just now?

Kotelnikov. [*Gazing at the crowd.*] There 's something stirring there. . . . A lady in black. . . . She has probably been taken ill. . . . They are leading her out. . . .

Sobinin. [*Gazing at the crowd.*] Hold the crown a bit higher. . . .

Father Ivan. Every man at the beginning doth set forth good wine; and when men have well drunk, then that which is worse: but thou hast kept the good wine until now. This beginning of miracles did Jesus in Cana of Galilee, and manifested forth His glory; and His disciples believed on Him. . . .

In the Crowd. I can't understand why they let hysterical women in here!

The Archbishop's Choir. [*Singing.*] Glory be to Thee, O Lord, glory be to Thee!

Patronikov. Don't buzz like a bumble-bee, Monsieur Sonnen-stein, and don't stand with your back to the altar. It is not done.

Sonnenstein. It's the young lady who's buzzing like a bee, it's not me. . . . ha ha ha!

The Acolyte. Let us all say with our whole soul, and with our whole mind let us say . . .

The Cathedral Choir. [*Singing.*] Lord, have mercy.

   [*The Deacon reads the long liturgical prayer, in the course of which the following conversation takes place.*[1]

In the Crowd. Sh-h-h! Quiet!
   But I too am being pushed!

The Choir. [*Singing.*] Lord, have mercy!

In the Crowd. Sh-h-h! Sh-h-h!
   Who's fainting? [*A groan. A movement in the crowd.*

Mme Kokoshkin. [*To the lady standing next to her*]. What's the matter? You see, my dear, it's just intolerable. If only they would open the door. . . . I'm dying from the heat.

In the Crowd. She's being led out, but she resists. . . . Who is she? —sh-h!

Sobinin. Oh, my God. . . .

In the Crowd. Yesterday, at the Hotel Europe, a woman poisoned herself.
   Yes, they say she was the wife of a doctor.
   Why did she do it, do you know?

Volguin. I hear someone crying. . . . The public is not behaving well.

Matveyev. The choristers are singing well to-day.

The Comic Actor. You and I ought to engage these choirs, Zakhar Ilyich!

Matveyev. What cheek, you muzzle-face! [*Laughter.*] Sh-h!

In the Crowd. Yes, they say she was a doctor's wife. . . . At the hotel. . . . With the fine example set by Mlle Riepin, this is now the fourth woman who has poisoned herself. Explain it to me, my dear fellow, what do these poisonings mean?
   It's an epidemic. Nothing else.
   You mean, a kind of imitativeness?
   Suicide is contagious!
   What a lot of psychopathic women there are now!
   Quiet! Stop walking about!
   Don't shout, please! [*A groan.*

[1] In the original the prayer is given in full; but it is left out in the copy published by Michael Tchekhov.

Mlle Riepin has poisoned the air with her death. All the
ladies have taken the contagion and gone mad about their
wrongs.

Even in the church the air is poisoned. Do you feel the
tension here?

[Here the Deacon ends the prayer.

The Archbishop's Choir. [*Singing.*] Lord, have mercy!

Father Ivan. For Thou art a merciful God, and the lover of men,
and to Thee we ascribe the glory, to the Father, and to the
Son, and to the Holy Ghost, now and for ever, world without
end.

The Choir. [*Singing.*] Amen!

Sobinin. I say, Kotelnikov!

Kotelnikov. Well?

Sobinin. Now . . . oh, great God! . . . Tatyana Riepin is
here. . . . She is here. . . .

Kotelnikov. You're off your head!

Sobinin. The lady in black . . . it's she. I recognized her.
. . . I saw her. . . .

Kotelnikov. There's no resemblance. . . . Except that she too
is a brunette, but nothing else.

The Deacon. Let us supplicate the Lord!

Kotelnikov. Don't whisper to me, it's not done. People are
watching you . . . .

Sobinin. For the love of God. . . . I can hardly stand on my
legs. It is she.   [*A groan.*

The Choir. [*Singing.*] Lord, have mercy!

In the Crowd. Quiet! Sh-h! Who's pushing there from
behind? Sh-h!

They've led her away behind the pillar. . . .

You can't get rid of the ladies anywhere. . . . Why don't
they stay at home?

One of the Public. [*Shouting.*] You keep quiet!

Father Ivan. [*Reading.*] O Lord our God, who in Thy saving
dispensation didst vouchsafe at Cana of Galilee . . . [*He
looks round.*] What a crowd! [*Continues reading.*] . . . by
Thy presence to declare matrimony honourable . . . [*Raising
his voice.*] I pray you, people keep quiet there! You are
hindering us from performing the ceremony. Don't walk
about the church, don't talk, don't make a noise, but stand
still and pray. Just so! You should have the fear of God
in you. [*Reading on.*] O Lord our God, who in Thy saving
dispensation didst vouchsafe at Cana of Galilee by Thy

presence to declare matrimony honourable, do Thou Thyself now also preserve in peace and concord Thy servants Peter and Vera, whom it hath pleased Thee to join one to the other. Make their marriage honourable; keep their bed undefiled; grant that their conversation may remain immaculate, and vouchsafe unto them to reach a good old age, with pure hearts, fulfilling Thy commandments. For Thou our God art a God of mercy and salvation, and to Thee we ascribe the glory with Thy Father unbegotten, and Spirit all holy, good and life-giving, now and for ever, world without end.

The Archbishop's Choir. [*Singing.*] Amen!

Sobinin. [*To Kotelnikov.*] Send someone for the police and tell them not to let any one in. . . .

Kotelnikov. Whom could they let in? The church as it is is packed full. Keep silent . . . don't whisper.

Sobinin. She . . . Tatyana is here.

Kotelnikov. You're raving. She's in the cemetery.

The Deacon. Assist, save, have mercy on us and preserve us, O God, by Thy grace!

The Cathedral Choir. [*Singing.*] Lord, have mercy!

The Deacon. The whole day perfect, holy, peaceful and sinless, let us ask the Lord.

The Cathedral Choir. [*Singing.*] Grant, O Lord!

[*The Deacon continues reading the short prayer, during which the following conversation takes place.*[1]

In the Crowd. That deacon will never finish with his 'Lord, have mercy,' and 'Lord, save us.'

I'm sick of standing.

There's a noise again. What a crowd!

Mme Olenin. Peter, you are trembling all over . . . you breathe with difficulty. . . . Aren't you well?

Sobinin. The lady in black . . . it's she. . . . It's our own fault.

Mme Olenin. What lady?

Sobinin. Tatyana is groaning. . . . I'm steadying myself, I'm trying to steady myself. . . . Kotelnikov is crushing my head with the crown. . . . I am all right. . . .

M. Kokoshkin. Vera is pale as death. Look, there are tears in her eyes. And he . . . look at him!

Mme Kokoshkin. I told her that the public would not behave well! I can't understand why she decided to be married

[1] The short prayer, given in the original copy, is left out by Michael Tchekhov.

here. Why didn't she go to the country? We ought to ask Father Ivan to get on quickly. She 's scared.

Voligun. Permit me to take my turn.

[*He takes the crown from Kotelnikov. The Deacon finishes his short prayer here.*]

The Choir. [*Singing.*] To Thee, O Lord!

Sobinin. Steady yourself, Vera, as I am doing . . . just so . . . The service will be over presently. We 'll go away at once. . . . It is she. . . .

Volguin. Sh-h-h!

Father Ivan. And vouchsafe us, O Lord, boldly and guiltlessly, to presume to call upon Thee, the heavenly God, as Father, and to say . . .

The Archbishop's Choir. [*Singing.*] Our Father which art in heaven, hallowed by Thy name, Thy kingdom come . . .

Matveyev. [*To his company of actors.*] Move on a bit, boys; I want to kneel down. [*Ke kneels down and bows to the ground.*] Thy will be done, as in heaven so in earth. Give us this day our bread for subsistence; and forgive us our debts, as we forgive our debtors . . .

The Archbishop's Choir. [*Singing.*] Thy will be done, as in heaven so in earth . . . our bread for subsistence . . .

Matveyev. Remember, O Lord, Thy deceased handmaid Tatyana and forgive her her trespasses, voluntary and involuntary, and forgive us and have mercy on us. . . . [*He gets up.*] It 's hot!

The Archbishop's Choir. [*Singing.*] And lead u . . . u . . . us not into temptation, but deliver us from e-e-evil!

Kotelnikov. [*To the Crown Prosecutor.*] A fly must have bitten our bridegroom. Look, how he trembles!

The Crown Prosecutor. What 's the matter with him?

Kotelnikov. He thought that the lady in black, who has just had hysterics, was Tatyana. A case of hallucination.

Father Ivan. For Thine is the kingdom, the power, and the glory, Father, Son, and Holy Ghost, now and for ever, world without end!

The Choir. Amen!

The Crown Prosecutor. See that he doesn't play any tricks!

Kotelnikov. He will hold out. He 's not that sort!

The Crown Prosecutor, Yes, he 's having a hard time of it!

Father Ivan. Peace be to all!

The Choir. And to thy spirit.

The Deacon. Let us bow our heads to the Lord!

The Choir. To Thee, O Lord!

In the Crowd. They'll be making a circuit round the altar presently.

Sh-h! Sh-h!

Has there been an inquest on the doctor's wife?

Not yet. They say the husband had deserted her. But they say that Sobinin too had deserted Mlle Riepin. Is it true?

Ye-s!

I remember the inquest on Mlle Riepin.

The Deacon. Let us supplicate the Lord!

The Choir. Lord, have mercy!

Father Ivan. [*Reading.*] O God, who madest all things by Thy might, and didst establish the world, and adorn the crown of all things which Thou hadst made, bless also with spiritual blessing this common cup, granting it unto them that are joined in the fellowship of matrimony. For blessed is Thy name, and glorified Thy kingdom, Father, Son, and Holy Ghost, now and for ever, world without end.

> [*Father Ivan hands the wine cup to Sobinin and Mme Olenin to drink.*

The Choir. Amen!

The Crown Prosecutor. See that he doesn't faint!

Kotelnikov. He's a strong brute. He'll go through it all right!

In the Crowd. Look here, boys, don't disperse. We will come out all together. Is Sipunov here?

Here I am! We shall have to surround the car and whistle for five minutes.

Father Ivan. Give me your hands. [*He ties Sobinin's and Mme Olenin's hands with a handkerchief.*] Is it tight?

The Crown Prosecutor. [*To the Student.*] Give me the crown, young man, and you carry the train.

The Archbishop's Choir. Rejoice, O Esaias; the Virgin conceived . . .

> [*Father Ivan makes a circuit round the altar, followed by the newly married couple and by their best men.*

The Archbishop's Choir. . . . and brought forth a Son, Emmanuel, God and Man: East is his name. . . .

Sobinin. [*To Volguin.*] Is this the end?

Volguin. Not yet.

The Archbishop's Choir. . . . Him we magnify, and the Virgin we call blessed.

> [*Father Ivan makes a circuit round the altar for the second time.*

The Archbishop's Choir. [*Singing.*] Holy Martyrs, ye who fought the good fight, and obtained the crown, intercede with the Lord to have mercy on our souls. . . .

Father Ivan. [*Making the third circuit and chanting.*] On our souls. . . .

Sobinin. My God, it's never going to end!

The Archbishop's Choir. [*Singing.*] Glory be to Thee, O Christ our God, Boast of the Apostles, Joy of the Martyrs, whose preaching is the Consubstantial Trinity.

An Officer from the Crowd. [*To Kotelnikov.*] Warn Sobinin that undergraduates and high-school boys are waiting outside to hiss him.

Kotelnikov. Thanks. [*To the Crown Prosecutor.*] How the business drags on! They will never stop officiating.

[*Wipes his face with his handkerchief.*

The Crown Prosecutor. But your hands are trembling. . . . What an effeminate lot you all are!

Kotelnikov. I keep on thinking of Tatyana. I have a feeling as though Sobinin is singing, and she's weeping.

Father Ivan. [*Taking the bridegroom's crown from Volguin. To Sobinin.*] Be magnified, O Bridegroom, as Abraham, and be blessed as Isaac, and be multiplied as Jacob, going thy way in peace, and fulfilling in righteousness the commandments of God.

A young Actor. What beautiful words to address to scoundrels.

Matveyev. God is the same to all.

Father Ivan. [*Taking the bride's crown from the Crown Prosecutor. To Mme Olenin.*] And thou, O Bride, be magnified as Sarah, and be joyful as Rebecca, and be multiplied as Rachel, delighting in thine own husband, keeping the ordinances of the law, for such was the good pleasure of God.

Among the Crowd. [*A general rush to the exit.*] Quiet! The service is not over yet.

Sh-h! Don't push!

The Deacon. Let us supplicate the Lord!

The Choir. Lord, have mercy!

Father Alexey. [*Taking off his dark glasses ; reading.*] O God, our God, who wast present at Cana of Galilee, and didst bless the marriage there, bless also these Thy servants, joined together by Thy Providence in the fellowship of matrimony; bless their comings in and goings out; multiply their life in good things and receive in Thy kingdom their crowns, preserving them unspotted, blameless, and undefiled, world without end.

The Choir. [*Singing.*] Amen!

Mme Olenin. [*To her brother.*] Tell them to get me a chair. I feel faint!

The Crown Prosecutor. Vera Alexandrovna, it will be over presently! Just a moment. . . . Steady yourself for a while, dear!

Mme Olenin. [*To her brother.*] Peter doesn't hear me. . . . He seems so dumbfounded. Oh, dear, dear, dear! . . . [*To Sobinin.*] Peter!

Father Ivan. Peace be to all!

The Choir. And to thy spirit!

The Deacon. Bow down your heads to the Lord!

Father Ivan. [*To Sobinin and Mme Olenin.*] The Father, the Son, and the Holy Ghost, the all-holy, consubstantial, and life-originating Trinity, the one Deity and Sovereignty, bless you and grant you long life, good offspring, increase in life and faith, and fill you with all the good things of the earth! And make you also worthy to enjoy the good things promised, through the intercession of the holy Mother of God, and of all the Saints, Amen! [*To Mme Olenin, with a smile.*] Kiss your husband!

Volguin. [*To Sobinin.*] Why do you stand still? Embrace her!
　　　　　[*The newly married couple embrace one another.*

Father Ivan. I congratulate you! May God . . .

Mme Kokoshkin. [*Coming to the bride.*] My dear, my darling. . . . I am so glad! I congratulate you!

Kotelnikov. [*To Sobinin.*] I congratulate you on the job. . . . Well, it's time you stopped getting pale, the whole rigmarole is over. . . .

The Deacon. Wisdom!
　　　　[*Friends offer their congratulations to the newly married couple.*

The Choir. [*Singing.*] More honourable than the Cherubim, and more glorious without comparison than the Seraphim, Thee who barest without corruption God the Word, O true Theotokos, Thee we magnify!
　　　　[*The crowd is hurrying out of church. Kouzma the verger is putting out the lights.*

Father Ivan. May Christ, our true God, who by His presence at Cana of Galilee made marriage honourable, may Christ through the intercession of His all-spotless Mother, of the holy, glorious and all-renowned Apostles, of the God-crowned and Isapostolic sovereigns Constantine and Helena, of the Holy Great Martyr Procopius, and of all the saints, have mercy and save us, for He is good and the lover of men.

The Choir. [*Singing.*] Amen. Lord, have mercy! Lord, have mercy! Lord, have mercy!

Ladies. [*To Mme Olenin.*] Congratulations, my dear. . . . May you live a hundred years. . . . [*Kisses.*

Sonnenstein. [*To Mme Olenin.*] Mme Sobinin, if I may say so, to put it in pure Russian language . . .

The Archbishop's Choir. [*Singing.*] Long life, long life! Long life!

Sobinin. Pardon, Vera! [*He takes Kotelnikov by the arm and leads him aside ; trembling and stammering.*] Come with me at once to the cemetery!

Kotelnikov. You are mad! It's night now! Whatever are you going to do there?

Sobinin. For the love of God, do come! I implore you. . . .

Kotelnikov. You must drive home with your bride now! You madman!

Sobinin. I don't care a damn, curse it, curse it a thousand times! I . . . am going . . . to have a mass said for the dead! . . . Oh, I am mad. . . . I nearly died. . . . Oh, Kotelnikov, Kotelnikov!

Kotelnikov. Come, come . . . [*Leads him to the bride.*]

[*After a while a piercing whistle is heard from the street. The people gradually leave the church. Only the Acolyte and Kouzma, the verger, remain.*

Kouzma. It's all no use. . . . No sense.

The Acolyte. What?

Kouzma. This wedding here. Every day we have weddings, christenings, buryings, but there's no sense in it all.

The Acolyte. And what exactly do you want?

Kouzma. Nothing. I'm just saying. . . . All this has no sense. . . . All of it.

The Acolyte. H'm. . . . [*Putting on his galoshes.*] Philosophize, and your head gets giddy. [*Walking out, his galoshes making a thudding noise.*] Good-bye! [*Exit.*

Kouzma. [*Alone.*] This afternoon we buried a gentleman, just now we had a wedding, to-morrow morning we shall have a christening. And it goes on without end. . . . Just so, with no sense. . . . [*A groan is heard.*

[*From behind the altar appear Father Ivan and Father Alexey in dark glasses.*

Father Ivan. He must have got a fine dowry, I suppose . . .

Father Alexey. Sure to have. . . .

Father Ivan. Just to think what life is! I too once courted a girl, I too once married and got a dowry, but it is all forgotten now in the full circle of time. [*Aloud.*] Kouzma! why have you put out all the candles? I shall tumble down in the darkness.

Kouzma. I thought you had gone already.

Father Ivan. Well, Father Alexey? Come and have tea with me?

Father Alexey. Thank you very much, Father Archpriest, but I have no time. I have still got to write a report.

Father Ivan. As you please.

The Lady in Black. [*Coming out from behind the pillar, staggering.*] Who is there! Take me away. . . . Take me away.

Father Ivan. What's the matter? Who's there? [*Frightened.*] What do you want here, madam?

Father Alexey. God, forgive us sinners. . . .

The Lady in Black. Take me away . . . take . . . [*Groaning.*] I am the sister of Ivanov, the officer . . . his sister . . .

Father Ivan. Why are you here?

The Lady in Black. I have taken poison! Out of hatred! Because he wronged her. . . . Why should he be happy? God . . . [*Crying out.*] Save me, save! [*Dropping on the floor.*] All must poison themselves . . . all! There's no justice. . . .

Father Alexey. [*In terror.*] What blasphemy! Lord, what blasphemy!

The Lady in Black. Out of hatred! . . . All must poison themselves. . . . [*Groaning and rolling on the floor.*] She is in her grave, and he . . . he . . . Through this wrong to woman God is profaned. . . . A woman wasted. . . .

Father Alexey. What blasphemy against religion! [*Clasping his hands.*] What blasphemy against life!

The Lady in Black. [*Tearing off her clothes and crying.*] Save me! Save me! Save me!

[*The curtain falls.*

(And all the rest I leave to the imagination of A. S. Souvorin.

ON THE HARMFULNESS OF TOBACCO

A STAGE MONOLOGUE IN ONE ACT [1]

THE CHARACTER

IVAN IVANOVICH NYUKHIN, a hen-pecked husband, whose wife keeps a music school and boarding-school for girls.

The scene represents a platform in a provincial club.

Nyukhin. [*With long side whiskers and clean-shaven upper lip, in an old, well-worn frock coat, entering with great dignity, bowing and adjusting his waistcoat.*] Ladies and gentlemen, so to say! [*Smoothing down his whiskers.*] It has been suggested to my wife that I should read here, for a charitable object, a popular lecture. Well, if I must lecture, I must—it is absolutely no matter to me. Of course, I am not a professor and hold no learned degrees, yet and nevertheless for the last thirty years, without stopping, I might even say to the injury of my own health and so on, I have been working on questions of a strictly scientific nature. I am a thinking man, and, imagine, at times even I compose scientific contributions; I mean, not precisely scientific, but, pardon my saying so, they are almost in the scientific line. By the way, the other day I wrote a long article entitled 'On the Harmfulness of Certain Insects.' My daughters like it immensely, especially the references to bugs; but after reading it I tore it to pieces. Surely, no matter how well you write, dispense with Persian powder [2] you cannot. We have got bugs even in our piano. . . . For the subject of my present lecture I have taken, so to say, the harm caused to mankind by the consumption of tobacco. I myself smoke, but my wife ordered me to lecture to-day on the harmfulness of tobacco, and therefore there is no help for it. On tobacco, well, let it be on tobacco—it is absolutely no matter to me; but to you, gentlemen, I suggest that you should regard my present lecture with all due seriousness, for fear that something unexpected may happen. Yet those

[1] Originally published in 1886.
[2] An insecticide, like Keating's.

who are afraid of a dry, scientific lecture, who do not care for such things, need not listen to it and may even leave. [*Adjusting his waistcoat.*] I particularly crave the attention of the members of the medical profession here present, who may gather from my lecture a great deal of useful information, since tobacco, apart from its harmful effects, is also used in medicine. Thus, for instance, if you place a fly in a snuff-box, it will probably die from derangement of the nerves. Tobacco, essentially, is a plant. . . . When I lecture I usually wink my right eye, but you must take no notice: it is through sheer nervousness. I am a very nervous man, generally speaking; and I started to wink my eye as far back as 1889, to be exact, on 13th September, on the very day when my wife gave birth to our, so to say, fourth daughter, Barbara. All my daughters were born on the 13th. Though [*looking at his watch*], in view of the short time at our disposal, I must not digress from the subject of the lecture. I must observe, by the way, that my wife keeps a music school and a private boarding-school; I mean to say, not exactly a boarding-school, but something in the nature of one. Between ourselves, my wife loves to complain of straitened circumstances; but she has put away in a safe nook some forty or fifty thousand roubles; as to myself, I have not a penny to bless myself with, not a *sou*— but, well, what's the good of dwelling on that? In the boarding-school it is my duty to look after the housekeeping. I buy the provisions, keep an eye on the servants, enter the expenses in a ledger, stitch together the exercise-books, exterminate bugs, take my wife's pet dog for a walk, catch mice. . . . Last night I had to give out flour and butter to the cook, as we were going to have pancakes to-day. Well, to be brief, to-day, when the pancakes were ready, my wife came into the kitchen to say that three of her pupils would have no pancakes, as they had swollen glands. So it happened that we had a few pancakes extra. What would you do with them? My wife first ordered those pancakes to be taken to the larder; but then she thought for a while, and after deliberation she said: 'You can have those pancakes, you scarecrow. . . .' When she is out of humour, she always addesses me like that: 'scarecrow' or 'viper' or 'Satan.' You see what a Satan I am. She's always out of humour. But I didn't masticate them properly, I just gulped them down, for I am always hungry. Yesterday, for instance, she gave me no dinner. 'It's no use,' she says, 'feeding you, scarecrow that you

are . . .' However [*looking at his watch*], I have strayed from
my subject, and have digressed somewhat from my theme.
Let us continue. Though, of course, you would rather hear
now a romance, or symphony, or some aria. . . . [*Singing.*]
'In the heat of the battle we shan't budge. . . .' I don't
remember where that comes from. . . . By the way, I have
forgotten to tell you that in my wife's music school, apart
from looking after the housekeeping, my duties also include
the teaching of mathematics, physics, chemistry, geography,
history, solfeggio, literature, etc. For dancing, singing, and
drawing my wife charges an extra fee, although it is I who
am the dancing and singing master. Our music school is at
No. 13 Five Dogs' Lane. That is probably why my life has
been so unlucky, through living in a house numbered thirteen.
Again, my daughters were born on the thirteenth, and our house
has thirteen windows. . . . But, well, what's the good dwelling on all this? My wife is at home at any hour for business
interviews, and the prospectus of the school can be had from
the porter here, at sixpence a copy. [*Taking a few copies from
his pocket.*] And, if you please, I myself can let you have some.
Each copy sixpence! Any one like a copy? [*A pause.*] No
one? Well, make it fourpence. [*A pause.*] How very annoying! Yes, the house is number thirteen. I am a failure at
everything; I have grown old, stupid. Now, I am lecturing,
and to look at me I am quite jolly, but I have such a longing
to shout at the top of my voice or to run away to the ends of
the earth. . . . And there is no one I can complain to, I even
want to cry. . . . You may say, You have your daughters.
. . . But what are daughters? I speak to them, and they
only laugh. . . . My wife has seven daughters. . . . No, I'm
sorry, I believe only six. . . . [*Vivaciously.*] Sure it's seven!
The eldest, Anna is twenty-seven; the youngest seventeen.
Gentlemen! [*Looking round.*] I am miserable, I have become
a fool, a nonentity, but, after all, you see before you the
happiest of fathers. After all, it ought to be like that, and
I dare not say it is not. But if only you knew! I have lived
with my wife for thirty-three years, and, I can say, those were
the best years of my life; I mean not precisely the best, but
generally speaking. They have passed, in a word, like one
happy moment; but strictly speaking, curse them all. [*Looking
round.*] I think, though, she has not come yet; she is not
here, and therefore I may say what I like. . . . I am terribly
afraid. . . . I am afraid when she looks at me. Well, as I

was just saying; my daughters don't get married, probably because they are shy, and also because men never have a chance of seeing them. My wife does not want to give parties, she never invites any one to dinner, she's a very stingy, ill-tempered, quarrelsome lady and therefore no one comes to the house, but . . . I can tell you in confidence [*Coming close to the footlights.*] . . . My wife's daughters can be seen on great feast days at the house of their aunt, Natalie Semion-ovna, that very same lady who suffers from rheumatism and always wears a yellow dress with black spots, as though she were covered all over with black beetles. There you get real food. And if my wife happens not to be there, then you can also. . . . [*Raising his elbow.*] I must observe that I get drunk on one wineglass, and on account of that I feel so happy and at the same time so sad that I cannot describe it to you. I then recall my youth, and for some reason I long to run away, to run right away. . . . Oh, if only you knew how I long to do it! [*Enthusiastically.*] To run away, to leave everything behind, to run without ever looking back. . . . Where to? It does not matter where . . . provided I could run away from that vile, mean, cheap life, which has turned me into a miserable old fool, into a miserable old idiot; to run away from that stupid, petty, ill-tempered, spiteful, malicious miser, my wife, who has been tormenting me for thirty-three years; to run away from the music, from the kitchen, from my wife's money affairs, from all those trifles and banalities. . . . To run away and then to stop somewhere far, far away in a field, and to stand stock-still like a tree, like a post, like a garden scarecrow, under the wide heaven, and to look all night long at the still, bright moon over my head, and to forget, to forget. . . . Oh, how much I long not to re-member! . . . How I long to tear off this old, shabby coat, which thirty-three years ago I wore at my wedding . . . [*tearing off his frock coat*] in which I always give lectures for charitable objects. . . . Take that! [*Stamping on the coat.*] Take that! I am old, poor, wretched, like this waistcoat, with its patched, shabby, ragged back. . . . [*Showing his back.*] I want nothing! I am better and cleaner than that; I was once young, I studied at the university, I had dreams, con-sidered myself a man. . . . Now I want nothing! Nothing but rest . . . rest! [*Looking back, he quickly puts on his frock coat.*] Behind the platform is my wife. . . . She has come and is waiting for me there. . . . [*Looking at his watch.*] The time is now over. . . . If she asks you, please, I implore you, tell her that the lecturer was . . . that the scarecrow, I mean myself, behaved with dignity. [*Looking aside, coughing.*] She is looking in my direction. . . . [*Raising his voice.*] Starting from the premise that tobacco contains a terrible poison, of which I have just spoken, smoking should in no circumstance be permitted, and I venture to hope, so to say, that this my lecture 'On the Harmfulness of Tobacco' will be of some profit to you. I have finished. Dixi et animam levavi!

[*Bows and walks off with dignity.*

STORIES

MY LIFE

THE STORY OF A PROVINCIAL

I

THE director said to me: 'I only keep you out of respect for your worthy father, or you would have gone long since.' I replied: 'You flatter me, your Excellency, but I suppose I am in a position to go.' And then I heard him saying: 'Take the fellow away, he is getting on my nerves.'

Two days later I was dismissed. Since I had grown up, to the great sorrow of my father, the municipal architect, I had changed my position nine times, going from one department to another, but all the departments were as like each other as drops of water; I had to sit and write, listen to inane and rude remarks, and just wait until I was dismissed.

When I told my father, he was sitting back in his chair with his eyes shut. His thin, dry face, with a dove-coloured tinge where he shaved (his face was like that of an old Catholic organist), wore an expression of meek submission. Without answering my greeting or opening his eyes, he said:

'If my dear wife, your mother, were alive, your life would be a constant grief to her. I can see the hand of Providence in her untimely death. Tell me, you unhappy boy,' he went on, opening his eyes, 'what am I do to with you?'

When I was younger my relations and friends knew what to do with me; some advised me to go into the army as a volunteer, others were for pharmacy, others for the telegraph service; but now that I was twenty-four and was going grey at the temples and had already tried the army and pharmacy and the telegraph service, and every possibility seemed to be exhausted, they gave me no more advice, but only sighed and shook their heads.

'What do you think of yourself?' my father went on. 'At your age other young men have a good social position, and just look at yourself: a lazy lout, a beggar, living on your father!'

And, as usual, he went on to say that young men were going to the dogs through want of faith, materialism, and conceit, and that amateur theatricals should be prohibited, because they seduce young people from religion and their duty.

'To-morrow we will go together, and you shall apologize to the director and promise to do your work conscientiously,' he concluded. 'You must not be without a position in society for a single day.'

'Please listen to me,' said I firmly, though I did not anticipate gaining anything by speaking. 'What you call a position in society is the privilege of capital and education. But people who are poor and uneducated have to earn their living by hard physical labour, and I see no reason why I should be an exception.'

'It is foolish and trivial of you to talk of physical labour,' said my father with some irritation. 'Do try to understand, you idiot, and get it into your brainless head, that in addition to physical strength you have a divine spirit; a sacred fire, by which you are distinguished from an ass or a reptile and brought nigh to God. This sacred fire has been kept alight for thousands of years by the best of mankind. Your great-grandfather, General Polozniev, fought at Borodino; your grandfather was a poet, an orator, and a marshal of the nobility; your uncle was an educationist; and I, your father, am an architect! Have all the Poloznievs kept the sacred fire alight for you to put it out?'

'There must be justice,' said I. 'Millions of people have to do manual labour.'

'Let them. They can do nothing else! Even a fool or a criminal can do manual labour. It is the mark of a slave and a barbarian, whereas the sacred fire is given only to a few!'

It was useless to go on with the conversation. My father worshipped himself and would not be convinced by anything unless he said it himself. Besides, I knew quite well that the annoyance with which he spoke of unskilled labour came not so much from any regard for the sacred fire, as from a secret fear that I should become a working man and the talk of the town. But the chief thing was that all my schoolfellows had long ago gone through the university and were making careers for themselves, and the son of the director of the State Bank was already a collegiate assessor, while I, an only son, was nothing! It was useless and unpleasant to go on with the conversation, but I still sat there and raised objections in the hope of making myself understood. The problem was simple and clear: how was I to earn my living? But he could not see its simplicity and kept on talking with sugary rounded phrases about Borodino and the sacred fire, and my uncle, a forgotten poet who wrote bad,

insincere verses, and he called me a brainless fool. But how
I longed to be understood! In spite of everything, I loved my
father and my sister, and from boyhood I have had a habit of
considering them, so strongly rooted that I shall probably never
get rid of it; whether I am right or wrong I am always afraid of
hurting them, and go in terror lest my father's thin neck should
go red with anger and he should have an apoplectic fit.

'It is shameful and degrading for a man of my age to sit in a
stuffy room and compete with a typewriting-machine,' I said.
'What has that to do with the sacred fire?'

'Still, it is intellectual work,' said my father. 'But that's
enough. Let us drop the conversation and I warn you that if
you refuse to return to your office and indulge your contemptible
inclinations, then you will lose my love and your sister's. I
shall cut you out of my will—that I swear, by God!'

With perfect sincerity, in order to show the purity of my
motives, by which I hope to be guided all through my life,
I said:

'The matter of inheritance does not strike me as important.
I renounce any rights I may have.'

For some unexpected reason these words greatly offended my
father. He went purple in the face.

'How dare you talk to me like that, you fool!' he cried to me
in a thin, shrill voice. 'You scoundrel!' And he struck me
quickly and dexterously with a familiar movement; once—
twice. 'You forget yourself!'

When I was a boy and my father struck me, I used to stand
bolt upright like a soldier and look him straight in the face;
and, exactly as if I were still a boy, I stood erect, and tried to
look into his eyes. My father was old and very thin, but his
spare muscles must have been as strong as whip-cord, for he
hit very hard.

I returned to the hall, but there he seized his umbrella and
struck me several times over the head and shoulders; at that
moment my sister opened the drawing-room door to see what
the noise was, but immediately drew back with an expression of
pity and horror, and said not one word in my defence.

My intention not to return to the office, but to start a new
working life, was unshakable. It only remained to choose the
kind of work—and there seemed to be no great difficulty about
that, because I was strong, patient, and willing. I was prepared
to face a monotonous, laborious life, of semi-starvation, filth,
and rough surroundings, always overshadowed with the thought

of finding a job and a living. And—who knows?—returning from work in Great Gentry Street, I might often envy Dolzhikov, the engineer, who lives by intellectual work, but I was happy in thinking of my coming troubles. I used to dream of intellectual activity, and to imagine myself a teacher, a doctor, a writer, but my dreams remained only dreams. A liking for intellectual pleasures—like the theatre and reading —grew into a passion with me, but I did not know whether I had any capacity for intellectual work. At school I had an unconquerable aversion for the Greek language, so that I had to leave when I was in the fourth class. Teachers were got to coach me up for the fifth class, and then I went into various departments, spending most of my time in perfect idleness, and this, I was told, was intellectual work.

My activity in the education department or in the municipal office required neither mental effort, nor talent, nor personal ability, nor creative spiritual impulse; it was purely mechanical, and such intellectual work seemed to me lower than manual labour. I despise it and I do not think that it for a moment justifies an idle, careless life, because it is nothing but a swindle, and only a kind of idleness. In all probability I have never known real intellectual work.

It was evening. We lived in Great Gentry Street—the chief street in the town—and our rank and fashion walked up and down it in the evenings, as there were no public gardens. The street was very charming, and was almost as good as a garden, for it had two rows of poplar trees, which smelt very sweet, especially after rain, and acacias, and tall trees, and apple trees hung over the fences and hedges. May evenings, the scent of the lilac, the hum of the cockchafers, the warm, still air—how new and extraordinary it all is, though spring comes every year! I stood by the gate and looked at the passers-by. With most of them I had grown up and played, but now my presence might upset them, because I was poorly dressed, in unfashionable clothes, and people made fun of my very narrow trousers and large, clumsy boots, and called them macaroni-on-steamboats. And I had a bad reputation in the town because I had no position and went to play billiards in low cafés, and had once been taken up, for no particular offence, by the political police.

In a large house opposite, Dolzhikov's, the engineer's, someone was playing the piano. It was growing dark and the stars were beginning to shine. And slowly, answering people's salutes, my father passed with my sister on his arm. He was wearing an old top hat with a broad curly brim.

'Look!' he said to my sister, pointing to the sky with the very umbrella with which he had just struck me. 'Look at the sky! Even the smallest stars are worlds! How insignificant man is in comparison with the universe.'

And he said this in a tone that seemed to convey that he found it extremely flattering and pleasant to be so insignificant. What an untalented man he was! Unfortunately, he was the only architect in the town, and during the last fifteen or twenty years I could not remember one decent house being built. When he had to design a house, as a rule he would draw first the hall and the drawing-room; as in olden days schoolgirls could only begin to dance by the fireplace, so his artistic ideas could only evolve from the hall and drawing-room. To them he would add the dining-room, nursery, study, connecting them with doors, so that in the end they were just so many passages, and each room had two or three doors too many. His houses were obscure, extremely confused, and limited. Every time, as though he felt something was missing, he had recourse to various additions, plastering them one on top of the other, and there would be various lobbies, and passages, and crooked staircases leading to the *entresol*, where it was only possible to stand in a stooping position, and where instead of a floor there would be a thin flight of stairs like a Russian bath, and the kitchen would always be under the house with a vaulted ceiling and a brick floor. The front of his houses always had a hard, stubborn expression, with stiff, timid lines, low, squat roofs, and fat, pudding-like chimneys surmounted with black cowls and squeaking weathercocks. And somehow all the houses built by my father were like each other, and vaguely reminded me of his top hat, and the stiff, obstinate back of his head. In the course of time the people of the town grew used to my father's lack of talent, which took root and became our style.

My father introduced the style into my sister's life. To begin with, he gave her the name of Cleopatra (and he called me Misail). When she was a little girl he used to frighten her by telling her about the stars and our ancestors; and explained the nature of life and duty to her at great length; and now when she was twenty-six he went on in the same way, allowing her to take no one's arm but his own, and somehow imagining that sooner or later an ardent young man would turn up and wish to enter into marriage with her out of admiration for his qualities. And she

adored my father, was afraid of him, and believed in his extraordinary intellectual powers.

It got quite dark and the street grew gradually empty. In
the house opposite the music stopped. The gate was wide open
and out into the street, careering with all its bells jingling, came
a *troika*. It was the engineer and his daughter going for a drive.
Time to go to bed!

I had a room in the house, but I lived in the courtyard in
a hut, under the same roof as the coach-house, which had been
built probably as a harness-room—for there were big nails in the
walls—but now it was not used, and my father for thirty years
had kept his newspapers there, which for some reason he had
bound half-yearly and then allowed no one to touch. Living
there I was less in touch with my father and his guests, and
I used to think that if I did not live in a proper room and did
not go to the house every day for meals, my father's reproach
that I was living on him lost some of its sting.

My sister was waiting for me. She had brought me supper
unknown to my father; a small piece of cold veal and a slice of
bread. In the family there were sayings: 'Money loves an
account,' or 'A copeck saves a rouble,' and so on, and my sister,
impressed by such wisdom, did her best to cut down expenses
and made us feed rather meagrely. She put the plate on the
table, sat on my bed, and began to cry.

'Misail,' she said, 'what are you doing to us?'

She did not cover her face, her tears ran down her cheeks and
hands, and her expression was sorrowful. She fell on the pillow,
gave way to her tears, trembling all over and sobbing.

'You have left your work again!' she said. 'How awful!'

'Do try to understand, sister!' I said, and because she cried I
was filled with despair.

As though it were deliberately arranged, the paraffin in my
little lamp ran out, and the lamp smoked and guttered, and the
old hooks in the wall looked terrible and their shadows flickered.

'Spare us!' said my sister, rising up. 'Father is in an awful
state, and I am ill. I shall go mad. What will become of you?'
she asked, sobbing and holding out her hands to me. 'I ask you,
I implore you, in the name of our dear mother, to go back to
your work.'

'I cannot, Cleopatra,' I said, feeling that only a little more
would make me give in. 'I cannot.'

'Why?' insisted my sister, 'why? If you have not made it
up with your chief, look for another place. For instance, why

shouldn't you work on the railway? I have just spoken to
Aniuta Blagovo, and she assures me you would be taken on, and
she even promised to do what she could for you. For goodness
sake, Misail, think! Think it over, I implore you!'

We talked a little longer and I gave in. I said that the
thought of working on the railway had never come into my head,
and that I was ready to try.

She smiled happily through her tears and clasped my hand,
and still she cried, because she could not stop, and I went into
the kitchen for paraffin.

II

Among the supporters of amateur theatricals, charity concerts,
and *tableaux vivants* the leaders were the Azhoguins, who lived
in their own house in Great Gentry Street. They used to lend
their house and assume the necessary trouble and expense.
They were a rich landowning family, and had about three
thousand dessiatins, with a magnificent farm in the neighbour-
hood, but they did not care for village life and lived in the town
summer and winter. The family consisted of a mother, a tall,
spare, delicate lady, who had short hair and wore a blouse and
a plain skirt *à l'anglaise*, and three daughters, who were spoken
of, not by their names, but as the eldest, the middle, and the
youngest; they all had ugly, sharp chins, and they were short-
sighted, high-shouldered, dressed in the same style as their
mother, had an unpleasant lisp, and yet they always took part
in every play and were always doing something for charity—
acting, reciting, singing. They were very serious and never
smiled, and even in burlesque operettas they acted without
gaiety and with a businesslike air, as though they were engaged
in bookkeeping.

I loved our plays, especially the rehearsals, which were
frequent, rather absurd, and noisy, and we were always given
supper after them. I had no part in the selection of the pieces
and the casting of the characters. I had to look after the stage.
I used to design the scenery and copy out the parts, and prompt
and make up. And I also had to look after the various effects
such as thunder, the singing of a nightingale, and so on. Having
no social position, I had no decent clothes, and during rehearsals
had to hold aloof from the others in the darkened wings and
shyly say nothing.

I used to paint the scenery in the Azhoguins' coach-house or yard. I was assisted by a house-painter, or, as he called himself, a decorating contractor, named Andrey Ivanov, a man of about fifty, tall and very thin and pale, with a narrow chest, hollow temples, and dark rings under his eyes; he was rather awful to look at. He had some kind of wasting disease, and every spring and autumn he was said to be on the point of death, but he would go to bed for a while and then get up and say with surprise: 'I'm not dead this time!'

In the town he was called Radish, and people said it was his real name. He loved the theatre as much as I, and no sooner did he hear that a play was in hand than he gave up all his work and went to the Azhoguins' to paint scenery.

The day after my conversation with my sister I worked from morning till night at the Azhoguins'. The rehearsal was fixed for seven o'clock, and an hour before it began all the players were assembled, and the eldest, the middle, and the youngest Miss Azhoguin were reading their parts on the stage. Radish, in a long, brown overcoat with a scarf wound round his neck, was standing, leaning with his head against the wall, looking at the stage with a rapt expression. Mrs Azhoguin went from guest to guest saying something pleasant to every one. She had a way of gazing into one's face and speaking in a hushed voice as though she were telling a secret.

'It must be difficult to paint scenery,' she said softly, coming up to me. 'I was just talking to Mrs Mufke about prejudice when I saw you come in. *Mon Dieu!* All my life I have struggled against prejudice. To convince the servants that all their superstitions are nonsense I always light three candles, and I begin all my important business on the thirteenth.'

The daughter of Dolzhikov, the engineer, was there, a handsome, plump, fair girl, dressed, as people said in our town, in Parisian style. She did not act, but at rehearsals a chair was put for her on the stage, and the plays did not begin until she appeared in the front row, to astonish everybody with the brilliance of her clothes. As coming from the metropolis, she was allowed to make remarks during rehearsals, and she did so with an affable, condescending smile, and it was clear that she regarded our plays as a childish amusement. It was said that she had studied singing at the Petersburg conservatoire and had sung for a winter season in opera. I liked her very much, and during rehearsals or the performance, I never took my eyes off her.

I had taken the book and began to prompt when suddenly my

sister appeared.   Without taking off her coat and hat she came
up to me and said:
'Please come!'
I went.   Behind the stage in the doorway stood Aniuta
Blagovo, also wearing a hat with a dark veil.   She was the
daughter of the vice-president of the court, who had been
appointed to our town years ago, almost as soon as the high
court was established.   She was tall and had a good figure, and
was considered indispensable for the *tableaux vivants*, and when
she represented a fairy or a muse, her face would burn with
shame; but she took no part in the plays, and would only look
in at rehearsals, on some business, and never enter the hall.   And
it was evident now that she had only looked in for a moment.

'My father has mentioned you,' she said dryly, not looking
at me and blushing. . . . 'Dolzhikov has promised to find you
something to do on the railway.   If you go to his house to-
morrow, he will see you.'
I bowed and thanked her for her kindness.
'And you must leave this,' she said, pointing to my book.
She and my sister went up to Mrs Azhoguin and began to
whisper, looking at me.
'Indeed,' said Mrs Azhoguin, coming up to me, and gazing
into my face.   'Indeed, if it takes you from your more serious
business'—she took the book out of my hands—'then you must
hand it over to someone else.   Don't worry, my friend.   It will
be all right.'
I said good-bye and left in some confusion.   As I went downstairs I saw my sister and Aniuta Blagovo going away; they were
talking animatedly, I suppose about my going on the railway,
and they hurried away.   My sister had never been to a rehearsal
before, and she was probably tortured by her conscience and
by her fear of my father finding out that she had been to the
Azhoguins' without permission.
The next day I went to see Dolzhikov at one o'clock.   The
man-servant showed me into a charming room, which was the
engineer's drawing-room and study.   Everything in it was
charming and tasteful, and to a man like myself, unused to such
things, very strange.   Costly carpets, huge chairs, bronzes,
pictures in gold and velvet frames; photographs on the walls of
beautiful women, clever, handsome faces, and striking attitudes;
from the drawing-room a door led straight into the garden, by a
veranda, and I saw lilac and a table laid for breakfast, rolls, and
a bunch of roses; and there was a smell of spring, and good

cigars, and happiness—and everything seemed to say, here lives a man who has worked and won the highest happiness here on earth. At the table the engineer's daughter was sitting reading a newspaper.

'Do you want my father?' she asked. 'He is having a shower-bath. He will be down presently. Please take a chair.'

I sat down.

'I believe you live opposite?' she asked after a short silence.

'Yes.'

'When I have nothing to do I look out of the window. You must excuse me,' she added, turning to her newspaper, 'and I often see you and your sister. She has such a kind, wistful expression.'

Dolzhikov came in. He was wiping his neck with a towel.

'Papa, this is Mr Polozniev,' said his daughter.

'Yes, yes. Blagovo spoke to me.' He turned quickly to me, but did not hold out his hand. 'But what do you think I can give you? I'm not bursting with situations. You are queer people!' he went on in a loud voice and as though he were scolding me. 'I get about twenty people every day, as though I were a department of state. I run a railway, sir. I employ hard labour; I need mechanics, navvies, joiners, well-sinkers, and you can only sit and write. That's all! You are all clerks!'

And he exhaled the same air of happiness as his carpets and chairs. He was stout, healthy, with red cheeks and a broad chest; he looked clean in his pink shirt and wide trousers, just like a china figure of a post-boy. He had a round, bristling beard—and not a single grey hair—and a nose with a slight bridge, and bright, innocent, dark eyes.

'What can you do?' he went on. 'Nothing! I am an engineer and well-to-do, but before I was given this railway I worked very hard for a long time. I was an engine-driver for two years, I worked in Belgium as an ordinary lubricator. Now, my dear man, just think—what work can I offer you?'

'I quite agree,' said I, utterly abashed, not daring to meet his bright, innocent eyes.

'Are you any good with the telegraph?' he asked after some thought.

'Yes. I have been in the telegraph service.'

'Mm. . . . Well, we'll see. Go to Dubechnia. There's a fellow there already. But he is a scamp.'

'And what will my duties be?' I asked.

'We'll see to that later. Go there now. I'll give orders.

But please don't get drunk and don't bother me with petitions or I 'll kick you out.'

He turned away from me without even a nod. I bowed to him and his daughter, who was reading the newspaper, and went out. I felt so miserable that when my sister asked how the engineer had received me, I could not utter a single word.

To go to Dubechnia I got up early in the morning at sunrise. There was not a soul in the street, the whole town was asleep, and my footsteps rang out with a hollow sound. The dewy poplars filled the air with a soft scent. I was sad and had no desire to leave the town. It seemed so nice and warm! I loved the green trees, the quiet sunny mornings, the ringing of the bells, but the people in the town were alien to me, tiresome, and sometimes even loathsome. I neither liked nor understood them.

I did not understand why or for what purpose those thirty-five thousand people lived. I knew that Kimry made a living by manufacturing boots, that Tula made samovars and guns, that Odessa was a port; but I did not know what our town was or what it did. The people in Great Gentry Street and two other clean streets had independent means and salaries paid by the Treasury, but how the people lived in the other eight streets which stretched parallel to each other for three miles and then were lost behind the hill—that was always an insoluble problem to me. And I am ashamed to think of the way they lived. They had neither public gardens, nor a theatre, nor a decent orchestra; the town and club libraries are used only by young Jews, so that books and magazines would lie for months uncut. The rich and the intelligentsia slept in close, stuffy bedrooms, with wooden beds infested with bugs; the children were kept in filthy dirty rooms called nurseries, and the servants, even when they were old and respectable, slept on the kitchen floor and covered themselves with rags. Except in Lent all the houses smelt of *bortsch*, and during Lent of sturgeon fried in sunflower oil. The food was unsavoury, the water unwholesome. On the town council, at the governor's, at the archbishop's, everywhere there had been talk for years about there being no good, cheap water-supply and of borrowing two hundred thousand roubles from the Treasury. Even the very rich people, of whom there were about thirty in the town, people who would lose a whole estate at cards, used to drink the bad water and talk passionately about the loan—and I could never understand this, for it seemed to me it would be simpler for them to pay up the two hundred thousand.

I did not know a single honest man in the whole town. My father took bribes, and imagined they were given to him out of respect for his spiritual qualities; the boys at the high school, in order to be promoted, went to lodge with the masters and paid them large sums; the wife of the military commandant took levies from the recruits during the recruiting, and even allowed them to stand her drinks, and once she was so drunk in church that she could not get up from her knees; during the recruiting the doctors also took bribes, and the municipal doctor and the veterinary surgeon levied taxes on the butchers' shops and public-houses; the district school did a trade in certificates which gave certain privileges in the civil service; the provosts took bribes from the clergy and churchwardens whom they controlled, and on the town council and various committees every one who came before them was pursued with: 'One expects thanks!'— and thereupon forty copecks had to change hands. And those who did not take bribes, like the high court officials, were stiff and proud, and shook hands with two fingers, and were distinguished by their indifference and narrow-mindedness. They drank and played cards, married rich women, and always had a bad, insidious influence on those round them. Only the girls had any moral purity; most of them had lofty aspirations and were pure and honest at heart; but they knew nothing of life, and believed that bribes were given to honour the spiritual qualities; and when they married, they soon grew old and weak, and were hopelessly lost in the mire of that vulgar, *bourgeois* existence.

III

A railway was being built in our district. On holidays and high days the town was filled with crowds of ragamuffins called 'railies,' of whom the people were afraid. I used often to see a miserable wretch with a bloody face, and without a hat, being dragged off by the police, and behind him was the proof of his crime, a samovar or some wet, newly washed linen. The 'railies' used to collect near the public houses and on the squares; and they drank, ate, and swore terribly, and whistled after the town prostitutes. To amuse these ruffians our shopkeepers used to make the cats and dogs drink vodka, or tie a kerosene-tin to a dog's tail, and whistle to make the dog come tearing along the street with the tin clattering after him, making him squeal with terror and think he had some frightful monster hard at his heels, so that he would rush out of the town and over the fields until he could run no more. We had several dogs in the town which were left with a permanent shiver and used to crawl about with their tails between their legs, and people said that they could not stand such tricks and had gone mad.

The station was being built five miles from the town. It was said that the engineer had asked for a bribe of fifty thousand roubles to bring the station nearer, but the municipality would only agree to forty; they would not give in to the extra ten thousand, and now the townspeople are sorry because they had to make a road to the station which cost them more. Sleepers and rails were fixed all along the line, and service-trains were running to carry building materials and labourers, and they were only waiting for the bridges upon which Dolzhikov was at work, and here and there the stations were not ready.

Dubechnia—the name of our first station—was seventeen versts from the town. I went on foot. The winter and spring corn was bright green, shining in the morning sun. The road was smooth and bright, and in the distance I could see in out-line the station, the hills, and the remote farmhouses. . . . How good it was out in the open! And how I longed to be filled with the sense of freedom, if only for that morning, to stop thinking of what was going on in the town, or of my needs, or even of eating! Nothing has so much prevented my living as the feeling of acute hunger, which makes my finest thoughts get mixed up with thoughts of porridge, cutlets, and fried fish. When I stand alone in the fields and look up at the larks hanging marvellously in the air, and bursting with hysterical song, I think: 'It would be nice to have some bread and butter.' Or when I sit in the road and shut my eyes and listen to the wonder-ful sounds of a May day, I remember how good hot potatoes smell. Being big and of a strong constitution I never have quite enough to eat, and so my chief sensation during the day is hunger, and so I can understand why so many people who are working for a bare living can talk of nothing but food.

At Dubechnia the station was being plastered inside, and the upper story of the water-tank was being built. It was close and smelt of lime, and the labourers were wandering lazily over piles of chips and rubbish. The signalman was asleep near his box with the sun pouring straight into his face. There was not a single tree. The telegraph wire gave a faint hum, and here and there birds had alighted on it. I wandered over the heaps, not knowing what to do, and remembered how when I asked the engineer what my duties would be, he had replied: 'We will see there.' But what was there to see in such a wilderness? The plasterers were talking about the foreman and about one Fyodor Vassilievich. I could not understand and was filled with embarrassment—physical embarrassment. I felt conscious of my arms and legs, and of the whole of my big body, and did not know what to do with them or where to go.

After walking for at least a couple of hours I noticed that from the station to the right of the line there were telegraph-poles which after about one and a half or two miles ended in a white stone wall. The labourers said it was the office, and I decided at last that I must go there.

It was a very old farmhouse, long unused. The wall of rough, white stone was decayed, and in places had crumbled away, and the roof of the wing, the blind wall of which looked towards the railway, had perished and was patched here and there with tin. Through the gates there was a large yard, overgrown with tall grass, and beyond that, an old house with Venetian blinds in the windows, and a high roof, brown with rot. On either side of the house, to right and left, were two symmetrical wings; the windows of one were boarded up, while by the other, the windows of which were open, there was a number of calves grazing. The last telegraph-pole stood in the yard, and the wire went from it to the wing with the blind wall. The door was open and I went in. By the table at the telegraph was sitting a man with a dark, curly head in a canvas coat; he glared at me sternly and askance, but he immediately smiled and said:

'How do you do, Little Profit?'

It was Ivan Cheprakov, my school friend, who was expelled, when he was in the second class, for smoking. Once, during the autumn, we were out catching goldfinches, starlings, and hawfinches, to sell them in the market early in the morning when our parents were still asleep.

We beat up flocks of starlings and shot at them with pellets, and then picked up the wounded, and some died in terrible agony—I can still remember how they moaned at night in my cage—and some recovered. And we sold them, and swore ourselves black in the face that they were male birds. Once in the market I had only one starling left, which I hawked about and finally sold for a copeck. 'A little profit!' I said to console myself, and from that time at school I was always known as 'Little Profit,' and even now, schoolboys and the townspeople sometimes use the name to tease me, though no one but myself remembers how it came about.

Cheprakov never was strong. He was narrow-chested, round-shouldered, long-legged. His tie looked like a piece of string, he had no waistcoat, and his boots were worse than mine—with the heels worn down. He blinked with his eyes and had an eager expression as though he were trying to catch something, and he was in a constant fidget.

'You wait,' he said, bustling about. 'Look here! . . . What was I saying just now?'

We began to talk. I discovered that the estate had till recently belonged to the Cheprakovs and only the previous autumn had passed to Dolzhikov, who thought it more profitable to keep his money in land than in shares, and had already bought three big estates in our district with the transfer of all mortgages. When Cheprakov's mother sold, she stipulated for the right to live in one of the wings for another two years and get her son a job in the office.

'Why shouldn't he buy?' said Cheprakov of the engineer. 'He gets a lot from the contractors. He bribes them all.'

Then he took me to dinner, deciding in his emphatic way that I was to live with him in the wing and board with his mother.

'She is a screw,' he said, 'but she will not take much from you.'

In the small rooms where his mother lived there was a queer jumble; even the hall and the passage were stacked with furniture, which had been taken from the house after the sale of the estate; and the furniture was old, and of redwood. Mrs Cheprakov, a very stout elderly lady, with slanting, Chinese eyes, sat by the window, in a big chair, knitting a stocking. She received me ceremoniously.

'It is Polozniev, mother,' said Cheprakov, introducing me. 'He is going to work here.'

'Are you a nobleman?' she asked in a strange, unpleasant voice as though she had boiling fat in her throat.

'Yes,' I answered.

'Sit down.'

The dinner was bad. It consisted only of a pie with unsweetened curds and some milk soup. Elena Nikifirovna, my hostess, was perpetually winking, first with one eye, then with the other. She talked and ate, but in her whole aspect there was a deathlike quality, and one could almost detect the smell of a corpse. Life hardly stirred in her, yet she had the air of being the lady of the manor, who had once had her serfs, and was the wife of a general, whose servants had to call him 'Your Excellency,' and when these miserable embers of life flared up in her for a moment, she would say to her son:

'Ivan, that is not the way to hold your knife!!'

Or she would say, gasping for breath, with the preciseness of a hostess labouring to entertain her guest:

'We have just sold our estate, you know. It is a pity, of course, we have got so used to being here, but Dolzhikov promised to make Ivan station-master at Dubechnia; so that we shan't have to leave. We shall live here on the station, which is the same as living on the estate. The engineer is such a nice man! Don't you think him very handsome?'

Until recently the Cheprakovs had been very well-to-do, but with the general's death everything changed. Elena Nikifirovna began to quarrel with the neighbours and to go to law, and she did not pay her bailiffs and labourers; she was always afraid of being robbed—and in less than ten years Dubechnia changed completely.

Behind the house there was an old garden run wild, overgrown with tall grass and brushwood. I walked along the terrace which was still well-kept and beautiful; through the glass door I saw a room with a parquet floor, which must have been the drawing-room. It contained an ancient piano, some engravings in mahogany frames on the walls—and nothing else. There was nothing left of the flower-garden but peonies and poppies, rearing their white and scarlet heads above the ground; on the paths, all huddled together, were young maples and elm trees, which had been stripped by the cows. The growth was dense and the garden seemed impassable, and only near the house, where there still stood poplars, firs, and some old lime trees, were there traces of the former avenues. Further on the garden was being cleared for a hay-field, and here it was no longer allowed to run wild, and one's mouth and eyes were no longer filled with spiders' webs, and a pleasant air was stirring. The further out one went, the more open it was, and there were cherry trees, plum trees, wide-spreading old apple trees, lichened and held up with props, and the pear trees were so tall that it was incredible that there could be pears on them. This part of the garden was let to the market-women of our town, and it was guarded from thieves and starlings by a peasant—an idiot who lived in a hut.

The orchard grew thinner and became a mere meadow running down to the river, which was overgrown with reeds and withy-beds. There was a pool by the mill-dam, deep and full of fish, and a little mill with a thatched roof ground and roared, and the frogs croaked furiously. On the water, which was as smooth as glass, circles appeared from time to time, and water-lilies trembled on the impact of a darting fish. The village of Dubechnia was on the other side of the river. The calm, azure pool was alluring with its promise of coolness and rest. And now all this, the pool, the mill, the comfortable banks of the river, belonged to the engineer!

And here my new work began. I received and dispatched telegrams, I wrote out various accounts and copied orders, claims, and reports, sent in to the office by our illiterate foremen and mechanics. But most of the day I did nothing, walking up and down the room waiting for telegrams, or I would tell the boy to stay in the wing, and go into the garden until the boy came to say the bell was ringing. I had dinner with Mrs Cheprakov. Meat was served very rarely; most of the dishes were made of milk, and on Wednesdays and Fridays we had Lenten fare, and the food was served in pink plates, which were called Lenten. Mrs Cheprakov was always blinking—the habit grew on her, and I felt awkward and embarrassed in her presence.

As there was not enough work for one, Cheprakov did nothing, but slept or went down to the pool with his gun to shoot ducks. In the evenings he got drunk in the village, or at the station, and before going to bed he would look in the glass and say:

'How are you, Ivan Cheprakov?'

When he was drunk, he was very pale and used to rub his hands and laugh, or rather neigh, 'He-he-he!' Out of bravado he would undress himself and run naked through the fields, and he used to eat flies and say they were a bit sour.

IV

Once after dinner he came running into the wing, panting, to say:

'Your sister has come to see you.'

I went out and saw a fly standing by the steps of the house. My sister had brought Aniuta Blagovo and a military gentleman in a summer uniform. As I approached I recognized the military gentleman as Aniuta's brother, the doctor.

'We've come to take you for a picnic,' he said, 'if you've no objection.'

My sister and Aniuta wanted to ask how I was getting on, but they were both silent and only looked at me. They felt that I didn't like my job, and tears came into my sister's eyes and Aniuta Blagovo blushed. We went into the orchard, the doctor first, and he said ecstatically:

'What air! By Jove, what air!'

He was just a boy to look at. He talked and walked like an undergraduate, and the look in his grey eyes was as lively, simple, and frank as that of a nice boy. Compared with his tall, handsome sister he looked weak and slight, and his little beard was thin and so was his voice—a thin tenor, though quite pleasant. He was away somewhere with his regiment and had come home on leave, and said that he was going to Petersburg in the autumn to take his M.D. He already had a family—a wife and three children; he had married young, in his second year at the university, and people said he was unhappily married and was not living with his wife.

'What is the time?' My sister was uneasy. 'We must go back soon, for my father would only let me be away until six o'clock.'

'Oh, your father,' sighed the doctor.

I made tea, and we drank it sitting on a carpet in front of the terrace, and the doctor, kneeling, drank from his saucer, and said that he was perfectly happy. Then Cheprakov fetched the key and unlocked the glass door and we all entered the house.

It was dark and mysterious and smelled of mushrooms, and our footsteps made a hollow sound as though there were a vault under the floor. The doctor stopped by the piano and touched the keys and it gave out a faint, tremulous, cracked but still melodious sound. He raised his voice and began to sing a romance, frowning and impatiently stamping his foot when he touched a broken key. My sister forgot about going home, but walked agitatedly up and down the room and said:

'I am happy! I am very, very happy!'

There was a note of surprise in her voice as though it seemed impossible to her that she should be happy. It was the first time in my life that I had seen her so gay. She even looked handsome. Her profile was not good, her nose and mouth somehow protruded and made her look as if she was always blowing, but she had beautiful, dark eyes, a pale, very delicate complexion, and a touching expression of kindness and sadness, and when she spoke she seemed very charming and even beautiful. Both she and I took after our mother; we were broadshouldered, strong, and sturdy, but her paleness was a sign of sickness, she often coughed, and in her eyes I often noticed the expression common to people who are ill, but who for some reason conceal it. In her present cheerfulness there was something childish and naïve, as though all the joy which had been suppressed and dulled during our childhood by a strict upbringing had suddenly awakened in her soul and rushed out into freedom.

But when evening came and the fly was brought round, my sister became very quiet and subdued, and sat in the fly as though it were a prison-van.

Soon they were all gone. The noise of the fly died away. . . . I remembered that Aniuta Blagavo had said not a single word to me all day.

'A wonderful girl!' I thought. 'A wonderful girl.'

Lent came and every day we had Lenten dishes. I was greatly depressed by my idleness and the uncertainly of my position, and, slothful, hungry, dissatisfied with myself, I wandered over the estate and only waited for an energetic mood to leave the place.

Once in the afternoon when Radish was sitting in our wing, Dolzhikov entered unexpectedly, very sunburnt, and grey with dust. He had been out on the line for three days and had come to Dubechnia on a locomotive and walked over. While he waited for the carriage which he had ordered to come out to meet him he went over the estate with his bailiff, giving orders in a loud voice, and then for a whole hour he sat in our wing and wrote letters. When telegrams came through for him, he himself tapped out the answers, while we stood there stiff and silent.

'What a mess!' he said, looking angrily through the accounts. 'I shall transfer the office to the station in a fortnight and I don't know what I shall do with you then.'

'I 've done my best, sir,' said Cheprakov.

'Quite so. I can see what your best is. You can only draw your wages.' The engineer looked at me and went on. 'You rely on getting introductions to make a career for yourself with as little trouble as possible. Well, I don't care about introductions. Nobody helped me. Before I had this line, I was an engine-driver. I worked in Belgium as an ordinary lubricator. And what are you doing here, Panteley?' he asked, turning to Radish. 'Going out drinking?'

For some reason or other he called all simple people Panteley, while he despised men like Cheprakov and myself, and called us drunkards, beasts, *canaille*. As a rule he was hard on petty officials, and paid and dismissed them ruthlessly without any explanation.

At last the carriage came for him. When he left he promised to dismiss us all in a fortnight; called the bailiff a fool, stretched himself out comfortably in the carriage, and drove away.

'Andrey Ivanich,' I said to Radish, 'will you take me on as a labourer?'

'Why! All right!'

We went together toward the town, and when the station and the farm were far behind us, I asked:

'Andrey Ivanich, why did you come to Dubechnia?'

'Firstly because some of my men are working on the line, and secondly to pay interest to Mrs Cheprakov. I borrowed fifty roubles from her last summer, and now I pay her one rouble a month interest.'

The decorator stopped and took hold of my coat.

'Misail Alexeich, my friend,' he went on, 'I take it that if a common man or a gentleman takes interest, he is a wrong-doer. The truth is not in him.'

Radish, looking thin, pale, and rather terrible, shut his eyes, shook his head, and muttered in a philosophic tone:

'The grub eats grass, rust eats iron, lies devour the soul. God save us miserable sinners!'

V

Radish was unpractical and he was no business man; he under-took more work than he could do, and when it came to payment he always lost his reckoning and so was always out on the wrong side. He was a painter, a glazier, a paper-hanger, and would even take on tiling, and I remember how he used to run about for days looking for tiles to make an insignificant profit. He was an excellent workman and would sometimes earn ten roubles a day, and but for his desire to be a master and to call himself a contractor, he would probably have made quite a lot of money.

He himself was paid by contract and paid me and the others by the day, between seventy-five copecks and a rouble per day. When the weather was hot and dry we did various outside jobs, chiefly painting roofs. Not being used to it, my feet got hot, as though I were walking over a red-hot oven, and when I wore felt boots my feet swelled. But this was only at the beginning. Later on I got used to it and everything went all right. I lived

among the people, to whom work was obligatory and un-
avoidable, people who worked like dray-horses, and knew
nothing of the moral value of labour, and never even used the
word 'labour' in their talk.   Among them I also felt like a dray-
horse, more and more imbued with the necessity and inevitability
of what I was doing, and this made my life easier, and saved me
from doubt.

At first everything amused me, everything was new.   It was
like being born again.   I could sleep on the ground and go barefoot—and found it exceedingly pleasant.   I could stand in a
crowd of simple folks, without embarrassing them, and when a
cab-horse fell down in the street, I used to run and help it up
without being afraid of soiling my clothes.   But, best of all, I
was living independently and was not a burden on any one.

The painting of roofs, especially when we mixed our own
paint, was considered a very profitable business, and therefore,
even such good workmen as Radish did not shun this rough and
tiresome work.   In short trousers, showing his lean, muscular
legs, he used to prowl over the roof like a stork, and I used to
hear him sigh wearily as he worked his brush:

'Woe, woe to us, miserable sinners!'

He could walk as easily on a roof as on the ground.   In spite
of his looking so ill and pale and corpse-like, his agility was
extraordinary; like any young man he would paint the cupola
and the top of the church without scaffolding, using only ladders
and a rope, and it was queer and strange when, standing there,
far above the ground, he would rise to his full height and cry
to the world at large:

'Grubs eat grass, rust eats iron, lies devour the soul!'

Or, thinking of something, he would suddenly answer his own
thought:

'Anything may happen!   Anything may happen!'

When I went home from work all the people sitting outside
their doors, the shop assistants, boys, and their masters, used to
shout after me and jeer spitefully, and at first it seemed mon-
strous and distressed me greatly.

'Little Profit,' they used to shout.   'House-painter!   Yellow
ochre!'

And no one treated me so unmercifully as those who had only
just risen above the people and had quite recently had to work
for their living.   Once in the market-place as I passed the iron-
monger's a can of water was spilled over me as if by accident,
and once a stick was thrown at me.   And once a fishmonger, a

grey-haired old man, stood in my way and looked at me morosely and said:

'It isn't you I'm sorry for, you fool, it's your father.'

And when my acquaintances met me they got confused. Some regarded me as a queer fish and a fool, and they were sorry for me; others did not know how to treat me and it was difficult to understand them. Once, in the daytime, in one of the streets off Great Gentry Street, I met Aniuta Blagovo. I was on my way to my work and was carrying two long brushes and a pot of paint. When she recognized me, Aniuta blushed.

'Please do not acknowledge me in the street,' she said nervously, sternly, in a trembling voice, without offering to shake hands with me, and tears suddenly gleamed in her eyes. 'If you must be like this, then, so—so be it, but please avoid me in public!'

I had left Great Gentry Street and was living in a suburb, called Makarikha, with my nurse Karpovna, a good-natured but gloomy old woman who was always looking for evil, and was frightened by her dreams, and saw omens and ill in the bees and wasps which flew into her room. And in her opinion my having become a working man boded no good.

'You are lost!' she said mournfully, shaking her head. 'Lost!'

With her in her little house lived her adopted son, Prokofyi, a butcher, a huge, clumsy fellow, of about thirty, with ginger hair and scrubby moustache. When he met me in the hall, he would silently and respectfully make way for me, and when he was drunk he would salute me with his whole hand. In the evenings he used to have supper, and through the wooden partition I could hear him snorting and snuffling as he drank glass after glass.

'Mother,' he would say in an undertone.

'Well?' Karpovna would reply. She was passionately fond of him. 'What is it, my son?'

'I'll do you a favour, mother. I'll feed you in your old age in this vale of tears, and when you die I'll bury you at my own expense. So I say and so I'll do.'

I used to get up every day before sunrise and go to bed early. We painters ate heavily and slept soundly, and only during the night would we have any excitement. I never quarrelled with my comrades. All day long there was a ceaseless stream of abuse, cursing and hearty good wishes, as, for instance, that one's eyes should burst, or that one might be carried off by cholera, but, all the same, among ourselves we were very friendly.

The men suspected me of being a religious crank and used to laugh at me good-naturedly, saying that even my own father denounced me, and they used to say that they very seldom went to church and that many of them had not been to confession for ten years, and they justified their laxness by saying that a decorator is among men like a jackdaw among birds.

My mates respected me and regarded me with esteem; they evidently liked my not drinking or smoking, and leading a quiet, steady life. They were only rather disagreeably surprised at my not stealing the oil, or going with them to ask our employers for a drink. The stealing of the employers' oil and paint was a custom with house-painters, and was not regarded as theft, and it was remarkable that even so honest a man as Radish would always come away from work with some white lead and oil. And even respectable old men who had their own houses in Makarikha were not ashamed to ask for tips, and when the men, at the beginning or end of a job, made up to some vulgar fool and thanked him humbly for a few pence, I used to feel sick and sorry.

With the customers they behaved like sly courtiers, and almost every day I was reminded of Shakespeare's Polonius.

'There will probably be rain,' a customer would say, staring at the sky.

'It is sure to rain,' the painters would agree.

'But the clouds aren't rain-clouds. Perhaps it won't rain.'

'No, sir. It won't rain. It won't rain, sure.'

Behind their backs they generally regarded the customers ironically, and when, for instance, they saw a gentleman sitting on his balcony with a newspaper, they would say:

'He reads newspapers, but he has nothing to eat.'

I never visited my people. When I returned from work I often found short, disturbing notes from my sister about my father; how he was very absent-minded at dinner, and then slipped away and locked himself in his study and did not come out for a long time. Such news upset me. I could not sleep, and I would go sometimes at night and walk along Great Gentry Street by our house, and look up at the dark windows, and try to guess if all was well within. On Sundays my sister would come to see me, but by stealth, as though she came not to see me, but our nurse. And if she came into my room she would look pale, with her eyes red, and at once she would begin to weep.

'Father cannot bear it much longer,' she would say. 'If, as

God forbid, something were to happen to him, it would be on your conscience all your life. It is awful, Misail! For mother's sake I implore you to mend your ways.'

'My dear sister,' I replied, 'how can I reform when I am convinced that I am acting according to my conscience? Do try to understand me!'

'I know you are obeying your conscience, but it ought to be possible to do so without hurting anybody.'

'Oh, saints above!' the old woman would sigh behind the door. 'You are lost. There will be a misfortune, my dear. It is bound to come.'

VI

One Sunday, Doctor Blagavo came to see me unexpectedly. He was wearing a white summer uniform over a silk shirt, and high glacé boots.

'I came to see you!' he began, gripping my hand in his hearty, undergraduate fashion. 'I hear of you every day and I have long intended to go and see you to have a heart-to-heart, as they say. Things are awfully boring in the town; there is not a living soul worth talking to. How hot it is, by Jove!' he went on, taking off his tunic and standing in his silk shirt. 'My dear fellow, let us have a talk.'

I was feeling bored and longing for other society than that of the decorators. I was really glad to see him.

'To begin with,' he said, sitting on my bed, 'I sympathize with you heartily, and I have a profound respect for your present way of living. In the town you are misunderstood and there is nobody to understand you, because, as you know, it is full of Gogolian pig-faces. But I guessed what you were at the picnic. You are a noble soul, an honest, high-minded man! I respect you and think it an honour to shake hands with you. To change your life so abruptly and suddenly as you did, you must have passed through a most trying spiritual process, and to go on with it now, to live scrupulously by your convictions, you must have to toil incessantly both in mind and in heart. Now, please tell me, don't you think that if you spent all this force of will, intensity, and power on something else, like trying to be a great scholar or an artist, your life would be both wider and deeper, and altogether more productive?'

We talked, and when we came to speak of physical labour, I expressed this idea: that it was necessary that the strong should not enslave the weak, and that the minority should not be parasites on the majority, always sucking up the finest sap, i.e. it was necessary that all without exception—the strong and the weak, the rich and the poor—should share equally in the struggle for existence, every man for himself, and in that respect there was no better means of levelling than physical labour and compulsory service for all.

'You think, then,' said the doctor, 'that all, without exception, should be employed in physical labour?'

'Yes.'

'But don't you think that if everybody, including the best people, thinkers and men of science, were to take part in the struggle for existence, each man for himself, and took to breaking stones and painting roofs, it would be a serious menace to progress?'

'Where is the danger?' I asked. 'Progress consists in deeds of love, in the fulfilment of the moral law. If you enslave no one, and are a burden upon no one, what further progress do you want?'

'But look here!' said Blagovo, suddenly losing his temper and getting up. 'I say! If a snail in its shell is engaged in self-perfection in obedience to the moral law—would you call that progress?'

'But why?' I was nettled. 'If you don't make your neighbours feed you, clothe you, carry you, defend you from your enemies, surely, that *is* progress amidst a life resting on slavery. My view is that that is the most real and, perhaps, the only possible, the only progress necessary.'

'The limits of universal progress, which is common to all men, are in infinity, and it seems to me strange to talk of a "possible" progress limited by our needs and temporal conceptions.'

'If the limits of progress are in infinity, as you say, then it means that its goal is indefinite,' I said. 'Think of living without knowing definitely what for!'

'Why not? Your "not knowing" is not so boring as your "knowing." I am climbing a ladder which is called progress, civilization, culture. I go on and on, not knowing definitely where I am going to, but surely it is worth while living for the sake of the wonderful ladder alone. And you know exactly what you are living for—that some should not enslave others, that the artist and the man who mixes his colours for him should dine equally well. But that is the *bourgeois*, kitchen side of life, and isn't it disgusting only to live for that? If some insects devour others, devil take them, let them! We need not think of them, they will perish and rot, however you save them from slavery—we must think of that great millennium which awaits all mankind in the distant future.'

Blagovo argued hotly with me, but it was noticeable that he was disturbed by some outside thought.

'Your sister is not coming,' he said, consulting his watch. 'Yesterday she was at our house and said she was going to see you. You go on talking about slavery, slavery,' he went on, 'but it is a special question, and all these questions are solved by mankind gradually.'

We began to talk of evolution. I said that every man decides the question of good and evil for himself, and does not wait for mankind to solve the question by virtue of gradual development. Besides, evolution is a stick with two ends. Side by side with the gradual development of humanitarian ideas, there is the gradual growth of ideas of a different kind. Serfdom is past, and capitalism is growing. And with ideas of liberation at their height the majority, just as in the days of Batay, feeds, clothes, and defends the minority; and is left hungry, naked, and defenceless. The state of things harmonizes beautifully with all your tendencies and movements, because the art of enslaving is also being gradually developed. We no longer flog our servants in the stables, but we give slavery more refined forms; at any rate, we are able to justify it in each separate case. Ideas remain ideas with us, but if we could, now, at the end of the nineteenth century, throw upon the working classes all our most unpleasant physiological functions, we should do so, and, of course, we should justify ourselves by saying that if the best people, thinkers and great scholars, had to waste their time on such functions, progress would be in serious jeopardy.

Just then my sister entered. When she saw the doctor, she was flurried and excited, and at once began to say that it was time for her to go home to her father.

'Cleopatra Alexeyevna,' said Blagovo earnestly, laying his hands on his heart, 'what will happen to your father if you spend half an hour with your brother and me?'

He was a simple kind of man and could communicate his cheerfulness to others. My sister thought for a minute and began to laugh, and suddenly got very happy, suddenly, unexpectedly, just as she did at the picnic. We went out into the fields and lay on the grass, and went on with our conversation and looked at the town, where all the windows facing the west looked golden in the setting sun.

After that Blagovo appeared every time my sister came to see me, and they always greeted each other as though their meeting was unexpected. My sister used to listen while the doctor and I argued, and her face was always joyful and rapturous, admiring and curious, and it seemed to me that a new world was slowly being discovered before her eyes, a world which she had not seen before even in her dreams, which now she was trying to divine; when the doctor was not there she was quiet and sad, and if, as she sat on my bed, she sometimes wept, it was for reasons of which she did not speak.

In August Radish gave us orders to go to the railway. A couple of days before we were 'driven' out of town, my father came to see me. He sat down and, without looking at me, slowly wiped his red face, then took out of his pocket our local paper and read out with deliberate emphasis on each word that a schoolfellow of my own age, the son of the director of the State Bank, had been appointed chief clerk of the Court of the Exchequer.

'And now, look at yourself,' he said, folding up the newspaper. 'You are a beggar, a vagabond, a scoundrel! Even the working class people and peasants get education to make themselves decent people, while you, a Polozniev, with famous, noble ancestors, go wallowing in the mire! But I did not come here to talk to you. I have given you up already.' He went on in a choking voice, as he stood up: 'I came here to find out where your sister is, you scoundrel! She left me after dinner. It is now past seven o'clock and she is not in. She has been going out lately without telling me, and she has been disrespectful— and I see your filthy, abominable influence at work. Where is she?'

He had in his hands the familiar umbrella, and I was already taken aback, and I stood stiff and erect, like a schoolboy, waiting for my father to thrash me, but he saw the glance I cast at the umbrella and this probably checked him.

'Live as you like!' he said. 'My blessing is gone from you.'

'Good God!' muttered my old nurse behind the door. 'You are lost. Oh! my heart feels some misfortune coming. I can feel it.'

I went to work on the railway. During the whole of August there was wind and rain. It was damp and cold; the corn had now been gathered in the fields, and on the big farms where the reaping was done with machines, the wheat lay not in sheaves, but in heaps; and I remember how those melancholy heaps grew

darker and darker every day, and the grain sprouted. It was
hard work; the pouring rain spoiled everything that we succeeded in finishing. We were not allowed either to live or to
sleep in the station buildings and had to take shelter in dirty,
damp, mud huts where the 'railies' had lived during the summer,
and at night I could not sleep from the cold and the bugs
crawling over my face and hands. And when we were working
near the bridges, then the 'railies' used to come out in a crowd
to fight the painters—which they regarded as sport. They used
to thrash us, steal our brushes, and to infuriate us and provoke
us to a fight they used to spoil our work, as when they smeared
the signal-boxes with green paint. To add to all our miseries
Radish began to pay us very irregularly. All the painting on
the line was given to one contractor, who subcontracted with
another, and he again with Radish, stipulating for twenty per
cent commission. The job itself was unprofitable; then came
the rains; time was wasted; we did not work and Radish had to
pay his men every day. The starving painters nearly came to
blows with him, called him a swindler, a blood-sucker, a Judas,
and he, poor man, sighed and in despair raised his hands to the
heavens and was continually going to Mrs Cheprakov to borrow
money.

VII

Came the rainy, muddy, dark autumn, bringing a slack time,
and I used to sit at home three days in the week without work,
or did various jobs outside painting; such as digging earth for
ballast for twenty copecks a day. Doctor Blagovo had gone to
Petersburg. My sister did not come to see me. Radish lay at
home ill, expecting to die every day.

And my mood was also autumnal; perhaps because when I
became a working man I saw only the seamy side of the life of
our town, and every day made fresh discoveries which brought
me to despair. My fellow townsmen, both those of whom I had
had a low opinion before, and those whom I had thought fairly
decent, now seemed to me base, cruel, and up to any dirty trick.
We poor people were tricked and cheated in the accounts, kept
waiting for hours in cold passages or in the kitchen, and we
were insulted and uncivilly treated. In the autumn I had to
paper the library and two rooms at the club. I was paid seven
copecks a piece, but was told to give a receipt for twelve copecks,
and when I refused to do it, a respectable gentleman in gold
spectacles, one of the stewards of the club, said to me:

'If you say another word, you scoundrel, I'll knock you down.'

And when a servant whispered to him that I was the son of Polozniev, the architect, then he got flustered and blushed, but he recovered himself at once and said:

'Damn him.'

In the shops we working men were sold bad meat, musty flour, and coarse tea. In church we were jostled by the police, and in the hospitals we were mulcted by the assistants and nurses, and if we could not give them bribes through poverty, we were given food in dirty dishes. In the post office the lowest official considered it his duty to treat us as animals and to shout rudely and insolently: 'Wait! Don't you come pushing your way in here!' Even the dogs, even they were hostile to us and hurled themselves at us with a peculiar malignancy. But what struck me most of all in my new position was the entire lack of justice, what the people call 'forgetting God.' Rarely a day went by without some swindle. The shopkeeper who sold us oil, the contractor, the workmen, the customers themselves, all cheated. It was an understood thing that our rights were never considered, and we always had to pay for the money we had earned, going with our hats off to the back door.

I was paper-hanging in one of the club-rooms, next the library, when, one evening as I was on the point of leaving, Dolzhikov's daughter came into the room carrying a bundle of books.

I bowed to her.

'Ah! How are you?' she said, recognizing me at once and holding out her hand. 'I am very glad to see you.'

She smiled and looked with a curious puzzled expression at my blouse and the pail of paste and the papers lying on the floor; I was embarrassed and she also felt awkward.

'Excuse my staring at you,' she said. 'I have heard so much about you. Especially from Doctor Blagovo. He is enthusiastic about you. I have met your sister; she is a dear, sympathetic girl, but I could not make her see that there is nothing awful in your simple life. On the contrary, you are the most interesting man in the town.'

Once more she glanced at the pail of paste and the paper and said:

'I asked Doctor Blagovo to bring us together, but he either forgot or had no time. However, we have met now. I should be very pleased if you would call on me. I do so want to have a talk. I am a simple person,' she said, holding out her hand,

'and I hope you will come and see me without ceremony. My father is away, in Petersburg.'

She went into the reading-room, with her dress rustling, and for a long time after I got home I could not sleep.

During that autumn some kind soul, wishing to relieve my existence, sent me from time to time presents of tea and lemons, or biscuits, or roast game. Karpovna said the presents were brought by a soldier, though from whom she did not know; and the soldier used to ask if I was well, if I had dinner every day, and if I had warm clothes. When the frost began the soldier came while I was out and brought a soft knitted scarf, which gave out a soft, hardly perceptible scent, and I guessed who my good fairy had been. For the scarf smelled of lily of the valley, Aniuta Blagovo's favourite scent.

Toward winter there was more work and things became more cheerful. Radish came to life again and we worked together in the cemetery church, where we scraped the holy shrine for gilding. It was a clean, quiet, and, as our mates said, a specially good job. We could do a great deal in one day, and so time passed quickly, imperceptibly. There was no swearing, nor laughing, nor loud altercations. The place compelled quiet and decency, and disposed one for tranquil, serious thoughts. Absorbed in our work, we stood or sat immovably, like statues; there was a dead silence, very proper to a cemetery, so that if a tool fell down, or the oil in the lamp spluttered, the sound would be loud and startling, and we would turn to see what it was. After a long silence one would hear a humming like that of a swarm of bees; in the porch, in an undertone, the funeral service was being read over a dead baby; or a painter painting a moon surrounded with stars on the cupola would begin to whistle quietly, and remembering suddenly that he was in a church, would stop; or Radish would sigh at his own thoughts: 'Anything may happen! Anything may happen!' or above our heads there would be the slow, mournful tolling of a bell, and the painters would say it must be a rich man being brought to the church. . . .

The days I spent in the peace of the little church, and during the evenings I played billiards, or went to the gallery of the theatre in the new serge suit I had bought with my own hard-earned money. They were already beginning plays and concerts at the Azhoguins', and Radish did the scenery by himself. He told me about the plays and *tableaux vivants* at the Azho-guins', and I listened to him enviously. I had a great longing to take part in the rehearsals, but I dared not go to the Azhoguins'.

A week before Christmas Doctor Blagovo arrived, and we resumed our arguments and played billiards in the evenings. When he played billiards he used to take off his coat, and unfasten his shirt at the neck, and generally try to look like a debauchee. He drank a little, but rowdily, and managed to spend in a cheap tavern like the Volga as much as twenty roubles in an evening.

Once more my sister came to see me, and when they met they expressed surprise, but I could see by her happy, guilty face that these meetings were not accidental. One evening when we were playing billiards the doctor said to me:

'I say, why don't you call on Miss Dolzhikov? You don't know Maria Victorovna. She is a clever, charming, simple creature.'

I told him how her father, the engineer, had received me in the spring.

'Nonsense!' laughed the doctor. 'The engineer is one thing and she is another. Really, my good fellow, you mustn't offend her. Go and see her some time. Let us go to-morrow evening. Will you?'

He persuaded me. Next evening I donned my serge suit and with some perturbation set out to call on Miss Dolzhikov. The footman did not seem to me so haughty and formidable, or the furniture so oppressive, as on the morning when I had come to ask for work. Maria Victorovna was expecting me and greeted me as an old friend and gave my hand a warm, friendly grip. She was wearing a grey dress with wide sleeves, and had her hair done in the style which, when it became the fashion a year later in our town, was called 'dog's ears.' The hair was combed back over the ears, and it made Maria Victorovna's face look broader, and she looked very like her father, whose face was broad and red and rather like a coachman's. She was handsome and elegant, but not young; about thirty to judge by her appearance, though she was not more than twenty-five.

'Dear doctor!' she said, making me sit down. 'How grateful I am to him. But for him, you would not have come. I am bored to death! My father has gone and left me alone, and I do not know what to do with myself.'

Then she began to ask where I was working, how much I got, and where I lived.

'Do you only spend what you earn on yourself?' she asked.

'Yes.'

'You are a happy man,' she replied. 'All the evil in life, it seems to me, comes from boredom and idleness, and spiritual emptiness, which are inevitable when one lives at other people's expense. Don't think I'm showing off. I mean it sincerely. It is dull and unpleasant to be rich. Win friends by just riches, they say, because as a rule there is and can be no such thing as just riches.'

She looked at the furniture with a serious, cold expression, as though she was making an inventory of it, and went on:

'Ease and comfort possess a magic power. Little by little they seduce even strong-willed people. Father and I used to live poorly and simply, and now you see how we live. Isn't it strange?' she said with a shrug. 'We spend twenty thousand roubles a year! In the provinces!'

'Ease and comfort must not be regarded as the inevitable privilege of capital and education,' I said. 'It seems to me possible to unite the comforts of life with work, however hard and dirty it may be. Your father is rich, but, as he says, he used to be a mechanic, and just a lubricator.'

She smiled and shook her head doubtfully.

'Papa sometimes eats *tiurya*,' she said, 'but only out of caprice.'

A bell rang and she got up.

'The rich and the educated ought to work like the rest,' she went on, 'and if there is to be any comfort, it should be accessible to all. There should be no privileges. However, that's enough philosophy. Tell me something cheerful. Tell me about the painters. What are they like? Funny?'

The doctor came. I began to talk about the painters, but, being unused to it, I felt awkward and talked solemnly and ponderously like an ethnographer. The doctor also told a few stories about working people. He rocked to and fro and cried and fell on his knees, and when he was depicting a drunkard, lay flat on the floor. It was as good as a play, and Maria Victorovna laughed until she cried. Then he played the piano and sang in his high-pitched tenor, and Maria Victorovna stood by him and told him what to sing and corrected him when he made a mistake.

'I hear you sing, too,' said I.

'Too?' cried the doctor. 'She is a wonderful singer, an artist, and you say—too? Careful, careful!'

'I used to study seriously,' she replied, 'but I have given it up now.'

She sat on a low stool and told us about her life in Petersburg, and imitated famous singers, mimicking their voices and mannerisms; then she sketched the doctor and myself in her album, not very well, but both were good likenesses. She laughed and made jokes and funny faces, and this suited her better than talking about unjust riches, and it seemed to me that what she had said about 'riches and comfort' came not from herself, but was just mimicry. She was an admirable comedian. I compared her mentally with the girls of our town, and not even the beautiful, serious Aniuta Blagovo could stand up against her; the difference was as vast as that between a wild and a garden rose.

We stayed to supper. The doctor and Maria Victorovna drank red wine, champagne, and coffee with cognac; they touched glasses and drank to friendship, to wit, to progress, to freedom, and never got drunk, but went rather red and laughed for no reason until they cried. To avoid being out of it I, too, drank red wine.

'People with talent and with gifted natures,' said Miss Dolzhikov, 'know how to live and go their own way; but ordinary people like myself know nothing and can do nothing by themselves; there is nothing for them but to find some deep social current and let themselves by borne by it.'

'Is it possible to find that which does not exist?' asked the doctor.

'It doesn't exist because we don't see it.'

'Is that so? Social currents are the invention of modern literature. They don't exist here.'

A discussion began.

'We have no profound social movements; nor have we had them,' said the doctor. 'Modern literature has invented a lot of things, and modern literature invented intellectual working men in village life, but go through all our villages and you will only find Mr Cheeky Snout in a jacket or black frock coat, who will make four mistakes in the word "one." Civilized life has not begun with us yet. We have the same savagery, the same slavery, the same triviality as we had five hundred years ago. Movements, currents—all that is so wretched and puerile mixed up with such vulgar, catch-penny interests—and one just cannot take it seriously. You may think you have discovered a large social movement, and you may follow it and devote your life in the modern fashion to such problems as the liberation of vermin from slavery, or the abolition of meat cutlets—

and I congratulate you, madam. But we have to learn, learn, learn, and there will be plenty of time for social movements; we are not up to them yet, and upon my soul, we don't understand anything at all about them.'

'You don't understand, but I do,' said Maria Victorovna. 'Good heavens! What a bore you are to-night.'

'It is our business to learn and learn, to try and accumulate as much knowledge as possible, because serious social movements come where there is knowledge, and the future happiness of mankind lies in science. Here's to science!'

'One thing is certain. Life must somehow be arranged differently,' said Maria Victorovna, after some silence and deep thought, 'and life as it has been up to now is worthless. Don't let us talk about it.'

When we left her the cathedral clock struck two.

'Did you like her?' asked the doctor. 'Isn't she a dear girl?'

We had dinner at Maria Victorovna's on Christmas Day, and then we went to see her every day during the holidays. There was nobody besides ourselves, and she was right when she said she had no friends in the town but the doctor and me. We spent most of the time talking, and sometimes the doctor would bring a book or a magazine and read aloud. After all, he was the first cultivated man I had met. I could not tell if he knew much, but he was always generous with his knowledge because he wished others to know too. When he talked about medicine, he was not like any of our local doctors, but he made a new and singular impression, and it seemed to me that if he had wished he could have become a genuine scientist. And perhaps he was the only person at that time who had any real influence over me. Meeting him and reading the books he gave me, I began gradually to feel a need for knowledge to inspire the tedium of my work. It seemed strange to me that I had not known before such things as that the whole world consisted of sixty elements. I did not know what oil of paint was, and that I could have got on without knowing these things. My acquaintance with the doctor raised me morally too. I used to argue with him, and though I usually stuck to my opinion, yet, through him, I came gradually to perceive that everything was not clear to me, and I tried to cultivate convictions as definite as possible so that the promptings of my conscience should be precise and have nothing vague about them. Nevertheless, educated and fine as he was, far and away the best man in the town, he was by no means perfect. There was something rather rude and priggish in his ways and in his trick of dragging talk down to discussion, and when he took off his coat and sat in his shirt and gave the footman a tip, it always seemed to me that culture was just a part of him, with the rest untamed Tartar.

After the holidays he left once more for Petersburg. He went in the morning and after dinner my sister came to see me. Without taking off her furs, she sat silent, very pale, staring in front of her. She began to shiver and seemed to be fighting against some illness.

'You must have caught a cold,' I said.

Her eyes filled with tears. She rose and went to Karpovna without a word to me, as though I had offended her. And a little later I heard her speaking in a tone of bitter reproach.

'Nurse, what have I been living for, up to now? What for? Tell me; haven't I wasted my youth? During the best years I have had nothing but making up accounts, pouring out tea, counting the copecks, entertaining guests, without a thought that there was anything better in the world! Nurse, try to understand me, I too have human desires and I want to live and they have made a housekeeper of me. It is awful, awful!'

She flung her keys against the door and they fell with a clatter in my room. They were the keys of the sideboard, the larder, the cellar, and the tea-chest—the keys my mother used to carry.

'Oh! Oh! Saints above!' cried my old nurse in terror. 'The blessed saints!'

When she left, my sister came into my room for her keys and said:

'Forgive me. Something strange has been going on in me lately.'

VIII

One evening when I came home late from Maria Victorovna's I found a young policeman in a new uniform in my room; he was sitting by the table reading.

'At last!' he said, getting up and stretching himself. 'This is the third time I have been to see you. The governor has ordered you to go and see him to-morrow at nine o'clock sharp. Don't be late.'

He made me give him a written promise to comply with his Excellency's orders and went away. This policeman's visit and the unexpected invitation to see the governor had a most depressing effect on me. From my early childhood I have had

a dread of gendarmes, police, legal officials, and I was tormented
with anxiety as though I had really committed a crime, and I
could not sleep. Nurse and Prokofyi were also upset and could
not sleep. And, to make things worse, nurse had an earache,
and moaned and more than once screamed out. Hearing I
could not sleep Prokofyi came quietly into my room with a little
lamp and sat by the table.

'You should have a drop of pepper-brandy,' he said after
some thought. 'In this vale of tears things go on all right
when you take a drop. And if mother had some pepper-brandy
poured into her ear she would be much better.'

About three he got ready to go to the slaughter-house to
fetch some meat. I knew I should not sleep until morning,
and to use up the time until nine, I went with him. We walked
with a lantern, and his boy Nicolka, who was about thirteen, and
had blue spots on his face and an expression like a murderer's,
drove behind us in a sledge, urging the horse on with hoarse cries.

'You will probably be punished at the governor's,' said
Prokofyi as we walked. 'There is a governor's rank, and an
archimandrite's rank, and an officer's rank, and a doctor's rank,
and every profession has its own rank. You don't keep to yours
and they won't allow it.'

The slaughter-house stood behind the cemetery, and till then
I had only seen it at a distance. It consisted of three dark sheds
surrounded by a grey fence, from which, when the wind was in
that direction in summer, there came an overpowering stench.
Now, as I entered the yard, I could not see the sheds in the darkness; I groped through horses and sledges, both empty and laden
with meat; and there were men walking about with lanterns and
swearing disgustingly. Prokofyi and Nicolka swore as filthily
and there was a continuous hum from the swearing and coughing
and the neighing of the horses.

The place smelled of corpses and offal, the snow was thawing
and already mixed with mud, and in the darkness it seemed to
me that I was walking through a pool of blood.

When we had filled the sledge with meat, we went to the
butcher's shop in the market-place. Day was beginning to
dawn. One after another the cooks came with baskets, and old
women in mantles. With an axe in his hand, wearing a white,
blood-stained apron, Prokofyi swore terrifically and crossed
himself, turning toward the church, and shouted so loud that
he could be heard all over the market, vowing that he sold his
meat at cost price and even at a loss. He cheated in weighing

and reckoning, the cooks saw it, but, dazed by his shouting, they did not protest, but only called him a gallows-bird.

Raising and dropping his formidable axe, he assumed picturesque attitudes and constantly uttered the sound 'Hak!' with a furious expression, and I was really afraid of his cutting off someone's head or hand.

I stayed in the butcher's shop the whole morning, and when at last I went to the governor's my fur coat smelled of meat and blood. My state of mind would have been appropriate for an encounter with a bear, armed with no more than a staff. I remember a long staircase with a striped carpet, and a young official in a frock coat with shining buttons, who silently indicated the door with both hands and went in to announce me. I entered the hall, where the furniture was most luxurious, but cold and tasteless, giving a most unpleasant impression—the tall, narrow pier-glasses, and the bright, yellow hangings over the windows; one could see that, though governors changed, the furniture remained the same. The young official again pointed with both hands to the door and I went toward a large, green table, by which stood a general with the Order of Vladimir at his neck.

'Mr Polozniev,' he began, holding a letter in his hand and opening his mouth wide so that it made a round O. 'I asked you to come to say this to you: Your esteemed father has applied verbally and in writing to the provincial marshal of nobility, to have you summoned and made to see the incongruity of your conduct with the title of nobleman which you have the honour to bear. His Excellency Alexander Pavlovich, justly thinking that your conduct may be subversive, and finding that persuasion may not be sufficient, without serious intervention on the part of the authorities, has given me his decision as to your case, and I agree with him.'

He said this quietly, respectfully, standing erect as if I was his superior, and his expression was not at all severe. He had a flabby, tired face, covered with wrinkles, with pouches under his eyes; his hair was dyed, and it was hard to guess his age from his appearance—fifty or sixty.

'I hope,' he went on, 'that you will appreciate Alexander Pavlovich's delicacy in applying to me, not officially, but privately. I have invited you unofficially not as a governor, but as a sincere admirer of your father's. And I ask you to change your conduct and to return to the duties proper to your rank, or, to avoid the evil effects of your example, to go to some other place where you are not known and where you may do what you like. Otherwise I shall have to resort to extreme measures.'

For half a minute he stood in silence staring at me open-mouthed.

'Are you a vegetarian?' he asked.

'No, Your Excellency, I eat meat.'

He sat down and took up a document, and I bowed and left.

It was not worth while going to work before dinner. I went home and tried to sleep, but could not because of the unpleasant, sickly feeling from the slaughter-house and my conversation with the governor. And so I dragged through till the evening and then, feeling gloomy and out of sorts, I went to see Maria Victorovna. I told her about my visit to the governor and she looked at me in bewilderment, as if she did not believe me, and suddenly she began to laugh merrily, heartily, stridently, as only good-natured, light-hearted people can.

'If I were to tell this in Petersburg!' she cried, nearly dropping with laughter, bending over the table. 'If I could tell them in Petersburg!'

IX

Now we saw each other often, sometimes twice a day. Almost every day, after dinner, she drove up to the cemetery and, as she waited for me, read the inscriptions on the crosses and monuments. Sometimes she came into the church and stood by my side and watched me working. The silence, the simple industry of the painters and gilders, Radish's good sense, and the fact that outwardly I was no different from the other artisans and worked as they did, in a waistcoat and old shoes, and that they addressed me familiarly—were new to her, and she was moved by it all. Once in her presence a painter who was working, at a door on the roof, called down to me:

'Misail, fetch me the white lead.'

I fetched him the white lead and as I came down the scaffolding she was moved to tears and looked at me and smiled.

'What a dear you are!' she said.

I have always remembered how when I was a child a green parrot got out of its cage in one of the rich people's houses and wandered about the town for a whole month, flying from one garden to another, homeless and lonely. And Maria Victorovna reminded me of the bird.

'Except to the cemetery,' she said with a laugh, 'I have

absolutely nowhere to go. The town bores me to tears. People read, sing, and twitter at the Azhoguins', but I cannot bear them lately. Your sister is shy, Miss Blagovo for some reason hates me. I don't like the theatre. What can I do with myself?'

When I was at her house I smelled of paint and turpentine, and my hands were stained. She liked that. She wanted me to come to her in my ordinary working clothes; but I felt awkward in them in her drawing-room, and as if I were in uniform, and so I always wore my new serge suit. She did not like that.

'You must confess,' she said once, 'that you have not got used to your new role. A working man's suit makes you feel awkward and embarrassed. Tell me, isn't it because you are not sure of yourself and are unsatisfied? Does this work you have chosen, this painting of yours, really satisfy you?' she asked merrily. 'I know paint makes things look nicer and wear better, but the things themselves belong to the rich and after all they are a luxury. Besides you have said more than once that everybody should earn his living with his own hands and you earn money, not bread. Why don't you keep to the exact meaning of what you say? You must earn bread, real bread, you must plough, sow, reap, thrash, or do something which has to do directly with agriculture, such as keeping cows, digging, or building houses. . . .'

She opened a handsome bookcase which stood by the writing-table and said:

'I'm telling you all this because I'm going to let you into my secret. *Voilà!* This is my agricultural library. Here are books on arable land, vegetable-gardens, orchard-keeping, cattle-keeping, bee-keeping: I read them eagerly and have studied the theory of everything thoroughly. It is my dream to go to Dubechnia as soon as March begins. It is wonderful there, amazing; isn't it? The first year I shall only be learning the work and getting used to it, and in the second year I shall begin to work thoroughly, without sparing myself. My father promised to give me Dubechnia as a present, and I am to do anything I like with it.'

She blushed and with mingled laughter and tears she dreamed aloud of her life at Dubechnia and how absorbing it would be. And I envied her. March would soon be here. The days were drawing out, and in the bright sunny afternoons the snow dripped from the roofs, and the smell of spring was in the air. I too longed for the country.

And when she said she was going to live at Dubechnia, I saw at once that I should be left alone in the town, and I felt jealous of the bookcase with her books about farming. I knew and cared nothing about farming and I was on the point of telling her that agriculture was work for slaves, but I recollected that my father had once said something of the sort and I held my peace.

Lent began. The engineer, Victor Ivanich, came home from Petersburg. I had begun to forget his existence. He came unexpectedly, not even sending a telegram. When I went there as usual in the evening, he was walking up and down the drawing-room, after a bath, with his hair cut, looking ten years younger, and talking. His daughter was kneeling by his trunks and taking out boxes, bottles, books, and handing them to Pavel, the footman. When I saw the engineer, I involuntarily stepped back and he held out both his hands and smiled and showed his strong, white, cab-driver's teeth.

'Here he is! Here he is! I'm very pleased to see you, Mr House-painter! Maria told me all about you and sang your praises. I quite understand you and heartily approve.' He took me by the arm and went on: 'It is much cleverer and more honest to be a decent workman than to spoil State paper and to wear a cockade. I myself worked with my hands in Belgium. I was an engine-driver for five years. . . .'

He was wearing a short jacket and comfortable slippers, and he shuffled along like a gouty man, waving and rubbing his hands; humming and buzzing and shrugging with pleasure at being at home again with his favourite shower-bath.

'There's no denying,' he said at supper, 'there's no denying that you are kind, sympathetic people, but somehow as soon as you gentlefolk take on manual labour or try to save the peasants, you reduce it all to sectarianism. You are a sectarian. You don't drink vodka. What is that but sectarianism?'

To please him I drank vodka. I drank wine, too. We ate cheese, sausages, pastries, pickles, and all kinds of dainties that the engineer had brought with him, and we sampled wines sent from abroad during his absence. They were excellent. For some reason the engineer had wines and cigars sent from abroad —duty free; somebody sent him caviare and sturgeon gratis; he did not pay rent for his house because his landlord supplied the railway with kerosene, and generally he and his daughter gave me the impression of having all the best things in the world at their service free of charge.

I went on visiting them, but with less pleasure than before. The engineer oppressed me and I felt cramped in his presence. I could not endure his clear, innocent eyes; his opinions bored me and were offensive to me, and I was distressed by the recollection that I had so recently been subordinate to this ruddy, well-fed man, and that he had been mercilessly rude to me. True he would put his arm round my waist and slap me kindly on the shoulder and approve of my way of living, but I felt that he despised my nullity just as much as before and only suffered me to please his daughter, and I could no longer laugh and talk easily, and I thought myself ill-mannered, and all the time was expecting him to call me Panteley as he did his footman Pavel. How my provincial, working man's pride rose up against him! I, a working man, a painter, going every day to the house of rich strangers, whom the whole town regarded as foreigners, and drinking their expensive wines and outlandish dishes! I could not reconcile this with my conscience. When I went to see them I sternly avoided those whom I met on the way, and looked askance at them like a real sectarian, and when I left the engineer's house I was ashamed of feeling so well fed.

But chiefly I was afraid of falling in love. Whether walking in the street, or working, or talking to my mates, I thought all the time of going to Maria Victorovna's in the evening, and always had her voice, her laughter, her movements with me. And always as I got ready to go to her, I would stand for a long time in front of the cracked mirror tying my necktie; my serge suit seemed horrible to me, and I suffered, but at the same time, despised myself for feeling so small. When she called to me from another room to say that she was not dressed yet and to ask me to wait a bit, and I could hear her dressing, I was agitated and felt as though the floor was sinking under me. And when I saw a woman in the street, even at a distance, I fell to comparing her figure with hers, and it seemed to me that all our women and girls were vulgar, absurdly dressed, and without manners; and such comparisons roused in me a feeling of pride; Maria Victorovna was better than all of them. And at night I dreamed of her and myself.

Once at supper the engineer and I ate a whole lobster. When I reached home I remembered that the engineer had twice called me 'my dear fellow,' and I thought that they treated me as they might have done a big, unhappy dog, separated from his master, and that they were amusing themselves with me, and that they would order me away like a dog when they were bored with me. I began to feel ashamed and hurt; went to the point of tears, as though I had been insulted, and, raising my eyes to the heavens, I vowed to put an end to it all.

Next day I did not go to the Dolzhikovs'. Late at night, when it was quite dark and pouring with rain, I walked up and down Great Gentry Street, looking at the windows. At the Azhoguins' everybody was asleep and the only light was in one of the top windows; old Mrs Azhoguin was sitting in her room embroidering by candle-light and imagining herself to be fighting against prejudice. It was dark in our house and opposite, at the Dolzhikovs', the windows were lit up, but it was impossible to see anything through the flowers and curtains. I kept on walking up and down the street; I was soaked through with the cold March rain. I heard my father come home from the club; he knocked at the door; in a minute a light appeared at a window and I saw my sister walking quickly with her lamp and hurriedly arranging her thick hair. Then my father paced up and down the drawing-room, talking and rubbing his hands, and my sister sat still in a corner, lost in thought, not listening to him. . . .

But soon they left the room and the light was put out. . . . I looked at the engineer's house and that too was now dark. In the darkness and the rain I felt desperately lonely, cast out at the mercy of fate, and I felt how, compared with my loneliness, and my suffering, actual and to come, all my work and all my desires and all that I had hitherto thought and read, were vain and futile. Alas! The activities and thoughts of human beings are not nearly so important as their sorrows! And not knowing exactly what I was doing I pulled with all my might at the bell at the Dolzhikovs' gate, broke it, and ran away down the street like a little boy, full of fear, thinking they would rush out at once and recognize me. When I stopped to take breath at the end of the street, I could hear nothing but the falling rain and far away a night-watchman knocking on a sheet of iron.

For a whole week I did not go to the Dolzhikovs'. I sold my serge suit. I had no work and I was once more half-starved, earning ten to twenty copecks a day, when possible, by disagreeable work. Floundering knee-deep in the mire, putting out all my strength, I tried to drown my memories and to punish myself for all the cheeses and preserves to which I had been treated at the engineer's. Still, no sooner did I go to bed, wet and hungry, than my untamed imagination set to work to evolve wonderful, alluring pictures, and to my amazement I confessed

that I was in love, passionately in love, and I fell sound asleep
feeling that the hard life had only made my body stronger and
younger.

One evening it began, most unseasonably, to snow, and the
wind blew from the north, exactly as if winter had begun again.
When I got home from work I found Maria Victorovna in my
room.   She was in her furs with her hands in her muff.

'Why don't you come to see me?' she asked, looking at me
with her bright sagacious eyes, and I was overcome with joy and
stood stiffly in front of her, just as I had done with my father
when he was going to thrash me; she looked straight into my
face and I could see by her eyes that she understood why I was
overcome.

'Why don't you come to see me?' she repeated.   'You don't
want to come?   I had to come to you.'

She got up and came close to me.

'Don't leave me,' she said, and her eyes filled with tears.
'I am lonely, utterly lonely.'

She began to cry and said, covering her face with her muff:

'Alone!   Life is hard, very hard, and in the whole world I
have no one but you.   Don't leave me!'

Looking for her handkerchief to dry her tears, she gave a
smile; we were silent for some time, then I embraced and kissed
her, and the pin in her hat scratched my face and drew blood.

And we began to talk as though we had been dear to each
other for a long, long time.

X

In a couple of days she sent me to Dubechnia and I was
beyond words delighted with it.   As I walked to the station, and
as I sat in the train, I laughed for no reason and people thought
me drunk.   There were snow and frost in the mornings still, but
the roads were getting dark, and there were rooks cawing above
them.

At first I thought of arranging the side wing opposite Mrs
Cheprakov's for myself and Maria, but it appeared that doves
and pigeons had taken up their abode there and it would be
impossible to cleanse it without destroying a great number of
nests.   We would have to live willy-nilly in the uncomfortable
rooms with Venetian blinds in the big house.   The peasants
called it a palace; there were more than twenty rooms in it, and
the only furniture was a piano and a child's chair, lying in the

attic, and even if Maria brought all her furniture from town we should not succeed in removing the impression of frigid emptiness and coldness. I chose three small rooms with windows looking on to the garden, and from early morning till late at night I was at work in them, glazing the windows, hanging paper, blocking up the chinks and holes in the floor. It was an easy, pleasant job. Every now and then I would run to the river to see if the ice was breaking and all the while I dreamed of the starlings returning. And at night when I thought of Maria I would be filled with an inexpressibly sweet feeling of an all-embracing joy to listen to the rats and the wind rattling and knocking above the ceiling; it was like an old hobgoblin coughing in the attic.

The snow was deep; there was a heavy fall at the end of March, but it thawed rapidly, as if by magic, and the spring floods rushed down so that by the beginning of April the starlings were already chattering and yellow butterflies fluttered in the garden. The weather was wonderful. Every day toward evening I walked towards the town to meet Masha, and how delightful it was to walk along the soft, drying road with bare feet! Half-way I would sit down and look at the town, not daring to go nearer. The sight of it upset me, I was always wondering how my acquaintances would behave toward me when they heard of my love. What would my father say? I was particularly worried by the idea that my life was becoming more complicated, and that I had entirely lost control of it, and that she was carrying me off like a balloon, God knows whither. I had already given up thinking how to make a living, and I thought—indeed, I cannot remember what I thought.

Masha used to come in a carriage. I would take a seat beside her and together, happy and free, we used to drive to Dubechnia. Or, having waited till sunset, I would return home, weary and disconsolate, wondering why Masha had not come, and then by the gate or in the garden I would find my darling. She would come by the railway and walk over from the station. What a triumph it was! In her plain, woollen dress, with a simple umbrella, but keeping a trim, fashionable figure and expensive, Parisian boots, she was a gifted actress playing the country girl. We used to go over the house, and plan out the rooms, and the paths, and the vegetable-garden, and the beehives. We already had chickens and ducks and geese which we loved because they were ours. We had oats, clover, buckwheat, and vegetable seeds all ready for sowing, and we used to examine them all and wonder what the crops would be like, and everything Masha said to me seemed extraordinarily clever and fine. This was the happiest time of my life.

Soon after Easter we were married in the parish church in the village of Kurilovka, three miles from Dubechnia. Masha wanted everything to be simple; by her wish our bridesmen were peasant boys, only one deacon sang, and we returned from the church in a little, shaky cart which she drove herself. My sister was the only guest from the town. Masha had sent her a note a couple of days before the wedding. My sister wore a white dress and white gloves. . . . During the ceremony she cried softly for joy and emotion, and her face had a maternal expression of infinite goodness. She was intoxicated with our happiness and smiled as though she were breathing a sweet perfume, and when I looked at her I understood that there was nothing in the world higher in her eyes than love, earthly love, and that she was always dreaming of love, secretly, timidly, yet passionately. She embraced Masha and kissed her, and, not knowing how to express her ecstasy, she said to her of me:

'He is a good man. A very good man.'

Before she left us, she put on her ordinary clothes, and took me into the garden to have a quiet talk.

'Father is very hurt that you have not written to him,' she said. 'You should have asked for his blessing. But, at heart, he is very pleased. He says that this marriage will raise you in the eyes of society, and that under Maria Victorovna's influence you will begin to adopt a more serious attitude toward life. In the evening now we talk about nothing but you; and yesterday he even said, "our Misail." I was delighted. He has evidently thought of a plan and I believe he wants to set you an example of magnanimity, and that he will be the first to talk of reconciliation. It is quite possible that one of these days he will come and see you here.'

She made the sign of the cross over me and said:

'Well, God bless you. Be happy. Aniuta Blagovo is a very clever girl. She says of your marriage that God has sent you a new ordeal. Well? Married life is not made up only of joy but of suffering as well. It is impossible to avoid it.'

Masha and I walked about three miles with her, and then walked home quietly and silently, as though it were a rest for both of us. Masha had her hand on my arm. We were at peace and there was no need to talk of love; after the wedding we grew closer to each other and dearer, and it seemed as though nothing could part us.

'Your sister is a dear, lovable creature,' said Masha, 'but looks as though she had lived in torture. Your father must be a terrible man.'

I began to tell her how my sister and I had been brought up and how absurd and full of torture our childhood had been. When she heard that my father had thrashed me quite recently she shuddered and clung to me.

'Don't tell me any more,' she said. 'It is too horrible.'

And now she did not leave me. We lived in the big house, in three rooms, and in the evenings we bolted the door that led to the empty part of the house, as though someone lived there whom we did not know and feared. I used to get up early, at dawn, and begin working. I repaired the carts; made paths in the garden, dug the flower beds, painted the roofs. When the time came to sow oats, I tried to plough and harrow and sow, and did it all conscientiously, and did not leave it all to the labourer. I used to get tired, and my face and feet used to burn with the rain and the sharp cold wind. But work in the fields did not attract me. I knew nothing about agriculture and did not like it; perhaps because my ancestors were not tillers of the soil and pure town blood ran in my veins. I loved nature dearly; I loved the fields and the meadows and the garden, but the peasant who turns the earth with his plough, shouting at his miserable horse, ragged and wet, with bowed shoulders, was to me an expression of wild, rude, ugly force, and as I watched his clumsy movements I could not help thinking of the long-past legendary life, when men did not yet know the use of fire. The fierce bull which led the herd, and the horses that stampeded through the village, filled me with terror, and all the large creatures, strong and hostile, a ram with horns, a gander, or a watch-dog seemed to me to be symbolical of some rough, wild force. These prejudices used to be particularly strong in me in bad weather, when heavy clouds hung over the black plough-lands. But worst of all was that when I was ploughing or sowing, and a few peasants stood and watched how I did it, I no longer felt the inevitability and necessity of the work and it seemed to me that I was trifling my time away.

I used to go through the gardens and the meadow to the mill. It was leased by Stiepan, a Kurilovka peasant; handsome, swarthy, with a black beard—an athletic appearance. He did not care for mill work and thought it tiresome and unprofitable, and he only lived at the mill to escape from home. He was a saddler and always smelled of tan and leather. He did not like talking, was slow and immovable, and used to hum 'U-lu-lu-lu,' sitting on the bank or in the doorway of the mill. Sometimes his wife and mother-in-law used to come from Kurilovka to see him; they were both fair, languid, soft, and they used to bow to him humbly and call him Stiepan Petrovich. And he would not answer their greeting with a word or a sign, but would turn where he sat on the bank and hum quietly: 'U-lu-lu-lu.' There would be a silence for an hour or two. His mother-in-law and his wife would whisper to each other, get up and look expectantly at him for some time, waiting for him to look at them, and then they would bow humbly and say in sweet, soft voices:

'Good-bye, Stiepan Petrovich.'

And they would go away. After that, Stiepan would put away the bundle of cracknels or the shirt they had left for him and sigh and give a wink in their direction and say:

'The female sex!'

The mill was worked with both wheels day and night. I used to help Stiepan, I liked it, and when he went away I was glad to take his place.

XI

After a spell of warm bright weather we had a season of bad roads. It rained and was cold all through May. The grinding of the millstones and the drip of the rain induced idleness and sleep. The floor shook, the whole place smelled of flour, and this too made one drowsy. My wife in a short fur coat and high rubber boots used to appear twice a day and she always said the same thing:

'Call this summer! It is worse than October!'

We used to have tea together and cook porridge, or sit together for hours in silence thinking the rain would never stop. Once when Stiepan went away to a fair, Masha stayed the night in the mill. When we got up we could not tell what time it was for the sky was overcast; the sleepy cocks at Dubechnia were crowing, and the corncrakes were calling in the meadow; it was very, very early. . . . My wife and I walked down to the pool and drew up the bow-net that Stiepan had put out in our presence the day before. There was one large perch in it and a crayfish angrily stretched out his claws.

'Let them go,' said Masha. 'Let them be happy too.'

Because we got up very early and had nothing to do, the day seemed very long, the longest in my life. Stiepan returned before dusk and I went back to the farmhouse.

'Your father came here to-day,' said Masha.

'Where is he?'

'He has gone. I did not receive him.'

Seeing my silence and feeling that I was sorry for my father, she said:

'We must be logical. I did not receive him and sent a message to ask him not to trouble us again and not to come and see us.'

In a moment I was outside the gates, striding toward the town to make it up with my father. It was muddy, slippery, cold. For the first time since our marriage I suddenly felt sad, and through my brain, tired with the long day, there flashed the thought that perhaps I was not living as I ought; I got more and more tired and was gradually overcome with weakness, inertia; I had no desire to move or to think, and after walking for some time, I waved my hand and went home.

In the middle of the yard stood the engineer in a leather coat with a hood. He was shouting:

'Where's the furniture? There was some good Empire furniture, pictures, vases. There's nothing left! Damn it, I bought the place with the furniture!'

Near him stood Moissey, Mrs Cheprakov's bailiff, fumbling with his cap; a lank fellow of about twenty-five, with a spotty face and little, impudent eyes; one side of his face was larger than the other as though he had been lain on.

'Yes, right honourable sir, you bought it without the furniture,' he said sheepishly. 'I remember that clearly.'

'Silence!' shouted the engineer, going red in the face, and beginning to shake, and his shout echoed through the garden.

XII

When I was busy in the garden or the yard, Moissey would stand with his hands behind his back and stare at me impertinently with his little eyes. And this used to irritate me to such an extent that I would put aside my work and go away.

We learned from Stiepan that Moissey had been Mrs Cheprakov's lover. I noticed that when people went to her for money they used to apply to Moissey first, and once I saw a peasant, a charcoal-burner, black all over, grovel at his feet. Sometimes after a whispered conversation Moissey would hand over the money himself without saying anything to his mistress, from which I concluded that the transaction was settled on his own account.

He used to shoot in our garden, under our very windows, steal food from our larder, borrow our horses without leave, and we were furious, feeling that Dubechnia was no longer ours, and Masha used to go pale and say:

'Have we to live another year and a half with these creatures?'

Ivan Cheprakov, the son, was a guard on the railway. During the winter he got very thin and weak, so that he got drunk on one glass of vodka, and felt cold out of the sun. He hated wearing his guard's uniform and was ashamed of it, but found his job profitable because he could steal candles and sell them. My new position gave him a mixed feeling of astonishment, envy, and vague hope that something of the sort might happen to him. He used to follow Masha with admiring eyes, and to ask me what I had for dinner nowadays, and his ugly, emaciated face used to wear a sweet, sad expression, and he used to twitch his fingers as though he could feel my happiness with them.

'I say, Little Profit,' he would say excitedly, lighting and relighting his cigarette—he always made a mess wherever he stood because he used to waste a whole box of matches on one cigarette—'I say, my life is about as beastly as it could be. Every little squirt of a soldier can shout: "Here, guard! Here!" I have such a lot in the trains and you know, mine's a rotten life! My mother has ruined me! I heard a doctor say in the train, if the parents are loose, their children become drunkards or criminals. That's it.'

Once he came staggering into the yard. His eyes wandered aimlessly and he breathed heavily; he laughed and cried, and said something in a kind of frenzy, and through his thickly uttered words I could only hear: 'My mother! Where is my mother?' and he wailed like a child crying because it has lost its mother in a crowd. I led him away into the garden and laid him down under a tree, and all that day and through the night Masha and I took it in turns to stay with him. He was sick and Masha looked with disgust at his pale, wet face and said:

'Are we to have these creatures on the place for another year and a half? It is awful! awful!'

And what a lot of trouble the peasants gave us! How many disappointments we had at the outset, in the spring, when we so longed to be happy! My wife built a school. I designed the school for sixty boys, and the zemstvo council approved the design, but recommended our building the school at Kurilovka, the big village, only three miles away; besides, the Kurilovka school, where the children of four villages, including that of Dubechnia, were taught, was old and inadequate and the floor was so rotten that the children were afraid to walk on it. At the end of March, Masha, by her own desire, was appointed trustee of the Kurilovka school, and at the beginning of April we called three parish meetings and persuaded the peasants that the school was old and inadequate, and that it was necessary to build a new one. A member of the zemstvo council and the elementary school inspector came down too and addressed them. After each meeting we were mobbed and asked for a pail of vodka; we felt stifled in the crowd and soon got tired and returned home dissatisfied and rather abashed. At last the peasants allotted a site for the school and undertook to cart the materials from the town. And as soon as the spring corn was sown, on the very first Sunday, carts set out from Kurilovka and Dubechnia to fetch the bricks for the foundations. They went at dawn and returned late in the evening. The peasants were drunk and said they were tired out.

The rain and the cold continued, as though deliberately, all through May. The roads were spoiled and deep in mud. When the carts came from town they usually drove, to our horror, into our yard! A horse would appear in the gate, straddling its forelegs, with its big belly heaving; before it came into the yard it would strain and heave and after it would come a ten-yard beam in a four-wheeled wagon, wet and slimy; alongside it, wrapped up to keep the rain out, never looking where he was going and splashing through the puddles, a peasant would walk with the skirt of his coat tucked up in his belt. Another cart would appear with planks; then a third with a beam; then a fourth . . . and the yard in front of the house would gradually be blocked up with horses, beams, planks. Peasants, men and women with their heads wrapped up and their skirts tucked up, would stare morosely at our windows, kick up a row, and insist on the lady of the house coming out to them; and they would curse and swear. And in a corner Moissey would stand, and it seemed to us that he delighted in our discomfiture.

'We won't cart any more!' the peasants shouted. 'We are tired to death! Let her go and cart it herself!'

Pale and scared, thinking they would any minute break into the house, Masha would send them money for a pail of vodka;

after which the noise would die down and the long beams would go jolting out of the yard.

When I went to look at the building my wife would get agitated and say:

'The peasants are furious. They might do something to you. No. Wait. I'll go with you.

We used to drive over to Kurilovka together and then the carpenters would ask for tips. The framework was ready for the foundations to be laid, but the masons never came, and when at last the masons did come it was apparent that there was no sand; somehow it had been forgotten that sand was wanted. Taking advantage of our helplessness, the peasants asked thirty copecks a load, although it was less than a quarter of a mile from the building to the river where the sand was to be fetched, and more than five hundred loads were needed. There were endless misunderstandings, wrangles, and continual begging. My wife was indignant, and the building contractor, Petrov, an old man of seventy, took her by the hand and said:

'You look here! Look here! Just get me sand and I'll find ten men and have the work done in two days. Look here!'

Sand was brought, but two, four days, a week passed, and still there yawned a ditch where the foundations were to be.

'I shall go mad,' cried my wife furiously. 'What wretches they are! What wretches!'

During these disturbances Victor Ivanich used to come and see us. He used to bring hampers of wine and dainties, and eat for a long time, and then go to sleep on the terrace and snore so that the labourers shook their heads and said:

'He's all right!'

Masha took no pleasure in his visits. She did not believe in him, and yet she used to ask his advice; when, after a sound sleep after dinner, he got up out of humour, and spoke disparagingly of our domestic arrangements, and said he was sorry he had ever bought Dubechnia which had cost him so much, and poor Masha looked miserably anxious and complained to him, he would yawn and say the peasants ought to be flogged.

He called our marriage and the life we were living a comedy, and used to say it was a caprice, a whimsy.

'She did the same sort of thing once before,' he told me. 'She fancied herself as an opera singer, and ran away from me. It took me two months to find her, and my dear fellow, I wasted a thousand roubles on telegrams alone.'

He had dropped calling me a sectarian or the House-painter;

and no longer approved of my life as a working man, but used to say:

'You are a queer fish! An abnormality. I don't venture to prophesy, but you will end badly!'

Masha slept poorly at nights and would sit by the window of our bedroom thinking. She no longer laughed and made faces at supper. I suffered, and when it rained, every drop cut into my heart like a bullet, and I could have gone on my knees to Masha and apologized for the weather. When the peasants made a row in the yard, I felt that it was my fault. I would sit for hours in one place, thinking only how splendid and how wonderful Masha was. I loved her passionately, and I was enraptured by everything she did and said. Her taste was for quiet indoor occupation; she loved to read for hours and to study; she, who knew about farm-work only from books, surprised us all by her knowledge, and the advice she gave was always useful, and when applied was never in vain. And in addition she had the fineness, the taste, and the good sense, the very sound sense which only very well-bred people possess.

To such a woman, with her healthy, orderly mind, the chaotic environment with its petty cares and dirty tittle-tattle, in which we lived, was very painful. I could see that, and I, too, could not sleep at night. My brain whirled and I could hardly choke back my tears. I tossed about, not knowing what to do.

I used to rush to town and bring Masha books, newspapers, sweets, flowers, and I used to go fishing with Stiepan, dragging for hours, neck-deep in cold water, in the rain, to catch an eel by way of varying our fare. I used humbly to ask the peasants not to shout, and I gave them vodka, bribed them, promised them anything they asked. And what a lot of other foolish things I did!

At last the rain stopped. The earth dried up. I used to get up in the morning and go into the garden—dew shining on the flowers, birds and insects shrilling, not a cloud in the sky, and the garden, the meadow, the river were so beautiful, perfect but for the memory of the peasants and the carts and the engineer. Masha and I used to drive out in a car to see how the oats were coming on. She drove and I sat behind; her shoulders were always a little hunched, and the wind would play with her hair.

'Keep to the right!' she shouted to the passers-by.

'You are like a coachman!' I once said to her.

'Perhaps. My grandfather, my father's father, was a coach-man. Didn't you know?' she asked, turning round, and immediately she began to mimic the way the coachmen shout and sing.

'Thank God!' I thought, as I listened to her. 'Thank God!' And again I remember the peasants, the carts, the engineer....

XIII

Doctor Blagovo came over on a bicycle. My sister began to come often. Once more we talked of manual labour and progress, and the mysterious Cross awaiting humanity in the remote future. The doctor did not like our life, because it interfered with our discussions, and he said it was unworthy of a free man to plough, and reap, and breed cattle, and that in time all such elementary forms of the struggle for existence would be left to animals and machines, while men would devote themselves exclusively to scientific investigation. And my sister always asked me to let her go home earlier, and if she stayed late, or for the night, she was greatly distressed.

'Good gracious, what a baby you are!' Masha used to say reproachfully. 'It is quite ridiculous.'

'Yes, it is absurd,' my sister would agree. 'I admit it is absurd, but what can I do if I have not the power to control myself. It always seems to me that I am doing wrong.'

During the haymaking my body, not being used to it, ached all over; sitting on the terrace in the evening, I would suddenly fall asleep and they would all laugh at me. They would wake me up and make me sit down to supper. I would be overcome with drowsiness and in a stupor saw lights, faces, plates, and heard voices without understanding what they were saying. And I used to get up early in the morning and take my scythe, or go to the school and work there all day.

When I was at home on holidays I noticed that my wife and sister were hiding something from me and even seemed to be avoiding me. My wife was tender with me as always, but she had some new thought of her own which she did not communicate to me. Certainly her exasperation with the peasants had increased and life was growing harder and harder for her, but she no longer complained to me. She talked more readily to the doctor than to me, and I could not understand why.

It was the custom in our province for the labourers to come to the farm in the evenings to be treated to vodka, even the girls having a glass. We did not keep the custom; the haymakers and the women used to come into the yard and stay until late in the evening, waiting for vodka, and then they went away cursing. And then Masha used to frown and relapse into silence or whisper irritably to the doctor:

'Savages! Barbarians!'

New-comers to the villages were received ungraciously, almost with hostility; like new arrivals at a school. At first we were looked upon as foolish, soft-headed people who had bought the estate because we did not know what to do with our money. We were laughed at. The peasants grazed their cattle in our pasture and even in our garden, drove our cows and horses into the village and then came and asked for compensation. The whole village used to come into our yard and declare loudly that in mowing we had cut the border of common land which did not belong to us; and as we did not know our boundaries exactly we used to take their word for it and pay a fine. But afterward it appeared that we had been in the right. They used to bark the young lime trees in our woods. A Dubechnia peasant, a money-lender, who sold vodka without a licence, bribed our labourers to help him cheat us in the most treacherous way; he substituted old wheels for the new on our wagons, stole our ploughing yokes and sold them back to us, and so on. But worst of all was the building at Kurilovka. There the women at night stole planks, bricks, tiles, iron; the bailiff and his assistants made a search; the women were each fined two roubles by the village council, and then the whole lot of them got drunk on the money.

When Masha found out, she would say to the doctor and my sister:

'What beasts! It is horrible, horrible!'

And more than once I heard her say she was sorry she had decided to build the school.

'You must understand,' the doctor tried to point out, 'that if you build a school or undertake any good work, it is not for the peasants, but for the sake of culture and the future. The worse the peasants are the more reason there is for building a school. Do understand!'

There was a lack of confidence in his voice, and it seemed to me that he hated the peasants as much as Masha.

Masha used often to go to the mill with my sister and they would say jokingly that they were going to have a look at Stiepan because he was so handsome. Stiepan, it appeared, was reserved and silent only with men, and in the company of women was free and talkative. Once when I went down to the river to bathe I involuntarily overheard a conversation. Masha and

Cleopatra, both in white, were sitting on the bank under the broad shade of a willow and Stiepan was standing near with his hands behind his back, saying:

'But are peasants human beings? Not they; they are, excuse me, brutes, beasts, and thieves. What does a peasant's life consist of? Eating and drinking, crying for cheaper food, brawling in taverns, without decent conversation, or behaviour or manners. Just an ignorant beast! He lives in filth, his wife and children live in filth; he sleeps in his clothes; takes the potatoes out of the soup with his fingers, drinks down a black-beetle with his *kvass*—because he won't trouble to fish it out!'

'It is because of their poverty!' protested my sister.

'What poverty? of course there is want, but there are different kinds of necessity. If a man is in prison, or is blind, say, or has lost his legs, then he is in a bad way and God help him; but if he is at liberty and in command of his senses, if he has eyes and hands and strength, then, good God, what more does he want? It is lamentable, my lady, ignorance, but not poverty. If you kind people, with your education, out of charity try to help him, then he will spend your money in drink, like the swine he is, or worse still, he will open a tavern and begin to rob the people on the strength of your money. You say—poverty. But does a rich peasant live any better? He lives like a pig, too, excuse me, clodhopper, a blusterer, a big-bellied blockhead, with a swollen red mug—makes me want to hit him in the eye, the blackguard. Look at Larion of Dubechina—he is rich, but all the same he barks the trees in your woods just like the poor; and he is a foul-mouthed brute, and his children are foul-mouthed, and when he is drunk he falls flat in the mud and goes to sleep. They are all worthless, my lady. It is just hell to live with them in the village. The village sticks in my gizzard, and I thank God, the King of Heaven, that I am well fed and clothed, and that I am a free man; I can live where I like, I don't want to live in the village and nobody can force me to do it. They say: "You have a wife." They say: "You are obliged to live at home with your wife." Why? I have not sold myself to her.'

'Tell me, Stiepan. Did you marry for love?' asked Masha.

'What love is there in a village?' Stiepan answered with a smile. 'If you want to know, my lady, it is my second marriage. I do not come from Kurilovka, but from Zalegosch, and I went to Kurilovka when I married. My father did not want to divide the land up between us—there are five of us. So I bowed to it and cut adrift and went to another village to my wife's family. My first wife died when she was young.

'What did she die of?'

'Foolishness. She used to sit and cry. She was always crying for no reason at all and so she wasted away. She used to drink herbs to make herself prettier and it must have ruined her inside. And my second wife at Kurilovka—what about her? A village woman, a peasant; that's all. When the match was being made I was nicely had; I thought she was young, nice to look at, and clean. Her mother was clean enough, drank coffee and, chiefly because they were a clean lot, I got married. Next day we sat down to dinner and I told my mother-in-law to fetch me a spoon. She brought me a spoon and I saw her wipe it with her finger. So that, thought I, is their cleanliness! I lived with them for a year and went away. Perhaps I ought to have married a town girl,' he went on after a silence. 'They say a wife is a helpmate to her husband. What do I want with a helpmate? I can look after myself. But you talk to me sensibly and soberly, without giggling all the while: "He-he-he!" What is life without a good talk?'

Stiepan suddenly stopped and relapsed into his dreary, monotonous 'U-lu-lu-lu.' That meant that he had noticed me.

Masha used often to visit the mill, she evidently took pleasure in her talks with Stiepan; he abused the peasants so sincerely and convincingly—and this attracted her to him. When she returned from the mill the idiot who looked after the garden used to shout after her:

'Palashka! Hullo, Palashka!' And he would bark at her like a dog: 'Bow-wow!'

And she would stop and stare at him as if she found in the idiot's barking an answer to her thought, and perhaps he attracted her as much as Stiepan's abuse. And at home she would find some unpleasant news awaiting her, as that the village geese had ruined the cabbages in the kitchen-garden, or that Larion had stolen the reins, and she would shrug her shoulders with a smile and say:

'What can you expect of such people?'

She was exasperated and a fury was gathering in her soul, and I, on the other hand, was getting used to the peasants and more and more attracted to them. For the most part, they were nervous, irritable, absurd people; they were people with suppressed imaginations, ignorant, with a bare, dull outlook, always dazed by the same thought of the grey earth, grey days, black bread; they were people driven to cunning, but like birds, they only hid their heads behind the trees—they could not reason. They did not come to us for the twenty roubles earned by haymaking, but for the half-pail of vodka, though they could buy four pails of vodka for the twenty roubles. Indeed they were dirty, drunken, and dishonest, but for all that one felt that the peasant life as a whole was sound at the core. However clumsy and brutal the peasant might look as he followed his antiquated plough, and however he might fuddle himself with vodka, still, looking at him more closely, one felt that there was something vital and important in him, something that was lacking in Masha and the doctor, for instance, namely, that he believes that the chief thing on earth is truth, that his and everybody's salvation lies in truth, and therefore above all else on earth he loves justice. I used to say to my wife that she was seeing the stain on the window, but not the glass itself; and she would be silent or, like Stiepan, she would hum, 'U-lu-lu-lu . . .' When she, good, clever actress that she was, went pale with fury and then harangued the doctor in a trembling voice about drunkenness and dishonesty, her blindness confounded and appalled me. How could she forget that her father, the engineer, drank, drank heavily, and that the money with which he bought Dubechnia was acquired by means of a whole series of impudent, dishonest swindles? How could she forget?

XIV

And my sister, too, was living with her own private thoughts which she hid from me. She used often to sit whispering with Masha. When I went up to her, she would shrink away, and her eyes would look guilty and full of entreaty. Evidently there was something going on in her soul of which she was afraid or ashamed. To avoid meeting me in the garden or being left alone with me she clung to Masha and I hardly ever had a chance to talk to her except at dinner.

One evening, on my way home from the school, I came quietly through the garden. It had already begun to grow dark. Without noticing me or hearing footsteps, my sister walked round an old wide-spreading apple tree, perfectly noiselessly like a ghost. She was in black, and walked very quickly, up and down, up and down, with her eyes on the ground. An apple fell from the tree, she started at the noise, stopped and pressed her hands to her temples. At that moment I went up to her.

In an impulse of tenderness, which suddenly came rushing to my heart, with tears in my eyes, somehow remembering our mother and our childhood, I took hold of her shoulders and kissed her.

'What is the matter?' I asked. 'You are suffering. I have seen it for a long time now. Tell me, what is the matter?'

'I am afraid . . .' she murmured, with a shiver.

'What's the matter with you?' I inquired. 'For God's sake, be frank!'

'I will, I will be frank. I will tell you the whole truth. It is so hard, so painful to conceal anything from you! . . . Misail, I am in love.' She went on in a whisper. 'Love, love. . . . I am happy, but I am afraid.'

I heard footsteps and Doctor Blagovo appeared among the trees. He was wearing a silk shirt and high boots. Clearly they had arranged a rendezvous by the apple tree. When she saw him she flung herself impulsively into his arms with a cry of anguish, as though he was being taken away from her:

'Vladimir! Vladimir!'

She clung to him, and gazed eagerly at him and only then I noticed how thin and pale she had become. It was especially noticeable through her lace collar, which I had known for years, for it now hung loosely about her slim neck. The doctor was taken aback, but controlled himself at once, and said, as he stroked her hair:

'That's enough. Enough! . . . Why are you so nervous? You see, I have come.'

We were silent for a time, bashfully glancing at each other. Then we all moved away and I heard the doctor saying to me:

'Civilized life has not yet begun with us. The old console themselves with saying that, if there is nothing now, there was something in the forties and the sixties; that is all right for the old ones, but we are young and our brains are not yet touched with senile decay. We cannot console ourselves with such illusions. The beginning of Russia was in 862, and civilized Russia, as I understand it, has not yet begun.'

But I could not bother about what he was saying. It was very strange, but I could not believe that my sister was in love, that she had just been walking with her hand on the arm of a stranger and gazing at him tenderly. My sister, poor, frightened, timid, downtrodden creature as she was, loved a

man who was already married and had children. I was full of
pity without knowing why; the doctor's presence was distasteful
to me and I could not make out what was to come of such a love.

XV

Masha and I drove over to Kurilovka for the opening of the
school.

'Autumn, autumn, autumn . . .' said Masha, looking about
her. Summer had passed. There were no birds and only the
willows were green.

Yes. Summer had passed. The days were bright and warm,
but it was fresh in the mornings; the shepherds went out in their
sheepskins, and the dew never dried all day on the asters in the
garden. There were continual mournful sounds and it was impossible to tell whether it was a shutter creaking on its rusty
hinges or the cranes flying—and one felt so well and so full of the
desire for life!

'Summer has passed . . .' said Masha. 'Now we can both
make up our accounts. We have worked hard and thought a
great deal and we are the better for it—all honour and praise to
us; we have improved ourselves; but have our successes had any
perceptible influence on the life around us, have they been of
any use to a single person? No! Ignorance, dirt, drunkenness, a terribly high rate of infant mortality—everything is just
as it was, and no one is any the better for your having ploughed
and sown and my having spent money and read books. Evidently we have only worked and broadened our minds for
ourselves.'

I was abashed by such arguments and did not know what to
think.

'From beginning to end we have been sincere,' I said, 'and if
a man is sincere, he is right.'

'Who denies that? We have been right but we have been
wrong in our way of setting about it. First of all, are not our
very ways of living wrong? You want to be useful to people,
but by the mere fact of buying an estate you make it impossible
to be so. Further, if you work, dress, and eat like a peasant you
lend your authority and approval to the clumsy clothes, and
their dreadful houses and their dirty beards. . . . On the other
hand, suppose you work for a long, long time, all your life, and
in the end obtain some practical results—what will your results
amount to, what can they do against such elemental forces as

wholesale ignorance, hunger, cold, and degeneracy? A drop in the ocean! Other methods of fighting are necessary, strong, bold, quick! If you want to be useful then you must leave the narrow circle of common activity and try to act directly on the masses! First of all, you need vigorous, noisy propaganda. Why are art and music, for instance, so much alive and so popular and so powerful? Because the musician or the singer influences thousands directly. Art, wonderful art!' She looked wistfully at the sky and went on: 'Art gives wings and carries you far, far away. If you are bored with dirt and pettifogging interests, if you are exasperated and outraged and indignant, rest and satisfaction are only to be found in beauty.'

As we approached Kurilovka the weather was fine, clear, and joyous. In the yards the peasants were thrashing and there was a smell of corn and straw. Behind the wattled fences the fruit trees were reddening and all around the trees were red or golden. In the church-tower the bells were ringing, the children were carrying ikons to the school and singing the Litany of the Virgin. And how clear the air was, and how high the doves soared!

The *Te Deum* was sung in the schoolroom. Then the Kurilovka peasants presented Masha with an ikon, and the Dubechina peasants gave her a large cracknel and a gilt salt-cellar. And Masha began to weep.

'And if we have said anything out of the way or have been discontented, please forgive us,' said an old peasant, bowing to us both.

As we drove home Masha looked back at the school. The green roof which I had painted glistened in the sun, and we could see it for a long time. And I felt that Masha's glances were glances of farewell.

XVI

In the evening she got ready to go to town.

She had often been to town lately to stay the night. In her absence I could not work, and felt listless and disheartened; our big yard seemed dreary, disgusting, and deserted; there were ominous noises in the garden, and without her the house, the trees, the horses were no longer 'ours.'

I never went out but sat all the time at her writing-table among her books on farming and agriculture, those deposed favourites, wanted no more, which looked out at me so shamefacedly from the bookcase. For hours together, while it struck seven, eight, nine, and the autumn night crept up as black as soot to the windows, I sat brooding over an old glove of hers, or the pen she always used, and her little scissors. I did nothing and saw clearly that everything I had done before, ploughing, sowing, and felling trees, had only been because she wanted it. And if she told me to clean out a well, when I had to stand waist-deep in water, I would go and do it, without trying to find out whether the well wanted a cleaning or not. And now, when she was away, Dubechnia with its squalor, its litter, its slamming shutters, with thieves prowling about it day and night, seemed to me like a chaos in which work was entirely useless. And why should I work, then? Why trouble and worry about the future, when I felt that the ground was slipping away from under me, that my position at Dubechnia was hollow, that, in a word, the same fate awaited me as had befallen the books on agriculture? Oh! what anguish it was at night, in the lonely hours, when I lay listening uneasily, as though I expected some-one any minute to call out that it was time for me to go away. I was not sorry to leave Dubechnia, my sorrow was for my love, for which it seemed that autumn had already begun. What a tremendous happiness it is to love and to be loved, and what a horror it is to feel that you are beginning to topple down from that lofty tower!

Masha returned from town toward evening on the following day. She was dissatisfied with something, but concealed it and said only: 'Why have the winter windows been put in? It will be stifling.' I opened two of the windows. We did not feel like eating, but we sat down and had supper.

'Go and wash your hands,' she said. 'You smell of putty.'

She had brought some new illustrated magazines from town and we both read them after supper. They had supplements with fashion-plates and patterns. Masha just glanced at them and put them aside to look at them carefully later on; but one dress, with a wide, bell-shaped skirt and big sleeves, interested her, and for a moment she looked at it seriously and attentively.

'That's not bad,' she said.

'Yes, it would suit you very well,' said I. 'Very well.'

And I admired the dress, only because she liked it, and went on tenderly:

'A wonderful, lovely dress! Lovely, wonderful Masha. My dear Masha.'

And tears began to drop on the fashion-plate.

'Wonderful Masha . . .' I murmured. 'Dear, darling Masha. . . .'

She went and lay down and I sat still for an hour and looked at the illustrations.

'You should not have opened the windows,' she called from the bedroom. 'I'm afraid it will be cold. Look how the wind is blowing in!'

I read the miscellany, about the preparation of cheap ink, and the size of the largest diamond in the world. Then I chanced on the picture of the dress she had liked and I imagined her at a ball, with a fan, and bare shoulders, a brilliant, dazzling figure, well up in music and painting and literature, and how insignificant and brief my share in her life seemed to be!

Our coming together, our marriage, was only an episode, one of many in the life of this lively, highly gifted creature. All the best things in the world, as I have said, were at her service, and she had them for nothing; even ideas and fashionable intellectual movements served her pleasure, a diversion in her existence, and I was only the coachman who drove her from one infatuation to another. Now I was no longer necessary to her; she would fly away and I should be left alone.

As if in answer to my thoughts a desperate scream suddenly came from the yard:

'Mur-der!'

It was a shrill female voice, and exactly as though it were trying to imitate it, the wind also howled dismally in the chimney. Half a minute passed and again it came through the sound of the wind, but as though from the other end of the yard:

'Mur-der!'

'Misail, did you hear that?' said my wife in a hushed voice. 'Did you hear?'

She came out of the bedroom in her nightgown, with her hair down, and stood listening and staring out of the dark window.

'Somebody is being murdered!' she muttered. 'It only wanted that!'

I took my gun and went out; it was very dark outside; a violent wind was blowing so that it was hard to stand up. I walked to the gate and listened; the trees were moaning; the wind went whistling through them, and in the garden the idiot's dog was howling. Beyond the gate it was pitch dark; there was not a light on the railway. And just by the wing, where the offices used to be, I suddenly heard a choking cry:

'Mur-der!'

'Who is there?' I called.

Two men were locked in a struggle. One had nearly thrown the other, who was resisting with all his might. And both were breathing heavily.

'Let go!' said one of them and I recognized Ivan Cheprakov. It was he who had cried out in a thin, falsetto voice. 'Let go, damn you, or I'll bite your hands!'

The other man I recognized as Moissey. I parted them and could not resist hitting Moissey in the face twice. He fell down, then got up, and I struck him again.

'He tried to kill me,' he muttered. 'I caught him creeping to his mother's drawer. . . . I tried to shut him up in the wing for safety.'

Cheprakov was drunk and did not recognize me. He stood gasping for breath as though trying to get enough wind to shriek again.

I left them and went back to the house. My wife was lying on the bed, fully dressed. I told her what had happened in the yard and did not keep back the fact that I had struck Moissey.

'Living in the country is horrible,' she said. 'And what a long night it is!'

'Mur-der!' we heard again, a little later.

'I'll go and part them,' I said.

'No. Let them kill each other,' she said with an expression of disgust.

She lay staring at the ceiling, listening, and I sat near her, not daring to speak and feeling that it was my fault that screams of 'murder' came from the yard and the night was so long.

We were silent and I waited impatiently for the light to peep in at the window. And Masha looked as though she had wakened from a long sleep and was astonished to find herself, so clever, so educated, so refined, cast away in this miserable provincial hole, among a lot of petty, shallow people, and to think that she could have so far forgotten herself as to have been carried away by one of them and to have been his wife for more than half a year. It seemed to me that we were all the same to her—myself, Moissey, Cheprakov; all swept together into the drunken, wild scream of 'murder'—myself, our marriage, our work, and the muddy roads of autumn: and when she breathed or stirred to make herself more comfortable I could read in her eyes: 'Oh, if the morning would come quicker!'

In the morning she went away.

I stayed at Dubechnia for another three days, waiting for her;

then I moved all our things into one room, locked it, and went to town. When I rang the bell at the engineer's, it was evening, and the lamps were alight in Great Gentry Street. Pavel told me that nobody was at home; Victor Ivanich had gone to Petersburg and Maria Victorovna must be at a rehearsal at the Azhoguins'. I remember the excitement with which I went to the Azhoguins', and how my heart thumped and sank within me, as I went upstairs and stood for a long while on the landing, not daring to enter that temple of the Muses! In the hall, on the table, on the piano, on the stage, there were candles burning; all in threes, for the first performance was fixed for the thirteenth, and the dress rehearsal was on Monday—the unlucky day. A fight against prejudice! All the lovers of dramatic art were assembled; the eldest, the middle, and the youngest Miss Azhoguin were walking about the stage, reading their parts. Radish was standing still in a corner all by himself, with his head against the wall, looking at the stage with adoring eyes, waiting for the beginning of the rehearsal. Everything was just the same!

I went toward my hostess to greet her, when suddenly everybody began to say 'Ssh' and to wave their hands to tell me not to make such a noise. There was a silence. The top of the piano was raised, a lady sat down, screwing up her short-sighted eyes at the music, and Masha stood by the piano, dressed up, beautiful, but beautiful in an odd new way, not at all like the Masha who used to come to see me at the mill in the spring. She began to sing:

'Why do I love thee, silent night?'

It was the first time since I had known her that I had heard her sing. She had a fine, rich, powerful voice, and to hear her sing was like eating a ripe, sweet-scented melon. She finished the song and was applauded. She smiled and looked pleased, made play with her eyes, stared at the music, plucked at her dress exactly like a bird which has broken out of its cage and preens its wings at liberty. Her hair was combed back over her ears, and she had a sly defiant expression on her face, as though she wished to challenge us all, or to shout at us, as though we were horses: 'Gee up, old things!'

And at that moment she must have looked very like her grandfather, the coachman.

'You here, too?' she asked, giving me her hand. 'Did you hear me sing? How did you like it?' And, without waiting

for me to answer she went on: 'You arrived very opportunely.
I'm going to Petersburg for a short time to-night. May I?'

At midnight I took her to the station. She embraced me
tenderly, probably out of gratitude, because I did not pester her
with useless questions, and she promised to write to me, and I
held her hands for a long time and kissed them, finding it hard
to keep back my tears, and not saying a word.

And when the train moved, I stood looking at the receding
lights, kissed her in my imagination and whispered:

'Masha dear, wonderful Masha! . . .'

I spent the night at Makarikha, at Karpovna's, and in the
morning I worked with Radish, upholstering the furniture at a
rich merchant's, who had married his daughter to a doctor.

XVII

On Sunday afternoon my sister came to see me and had tea
with me.

'I read a great deal now,' she said, showing me the books she
had got out of the town library on her way. 'Thanks to your
wife and Vladimir. They awakened my self-consciousness.
They saved me and have made me feel that I am a human being.
I used not to sleep at night for worrying: "What a lot of sugar
has been wasted during the week!" "The cucumbers must not
be oversalted." I don't sleep now, but I have quite different
thoughts. I am tormented with the thought that half my life
has passed so foolishly and half-heartedly. I despise my old
life. I am ashamed of it. And I regard my father now as an
enemy. Oh, how grateful I am to your wife! And Vladimir.
He is such a wonderful man! They opened my eyes.'

'It is not good that you can't sleep,' I said.

'You think I am ill? Not a bit. Vladimir sounded me and
says I am perfectly healthy. But health is not the point. That
doesn't matter so much. . . . Tell me, am I right?'

She needed moral support. That was obvious. Masha had
gone, Doctor Blagovo was in Petersburg, and there was no one
except myself in the town who could tell her that she was right.
She fixed her eyes on me, trying to read my inmost thoughts,
and if I were sad in her presence, she always took it upon herself
and was depressed. I had to be continually on my guard, and
when she asked me if she was right, I hastened to assure her that
she was right and that I had a profound respect for her.

'You know, they have given me a part at the Azhougins',' she went on. 'I wanted to act. I want to live. I want to drink deep of life; I have no talent whatever, and my part is only ten lines, but it is immeasurably finer and nobler than pouring out tea five times a day and watching to see that the cook does not eat the sugar left over. And most of all I want to let father see that I too can protest.'

After tea she lay down on my bed and stayed there for some time, with her eyes closed, and her face very pale.

'Just weakness!' she said, as she got up. 'Vladimir said all town girls and women are anaemic from lack of work. What a clever man Vladimir is! He is right; wonderfully right! We do need work!'

Two days later she came to rehearsal at the Azhoguins' with her part in her hand. She was in black, with a garnet necklace, and a brooch that looked at a distance like a pasty, and she had enormous earrings, in each of which sparkled a diamond. I felt uneasy when I saw her; I was shocked by her lack of taste. The others noticed too that she was unsuitably dressed and that her earrings and diamonds were out of place. I saw their smiles and heard someone say jokingly: 'Cleopatra of Egypt!'

She was trying to be fashionable, and easy, and assured, and she seemed affected and odd. She lost her simplicity and her charm.

'I just told father that I was going to a rehearsal,' she began, coming up to me, 'and he shouted that he would take his blessing from me, and he nearly struck me. Fancy,' she added, glancing at her part, 'I don't know my part. I'm sure to make a mistake. Well, the die is cast,' she said excitedly; 'the die is cast.'

She felt that all the people were looking at her and were all amazed at the important step she had taken and that they were all expecting something remarkable from her, and it was impossible to convince her that nobody took any notice of such small uninteresting persons as she and I.

She had nothing to do until the third act, and her part, a guest, a country gossip, consisted only in standing by the door, as if she were overhearing something, and then speaking a short monologue. For at least an hour and a half before her cue, while the others were walking, reading, having tea, quarrelling, she never left me and kept on mumbling her part, and dropping her written copy, imagining that everybody was looking at her, and waiting for her to come on, and she patted her hair with a trembling hand and said:

'I'm sure to make a mistake. . . . You don't know how
awful I feel! I am as terrified as if I were going to the scaffold.'

At last her cue came.

'Cleopatra Alexeyevna—your cue!' said the manager.

She walked on to the middle of the stage with an expression of
terror on her face; she looked ugly and stiff, and for half a
minute was speechless, perfectly motionless, except for her large
earrings which wobbled on either side of her face.

'You can read your part, the first time,' said someone.

I could see that she was trembling so that she could neither
speak nor open her part, and that she had entirely forgotten the
words and I had just made up my mind to go up and say something to her when she suddenly dropped down on her knees in
the middle of the stage and sobbed loudly.

There was a general stir and uproar. And I stood quite still
by the wings, shocked by what had happened, not understanding
at all, not knowing what to do. I saw them lift her up and lead
her away. I saw Aniuta Blagovo come up to me. I had not
seen her in the hall before and she seemed to have sprung up
from the floor. She was wearing a hat and veil, and as usual
looked as if she had only dropped in for a minute.

'I told her not to try to act,' she said angrily, biting out each
word, with her cheeks blushing. 'It is folly! You ought to
have stopped her!'

Mrs Azhoguin came up in a short jacket with short sleeves.
She had tobacco ash on her thin, flat bosom.

'My dear, it is too awful!' she said, wringing her hands, and as
usual, staring into my face. 'It is too awful! . . . Your sister
is in a condition. . . . She is going to have a baby! You must
take her away at once. . . .'

In her agitation she breathed heavily. And behind her, stood
her three daughters, all thin and flat-chested like herself, and all
huddled together in their dismay. They were frightened, overwhelmed just as if a convict had been caught in the house.
What a shame! How awful! And this was the family that
had been fighting the prejudices and superstitions of mankind
all their lives; evidently they thought that all the prejudices and
superstitions of mankind were to be found in burning three
candles and in the number thirteen, or the unlucky day—
Monday.

'I must request . . . request . . .' Mrs Azhoguin kept on
saying, compressing her lips and accentuating the *quest*, 'I
must request you to take her away.'

XVIII

A little later my sister and I were walking along the street. I covered her with the skirt of my overcoat; we hurried along through by-streets, where there were no lamps, avoiding the passers-by, and it was like a flight. She did not weep any more, but stared at me with dry eyes. It was about twenty minutes' walk to Makarikha, whither I was taking her, and in that short time we went over the whole of our lives, and talked over everything, and considered the position and pondered. . . .

We decided that we could not stay in the town, and that when I could get some money, we would go to some other place. In some of the houses the people were asleep already, and in others they were playing cards; we hated those houses, were afraid of them, and we talked of the fanaticism, callousness, and nullity of these respectable families, these lovers of dramatic art whom we had frightened so much, and I wondered how those stupid, cruel, slothful, dishonest people were better than the drunken and superstitious peasants of Kurilovka, or how they were better than animals, which also lose their heads when some accident breaks the monotony of their lives, which are limited by their instincts. What would happen to my sister if she stayed at home? What moral torture would she have to undergo, talking to my father and meeting acquaintances every day? I imagined it all and there came into my memory people I had known who had been gradually dropped by their friends and relations, and I remembered the tortured dogs which had gone mad, and sparrows plucked alive and thrown into the water—and a whole long series of dull, protracted sufferings which I had seen going on in the town since my childhood; and I could not conceive what the thirty-five thousand inhabitants lived for, why they read the Bible, why they prayed, why they skimmed books and magazines. What good was all that had been written and said, if they were in the same spiritual darkness and had the same hatred of freedom as if they were living hundreds and hundreds of years ago? The builder spends his time putting up houses all over the town, and yet would go down to his grave saying 'galdary' for 'gallery.' And the thirty-five thousand inhabitants had read and heard of truth and mercy and freedom for generations, but to the bitter end they would go on lying from morning to night, tormenting one another, fearing and hating freedom as a deadly enemy.

'And so, my fate is decided,' said my sister when we reached home. 'After what has happened I can never go *there* again. My God, how good it is! I feel at peace.'

She lay down at once. Tears shone on her eyelashes, but her expression was happy. She slept soundly and softly, and it was clear that her heart was easy and that she was at rest. For a long, long time she had not slept so well.

So we began to live together. She was always singing and said she felt very well, and I took back the books we had borrowed from the library unread, because she gave up reading; she only wanted to dream and to talk of the future. She would hum as she mended my clothes or helped Karpovna with the cooking, or talk of her Vladimir, of his mind, and his goodness, and his fine manners, and his extraordinary learning. And I agreed with her, though I no longer liked the doctor. She wanted to work, to be independent, and to live by herself, and she said she would become a school-teacher or a nurse as soon as her health allowed, and she would scrub the floors and do her own washing. She loved her unborn baby passionately, and she knew already the colour of his eyes and the shape of his hands and how he laughed. She liked to talk of his upbringing, and since the best man on earth was Vladimir, all her ideas were reduced to making the boy as charming as his father. There was no end to her chatter, and everything she talked about filled her with a lively joy. Sometimes I, too, rejoiced, though I knew not why.

She must have infected me with her dreaminess, for I, too, read nothing and just dreamed. In the evenings, in spite of being tired, I used to pace up and down the room with my hands in my pockets, talking about Masha.

'When do you think she will return?' I used to ask my sister. 'I think she'll be back at Christmas. Not later. What is she doing there?'

'If she doesn't write to you, it means she must be coming soon.'

'True,' I would agree, though I knew very well that there was nothing to make Masha return to our town.

I missed her very much, but I could not help deceiving myself and wanted others to deceive me. My sister was longing for her doctor, I for Masha, and we both laughed and talked and never saw that we were keeping Karpovna from sleeping. She would lie on the stove and murmur:

'The samovar tinkled this morning. Tink-led! That bodes nobody any good, my merry friends!'

Nobody came to the house except the postman who brought my sister letters from the doctor, and Prokofyi, who used to come in sometimes in the evening and glance secretly at my sister, and then go into the kitchen and say:

'Every class has its ways, and if you 're too proud to understand that, the worse for you in this vale of tears.'

He loved the expression — vale of tears. And — about Christmas time—when I was going through the market, he called me into his shop, and without giving me his hand, de clared that he had some important business to discuss. He was red in the face with the frost and with vodka; near him by the counter stood Nicolka of the murderous face, holding a bloody knife in his hand.

'I want to be blunt with you,' began Prokofyi. 'This business must not happen because, as you know, people will neither forgive you nor us for such a vale of tears. Mother, of course, is too dutiful to say anything unpleasant to you herself, and tell you that your sister must go somewhere else because of her condition, but I don't want it either, because I do not approve of her behaviour.'

I understood and left the shop. That very day my sister and I went to Radish's. We had no money for a cab, so we went on foot; I carried a bundle with all our belongings on my back, my sister had nothing in her hands, and she was breathless and kept coughing and asking if we would soon be there.

XIX

At last there came a letter from Masha.

'My dear, kind M. A.,' she wrote, 'my brave, sweet angel, as the old painter calls you, good-bye. I am going to America with my father for the exhibition. In a few days I shall be on the ocean—so far from Dubechnia. It is awful to think of! It is vast and open like the sky and I long for it and freedom. I rejoice and dance about and you see how incoherent my letter is. My dear Misail, give me my freedom. Quick, snap the thread which still holds and binds us. My meeting and knowing you was a ray from heaven, which brightened my existence. But, you know, my becoming your wife was a mistake, and the knowledge of the mistake weighs me down, and I implore you on my knees, my dear, generous friend, quick—quick—before I go over the sea—wire that you will agree to correct our mutual mistake, remove then the only burden on my wings, and my father, who will be responsible for the whole business, has promised me not to overwhelm you with formalities. So, then, I am free of the whole world? Yes?

'Be happy. God bless you. Forgive my wickedness.

'I am alive and well. I am squandering money on all sorts of follies, and every minute I thank God that such a wicked woman as I am has no children. I am singing and I am a success, but it is not a passing whim. No. It is my haven, my convent cell where I go for rest. King David had a ring with an inscription: "Everything passes." When one is sad, these words make one cheerful; and when one is cheerful, they make one sad. And I have got a ring with the words written in Hebrew, and this talisman will keep me from losing my heart and head. Or does one need nothing but consciousness of freedom, because, when one is free, one wants nothing, nothing, nothing? Snap the thread then. I embrace you and your sister warmly. Forgive and forget your M.'

My sister had one room. Radish, who had been ill and was recovering, was in the other. Just as I received this letter, my sister went into the painter's room and sat by his side and began to read to him. She read Ostrovsky or Gogol to him every day, and he used to listen, staring straight in front of him, never laughing, shaking his head, and every now and then muttering to himself:

'Anything may happen! Anything may happen!'

If there was anything ugly in what she read, he would say vehemently, pointing to the book:

'There it is! Lies! That's what lies do!'

Stories used to attract him by their contents as well as by their moral and their skilfully complicated plot, and he used to marvel at *him*, though he never called *him* by his name.

'How well *he* has managed it.'

Now my sister read a page quickly and then stopped, because her breath failed her. Radish held her hand, and moving his dry lips he said in a hoarse, hardly audible voice:

'The soul of the righteous is white and smooth as chalk; and the soul of the sinner is as a pumice-stone. The soul of the righteous is clear oil, and the soul of the sinner is coal-tar. We must work and sorrow and pity,' he went on. 'And if a man does not work and sorrow he will not enter the kingdom of heaven. Woe, woe to the well fed, woe to the strong, woe to the rich, woe to the usurers! They will not see the kingdom of heaven. Grubs eat grass, rust eats iron . . .'

'And lies devour the soul,' said my sister, laughing.

I read the letter once more. At that moment the soldier came into the kitchen who had brought in twice a week, without saying from whom, tea, French bread, and game, all smelling of scent. I had no work and used to sit at home for days together, and probably the person who sent us the bread knew that we were in want.

I heard my sister talking to the soldier and laughing merrily. Then she lay down and ate some bread and said to me:

'When you wanted to get away from the office and become a house-painter, Aniuta Blagovo and I knew from the very beginning that you were right, but we were afraid to say so. Tell me, what power is it that keeps us from saying what we feel? There's Aniuta Blagovo. She loves you, adores you, and she knows that you are right. She loves me, too, like a sister, and she knows that I am right, and in her heart she envies me, but some power prevents her coming to see us. She avoids us. She is afraid.'

My sister folded her hands across her bosom and said rapturously:

'If you only knew how she loves you! She confessed it to me and to no one else, very hesitatingly, in the dark. She used to take me out into the garden, into the dark, and begin to tell me in a whisper how dear you were to her. You will see that she will never marry because she loves you. Are you sorry for her?'

'Yes.'

'It was she sent the bread. She is funny. Why should she hide herself? I used to be silly and stupid, but I left all that and I am not afraid of any one, and I think and say aloud what I like—and I am happy. When I lived at home I had no notion of happiness, and now I would not change places with a queen.'

Doctor Blagovo came. He had now his diploma and was now living in the town, at his father's, taking a rest. After which he said he would go back to Petersburg. He wanted to devote himself to vaccination against typhus, and, I believe, cholera; he wanted to go abroad to increase his knowledge and then to become a university professor. He had already left the army and wore serge clothes, with well-cut coats, wide trousers, and expensive ties. My sister was enraptured with his pins and studs and his red silk handkerchief, which, out of swagger, he wore in his outside breast-pocket. Once, when we had nothing to do, she and I fell to counting up his suits and came to the conclusion

that he must have at least ten. It was clear that he still loved
my sister, but never once, even in joke, did he talk of taking her
to Petersburg or abroad with him, and I could not imagine what
would happen to her if she lived, or what was to become of her
child. But she was happy in her dreams and would not think
seriously of the future. She said he could go wherever he liked
and even cast her aside, if only he were happy himself, and what
had been was enough for her.

Usually when he came to see us he would sound her very
carefully, and ask her to drink some milk with some medicine
in it. He did so now. He sounded her and made her drink a
glass of milk, and the room began to smell of creosote.

'That's a good girl,' he said, taking the glass from her. 'You
must not talk much, and you have been chattering like a magpie
lately. Please, be quiet.'

She began to laugh and he came into Radish's room, where I
was sitting, and tapped me affectionately on the shoulder.

'Well, old man, how are you?' he asked, bending over the
patient.

'Sir,' said Radish, only just moving his lips. 'Sir, I make so
bold . . . We are all in the hands of God, and we must all die.
. . . Let me tell you the truth, sir. . . . You will never enter
the kingdom of heaven.'

And suddenly I lost consciousness and was caught up into a
dream: it was winter, at night, and I was standing in the yard of
the slaughter-house with Prokofyi by my side, smelling of
pepper-brandy; I pulled myself together and rubbed my eyes
and then I seemed to be going to the governor's for an explanation. Nothing of the kind ever happened to me, before or after,
and I can only explain these strange dreams like memories,
by ascribing them to overstrain of the nerves. I lived again
through the scene in the slaughter-house and the conversation
with the governor, and at the same time I was conscious of its
unreality.

When I came to myself I saw that I was not at home, but
standing with the doctor by a lamp in the street.

'It is sad, sad,' he was saying with tears running down his
cheeks. 'She is happy and always laughing and full of hope.
But, poor darling, her condition is hopeless. Old Radish hates
me and keeps trying to make me understand that I have wronged
her. In his way he is right, but I have my point of view, too,
and I do not repent of what has happened. It is necessary to
love. We must all love. That's true, isn't it? Without love

there would be no life, and a man who avoids and fears love is not free.'

We gradually passed to other subjects. He began to speak of science and his dissertation which had been very well received in Petersburg. He spoke enthusiastically and thought no more of my sister, or of his grief, or of myself. Life was carrying him away. She has America and a ring with an inscription, I thought, and he has his medical degree and his scientific career, and my sister and I are left with the past.

When we parted I stood beneath the lamp and read my letter again. And I remembered vividly how she came to me at the mill that spring morning and lay down and covered herself with my fur coat—pretending to be just a peasant woman. And another time—also in the early morning—when we pulled the bow-net out of the water, and the willows on the bank showered great drops of water on us and we laughed. . . .

All was dark in our house in Great Gentry Street. I climbed the fence, and, as I used to do in the old days, I went into the kitchen by the back door to get a little lamp. There was nobody in the kitchen. On the stove the samovar was singing merrily, all ready for my father. 'Who pours out my father's tea now?' I thought. I took the lamp and went on to the shed and made a bed of old newspapers and lay down. The nails in the wall looked ominous as before and their shadows flickered. It was cold. I thought I saw my sister coming in with my supper, but I remembered at once that she was ill at Radish's, and it seemed strange to me that I should have climbed the fence and be lying in the cold shed. My mind was blurred and filled with fantastic imaginations.

A bell rang; sounds familiar from childhood; first the wire rustled along the wall, and then there was a short, melancholy tinkle in the kitchen. It was my father returning from the club. I got up and went into the kitchen. Aksinya, the cook, clapped her hands when she saw me and began to cry.

'Oh, my dear,' she said in a whisper. 'Oh, my dear! My God!'

And in her agitation she began to pluck at her apron. On the window-sill were two large bottles of berries soaking in vodka. I poured out a cup and gulped it down, for I was very thirsty. Aksinya had just scrubbed the table and the chairs, and the kitchen had the good smell which kitchens always have when the cook is clean and tidy. This smell and the trilling of the cricket used to entice us into the kitchen when we were children, and there we used to be told fairy-tales, and we played at kings and queens. . . .

'And where is Cleopatra?' asked Aksinya hurriedly, breathlessly. 'And where is your hat, sir? And they say your wife has gone to Petersburg.'

She had been with us in my mother's time and used to bathe Cleopatra and me in a tub, and we were still children to her, and it was her duty to correct us. In a quarter of an hour or so she laid bare all her thoughts, which she had been storing up in her quiet kitchen all the time I had been away. She said the doctor ought to be made to marry Cleopatra—we would only have to frighten him a bit and make him send in a nicely written application, and then the archbishop would dissolve his first marriage, and it would be a good thing to sell Dubechnia without saying anything to my wife, and to bank the money in my own name; and if my sister and I went on our knees to our father and asked him nicely, then perhaps he would forgive us; and we ought to pray to the Holy Mother to intercede for us. . . .

'Now, sir, go and talk to him,' she said, when we heard my father's cough. 'Go, speak to him, and beg his pardon. He won't bite your head off.'

I went in. My father was sitting at his desk working on the plan of a bungalow with Gothic windows and a stumpy tower like the look-out of a fire-station—an immensely stiff and inartistic design. As I entered the study I stood so that I could not help seeing the plan. I did not know why I had come to my father, but I remember that when I saw his thin face, red neck, and his shadow on the wall, I wanted to throw my arms round him and, as Aksinya had bid me, to beg his pardon humbly; but the sight of the bungalow with the Gothic windows and the stumpy tower stopped me.

'Good evening,' I said.

He glanced at me and at once cast his eyes down on his plan.

'What do you want?' he asked after a while.

'I came to tell you that my sister is very ill. She is dying,' I said dully.

'Well?' My father sighed, took off his spectacles and laid them on the table. 'As you have sown, so you must reap. I want you to remember how you came to me two years ago, and on this very spot I asked you to give up your delusions, and I reminded you of your honour; your duty, your obligations to your ancestors, whose traditions must be kept sacred. Did you listen to me? You spurned my advice and clung to your wicked opinions; furthermore, you dragged your sister into your abominable delusions and brought about her downfall and her shame. Now you are both suffering for it. As you have sown, so you must reap.'

He paced up and down the study as he spoke. Probably he thought that I had come to him to admit that I was wrong, and probably he was waiting for me to ask his help for my sister and myself. I was cold, and I shook as though I were in a fever, and I spoke with difficulty in a hoarse voice.

'And I must ask you to remember,' I said, 'that on this very spot I implored you to try to understand me, to reflect, and to think what we were living for and to what end, and your answer was to talk about my ancestors and my grandfather who wrote verses. Now you are told that your only daughter is in a hope-less condition and you talk of ancestors and traditions! . . And you can maintain such frivolity when death is near and you have only five or ten years left to live!'

'Why did you come here?' asked my father sternly, evidently affronted at my reproaching him with frivolity.

'I don't know. I love you. I am more sorry than I can say that we are so far apart. That is why I came. I still love you, but my sister has finally broken with you. She does not forgive you and will never forgive you. Your very name fills her with hatred of her past life.'

'And who is to blame?' cried my father. 'You, you scoundrel!'

'Yes. Say that I am to blame,' I said. 'I admit that I am to blame for many things, but why is your life, which you have tried to force on us, so tedious and frigid and ungracious, why are there no people in any of the houses you have built during the last thirty years from whom I could learn how to live and how to avoid such suffering? These houses of yours are infernal dungeons in which mothers and daughters are persecuted, children are tortured. . . . My poor mother! My unhappy sister! One needs to drug oneself with vodka, cards, scandal; cringe, play the hypocrite, and go on year after year designing rotten houses, not to see the horror that lurks in them. Our town has been in existence for hundreds of years, and during the whole of that time it has not given the country one useful man—not one! You have strangled in embryo everything that was alive and joyous! A town of shopkeepers, publicans, clerks, and hypocrites, an aimless, futile town, and not a soul would be the worse if it were suddenly razed to the ground.'

'I don't want to hear you, you scoundrel,' said my father, taking a ruler from his desk. 'You are drunk! You dare come into your father's presence in such a state! I tell you for the last time, and you can tell this to your strumpet of a sister, that you will get nothing from me. I have torn my disobedient children out of my heart, and if they suffer through their disobedience and obstinacy I have no pity for them. You may go back where you came from! God has been pleased to punish me through you. I will humbly bear my punishment and, like Job, I find consolation in suffering and unceasing toil. You shall not cross my threshold until you have mended your ways. I am a just man, and everything I say is practical good sense, and if you had any regard for yourself, you would remember what I have said, and what I am saying now.'

I threw up my hands and went out; I do not remember what happened that night or next day.

They say that I went staggering through the street without a hat, singing aloud, with crowds of little boys shouting after me:

'Little Profit! Little Profit!'

XX

If I wanted to order a ring, I would have it inscribed: 'Nothing passes.' I believe that nothing passes without leaving some trace, and that every little step has some meaning for the present and the future life.

What I lived through was not in vain. My great misfortunes, my patience, moved the hearts of the people of the town and they no longer call me 'Little Profit,' they no longer laugh at me and throw water over me as I walk through the market. They got used to my being a working man and see nothing strange in my carrying paint-pots and glazing windows; on the contrary, they give me orders, and I am considered a good workman and the best contractor, after Radish, who, though he recovered and still paints the cupolas of the church without scaffolding, is not strong enough to manage the men, and I have taken his place and go about the town touting for orders, and take on and sack the men, and borrow money at exorbitant interest. And now that I am a contractor I can understand how it is possible to spend several days hunting through the town for slaters to carry out a trifling order. People are polite to me, and address me respectfully and give me tea in the houses where I work, and send the servant to ask me if I would like dinner. Children and girls often come and watch me with curious, sad eyes.

Once I was working in the governor's garden, painting the summer-house marble. The governor came into the summer-house, and having nothing better to do, began to talk to me, and I reminded him how he had once sent for me to caution me. For a moment he stared at my face, opened his mouth like a round O, waved his hands, and said:

'I don't remember.'

I am growing old, taciturn, crotchety, strict; I seldom laugh, and people say I am growing like Radish, and, like him, I bore the men with my aimless moralizing.

Maria Victorovna, my late wife, lives abroad, and her father is making a railway somewhere in the eastern provinces and buying land there. Doctor Blagovo is also abroad. Dubechnia has passed to Mrs Cheprakov, who bought it from the engineer after haggling him into a twenty-per-cent reduction in the price. Moissey walks about in a bowler hat; he often drives into town in a trap and stops outside the bank. People say he has already bought an estate on a mortgage, and is always inquiring at the bank about Dubechnia, which he also intends to buy. Poor Ivan Cheprakov used to hang about the town, doing nothing and drinking. I tried to give him a job in our business, and for a time he worked with us painting roofs and glazing, and he rather took to it, and, like a regular house-painter, he stole the oil, and asked for tips, and got drunk. But it soon bored him. He got tired of it and went back to Dubechnia, and some time later I was told by the peasants that he had been inciting them to kill Moissey one night and rob Mrs Cheprakov.

My father has got very old and bent, and just takes a little walk in the evening near his house.

When we had the cholera, Prokofyi cured the shopkeepers with pepper-brandy and tar and took money for it, and as I read in the newspaper, he was flogged for libelling the doctors as he sat in his shop. His boy Nicolka died of cholera. Karpovna is still alive, and still loves and fears her Prokofyi. Whenever she sees me she sadly shakes her head and says with a sigh:

'Poor thing. You are lost!'

On week-days I am busy from early morning till late at night. And on Sundays and holidays I take my little niece (my sister expected a boy, but a girl was born) and go with her to the cemetery, where I stand or sit and look at the grave of my dear one, and tell the child that her mother is lying there.

Sometimes I find Aniuta Blagovo by the grave. We greet each other and stand silently, or we talk of Cleopatra, and the child, and the sadness of this life. Then we leave the cemetery and walk in silence and she lags behind—on purpose, to avoid staying with me. The little girl, joyful, happy, with her eyes half-closed against the brilliant sunlight, laughs and holds out her little hands to her, and we stop and together we fondle the darling child.

And when we reach the town, Aniuta Blagovo, blushing and agitated, says good-bye, and walks on alone, serious and circumspect. . . . And, to look at her, none of the passers-by could imagine that she had just been walking by my side and even fondling the child.

THE HOUSE WITH THE MEZZANINE

(A PAINTER'S STORY)

I

It happened nigh on seven years ago, when I was living in one of the districts of the J. province, on the estate of Bielokurov, a landowner, a young man who used to get up early, dress himself in a long overcoat, drink beer in the evenings, and all the while complain to me that he could nowhere find any one in sympathy with his ideas. He lived in a little house in the orchard, and I lived in the old manor-house, in a huge pillared hall where there was no furniture except a large divan, on which I slept, and a table at which I used to play patience. Even in calm weather there was always a moaning in the chimney, and in a storm the whole house would rock and seem as though it must split, and it was quite terrifying, especially at night, when all the ten great windows were suddenly lit up by a flash of lightning.

Doomed by fate to permanent idleness, I did positively nothing. For hours together I would sit and look through the windows at the sky, the birds, the trees, and read my letters over and over again, and then for hours together I would sleep. Sometimes I would go out and wander aimlessly until evening.

Once on my way home I came unexpectedly on a strange

farmhouse. The sun was already setting, and the lengthening shadows were thrown over the ripening corn. Two rows of closely planted tall fir trees stood like two thick walls, forming a sombre, magnificent avenue. I climbed the fence and walked up the avenue, slipping on the fir needles which lay two inches thick on the ground. It was still, dark, and only here and there in the tops of the trees shimmered a bright gold light casting the colours of the rainbow on a spider's web. The smell of the firs was almost suffocating. Then I turned into an avenue of limes. And here too were desolation and decay; the dead leaves rustled mournfully beneath my feet, and there were lurking shadows among the trees. To the right, in an old orchard, a yellow-hammer sang a faint reluctant song, and he too must have been old. The lime trees soon came to an end and I came to a white house with a terrace and a mezzanine, and suddenly a vista opened upon a farmyard with a pond and a bathing-shed, and a row of green willows, with a village beyond, and above it stood a tall, slender belfry, on which glowed a cross catching the light of the setting sun. For a moment I was possessed with a sense of enchantment, intimate, particular, as though I had seen the scene before in my childhood.

By the white stone gate surmounted with stone lions, which led from the yard into the field, stood two girls. One of them, the elder, thin, pale, very handsome, with masses of chestnut hair and a little stubborn mouth, looked rather prim and scarcely glanced at me; the other, who was quite young— seventeen or eighteen, no more, also thin and pale, with a big mouth and big eyes, looked at me in surprise as I passed, said something in English and looked confused, and it seemed to me that I had always known their dear faces. And I returned home feeling as though I had awoken from a pleasant dream.

Soon after that, one afternoon, when Bielokurov and I were walking near the house, suddenly there came into the yard a spring-carriage in which sat one of the two girls, the elder. She had come to ask for subscriptions to a fund for those who had suffered in a recent fire. Without looking at us, she told us very seriously how many houses had been burned down in Sianov, how many men, women, and children had been left without shelter, and what had been done by the committee of which she was a member. She gave us the list for us to write our names, put it away, and began to say good-bye.

'You have completely forgotten us, Piotr Petrovich,' she said to Bielkurov, as she gave him her hand. 'Come and see us, and

if Mr N.'—she said my name—'would like to see how the
admirers of his talent live and would care to come and see us,
then mother and I would be very pleased.'

I bowed.

When she had gone Piotr Petrovitch began to tell me about
her. The girl, he said, was of a good family and her name was
Lydia Volchaninov, and the estate, on which she lived with her
mother and sister, was called, like the village on the other side
of the pond, Sholkovka. Her father had once occupied an
eminent position in Moscow and died a privy councillor. Not-
withstanding their large means, the Volchaninovs always lived
in the village, summer and winter, and Lydia was a teacher in
the zemstvo school at Sholkovka and earned twenty-five
roubles a month. She only spent what she earned on herself
and was proud of her independence.

'They are an interesting family,' said Bielokurov. 'We
ought to go and see them. They will be very glad to see
you.'

One afternoon, during a holiday, we remembered the Volchaninovs and went over to Sholkovka. They were all at home.
The mother, Ekaterina Pavlovna, had obviously once been
handsome, but now she was stouter than her age warranted,
suffered from asthma, was melancholy and absent-minded as
she tried to entertain me with talk about painting. When she
heard from her daughter that I might perhaps come over to
Sholkovka, she hurriedly called to mind a few of my landscapes
which she had seen in exhibitions in Moscow, and now she asked
what I had tried to express in them. Lydia, or as she was called
at home, Lyda, talked more to Bielokurov than to me. Seriously
and without a smile, she asked him why he did not work for the
zemstvo and why up till now he had never been to a zemstvo
meeting.

'It is not right of you, Piotr Petrovich,' she said reproachfully.
'It is not right. It is a shame.'

'True, Lyda, true,' said her mother. 'It is not right.'

'All our district is in Balaguin's hands,' Lyda went on,
turning to me. 'He is the chairman of the council and all the
jobs in the district are given to his nephews and brothers-in-law,
and he does exactly as he likes. We ought to fight him. The
young people ought to form a strong party; but you see what our
young men are like. It is a shame, Piotr Petrovich.'

The younger sister, Genya, was silent during the conversation
about the zemstvo. She did not take part in serious conversa-

tions, for by the family she was not considered grown-up, and they gave her her baby name, Missyuss, because as a child she used to call her English governess that. All the time she examined me curiously and when I looked at the photograph album she explained: 'This is my uncle. . . . That is my godfather,' and fingered the portraits, and at the same time touched me with her shoulder in a childlike way, and I could see her small, undeveloped bosom, her thin shoulders, her long, slim waist tightly drawn in by a belt.

We played croquet and lawn-tennis, walked in the garden, had tea, and then a large supper. After the huge pillared hall, I felt out of tune in the small cosy house, where there were no oleographs on the walls and the servants were treated considerately, and everything seemed to me young and pure, through the presence of Lyda and Missyuss, and everything was decent and orderly. At supper Lyda again talked to Bielokurov about the zemstvo, about Balaguin, about school libraries. She was a lively, sincere, serious girl, and it was interesting to listen to her, though she spoke at length and in a loud voice—perhaps because she was used to holding forth at school. On the other hand, Piotr Petrovich, who from his university days had retained the habit of reducing any conversation to a discussion, spoke tediously, slowly, and deliberately, with an obvious desire to be taken for a clever and progressive man. He gesticulated and upset the sauce with his sleeve and it made a large pool on the table-cloth, though nobody but myself seemed to notice it.

When we returned home the night was dark and still.

'I call it good breeding,' said Bielokurov, with a sigh, 'not so much not to upset the sauce on the table, as not to notice it when someone else has done it. Yes. An admirable intellectual family. I'm rather out of touch with nice people. Ah! terribly. And all through business, business, business!'

He went on to say what hard work being a good farmer meant. And I thought: What a stupid, lazy lout! When we talked seriously he would drag it out with his awful drawl—er, er, er— and he works just as he talks—slowly, always behindhand, never up to time; and as for being businesslike, I don't believe it, he often keeps letters given him to post for weeks in his pocket.

'The worst of it is,' he murmured as he walked along by my side—'the worst of it is that you go working away and never get any sympathy from anybody.'

II

I began to frequent the Volchaninovs' house. Usually I sat on the bottom step of the veranda. I was filled with dissatisfaction, vague discontent with my life, which had passed so quickly and uninterestingly, and I thought all the while how good it would be to tear out of my breast my heart which had grown so weary. There would be talk going on on the terrace, the rustling of dresses, the fluttering of the pages of a book. I soon got used to Lyda receiving the sick all day long, and distributing books, and I used often to go with her to the village, bareheaded, under an umbrella. And in the evening she would hold forth about the zemstvo and schools. She was very handsome, subtle, correct, and her lips were thin and sensitive, and whenever a serious conversation started she would say to me dryly:

'This won't interest you.'

I was not sympathetic to her. She did not like me because I was a landscape-painter, and in my pictures did not paint the suffering of the masses, and I seemed to her indifferent to what she believed in. I remember once driving along the shore of Lake Baikal, and I met a Bouryat girl, in shirt and trousers of Chinese cotton, on horseback: I asked her if she would sell me her pipe and, while we were talking, she looked with scorn at my European face and hat, and in a moment she got bored with talking to me, whooped, and galloped away. And in exactly the same way Lyda despised me as a stranger. Outwardly she never showed her dislike of me, but I felt it, and, as I sat on the bottom step of the terrace, I had a certain irritation and said that treating the peasants without being a doctor meant deceiving them, and that it is easy to be a benefactor when one owns four thousand acres.

Her sister, Missyuss, had no such cares and spent her time in complete idleness, like myself. As soon as she got up in the morning she would take a book and read it on the terrace, sitting far back in a lounge chair so that her feet hardly touched the ground, or she would hide herself with her book in the lime-walk, or she would go through the gate into the field. She would read all day long, eagerly poring over the book, and only through her looking fatigued, dizzy, and pale sometimes, was it possible to guess how much her reading exhausted her. When she saw me come she would blush a little and leave her book, and, looking into my face with her big eyes, she would tell me of things that had happened, how the chimney in the servants' room had caught fire, or how the labourer had caught a large fish in the pond. On week-days she usually wore a bright-coloured blouse and a dark-blue skirt. We used to go out together and pluck cherries for jam, in the boat, and when she jumped to reach a cherry, or pulled the oars, her thin, round arms would shine through her wide sleeves. Or I would make a sketch and she would stand and watch me breathlessly.

One Sunday, at the end of June, I went over to the Volchaninovs, in the morning about nine o'clock. I walked through the park, avoiding the house, looking for mushrooms, which were very plentiful that summer, and marking them so as to pick them later with Genya. A warm wind was blowing. I met Genya and her mother, both in bright Sunday dresses, going home from church, and Genya was holding her hat against the wind. They told me they were going to have tea on the terrace.

As a man without a care in the world, seeking somehow to justify his constant idleness, I have always found such festive mornings in a country house wholly attractive. When the green garden, still moist with dew, shines in the sun and seems happy, and when the terrace smells of mignonette and oleander, and the young people have just returned from church and drink tea in the garden, and when they are all so gaily dressed and so merry, and when you know that all these healthy, satisfied, beautiful people will do nothing all day long, then you long for all life to be like that. So I thought then as I walked through the garden, quite prepared to drift like that without occupation or purpose, all through the day, all through the summer.

Genya carried a basket and she looked as though she knew that she would find me there. We gathered mushrooms and talked, and whenever she asked me a question she stood in front of me to see my face.

'Yesterday,' she said, 'a miracle happened in our village. Pelagueya, the cripple, has been ill for a whole year, and no doctors or medicines were any good, but yesterday an old woman muttered over her and she got better.'

'That's nothing,' I said. 'One should not go to sick people and old women for miracles. Is not health a miracle? And life itself? A miracle is something incomprehensible.'

'And you are not afraid of the incomprehensible?'

'No. I like to face things I do not understand and I do not submit to them. I am superior to them. Man must think himself higher than lions, tigers, stars, higher than anything in nature, even higher than that which seems incomprehensible and miraculous. Otherwise he is not a man, but a mouse which is afraid of everything.'

Genya thought that I, as an artist, knew a great deal and could guess what I did not know. She wanted me to lead her into the region of the eternal and the beautiful, into the highest world, with which, as she thought, I was perfectly familiar, and she talked to me of God, of eternal life, of the miraculous. And I, who did not admit that I and my imagination would perish for ever, would reply: 'Yes. Men are immortal. Yes, eternal life awaits us.' And she would listen and believe me and never asked for proof.

As we approached the house she suddenly stopped and said: 'Our Lyda is a remarkable person, isn't she? I love her dearly and would gladly sacrifice my life for her at any time. But tell me'—Genya touched my sleeve with her finger—'but tell me, why do you argue with her all the time? Why are you so irritated?'

'Because she is not right.'

Genya shook her head and tears came to her eyes.

'How incomprehensible!' she muttered.

At that moment Lyda came out, and she stood by the balcony with a riding-whip in her hand, and looked very fine and pretty in the sunlight as she gave some orders to a farm-hand. Bustling about and talking loudly, she tended two or three of her patients, and then with a businesslike, preoccupied look she walked through the house, opening one cupboard after another, and at last went off to the attic; it took some time to find her for dinner and she did not come until we had finished the soup. Somehow I remember all these little details and love to dwell on them, and I remember the whole of that day vividly, though nothing particular happened. After dinner Genya read, lying in her lounge chair, and I sat on the bottom step of the terrace. We were silent. The sky was overcast and a thin fine rain began to fall. It was hot, the wind had dropped, and it seemed the day would never end. Ekaterina Pavlovna came out on to the terrace with a fan, looking very sleepy.

'Oh, mamma,' said Genya, kissing her hand. 'It is not good for you to sleep during the day.'

They adored each other. When one went into the garden, the other would stand on the terrace and look at the trees and call: 'Hallo, Genya!' or 'Mamma, dear, where are you?'

They always prayed together and shared the same faith, and they understood each other very well, even when they were silent. And they treated other people in exactly the same way. Ekaterina Pavlovna also soon got used to me and became attached to me, and when I did not run up for a few days she would send to inquire if I was well. And she too used to look admiringly at my sketches, and with the same frank loquacity she would tell me things that happened, and she would confide her domestic secrets to me.

She revered her elder daughter. Lyda never came to her for caresses, and only talked about serious things: she went her own way and to her mother and sister she was as sacred and enigmatic as the admiral, sitting in his cabin, to his sailors.

'Our Lyda is a remarkable person,' her mother would often say; 'isn't she?'

And, now, as the soft rain fell, we spoke of Lyda.

'She is a remarkable woman,' said her mother, and added in a low voice like a conspirator's as she looked round, 'such as she have to be looked for with a lamp in broad daylight, though, you know, I am beginning to be anxious. The school, pharmacies, books—all very well, but why go to such extremes? She is twenty-three and it is time for her to think seriously about herself. If she goes on with her books and her pharmacies she won't know how life has passed. . . . She ought to marry.'

Genya, pale with reading, and with her hair ruffled, looked up and said, as if to herself, as she glanced at her mother:

'Mamma, dear, everything depends on the will of God.'

And once more she plunged into her book.

Bielokurov came over in a *poddiovka*, wearing an embroidered shirt. We played croquet and lawn-tennis, and when it grew dark we had a long supper, and Lyda once more spoke of her schools and Balaguin, who had got the whole district into his own hands. As I left the Volchaninovs that night I carried away an impression of a long, long idle day, with a sad consciousness that everything ends, however long it may be. Genya took me to the gate and perhaps, because she had spent the whole day with me from the beginning to end, I felt somehow lonely without her, and the whole kindly family was dear to me; and for the first time during the whole of that summer I had a desire to work.

'Tell me why you lead such a monotonous life,' I asked Bielokurov, as we went home. 'My life is tedious, dull, monotonous, because I am a painter, a queer fish, and have been worried all my life with envy, discontent, disbelief in my work: I am always poor, I am a vagabond, but you are a wealthy, normal man, a landowner, a gentleman—why do you live so tamely and take so little from life? Why, for instance, haven't you fallen in love with Lyda or Genya?'

'You forget that I love another woman,' answered Bielokurov.

He meant his mistress Lyubov Ivanovna, who lived with him in the orchard house. I used to see the lady every day, very stout, podgy, pompous, like a fatted goose, walking in the garden in a Russian head-dress, always with a sunshade, and the servants used to call her to meals or tea. Three years ago she rented a part of his house for the summer, and stayed on to live with Bielokurov, apparently for ever. She was ten years older than he and managed him very strictly, so that he had to ask her permission to go out. She would often sob and make horrible noises like a man with a cold, and then I used to send and tell her that if she did not stop I would go away. Then she would stop.

When we reached home, Bielokurov sat down on the divan and frowned and brooded, and I began to pace up and down the hall, feeling a sweet stirring in me, exactly like a stirring of love. I wanted to talk about the Volchaninovs.

'Lyda could only fall in love with a zemstvo worker like herself, someone who is run off his legs with hospitals and schools,' I said. 'For the sake of a girl like that a man might not only become a zemstvo worker, but might even become worn out, like the tale of the iron boots. And Missyuss? How charming Missyuss is!'

Bielokurov began to talk at length and with his drawling er-er-ers of the disease of the century—pessimism. He spoke confidently and argumentatively. Hundreds of miles of deserted, monotonous, blackened steppe could not so forcibly depress the mind as a man like that, sitting and talking and showing no signs of going away.

'The point is neither pessimism nor optimism,' I said irritably, 'but that ninety-nine out of a hundred have no sense.'

Bielokurov took this to mean himself, was offended, and went away.

III

'The prince is on a visit to Malozyomov and sends you his regards,' said Lyda to her mother, as she came in and took off her gloves. 'He told me many interesting things. He promised to bring forward in the zemstvo council the question of a medical station at Malozyomov, but he says there is little hope.' And turning to me, she said: 'Forgive me, I keep forgetting that you are not interested.'

I felt irritated.

'Why not?' I asked and shrugged my shoulders. 'You don't care about my opinion, but I assure you, the question greatly interests me.'

'Yes?'

'In my opinion there is absolutely no need for a medical station at Malozyomov.'

My irritation affected her; she gave a glance at me, half closed her eyes and said:

'What is wanted then? Landscapes?'

'Not landscapes either. Nothing is wanted there.'

She finished taking off her gloves and took up a newspaper which must have come by post; a moment later, she said quietly, apparently controlling herself:

'Last week Anna died in childbirth, and if a medical man had been available she would have lived. However, I suppose landscape-painters are entitled to their opinions.'

'I have a very definite opinion, I assure you,' said I, and she took refuge behind the newspaper, as though she did not wish to listen. 'In my opinion medical stations, schools, libraries, pharmacies, under existing conditions, only lead to slavery. The masses are caught in a vast chain; you do not cut it but only add new links to it. That is my opinion.'

She looked at me and smiled mockingly, and I went on, striving to catch the thread of my ideas.

'It does not matter that Anna should die in childbirth, but it does matter that all these Annas, Marfas, Pelagueyas, from dawn to sunset should be grinding away, ill from overwork, all their lives worried about their starving sickly children; all their lives they are afraid of death and disease, and have to be looking after themselves; they fade in youth, grow old very early, and die in filth and dirt; their children as they grow up go the same way and hundreds of years slip by and millions of people live worse than animals—in constant dread of never having a crust to eat; but the horror of their position is that they have no time to think of their souls, no time to remember that they are made in the likeness of God; hunger, cold, animal fear, incessant work, like drifts of snow block all the ways to spiritual activity, to the very thing that distinguishes man from the animals, and is the only thing indeed that makes life worth living. You come to their assistance with hospitals and schools, but you do not free them from their fetters; on the contrary, you enslave them even more, since by introducing new prejudices into their lives, you increase the number of their demands, not to mention the fact that they have to pay the zemstvo for their drugs and pamphlets, and therefore, have to work harder than ever.'

'I will not argue with you,' said Lyda. 'I have heard all that.' She put down her paper. 'I will only tell you one thing, it is no good sitting with folded hands. It is true, we do not save mankind, and perhaps we do make mistakes, but we do what we can and we are right. The highest and most sacred truth for an educated being is to help his neighbours, and we do what we can to help. You do not like it, but it is impossible to please everybody.'

'True, Lyda, true,' said her mother.

In Lyda's presence her courage always failed her, and as she talked she would look timidly at her, for she was afraid of saying something foolish or out of place; and she never contradicted, but would always agree: 'True, Lyda, true.'

'Teaching peasants to read and write, giving them little moral pamphlets and medical assistance, cannot decrease either ignorance or mortality, just as the light from your windows cannot illuminate this huge garden,' I said. 'You give nothing by your interference in the lives of these people. You only create new demands, and a new compulsion to work.'

'Ah! My God, but we must do something!' said Lyda exasperatedly, and I could tell by her voice that she thought my opinions negligible and despised me.

'It is necessary,' I said, 'to free people from hard physical work. It is necessary to relieve them of their yoke, to give them breathing space, to save them from spending their whole lives in the kitchen or the byre, in the fields; they should have time to take thought of their souls, of God and to develop their spiritual capacities. Every human being's salvation lies in spiritual activity—in his continual search for truth and the meaning of life. Give them some relief from rough, animal labour, let them feel free, then you will see how ridiculous at bottom your pamphlets and pharmacies are. Once a human being is aware of his vocation, then he can only be satisfied with religion, service, art, and not with trifles like that.'

'Free them from work?' Lyda gave a smile. 'Is that possible?'

'Yes. . . . Take upon yourself a part of their work. If we all, in town and country, without exception, agreed to share the work which is being spent by mankind in the satisfaction of physical demands, then none of us would have to work more than two of three hours a day. If all of us, rich and poor, worked three hours a day the rest of our time would be free. And then to be still less dependent on our bodies, we should invent machines to do the work and we should try to reduce our demands to the minimum. We should toughen ourselves and our children would not be afraid of hunger and cold, and we should not be anxious about their health, as Anna, Maria, Pelagueya were anxious. Then supposing we did not bother about doctors and pharmacies, and did away with tobacco factories and distilleries—what a lot of free time we should have! We would give our leisure to service and the arts. Just as peasants all work together to repair the roads, so the whole community would work together to seek truth and the meaning of life, and, I am sure of it—truth would be found very soon, man would get rid of his continual, poignant, depressing fear of death and even of death itself.'

'But you contradict yourself,' said Lyda. 'You talk about service and deny education.'

'I deny the education of a man who can only use it to read the signs on the public-houses and possibly a pamphlet which he is incapable of understanding—the kind of education we have had from the time of Rurik; and village life has remained exactly as it was then. Not education is wanted but freedom for the full development of spiritual capacities. Not schools are wanted but universities.'

'You deny medicine too.'

'Yes. It should only be used for the investigation of diseases, as natural phenomena, not for their cure. It is no good curing diseases if you don't cure their causes. Remove the chief cause—physical labour, and there will be no diseases. I don't acknowledge the science which cures,' I went on excitedly. 'Science and art, when they are true, are directed not to temporary or private purposes, but to the eternal and the general—they seek the truth and the meaning of life, they seek God, the soul, and when they are harnessed to passing needs and activities, like pharmacies and libraries, then they only complicate and encumber life. We have any number of doctors, pharmacists, lawyers, and highly educated people, but we have no biologists, mathematicians, philosophers, poets. All our intellectual and spiritual energy is wasted on temporary passing needs. . . . Scientists, writers, painters work and work, and thanks to them the comforts of life grow greater every day, the demands of the body multiply, but we are still a long way from the truth and man still remains the most rapacious and unseemly of animals, and everything tends to make the majority of mankind degenerate and more and more lacking in vitality. Under such conditions the life of an artist has no meaning, and the more talented he is, the more strange and incomprehensible his position is, since it only amounts to his working for the amusement of the predatory, disgusting animal, man, and supporting the existing state of things. And I don't want to work and will not. . . . Nothing is wanted, so let the world go to hell.'

'Missyuss, go away,' said Lyda to her sister, evidently thinking my words dangerous to so young a girl.

Genya looked sadly at her sister and mother and went out.

'People generally talk like that,' said Lyda, 'when they want to excuse their indifference. It is easier to deny hospitals and schools than to come and teach.'

'True, Lyda, true,' her mother agreed.

'You say you will not work,' Lyda went on. 'Apparently you set a high price on your work, but do stop arguing. We shall never agree, since I value the most imperfect library or pharmacy, of which you spoke so scornfully just now, more than all the landscapes in the world.' And at once she turned to her mother and began to talk in quite a different tone: 'The prince has got very thin, and is much changed since the last time he was here. The doctors are sending him to Vichy.'

She talked to her mother about the prince to avoid talking to me. Her face was burning, and, in order to conceal her agitation, she bent over the table as if she were short-sighted and made a show of reading the newspaper. My presence was distasteful to her. I took my leave and went home.

IV

All was quiet outside: the village on the other side of the pond was already asleep, not a single light was to be seen, and on the pond there was only the faint reflection of the stars. By the gate with the stone lions stood Genya, waiting to accompany me.

'The village is asleep,' I said, trying to see her face in the darkness, and I could see her dark sad eyes fixed on me. 'The innkeeper and the horse-stealers are sleeping quietly, and decent people like ourselves quarrel and irritate each other.'

It was a melancholy August night—melancholy because it already smelled of the autumn; the moon rose behind a purple cloud and hardly lighted the road and the dark fields of winter corn on either side. Stars fell frequently, Genya walked beside me on the road and tried not to look at the sky, to avoid seeing the falling stars, which somehow frightened her.

'I believe you are right,' she said, trembling in the evening chill. 'If people could give themselves to spiritual activity, they would soon burst everything.'

'Certainly. We are superior beings, and if we really knew all the power of the human genius and lived only for higher purposes, then we should become like gods. But this will never be. Mankind will degenerate and of their genius not a trace will be left.'

When the gate was out of sight Genya stopped and hurriedly shook my hand.

'Good night,' she said, trembling; her shoulders were covered only with a thin blouse and she was shivering with cold. 'Come to-morrow.'

I was filled with a sudden dread of being left alone with my inevitable dissatisfaction with myself and people, and I, too, tried not to see the falling stars.

'Stay with me a little longer,' I said. 'Please.' I loved Genya, and she must have loved me, because she used to meet me and walk with me, and because she looked at me with tender admiration. How thrillingly beautiful her pale face was, her thin nose, her arms, her slenderness, her inactivity, her constant reading. And her mind? I suspected her of having an unusual intellect; I was fascinated by the breadth of her views, perhaps because she thought differently from the strong, handsome Lyda, who did not love me. Genya liked me as a painter, I had conquered her heart by my talent, and I longed passionately to paint only for her, and I dreamed of her as my little queen, who would one day possess with me the trees, the fields, the river, the dawn, all nature, wonderful and fascinating, with whom, as with them, I have felt hopeless and useless.

'Stay with me a moment longer,' I called. 'I implore you.'

I took off my overcoat and covered her childish shoulders. Fearing that she would look queer and ugly in a man's coat, she began to laugh and threw it off, and as she did so, I embraced her and began to cover her face, her shoulders, her arms with kisses.

'Till to-morrow,' she whispered timidly as though she was afraid to break the stillness of the night. She embraced me: 'We have no secrets from one another. I must tell mamma and my sister. . . . Is it so terrible? Mamma will be pleased. Mamma loves you, but Lyda!'

She ran to the gates.

'Good-bye,' she called out.

For a couple of minutes I stood and heard her running. I had no desire to go home, there was nothing there to go for. I stood for a while lost in thought, and then quietly dragged myself back, to have one more look at the house in which she lived, the dear, simple, old house, which seemed to look at me with the windows of the mezzanine for eyes, and to understand everything. I walked past the terrace, sat down on a bench by the lawn-tennis court, in the darkness under an old elm tree, and looked at the house. In the windows of the mezzanine, where Missyuss had her room, shone a bright light, and then a faint green glow. The lamp had been covered with a shade. Shadows began to move. . . . I was filled with tenderness and a calm satisfaction, to think that I could let myself be carried away and fall in love, and at the same time I felt uneasy at the thought that only a few yards away in one of the rooms of the house lay Lyda who did not love me, and perhaps hated me. I sat and waited to see if Genya would come out. I listened attentively and it seemed to me they were sitting in the mezzanine.

An hour passed. The green light went out, and the shadows were no longer visible. The moon hung high above the house and lit the sleeping garden and the avenues; I could distinctly see the dahlias and roses in the flower-bed in front of the house, and all seemed to be of one colour. It was very cold. I left the garden, picked up my overcoat in the road, and walked slowly home.

Next day after dinner when I went to the Volchaninovs', the glass door was wide open. I sat down on the terrace expecting Genya to come from behind the flower-bed or from out of the rooms; then I went into the drawing-room and the dining-room. There was not a soul to be seen. From the dining-room I went down a long passage into the hall, and then back again. There were several doors in the passage and behind one of them I could hear Lyda's voice:

'To the crow somewhere . . . God . . .'—she spoke slowly

and distinctly, and was probably dictating—'. . . God sent a piece of cheese. . . . To the crow . . . somewhere . . . Who is there?' she called out suddenly as she heard my footsteps.

'It is I.'

'Oh! excuse me. I can't come out just now. I am teaching Masha.'

'Is Ekaterina Pavlovna in the garden?'

'No. She and my sister left to-day for my aunt's in Penza, and in the winter they are probably going abroad,' She added after a short silence: 'To the crow somewhere God sent a pi-ece of cheese. Have you got that?'

I went out into the hall, and, without a thought in my head, stood and looked out at the pond and the village, and still I heard:

'A piece of cheese. . . . To the crow somewhere God sent a piece of cheese.'

And I left the house by the way I had come the first time, only reversing the order, from the yard into the garden, past the house, then along the lime-walk. Here a boy overtook me and handed me a note: 'I have told my sister everything and she insists on my parting from you,' I read. 'I could not hurt her by disobeying. God will give you happiness. If you knew how bitterly mamma and I have cried!'

Then through the fir avenue and the rotten fence. . . . Over the fields where the corn was ripening and the quails piped, cows and shackled horses now were browsing. Here and there on the hills the winter corn was already showing green. A sober, workaday mood possessed me and I was ashamed of all I had said at the Volchaninovs', and once more it became tedious to go on living. I went home, packed my things, and left that evening for Petersburg.

I never saw the Volchaninovs again. Lately on my way to the Crimea I met Bielokurov at a station. As of old he was in a *poddiovka*, wearing an embroidered shirt, and when I asked after his health, he replied: 'Quite well, thanks be to God.' He began to talk. He had sold his estate and bought another, smaller one in the name of Lyubov Ivanovna. He told me a little about the Volchaninovs. Lyda, he said, still lived at Sholkovka and taught the children in the school, little by little she succeeded in gathering round herself a circle of sympathetic people, who formed a strong party, and at the last zemstvo election they drove out Balaguin, who up till then had had the whole district in his hands. Of Genya Bielokurov said that she did not live at home and he did not know where she was.

I have already begun to forget about the house with the mezzanine, and only now and then, when I am working or reading, suddenly—without rhyme or reason—I remember the green light in the window, and the sound of my own footsteps as I walked through the fields that night, when I was in love, rubbing my hands to keep them warm. And even more rarely when I am sad and lonely, I begin already to recollect and it seems to me that I, too, am being remembered and waited for, and that we shall meet. . . .

Missyuss, where are you?

TYPHUS

In a smoking compartment of the mail-train from Petersburg to Moscow sat a young lieutenant, Klimov by name. Opposite him sat an elderly man with a clean-shaven, shipmaster's face, to all appearances a well-to-do Finn or Swede, who all through the journey smoked a pipe and talked round and round the same subject.

'Ha! you are an officer! My brother is also an officer, but he is a sailor. He is a sailor and is stationed at Kronstadt. Why are you going to Moscow?'

'I am stationed there.'

'Ha! Are you married?'

'No. I live with my aunt and sister.'

'My brother is also an officer, but he is married and has a wife and three children. Ha!'

The Finn looked surprised at something, smiled broadly and fatuously as he exclaimed, 'Ha!' and every now and then blew through the stem of his pipe. Klimov, who was feeling rather unwell, and not at all inclined to answer questions, hated him with all his heart. He thought how good it would be to snatch his gurgling pipe out of his hands and throw it under the seat and to order the Finn himself into another car.

'They are awful people, these Finns and . . . Greeks,' he thought. 'Useless, good-for-nothing, disgusting people. They only cumber the earth. What is the good of them?'

And the thought of Finns and Greeks filled him with a kind

of nausea. He tried to compare them with the French and the Italians, but the idea of those races somehow roused in him the notion of organ-grinders, naked women, and the foreign oleographs which hung over the chest of drawers in his aunt's house.

The young officer felt generally out of sorts. There seemed to be no room for his arms and legs, though he had the whole seat to himself; his mouth was dry and sticky, his head was heavy, and his clouded thoughts seemed to wander at random, not only in his head, but also outside it among the seats and the people looming in the darkness. Through the turmoil in his brain, as through a dream, he heard the murmur of voices, the rattle of the wheels, the slamming of doors. Bells, whistles, conductors, the tramp of the people on the platforms came oftener than usual. The time slipped by quickly, imperceptibly, and it seemed that the train stopped every minute at a station as now and then there would come up the sound of metallic voices:

'Is the post ready?'

'Ready.'

It seemed to him that the stove-heater came in too often to look at the thermometer, and that trains never stopped passing and his own train was always roaring over bridges. The noise, the whistle, the Finn, the tobacco smoke—all mixed with the ominous shifting of misty shapes, weighed on Klimov like an intolerable nightmare. In terrible anguish he lifted up his aching head, looked at the lamp whose light was encircled with shadows and misty spots; he wanted to ask for water, but his dry tongue would hardly move, and he had hardly strength enough to answer the Finn's questions. He tried to lie down more comfortably and sleep, but he did not succeed; the Finn fell asleep several times, woke up and lighted his pipe, talked to him with his 'Ha!' and went to sleep again; and the lieutenant could still not find room for his legs on the seat, and all the while the ominous figures shifted before his eyes.

At Spirov he got out to have a drink of water. He saw some people sitting at a table eating hurriedly.

'How can they eat?' he thought, trying to avoid the smell of roast meat in the air and seeing the chewing mouths, for both seemed to him utterly disgusting and made him feel sick.

A handsome lady was talking to a military man in a red cap, and she showed magnificent white teeth when she smiled; her smile, her teeth, the lady herself produced in Klimov the same impression of disgust as the ham and the fried cutlets. He could not understand how the military man in the red cap could bear to sit near her and look at her healthy smiling face.

After he had drunk some water, he went back to his place. The Finn sat and smoked. His pipe gurgled and sucked like a galosh full of holes in dirty weather.

'Ha!' with some surprise. 'What station is this?'

'I don't know,' said Klimov, lying down and shutting his mouth to keep out the acrid tobacco smoke.

'When do we get to Tver?'

'I don't know. I am sorry, I. . . . I can't talk. I am not well. I have a cold.'

The Finn knocked out his pipe against the window-frame and began to talk of his brother, the sailor. Klimov paid no more attention to him and thought in agony of his soft, comfortable bed, of the bottle of cold water, of his sister Katy, who knew so well how to tuck him up and cosset him. He even smiled when there flashed across his mind his soldier-servant Pavel, taking off his heavy, close-fitting boots and putting water on the table. It seemed to him that he would only have to lie on his bed and drink some water and his nightmare would give way to a sound, healthy sleep.

'Is the post ready?' came a dull voice from a distance.

'Ready,' answered a loud, bass voice almost by the very window.

It was the second or third station from Spirov.

Time passed quickly, seemed to gallop along, and there would be no end to the bells, whistles, and stops. In despair Klimov pressed his face into the corner of the cushion, held his head in his hands, and again began to think of his sister Katy and his orderly Pavel; but his sister and his orderly got mixed up with the looming figures and whirled about and disappeared. His breath, thrown back from the cushion, burned his face, and his legs ached and a draught from the window poured into his back, but, painful though it was, he refused to change his position. . . . A heavy, drugging torpor crept over him and chained his limbs.

When at length he raised his head, the car was quite light. The passengers were putting on their overcoats and moving about. The train stopped. Porters in white aprons and number-plates bustled about the passengers and seized their boxes. Klimov put on his greatcoat mechanically and left the train, and he felt as though it were not himself walking, but someone else, a stranger, and he felt that he was accompanied by the heat of the train, his thirst, and the ominous, lowering figures which all night long had prevented his sleeping. Mechanically he got his luggage and took a cab. The cabman charged him one rouble and twenty-five copecks for driving him to Povarska Street, but he did not haggle and submissively took his seat in the sledge. He could still grasp the difference in numbers, but money had no value to him whatever.

At home Klimov was met by his aunt and his sister Katy, a girl of eighteen. Katy had a copy-book and a pencil in her hands as she greeted him, and he remembered that she was preparing for a teacher's examination. He took no notice of her greetings and questions, but gasped from the heat, and walked aimlessly through the rooms until he reached his own, and then he fell prone on the bed. The Finn, the red cap, the lady with the white teeth, the smell of roast meat, the shifting spot in the lamp, filled his mind and he lost consciousness and did not hear the frightened voices near him.

When he came to himself he found himself in bed, undressed, and noticed the water-bottle and Pavel, but it did not make him any more comfortable nor easy. His legs and arms, as before, felt cramped, his tongue clove to his palate, and he could hear the bubble of the Finn's pipe. . . . By the bed, growing out of Pavel's broad back, a stout, black-bearded doctor was bustling.

'All right, all right, my lad,' he murmured. 'Excellent, excellent. . . . Jist so, jist so. . . .'

The doctor called Klimov 'my lad.' Instead of 'just so,' he said 'jist saow,' and instead of 'yes,' 'yies.'

'Yies, yies, yies,' he said. 'Jist saow, jist saow. . . . Don't be downhearted!'

The doctor's quick, careless way of speaking, his well-fed face, and the condescending tone in which he said 'my lad' exasperated Klimov.

'Why do you call me "my lad"?' he moaned. 'Why this familiarity, damn it all?'

And he was frightened by the sound of his own voice. It was so dry, weak, and hollow that he could hardly recognize it.

'Excellent, excellent,' murmured the doctor, not at all offended. 'Yies, yies. You musn't be cross.'

And at home the time galloped away as alarmingly quickly as in the train. . . . The light of day in his bedroom was every now and then changed to the dim light of evening. . . . The doctor never seemed to leave the bedside, and his 'Yies, yies, yies,' could be heard at every moment. Through the room stretched an endless row of faces: Pavel, the Finn, Captain

Yaroshevich, Sergeant Maximenko, the red cap, the lady with the white teeth, the doctor. All of them talked, waved their hands, smoked, ate. Once in broad daylight Klimov saw his regimental priest, Father Alexander, in his stole and with the service-book in his hands, standing by the bedside and muttering something with such a serious expression as Klimov had never seen him wear before. The lieutenant remembered that Father Alexander used to call all the Catholic officers Poles, and wishing to make the priest laugh, he exclaimed:

'Father, Yaroshevich the Pole has fled to the woods.'

But Father Alexander, usually a gay, light-hearted man, did not laugh and looked even more serious, and made the sign of the cross over Klimov. At night, one after the other, there would come slowly creeping in and out two shadows. They were his aunt and his sister. The shadow of his sister would kneel down and pray; she would bow to the ikon, and her grey shadow on the wall would bow, too, so that two shadows prayed to God. And all the time there was a smell of roast meat and of the Finn's pipe, but once Klimov could detect a distinct smell of incense. He nearly vomited and cried:

'Incense! Take it away.'

There was no reply. He could only hear priests chanting in an undertone and someone running on the stairs.

When Klimov recovered from his delirium there was not a soul in the bedroom. The morning sun blazed through the window and the drawn curtains, and a trembling beam, thin and keen as a sword, played on the water-bottle. He could hear the rattle of wheels—that meant there was no more snow in the streets. The lieutenant looked at the sunbeam, at the familiar furniture and the door, and his first inclination was to laugh. His chest and stomach trembled with a sweet, happy, tickling laughter. From head to foot his whole body was filled with a feeling of infinite happiness, like that which the first man must have felt when he stood erect and beheld the world for the first time. Klimov had a passionate longing for people, movement, talk. His body lay motionless; he could only move his hands, but he hardly noticed it, for his whole attention was fixed on little things. He was delighted with his breathing and with his laughter; he was delighted with the existence of the water-bottle, the ceiling, the sunbeam, the ribbon on the curtain. God's world, even in such a narrow corner as his bedroom, seemed to him beautiful, varied, great. When the doctor appeared the lieutenant thought how nice his medicine was, how nice and sympathetic the doctor was, how nice and interesting people were, on the whole.

'Yies, yies, yies,' said the doctor. 'Excellent, excellent. Now we are well again. Jist saow. Jist saow.'

The lieutenant listened and laughed gleefully. He remembered the Finn, the lady with the white teeth, the train, and he wanted to eat and smoke.

'Doctor,' he said, 'tell them to bring me a slice of rye bread and salt, and some sardines. . . .'

The doctor refused. Pavel did not obey his order and refused to go for bread. The lieutenant could not bear it and began to cry like a thwarted child.

'Ba-by,' the doctor laughed. 'Mamma! Hushaby!'

Klimov also began to laugh, and when the doctor had gone, he fell sound asleep. He woke up with the same feeling of joy and happiness. His aunt was sitting by his bed.

'Oh, aunty!' He was very happy. 'What has been the matter with me?'

'Typhus.'

'I say! And now I am well, quite well! Where is Katy?'

'She is not at home. She has probably gone to see someone after her examination.'

The old woman bent over her stocking as she said this; her lips began to tremble; she turned her face away and suddenly began to sob. In her grief, she forgot the doctor's orders and cried:

'Oh! Katy! Katy! Our angel is gone from us! She is gone!'

She dropped her stocking and stooped down for it, and her cap fell off her head. Klimov stared at her grey hair, could not understand, was alarmed for Katy, and asked.

'But where is she, aunty?'

The old woman, who had already forgotten Klimov and remembered only her grief, said:

'She caught typhus from you and . . . and died. She was buried the day before yesterday.'

This sudden appalling piece of news came home to Klimov's mind, but dreadful and shocking though it was it could not subdue the animal joy which thrilled through the convalescent lieutenant. He cried, laughed, and soon began to complain that he was given nothing to eat.

Only a week later, when, supported by Pavel, he walked in a dressing-gown to the window, and saw the grey spring sky and heard the horrible rattle of some old rails being carted past, then

his heart ached with sorrow and he began to weep and pressed
his forehead against the window-frame.

'How unhappy I am!' he murmured. 'My God, how unhappy I am!'

And joy gave way to his habitual weariness and a sense of his
irreparable loss.

GOOSEBERRIES

From early morning the sky had been overcast with clouds; the
day was still, cool, and wearisome, as usual on grey, dull days
when the clouds hang low over the fields and it looks like rain,
which never comes. Ivan Ivanich, the veterinary surgeon, and
Bourkin, the schoolmaster, were tired of walking and the fields
seemed endless to them. Far ahead they could just see the
windmills of the village of Mirousky, to the right stretched away
to disappear behind the village a line of hills, and they knew that
it was the bank of the river; meadows, green willows, farmhouses; and from one of the hills there could be seen a field as
endless, telegraph posts, and the train, looking from a distance
like a crawling caterpillar, and in clear weather even the town.
In the calm weather when all nature seemed gentle and melancholy, Ivan Ivanich and Bourkin were filled with love for the
fields and thought how grand and beautiful the country was.

'Last time, when we stopped in Prokufyi's shed,' said Bourkin,
'you were going to tell me a story.'

'Yes. I wanted to tell you about my brother.'

Ivan Ivanich took a deep breath and lighted his pipe before
beginning his story, but just then the rain began to fall. And
in about five minutes it came pelting down and showed no signs
of stopping. Ivan Ivanich stopped and hesitated; the dogs,
wet through, stood with their tails between their legs and
looked at them mournfully.

'We ought to take shelter,' said Bourkin. 'Let us go to
Aliokhin. It is close by.'

'Very well.'

They took a short cut over a stubble field and then bore to
the right, until they came to the road. Soon there appeared
poplars, a garden, the red roofs of granaries; the river began to

glimmer and they came to a wide road with a mill and a white bathing-shed. It was Sophino, where Aliokhin lived.

The mill was working, drowning the sound of the rain, and the dam shook. Round the carts stood wet horses, hanging their heads, and men were walking about with their heads covered with sacks. It was wet, muddy, and unpleasant, and the river looked cold and sullen. Ivan Ivanich and Bourkin felt wet and uncomfortable through and through; their feet were tired with walking in the mud, and they walked past the dam to the barn in silence as though they were angry with each other.

In one of the barns a winnowing machine was working, sending out clouds of dust. On the threshold stood Aliokhin himself, a man of about forty, tall and stout, with long hair, more like a professor or a painter than a farmer. He was wearing a grimy white shirt and rope belt, and pants instead of trousers; and his boots were covered with mud and straw. His nose and eyes were black with dust. He recognized Ivan Ivanich and was apparently very pleased.

'Please, gentlemen,' he said, 'go to the house. I 'll be with you in a minute.'

The house was large and two-storied. Aliokhin lived downstairs in two vaulted rooms with little windows designed for the farm-hands; the farmhouse was plain, and the place smelled of rye bread and vodka and leather. He rarely used the reception-rooms, only when guests arrived. Ivan Ivanich and Bourkin were received by a chambermaid; such a pretty young woman that both of them stopped and exchanged glances.

'You cannot imagine how glad I am to see you, gentlemen,' said Aliokhin, coming after them into the hall. 'I never expected you. Pelagueya,' he said to the maid, 'give my friends a change of clothes. And I will change, too. But I must have a bath. I haven't had one since the spring. Wouldn't you like to come to the bathing-shed? And meanwhile our things will be got ready.'

Pretty Pelagueya, dainty and sweet, brought towels and soap and Aliokhin led his guests to the bathing-shed.

'Yes,' he said, 'it is a long time since I had a bath. My bathing-shed is all right, as you see. My father and I put it up, but somehow I have no time to bathe.'

He sat down on the step and lathered his long hair and neck, and the water round him became brown.

'Yes. I see,' said Ivan Ivanich heavily, looking at his head.

'It is a long time since I bathed,' said Aliokhin shyly, as he soaped himself again, and the water round him became dark blue, like ink.

Ivan Ivanich came out of the shed, plunged into the water with a splash, and swam about in the rain, flapping his arms, and sending waves back, and on the waves tossed white lilies; he swam out to the middle of the pool and dived, and in a minute came up again in another place and kept on swimming and diving, trying to reach the bottom. 'Ah! how delicious!' he shouted in his glee. 'How delicious!' He swam to the mill, spoke to the peasants, and came back, and in the middle of the pool he lay on his back to let the rain fall on his face. Bourkin and Aliokhin were already dressed and ready to go, but he kept on swimming and diving.

'Delicious,' he said. 'Too delicious!'

'You've had enough,' shouted Bourkin.

They went to the house. And only when the lamp was lit in the large drawing-room upstairs, and Bourkin and Ivan Ivanich, dressed in silk dressing-gowns and warm slippers, lounged in chairs, and Aliokhin himself, washed and brushed, in a new frock coat, paced up and down evidently delighting in the warmth and cleanliness and dry clothes and slippers, and pretty Pelagueya, noiselessly tripping over the carpet and smiling sweetly, brought in tea and jam on a tray, only then did Ivan Ivanich begin his story, and it was as though he was being listened to not only by Bourkin and Aliokhin, but also by the old and young ladies and the officer who looked down so staidly and tranquilly from the golden frames.

'We are two brothers,' he began, 'I, Ivan Ivanich, and Nicholai Ivanich, two years younger. I went in for study and became a veterinary surgeon, while Nicholai was at the Exchequer Court when he was nineteen. Our father, Tchimsha-Himalaysky, was a cantonist, but he died with an officer's rank and left us his title of nobility and a small estate. After his death the estate went to pay his debts. However, we spent our childhood there in the country. We were just like peasants' children, spent days and nights in the fields and the woods, minded the house, barked the lime trees, fished, and so on. . . . And you know once a man has fished, or watched the fieldfares hovering in flocks over the village in the bright, cool, autumn days, he can never really be a townsman, and to the day of his death he will be drawn to the country. My brother pined away in the Exchequer. Years passed and he sat in the same place, wrote out the same documents, and thought of one thing,

how to get back to the country. And little by little his distress
became a definite disorder, a fixed idea—to buy a small farm
somewhere by the bank of a river or a lake.

'He was a good fellow and I loved him, but I never sympa-
thized with the desire to shut oneself up on one's own farm. It
is a common saying that a man needs only six feet of land. But
surely a corpse wants that, not a man. And I hear that our
intellectuals have a longing for the land and want to acquire
farms. But it all comes down to the six feet of land. To leave
town, and the struggle and the swim of life, and go and hide
yourself in a farmhouse is not life—it is egoism, laziness; it is a
kind of monasticism, but monasticism without action. A man
needs, not six feet of land, not a farm, but the whole earth, all
nature, where in full liberty he can display all the properties and
qualities of the free spirit.

'My brother Nicholai, sitting in his office, would dream of
eating his own *schi*, with its savoury smell floating across the
farmyard; and of eating out in the open air, and of sleeping in
the sun, and of sitting for hours together on a seat by the gate
and gazing at the fields and the forest. Books on agriculture
and the hints in almanacs were his joy, his favourite spiritual
food; and he liked reading newspapers, but only the advertisements of land to be sold, so many acres of arable and grass land,
with a farmhouse, river, garden, mill, and mill-pond. And he
would dream of garden walls, flowers, fruits, nests, carp in the
pond, don't you know, and all the rest of it. These fantasies
of his used to vary according to the advertisements he found,
but somehow there was always a gooseberry bush in every one.
Not a house, not a romantic spot could he imagine without its
gooseberry bush.

'"Country life has its advantages," he used to say. "You
sit on the veranda drinking tea and your ducklings swim on the
pond, and everything smells good . . . and there are gooseberries."

'He used to draw out a plan of his estate and always the same
things were shown on it: (*a*) Farmhouse, (*b*) cottage, (*c*) vegetable garden, (*d*) gooseberry bush. He used to live meagrely
and never had enough to eat and drink, dressed God knows how,
exactly like a beggar, and always saved and put his money into
the bank. He was terribly stingy. It used to hurt me to see
him, and I used to give him money to go away for a holiday, but
he would put that away, too. Once a man gets a fixed idea,
there's nothing to be done.

'Years passed; he was transferred to another province. He completed his fortieth year and was still reading advertisements in the papers and saving up his money. Then I heard he was married. Still with the same idea of buying a farmhouse with a gooseberry bush, he married an elderly, ugly widow, not out of any feeling for her, but because she had money. With her he still lived stingily, kept her half-starved, and put the money into the bank in his own name. She had been the wife of a postmaster and was used to good living, but with her second husband she did not even have enough black bread; she pined away in her new life, and in three years or so gave up her soul to God. And my brother never for a moment thought himself to blame for her death. Money, like vodka, can play queer tricks with a man. Once in our town a merchant lay dying. Before his death he asked for some honey, and he ate all his notes and scrip with the honey so that nobody should get it. Once I was examining a herd of cattle at a station and a horse-jobber fell under the engine, and his foot was cut off. We carried him into the waiting-room, with the blood pouring down —a terrible business—and all the while he kept on asking anxiously for his foot; he had twenty-five roubles in his boot and did not want to lose them.'

'Keep to your story,' said Bourkin.

'After the death of his wife,' Ivan Ivanich continued, after a long pause, 'my brother began to look out for an estate. Of course you may search for five years, and even then buy a pig in a poke. Through an agent my brother Nicholai raised a mortgage and bought three hundred acres with a farmhouse, a cottage, and a park, but there was no orchard, no gooseberry bush, no duck-pond; there was a river, but the water in it was coffee-coloured because the estate lay between a brick-yard and a gelatine factory. But my brother Nicholai was not worried about that; he ordered twenty gooseberry bushes and settled down to a country life.

'Last year I paid him a visit. I thought I'd go and see how things were with him. In his letters my brother called his estate Tchimbarshov Corner, or Himalayskoe. I arrived at Himalayskoe in the afternoon. It was hot. There were ditches, fences, hedges, rows of young fir trees, trees everywhere, and there was no telling how to cross the yard or where to put your horse. I went to the house and was met by a red-haired dog, as fat as a pig. He tried to bark but felt too lazy. Out of the kitchen came the cook, barefooted, and also as fat as a pig, and said that the master was having his afternoon rest. I went in to my brother and found him sitting on his bed with his knees covered with a blanket; he looked old, stout, flabby; his cheeks, nose, and lips were pendulous. I half expected him to grunt like a pig.

'We embraced and shed a tear of joy and also of sadness to think that we had once been young, but were now both going grey and nearing death. He dressed and took me to see his estate.

'"Well? How are you getting on?" I asked.

'"All right, thank God. I am doing very well."

'He was no longer the poor, tired official, but a real landowner and a person of consequence. He had got used to the place and liked it, ate a great deal, took Russian baths, was growing fat, had already gone to law with the parish and the two factories, and was much offended if the peasants did not call him "Your Lordship." And, like a good landowner, he looked after his soul and did good works pompously, never simply. What good works? He cured the peasants of all kinds of diseases with soda and castor-oil, and on his birthday he would have a thanksgiving service held in the middle of the village, and would treat the peasants to half a bucket of vodka, which he thought the right thing to do. Ah, those horrible buckets of vodka! One day a greasy landowner will drag the peasants before the zemstvo court for trespass, and the next, if it's a holiday, he will give them a bucket of vodka, and they drink and shout "Hooray!" and lick his boots in their drunkenness. A change to good eating and idleness always fills a Russian with the most preposterous self-conceit. Nicholai Ivanich, who, when he was in the Exchequer, was terrified to have an opinion of his own, now imagined that what he said was law. "Education is necessary for the masses, but they are not fit for it." "Corporal punishment is generally harmful, but in certain cases it is useful and indispensable."

'"I know the people and I know how to treat them," he would say. "The people love me. I have only to raise my finger and they will do as I wish."

'And all this, mark you, was said with a kindly smile of wisdom. He was constantly saying: "We noblemen," or "I, as a nobleman." Apparently he had forgotten that our grandfather was a peasant and our father a common soldier. Even our family name, Tchimsha-Himalaysky, which is really an absurd one, seemed to him full-sounding, distinguished, and very pleasing.

'But my point does not concern him so much as myself. I want to tell you what a change took place in me in those few hours while I was in his house. In the evening, while we were having tea, the cook laid a plateful of gooseberries on the table. They had not been bought, but were his own gooseberries, plucked for the first time since the bushes were planted. Nicholai Ivanich laughed with joy and for a minute or two he looked in silence at the gooseberries with tears in his eyes. He could not speak for excitement, then put one into his mouth, glanced at me in triumph, like a child at last being given its favourite toy, and said:

'"How good they are!"

'He went on eating greedily, and saying all the while:

'"How good they are! Do try one!"

'It was hard and sour, but, as Pushkin said, the illusion which exalts us is dearer to us than ten thousand truths. I saw a happy man, one whose dearest dream had come true, who had attained his goal in life, who had got what he wanted, and was pleased with his destiny and with himself. In my idea of human life there is always some alloy of sadness, but now at the sight of a happy man I was filled with something like despair. And at night it grew on me. A bed was made up for me in the room near my brother's and I could hear him, unable to sleep, going again and again to the plate of gooseberries. I thought: "After all, what a lot of contented, happy people there must be! What an overwhelming power that means! I look at this life and see the arrogance and the idleness of the strong, the ignorance and bestiality of the weak, the horrible poverty everywhere, over-crowding, drunkenness, hypocrisy, falsehood. . . . Meanwhile in all the houses, all the streets, there is peace; out of fifty thousand people who live in our town there is not one to kick against it all. Think of the people who go to the market for food: during the day they eat; at night they sleep, talk nonsense, marry, grow old, piously follow their dead to the cemetery; one never sees or hears those who suffer, and all the horror of life goes on somewhere behind the scenes. Everything is quiet, peaceful, and against it all there is only the silent protest of statistics; so many go mad, so many gallons are drunk, so many children die of starvation. . . . And such a state of things is obviously what we want; apparently a happy man only feels so because the unhappy bear their burden in silence, but for which happiness would be impossible. It is a general hypnosis. Every happy man should have someone with a little hammer at his door to knock and remind him that there are unhappy people, and that, however happy he may be, life will sooner or later show its claws, and some misfortune will befall him—illness, poverty, loss, and then no one will see or hear him, just as he now neither sees nor hears others. But there is no man with a hammer, and the happy go on living, just a little fluttered with the petty cares of every day, like an aspen tree in the wind—and everything is all right.'

'That night I was able to understand how I, too, had been content and happy,' Ivan Ivanich went on, getting up. 'I, too, at meals or out hunting, used to lay down the law about living, and religion, and governing the masses. I, too, used to say that teaching is light, that education is necessary, but that for simple folk reading and writing is enough for the present. Freedom is a boon, I used to say, as essential as the air we breathe, but we must wait. Yes—I used to say so, but now I ask: Why do we wait?' Ivan Ivanich glanced angrily at Bourkin. 'Why do we wait, I ask you? What considerations keep us fast? I am told that we cannot have everything at once, and that every idea is realized in time. But who says so? Where is the proof that it is so? You refer me to the natural order of things, to the law of cause and effect, but is there order or natural law in that I, a living, thinking creature, should stand by a ditch until it fills up, or is narrowed, when I could jump it or throw a bridge over it? Tell me, I say, why should we wait? Wait, when we have no strength to live, and yet must live and are full of the desire to live!

'I left my brother early the next morning, and from that time on I found it impossible to live in town. The peace and the quiet of it oppress me. I dare not look in at the windows, for nothing is more dreadful to see than the sight of a happy family, sitting round a table, having tea. I am an old man now and am no good for the struggle. I commenced late. I can only grieve within my soul, and fret and sulk. At night my head buzzes with the rush of my thoughts and I cannot sleep. . . . Ah! If I were young!'

Ivan Ivanich walked excitedly up and down the room and repeated:

'If I were young.'

He suddenly walked up to Aliokhin and shook him first by one hand and then by the other.

'Pavel Konstantinich,' he said in a voice of entreaty, 'don't be satisfied, don't let yourself be lulled to sleep! While you are young, strong, wealthy, do not cease to do good! Happiness does not exist, nor should it, and if there is any meaning or purpose in life, they are not in our peddling little happiness, but in something reasonable and grand. Do good!'

Ivan Ivanich said this with a piteous supplicating smile, as though he were asking a personal favour.

Then they all three sat in different corners of the drawing-room and were silent. Ivan Ivanich's story had satisfied neither Bourkin nor Aliokhin. With the generals and ladies looking down from their gilt frames, seeming alive in the firelight, it was tedious to hear the story of a miserable official who ate gooseberries. . . . Somehow they had a longing to hear and to speak of charming people, and of women. And the mere fact of sitting in the drawing-room where everything—the lamp with its coloured shade, the chairs, and the carpet under their feet—told how the very people who now looked down at them from their frames once walked, and sat and had tea there, and the fact that pretty Pelagueya was near—was much better than any story.

Aliokhin wanted very much to go to bed; he had to get up for his work very early, about two in the morning, and now his eyes were closing, but he was afraid of his guests saying something interesting without his hearing it, so he would not go. He did not trouble to think whether what Ivan Ivanich had been saying was clever or right; his guests were talking of neither groats, nor hay, nor tar, but of something which had no bearing on his life, and he liked it and wanted them to go on. . . .

'However, it's time to go to bed,' said Bourkin, getting up. 'I will wish you good night.'

Aliokhin said good night and went downstairs, and left his guests. Each had a large room with an old wooden bed and carved ornaments; in the corner was an ivory crucifix; and their wide, cool beds, made by pretty Pelagueya, smelled sweetly of clean linen.

Ivan Ivanich undressed in silence and lay down.

'God forgive me, a wicked sinner,' he murmured, as he drew the clothes over his head.

A smell of burning tobacco came from his pipe which lay on the table, and Bourkin could not sleep for a long time and was worried because he could not make out where the unpleasant smell came from.

The rain beat against the windows all night long.

IN EXILE

OLD Simeon, whose nickname was Brains, and a young Tartar, whose name nobody knew, were sitting on the bank of the river by a wood fire. The other three ferrymen were in the hut. Simeon who was an old man of about sixty, skinny and tooth-less, but broad-shouldered and healthy, was drunk. He would long ago have gone to bed, but he had a bottle in his pocket and was afraid of his comrades asking him for vodka. The Tartar was ill and miserable, and, pulling his rags about him, he went on talking about the good things in the province of Simbirsk, and what a beautiful and clever wife he had left at home. He was not more than twenty-five, and now, by the light of the wood fire, with his pale, sorrowful, sickly face, he looked a mere boy.

'Of course, it is not a paradise here,' said Brains, 'you see, water, the bare bushes by the river, clay everywhere—nothing else. . . . It is long past Easter and there is still ice on the water and this morning there was snow. . . .'

'Bad! Bad!' said the Tartar with a frightened look.

A few yards away flowed the dark, cold river, muttering, dash-ing against the holes in the clayey bank as it tore along to the distant sea. By the bank they were sitting on, loomed a great barge, which the ferrymen call a *karbass*. Far away and away, flashing out, flaring up, were fires crawling like snakes—last year's grass being burned. And behind the water again was darkness. Little banks of ice could be heard knocking against the barge. . . . It was very damp and cold. . . .

The Tartar glanced at the sky. There were as many stars as at home, and the darkness was the same, but something was missing. At home in the Simbirsk province the stars and the sky were altogether different.

'Bad! Bad!' he repeated.

'You will get used to it,' said Brains with a laugh. 'You are young yet and foolish; the milk is hardly dry on your lips, and in your folly you imagine that there is no one unhappier than you, but there will come a time when you will say: God give every one such a life! Just look at me. In a week's time the floods will be gone, and we will fix a ferry here, and all of you will go away into Siberia and I shall stay here, going to and fro.

I have been living thus for the last two-and-twenty years, but, thank God, I want nothing. God give everybody such a life.'

The Tartar threw some branches on to the fire, crawled near to it, and said:

'My father is sick. When he dies, my mother and my wife have promised to come here.'

'What do you want your mother and your wife for?' asked Brains. 'Just foolishness, my friend. It's the devil tempting you, plague take him, Don't listen to the Evil One. Don't give way to him. When he talks to you about women you should answer him sharply: "I don't want them!" When he talks of freedom, you should stick to it and say: "I don't want it. I want nothing! No father, no mother, no wife, no freedom, no home, no love! I want nothing." Plague take 'em all.'

Brains took a swig at his bottle and went on:

'My brother, I am not an ordinary peasant. I don't come from the servile masses. I am the son of a deacon, and when I was a free man at Rursk, I used to wear a frock coat, and now I have brought myself to such a point that I can sleep naked on the ground and eat grass. God give such a life to everybody. I want nothing. I am afraid of nobody and I think there is no man richer or freer than I. When they sent me here from Russia I set my teeth at once and said: "I want nothing!" The devil whispers to me about my wife and my kindred, and about freedom, and I say to him: "I want nothing!" I stuck to it, and, you see, I live happily and have nothing to grumble at. If a man gives the devil the least opportunity and listens to him just once, then he is lost and has no hope of salvation: he will be over ears in the mire and will never get out. Not only peasants the like of you are lost, but the nobly born and the educated also. About fifteen years ago a certain nobleman was banished here from Russia. He had had some trouble with his brothers and had made a forgery in a will. People said he was a prince or a baron, but perhaps he was only a high official—who knows? Well, he came here and at once bought a house and land in Moukhzyink. "I want to live by my own work," said he, "in the sweat of my brow, because I am no longer a nobleman but an exile." "Why," said I, "God help you, for that is good." He was a young man then, ardent and eager; he used to mow and go fishing, and he would ride sixty miles on horseback. Only one thing was wrong; from the very beginning he was always driving to the post office at Guyrin. He used to sit in my boat and sigh: "Ah! Simeon, it is a long time since they sent me any money from home." "You are better without money, Vassili Andreich," said I. "What's the good of it? You just throw away the past, as though it had never happened, as though it were only a dream, and start life afresh. Don't listen to the devil," I said, "he won't do you any good, and he will only tighten the noose. You want money now, but in a little while you will want something else, and then more and more. If," said I, "you want to be happy you must want nothing. Exactly. . . . If," I said, "fate has been hard on you and me, it is no good asking her for charity and falling at her feet. We must ignore her and laugh at her." That's what I said to him. . . . Two years later I ferried him over and he rubbed his hands and laughed. "I'm going," said he, "to Guyrin to meet my wife. She has taken pity on me, she says, and she is coming here. She is very kind and good." And he gave a gasp of joy. Then one day he came with his wife, a beautiful young lady with a little girl in her arms and a lot of luggage. And Vassili Andreich kept turning and looking at her and could not look at her or praise her enough. "Yes, Simeon, my friend, even in Siberia people live." Well, thought I, all right, you won't be content. And from that time on, mark you, he used to go to Guyrin every week to find out if money had been sent from Russia. A terrible lot of money was wasted. "She stays here," said he, "for my sake, and her youth and beauty wither away here in Siberia. She shares my bitter lot with me," said he, "and I must give her all the pleasure I can afford. . . .' To make his wife happier he took up with the officials and any kind of rubbish. And they couldn't have company without giving food and drink, and they must have a piano and a fluffy little dog on the sofa—bad cess to it. . . . Luxury, in a word, all kinds of tricks. My lady did not stay with him long. How could she? Clay, water, cold, no vegetables, no fruit; uneducated people and drunkards, with no manners, and she was a pretty pampered young lady from the metropolis. . . . Of course she got bored. And her husband was no longer a gentleman, but an exile—quite a different matter. Three years later, I remember, on the eve of the Assumption, I heard shouts from the other bank. I went over in the ferry and saw my lady, all wrapped up, with a young gentleman, a government official, in a troika. . . . I ferried them across, they got into the carriage and disappeared, and I saw no more of them. Toward the morning Vassili Andreich came racing up in a coach and pair. "Has my wife been across, Simeon, with a gentleman in spectacles?" "She has," said I,

"but you might as well look for the wind in the fields." He
raced after them and kept it up for five days and nights. When
he came back he jumped on to the ferry and began to knock his
head against the side and to cry aloud. "You see," said I
"there you are." And I laughed and reminded him: "Even in
Siberia people live." But he went on beating his head harder
than ever. . . . Then he got the desire for freedom. His wife
had gone to Russia and he longed to go there to see her and take
her away from her lover. And he began to go to the post
office every day, and then to the authorities of the town. He
was always sending applications or personally handing them to
the authorities, asking to have his term remitted and to be
allowed to go, and he told me that he had spent over two
hundred roubles on telegrams. He sold his land and mortgaged
his house to the money-lenders. His hair went grey, he grew
round-shouldered, and his face got yellow and consumptive-
looking. He used to cough whenever he spoke and tears used
to come into his eyes. He spent eight years on his applications,
and at last he became happy again and lively: he had thought
of a new dodge. His daughter, you see, had grown up. He
doted on her and could never take his eyes off her. And, indeed,
she was very pretty, dark and clever. Every Sunday he used to
go to church with her at Guyrin. They would stand side by
side on the ferry, and she would smile and he would devour
her with his eyes. "Yes, Simeon," he would say. "Even in
Siberia people live. Even in Siberia there is happiness. Look
what a fine daughter I have. You wouldn't find one like her in
a thousand miles' journey." "She's a nice girl," said I. "Oh,
yes." . . . And I thought to myself: "You wait. . . . She is
young. Young blood will have its way; she wants to live and
what life is there here?" And she began to pine away. . . .
Wasting, wasting away, she withered away, fell ill and had
to keep to her bed. . . . Consumption. That's Siberian happiness, plague take it; that's Siberian life. . . . He rushed all
over the place after the doctors and dragged them home with
him. If he heard of a doctor or a quack three hundred miles off
he would rush off after him. He spent a terrific amount of
money on doctors and I think it would have been much better
spent on drink. All the same she had to die. No help for it.
Then it was all up with him. He thought of hanging himself,
and of trying to escape to Russia. That would be the end of
him. He would try to escape: he would be caught, tried, penal
servitude, flogging.'

'Good! Good!' muttered the Tartar with a shiver. 'What is good?' asked Brains.

'Wife and daughter. What does penal servitude and suffering matter? He saw his wife and his daughter. You say one should want nothing. But nothing—is evil! His wife spent three years with him. God gave him that. Nothing is evil, and three years is good. Why don't you understand that?'

Trembling and stammering as he groped for Russian words, of which he knew only a few, the Tartar began to say: 'God forbid he should fall ill among strangers, and die and be buried in the cold sodden earth, and then, if his wife could come to him if only for one day or even for one hour, he would gladly endure any torture for such happiness, and would even thank God. Better one day of happiness than nothing.'

Then once more he said what a beautiful, clever wife he had left at home, and with his head in his hands he began to cry and assured Simeon that he was innocent, and had been falsely accused. His two brothers and his uncle had stolen some horses from a peasant and beaten the old man nearly to death, and the community never looked into the matter at all, and judgment was passed by which all three brothers were exiled to Siberia, while his uncle, a rich man, remained at home.

'You will get used to it,' said Simeon.

The Tartar relapsed into silence and stared into the fire with his eyes red from weeping; he looked perplexed and frightened, as if he could not understand why he was in the cold and the darkness, among strangers, and not in the province of Simbirsk. Brains lay down near the fire, smiled at something, and began to say in an undertone:

'But what a joy she must be to your father,' he muttered after a pause. 'He loves her and she is a comfort to him, eh? But, my man, don't tell me. He is a strict, harsh old man. And girls don't want strictness; they want kisses and laughter, scents and pomade. Yes. . . . Ah! What a life!' Simeon swore heavily. 'No more vodka! That means bedtime. What! I'm going, my man.'

Left alone, the Tartar threw more branches on the fire, lay down, and, looking into the blaze, began to think of his native village and of his wife; if she could come if only for a month, or even a day, and then, if she liked, go back again! Better a month or even a day, than nothing. But even if his wife kept her promise and came, how could he provide for her? Where was she to live?

'If there is nothing to eat; how are we to live?' asked the Tartar aloud.

For working at the oars day and night he was paid two copecks a day; the passengers gave tips, but the ferrymen shared them out and gave nothing to the Tartar, and only laughed at him. And he was poor, cold, hungry, and fearful. . . . With his whole body aching and shivering he thought it would be good to go into the hut and sleep; but there was nothing to cover himself with, and it was colder there than on the bank. He had nothing to cover himself with there, but he could make up a fire. . . .

In a week's time, when the floods had subsided and the ferry would be fixed up, all the ferrymen except Simeon would not be wanted any longer and the Tartar would have to go from village to village, begging and looking for work. His wife was only seventeen; beautiful, soft, and shy. . . . Could she go unveiled begging through the villages. No. The idea of it was horrible.

It was already dawn. The barges, the bushy willows above the water, the swirling flood began to take shape, and up above in a clayey cliff a hut thatched with straw, and above that the straggling houses of the village, where the cocks had begun to crow.

The ginger-coloured clay cliff, the barge, the river, the strange wild people, hunger, cold, illness—perhaps all these things did not really exist. Perhaps, thought the Tartar, it was only a dream. He felt that he must be asleep, and he heard his own snoring. . . . Certainly he was at home in the Simbirsk province; he had but to call his wife and she would answer; and his mother was in the next room. . . . But what awful dreams there are! Why? The Tartar smiled and opened his eyes. What river was that? The Volga?

It was snowing.

'Hi! Ferry!' someone shouted on the other bank. '*Karba-a-ass!*'

The Tartar awoke and went to fetch his mates to row over to the other side. Hurrying into their sheepskins, swearing sleepily in hoarse voices, and shivering from the cold, the four men appeared on the bank. After their sleep, the river, from which there came a piercing blast, seemed to them horrible and disgusting. They stepped slowly into the barge. . . . The Tartar and the three ferrymen took the long, broad-bladed oars, which in the dim light looked like a crab's claw, and Simeon flung himself with his belly against the tiller. And on the other side the voice kept on shouting, and a revolver was fired twice, for the man probably thought the ferrymen were asleep or gone to the village inn.

'All right. Plenty of time!' said Brains in the tone of one who was convinced that there is no need for hurry in this world —and indeed there is no reason for it.

The heavy, clumsy barge left the bank and heaved through the willows, and by the willows slowly receding it was possible to tell that the barge was moving. The ferrymen plied the oars with a slow measured stroke; Brains hung over the tiller with his stomach pressed against it and swung from side to side. In the dim light they looked like men sitting on some antediluvian animal with long limbs, swimming out to a cold dismal nightmare country.

They got clear of the willows and swung out into mid-stream. The thud of the oars and the splash could be heard on the other bank and shouts came: 'Quicker! Quicker!' After another ten minutes the barge bumped heavily against the landing-stage.

'And it is still snowing, snowing all the time,' Simeon murmured, wiping the snow off his face. 'God knows where it comes from!'

On the other side a tall, lean old man was waiting in a short fox-fur coat and a white astrakhan hat. He was standing some distance from his horses and did not move; he had a stern concentrated expression as if he were trying to remember something and were furious with his recalcitrant memory. When Simeon went up to him and took off his hat with a smile he said:

'I'm in a hurry to get to Anastasievka. My daughter is worse again and they tell me there's a new doctor at Anastasievka.'

The coach was clamped on to the barge and they rowed back. All the while as they rowed the man, whom Simeon called Vassili Andreich, stood motionless, pressing his thin lips tight and staring in front of him. When the driver craved leave to smoke in his presence, he answered nothing, as if he did not hear. And Simeon hung over the rudder and looked at him mockingly and said:

'Even in Siberia people live. L-i-v-e!'

On Brains's face was a triumphant expression as if he were proving something, as if pleased that things had happened just as he thought they would. The unhappy, helpless look of the man in the fox-fur coat seemed to give him great pleasure.

'The roads are now muddy, Vassili Andreich,' he said, when

the horses had been harnessed on the bank. 'You'd better wait a couple of weeks, until it gets dryer. . . . If there were any point in going—but you know yourself that people are always on the move day and night and there's no point in it. Sure!'

Vassili Andreich said nothing, gave him a tip, took his seat in the coach and drove away.

'Look! He's gone galloping after the doctor!' said Simeon, shivering in the cold. 'Yes. To look for a real doctor, trying to overtake the wind in the fields, and catch the devil by the tail, plague take him! What queer fish there are! God forgive me, a miserable sinner.'

The Tartar went up to Brains, and, looking at him with mingled hatred and disgust, trembling, and mixing Tartar words up with his broken Russian, said:

'He good . . . good. And you . . . bad! You are bad! The gentleman is a good soul, very good, and you are a beast, you are bad! The gentleman is alive and you are dead. . . . God made man that he should be alive, that he should have happiness, sorrow, grief, and you want nothing, so you are not alive, but a stone! A stone wants nothing and so do you. . . . You are a stone—and God does not love you and the gentleman He does.'

They all began to laugh: the Tartar furiously knit his brows, waved his hand, drew his rags round him, and went to the fire. The ferrymen and Simeon went slowly to the hut.

'It's cold,' said one of the ferrymen hoarsely, as he stretched himself on the straw with which the damp, clay floor was covered.

'Yes. It's not warm,' another agreed. . . . 'It's a hard life.'

All of them lay down. The wind blew the door open. The snow drifted into the hut. Nobody could bring himself to get up and shut the door; it was cold, but they put up with it.

'And I am happy,' muttered Simeon as he fell asleep. 'God give such a life to everybody.'

'You certainly are the devil's own. Even the devil don't need to take you.'

Sounds like the barking of a dog came from outside.

'Who is that? Who is there?'

'It's the Tartar crying.'

'Oh! he's a queer fish.'

'He'll get used to it!' said Simeon, and at once he fell asleep. Soon the others slept too and the door was left open.

THE LADY WITH THE TOY DOG

I

IT was reported that a new face had been seen on the quay; a lady with a little dog. Dimitri Dimitrich Gomov, who had been a fortnight at Yalta and had got used to it, had begun to show an interest in new faces. As he sat in the pavilion at Verné's he saw a young lady, blonde and fairly tall, and wearing a broad-brimmed hat, pass along the quay. After her ran a white Pomeranian.

Later he saw her in the park and in the square several times a day. She walked by herself, always in the same broad-brimmed hat, and with this white dog. Nobody knew who she was, and she was spoken of as the lady with the toy dog.

'If,' thought Gomov, 'if she is here without a husband or a friend, it would be as well to make her acquaintance.'

He was not yet forty, but he had a daughter of twelve and two boys at school. He had married young, in his second year at the university, and now his wife seemed half as old again as himself. She was a tall woman, with dark eyebrows, erect, grave, stolid, and she thought herself an intellectual woman. She read a great deal, called her husband not Dimitri, but Demitri, and in his private mind he thought her short-witted, narrow-minded, and ungracious. He was afraid of her and disliked being at home. He had begun to betray her with other women long ago, betrayed her frequently, and probably for that reason nearly always spoke ill of women, and when they were discussed in his presence he would maintain that they were an inferior race.

It seemed to him that his experience was bitter enough to give him the right to call them any name he liked, but he could not live a couple of days without the 'inferior race.' With men he was bored and ill at ease, cold and unable to talk, but when he was with women, he felt easy and knew what to talk about, and how to behave, and even when he was silent with them he felt quite comfortable. In his appearance as in his character, indeed in his whole nature, there was something attractive, indefinable, which drew women to him and charmed them; he knew it, and he, too, was drawn by some mysterious power to them.

His frequent, and, indeed, bitter experiences had taught him long ago that every affair of that kind, at first a divine diversion, a delicious smooth adventure, is in the end a source of worry for a decent man, especially for men like those at Moscow who are slow to move, irresolute, domesticated, for it becomes at last an acute and extraordinarily complicated problem and a nuisance. But whenever he met and was interested in a new woman, then his experience would slip away from his memory, and he would long to live, and everything would seem so simple and amusing.

And it so happened that one evening he dined in the gardens, and the lady in the broad-brimmed hat came up at a leisurely pace and sat at the next table. Her expression, her gait, her dress, her coiffure told him that she belonged to society, that she was married, that she was paying her first visit to Yalta, that she was alone, and that she was bored. . . . There is a great deal of untruth in the gossip about the immorality of the place. He scorned such tales, knowing that they were for the most part concocted by people who would be only too ready to sin if they had the chance, but when the lady sat down at the next table, only a yard or two away from him, his thoughts were filled with tales of easy conquests, of trips to the mountains; and he was suddenly possessed by the alluring idea of a quick transitory liaison, a moment's affair with an unknown woman whom he knew not even by name.

He beckoned to the little dog, and when it came up to him, wagged his finger at it. The dog began to growl. Gomov again wagged his finger.

The lady glanced at him and at once cast her eyes down.

'He won't bite,' she said and blushed.

'May I give him a bone?'—and when she nodded emphatically, he asked affably: 'Have you been in Yalta long?'

'About five days.'

'And I am just dragging through my second week.'

They were silent for a while.

'Time goes quickly,' she said, 'and it is amazingly boring here.'

'It is the usual thing to say that it is boring here. People live quite happily in dull holes like Bieliev or Zhidra, but as soon as they come here they say: "How boring it is! The very dregs of dullness!" One would think they came from Spain.'

She smiled. Then both went on eating in silence as though

they did not know each other; but after dinner they went off together—and then began an easy, playful conversation as though they were perfectly happy, and it was all one to them where they went or what they talked of. They walked and talked of how the sea was strangely luminous; the water lilac, so soft and warm, and athwart it the moon cast a golden streak. They said how stifling it was after the hot day. Gomov told her how he came from Moscow and was a philologist by education, but in a bank by profession; and how he had once wanted to sing in opera, but gave it up; and how he had two houses in Moscow. . . . And from her he learned that she came from Petersburg, was born there, but married at S. where she had been living for the last two years; that she would stay another month at Yalta, and perhaps her husband would come for her, because, he too, needed a rest. She could not tell him what her husband was — provincial administration or zemstvo council—and she seemed to think it funny. And Gomov found out that her name was Anna Sergueyevna.

In his room at night, he thought of her and how they would meet next day. They must do so. As he was going to sleep, it struck him that she could only lately have left school, and had been at her lessons even as his daughter was then; he remembered how bashful and *gauche* she was when she laughed and talked with a stranger—it must be, he thought, the first time she had been alone, and in such a place with men walking after her and looking at her and talking to her, all with the same secret purpose which she could not but guess. He thought of her slender white neck and her pretty, grey eyes.

'There is something touching about her,' he thought as he began to fall asleep.

II

A week passed. It was a blazing day. Indoors it was stifling, and in the streets the dust whirled along. All day long he was plagued with thirst and he came into the pavilion every few minutes and offered Anna Sergueyevna an iced drink or an ice. It was impossibly hot.

In the evening, when the air was fresher, they walked to the jetty to see the steamer come in. There was quite a crowd all gathered to meet somebody, for they carried bouquets. And among them were clearly marked the peculiarities of Yalta: the elderly ladies were youthfully dressed and there were many generals.

The sea was rough and the steamer was late, and before it turned into the jetty it had to do a great deal of manœuvring. Anna Sergueyevna looked through her lorgnette at the steamer and the passengers as though she were looking for friends, and when she turned to Gomov, her eyes shone. She talked much and her questions were abrupt, and she forgot what she had said; and then she lost her lorgnette in the crowd.

The well-dressed people went away, the wind dropped, and Gomov and Anna Sergueyevna stood as though they were waiting for somebody to come from the steamer. Anna Sergueyevna was silent. She smelled her flowers and did not look at Gomov.

'The weather has got pleasanter toward evening,' he said. 'Where shall we go now? Shall we take a carriage?'

She did not answer.

He fixed his eyes on her and suddenly embraced her and kissed her lips, and he was kindled with the perfume and the moisture of the flowers; at once he started and looked round; had not someone seen?'

'Let us go to your——' he murmured.

And they walked quickly away.

Her room was stifling, and smelled of scents which she had bought at the Japanese shop. Gomov looked at her and thought: 'What strange chances there are in life!' From the past there came the memory of earlier good-natured women, gay in their love, grateful to him for their happiness, short though it might be; and of others—like his wife—who loved without sincerity, and talked overmuch and affectedly, hysterically, as though they were protesting that it was not love, nor passion, but something more important; and of the few beautiful cold women, into whose eyes there would flash suddenly a fierce expression, a stubborn desire to take, to snatch from life more than it can give; they were no longer in their first youth, they were capricious, unstable, domineering, imprudent, and when Gomov became cold toward them then their beauty roused him to hatred, and the lace on their lingerie reminded him of the scales of fish.

But here there was the shyness and awkwardness of inexperienced youth, a feeling of constraint; an impression of perplexity and wonder, as though someone had suddenly knocked at the door. Anna Sergueyevna, 'the lady with the toy dog,' took what had happened somehow seriously, with a particular gravity, as though thinking that this was her downfall and very strange and improper. Her features seemed to sink and wither, and on either side of her face her long hair hung mournfully down; she sat crestfallen and musing, exactly like a woman taken in sin in some old picture.

'It is not right,' she said. 'You are the first to lose respect for me.'

There was a melon on the table. Gomov cut a slice and began to eat it slowly. At least half an hour passed in silence.

Anna Sergueyevna was very touching; she irradiated the purity of a simple, devout, inexperienced woman; the solitary candle on the table hardly lighted her face, but it showed her very wretched.

'Why should I cease to respect you?' asked Gomov. 'You don't know what you are saying.'

'God forgive me!' she said, and her eyes filled with tears. 'It is horrible.'

'You seem to want to justify yourself.'

'How can I justify myself? I am a wicked, low woman and I despise myself. I have no thought of justifying myself. It is not my husband that I have deceived, but myself. And not only now but for a long time past. My husband may be a good honest man, but he is a lackey. I do not know what work he does, but I do know that he is a lackey in his soul. I was twenty when I married him. I was overcome by curiosity. I longed for something. "Surely," I said to myself, "there is another kind of life." I longed to live! To live, and to live. . . . Curiosity burned me up. . . . You do not understand it, but I swear by God, I could no longer control myself. Something strange was going on in me. I could not hold myself in. I told my husband that I was ill and came here. . . . And here I have been walking about dizzily, like a lunatic. . . . And now I have become a low, filthy woman whom everybody may despise.'

Gomov was already bored; her simple words irritated him with their unexpected and inappropriate repentance; but for the tears in her eyes he might have thought her to be joking or playing a part.

'I do not understand,' he said quietly. 'What do you want?'

She hid her face in his bosom and pressed close to him.

'Believe, believe me, I implore you,' she said. 'I love a pure, honest life, and sin is revolting to me. I don't know myself what I am doing. Simple people say: "The devil entrapped me," and I can say of myself: "The Evil One tempted me."'

'Don't, don't,' he murmured.

He looked into her staring, frightened eyes, kissed her, spoke quietly and tenderly, and gradually quieted her and she was happy again, and they both began to laugh.

Later, when they went out, there was not a soul on the quay; the town with its cypresses looked like a city of the dead, but the sea still roared and broke against the shore; a boat swung on the waves; and in it sleepily twinkled the light of a lantern.

They found a cab and drove out to the Oreanda.

'Just now in the hall,' said Gomov, 'I discovered your name written on the board—von Didenitz. Is your husband a German?'

'No. His grandfather, I believe, was a German, but he himself is an Orthodox Russian.'

At Oreanda they sat on a bench, not far from the church, looked down at the sea and were silent. Yalta was hardly visible through the morning mist. The tops of the hills were shrouded in motionless white clouds. The leaves of the trees never stirred, the cicadas trilled, and the monotonous dull sound of the sea, coming up from below, spoke of the rest, the eternal sleep awaiting us. So the sea roared when there was neither Yalta nor Oreanda, and so it roars and will roar, dully, indifferently when we shall be no more. And in this continual indifference to the life and death of each of us, lives pent up, the pledge of our eternal salvation, of the uninterrupted movement of life on earth and its unceasing perfection. Sitting side by side with a young woman, who in the dawn seemed so beautiful, Gomov, appeased and enchanted by the sight of the fairy scene, the sea, the mountains, the clouds, the wide sky, thought how at bottom, if it were thoroughly explored, everything on earth was beautiful, everything, except what we ourselves think and do when we forget the higher purposes of life and our own human dignity.

A man came up—a coast-guard—gave a look at them, then went away. He, too, seemed mysterious and enchanted. A steamer came over from Feodossia, by the light of the morning star, its own lights already put out.

'There is dew on the grass,' said Anna Sergueyevna after a silence.

'Yes. It is time to go home.'

They returned to the town.

Then every afternoon they met on the quay, and lunched

together, dined, walked, enjoyed the sea. She complained that
she slept badly, that her heart beat alarmingly. She would ask
the same question over and over again, and was troubled now by
jealousy, now by fear that he did not sufficiently respect her.
And often in the square or the gardens, when there was no one
near, he would draw her close and kiss her passionately. Their
complete idleness, these kisses in the full daylight, given timidly
and fearfully lest any one should see, the heat, the smell of the
sea and the continual brilliant parade of leisured, well-dressed,
well-fed people almost regenerated him. He would tell Anna
Sergueyevna how delightful she was, how tempting. He was
impatiently passionate, never left her side, and she would often
brood, and even asked him to confess that he did not respect her,
did not love her at all, and only saw in her a loose woman.
Almost every evening, rather late, they would drive out of the
town, to Oreanda, or to the waterfall; and these drives were
always delightful, and the impressions won during them were
always beautiful and sublime.

They expected her husband to come. But he sent a letter
in which he said that his eyes were bad and implored his wife
to come home. Anna Sergueyevna began to worry.

'It is a good thing I am going away,' she would say to Gomov.
'It is fate.'

She went in a carriage and he accompanied her. They drove
for a whole day. When she took her seat in the car of an
express train and when the second bell sounded, she said:

'Let me have another look at you. . . . Just one more look.
Just as you are.'

She did not cry, but was sad and low-spirited, and her lips
trembled.

'I will think of you—often,' she said. 'Good-bye. Good-
bye. Don't think ill of me. We part for ever. We must,
because we ought not to have met at all. Now, good-bye.'

The train moved off rapidly. Its lights disappeared, and in a
minute or two the sound of it was lost, as though everything
were agreed to put an end to this sweet, oblivious madness.
Left alone on the platform, looking into the darkness, Gomov
heard the trilling of the grasshoppers and the humming of the
telegraph-wires, and felt as though he had just woken up. And
he thought that it had been one more adventure, one more
affair, and it also was finished and had left only a memory. He
was moved, sad, and filled with a faint remorse; surely the
young woman, whom he would never see again, had not been

happy with him; he had been kind to her, friendly, and sincere, but still in his attitude toward her, in his tone and caresses, there had always been a thin shadow of raillery, the rather rough arrogance of the successful male aggravated by the fact that he was twice as old as she. And all the time she had called him kind, remarkable, noble, so that he was never really himself to her, and had involuntarily deceived her. . . .

Here at the station, the smell of autumn was in the air, and the evening was cool.

'It is time for me to go north,' thought Gomov, as he left the platform. 'It is time.'

III

At home in Moscow, it was already like winter; the stoves were heated, and in the mornings, when the children were getting ready to go to school, and had their tea, it was dark and their nurse lighted the lamp for a short while. The frost had already begun. When the first snow falls, the first day of driving in sledges, it is good to see the white earth, the white roofs; one breathes easily, eagerly, and then one remembers the days of youth. The old lime trees and birches, white with hoar-frost, have a kindly expression; they are nearer to the heart than cypresses and palm trees, and with the dear familiar trees there is no need to think of mountains and the sea.

Gomov was a native of Moscow. He returned to Moscow on a fine frosty day, and when he donned his fur coat and warm gloves, and took a stroll through Petrovka, and when on Saturday evening he heard the church-bells ringing, then his recent travels and the places he had visited lost all their charms. Little by little he sank back into Moscow life, read eagerly three newspapers a day, and said that he did not read Moscow papers as a matter of principle. He was drawn into a round of restaurants, clubs, dinner-parties, parties, and he was flattered to have his house frequented by famous lawyers and actors, and to play cards with a professor at the university club. He could eat a whole plateful of hot *sielianka*.

So a month would pass, and Anna Sergueyevna, he thought, would be lost in the mists of memory and only rarely would she visit his dreams with her touching smile, just as other women had done. But more than a month passed, full winter came, and in his memory everything was clear, as though he had parted from Anna Sergueyevna only yesterday. And his memory was lit by a light that grew ever stronger. No matter how, through the voices of his children saying their lessons, penetrating to the evening stillness of his study, through hearing a song, or the music in a restaurant, or the snow-storm howling in the chimney, suddenly the whole thing would come to life again in his memory: the meeting on the jetty, the early morning with the mists on the mountains, the steamer from Feodossia and their kisses. He would pace up and down his room and remember it all and smile, and then his memories would drift into dreams, and the past was confused in his imagination with the future. He did not dream at night of Anna Sergueyevna, but she followed him everywhere, like a shadow, watching him. As he shut his eyes, he could see her, vividly, and she seemed handsomer, tenderer, younger than in reality; and he seemed to himself better than he had been at Yalta. In the evenings she would look at him from the bookcase, from the fireplace, from the corner; he could hear her breathing and the soft rustle of her dress. In the street he would gaze at women's faces to see if there were not one like her. . . .

He was filled with a great longing to share his memories with someone. But at home it was impossible to speak of his love, and away from home—there was no one. Impossible to talk of her to the other people in the house and the men at the bank. And talk of what? Had he loved then? Was there anything fine, romantic, or elevating or even interesting in his relations with Anna Sergueyevna? And he would speak vaguely of love, of women, and nobody guessed what was the matter, and only his wife would raise her dark eyebrows and say:

'Demitri, the role of coxcomb does not suit you at all.'

One night, as he was coming out of the club with his partner, an official, he could not help saying:

'If only I could tell what a fascinating woman I met at Yalta.'

The official seated himself in his sledge and drove off, but suddenly called:

'Dimitri Dimitrich!'

'Yes?'

'You were right. The sturgeon was tainted.'

These banal words suddenly roused Gomov's indignation. They seemed to him degrading and impure. What barbarous customs and people!

What preposterous nights, what dull, empty days! Furious card-playing, gormandizing, drinking, endless conversations about the same things, futile activities and conversations taking up the best part of the day and all the best of man's forces, leaving only a stunted, wingless life, just rubbish; and to go away and escape was impossible—one might as well be in a lunatic asylum or in prison with hard labour.

Gomov did not sleep that night, but lay burning with indignation, and then all next day he had a headache. And the following night he slept badly, sitting up in bed and thinking, or pacing from corner to corner of his room. His children bored him, the bank bored him, and he had no desire to go out or speak to any one.

In December when the holidays came he prepared to go on a journey and told his wife he was going to Petersburg to present a petition for a young friend of his—and went to S. Why? He did not know. He wanted to see Anna Sergueyevna, to talk to her, and if possible to arrange an assignation.

He arrived at S. in the morning and occupied the best room in the hotel, where the whole floor was covered with a grey canvas, and on the table there stood an inkstand grey with dust, adorned with a horseman on a headless horse holding a net in his raised hand. The porter gave him the necessary information: von Didenitz; Old Goncharna Street, his own house—not far from the hotel; lives well, has his own horses, every one knows him.

Gomov walked slowly to Old Goncharna Street and found the house. In front of it was a long, grey fence spiked with nails.

'No getting over a fence like that,' thought Gomov, glancing from the windows to the fence.

He thought: 'To-day is a holiday and her husband is probably at home. Besides it would be tactless to call and upset her. If he sent a note then it might fall into her husband's hands and spoil everything. It would be better to wait for an opportunity.' And he kept on walking up and down the street, and round the fence, waiting for his opportunity. He saw a beggar go in at the gate and the dogs attack him. He heard a piano and the sounds came faintly to his ears. It must be Anna Sergueyevna playing. The door suddenly opened and out of it came an old woman, and after her ran the familiar white Pomeranian. Gomov wanted to call the dog, but his heart suddenly began to thump and in his agitation he could not remember the dog's name.

He walked on, and more and more he hated the grey fence and thought with a gust of irritation that Anna Sergueyevna had already forgotten him, and was perhaps already amusing herself with someone else, as would be only natural in a young woman forced from morning to night to behold the accursed fence. He returned to his room and sat for a long time on the sofa, not knowing what to do. Then he dined and afterward slept for a long while.

'How idiotic and tiresome it all is,' he thought as he awoke and saw the dark windows; for it was evening. 'I've had sleep enough, and what shall I do to-night?'

He sat on his bed, which was covered with a cheap, grey blanket, exactly like those used in a hospital, and tormented himself.

'So much for the lady with the toy dog. . . . So much for the great adventure. . . . Here you sit.'

However, in the morning, at the station, his eye had been caught by a poster with large letters: 'First Performance of *The Geisha*.' He remembered that and went to the theatre.

'It is quite possible she will go to the first performance,' he thought.

The theatre was full and, as usual in all provincial theatres, there was a thick mist above the lights, the gallery was noisily restless; in the first row before the opening of the performance stood the local dandies with their hands behind their backs, and there in the governor's box, in front, sat the governor's daughter, and the governor himself sat modestly behind the curtain and only his hands were visible. The curtain quivered; the orchestra tuned up for a long time, and while the audience were coming in and taking their seats, Gomov gazed eagerly round.

At last Anna Sergueyevna came in. She took her seat in the third row, and when Gomov glanced at her his heart ached and he knew that for him there was no one in the whole world nearer, dearer, and more important than she; she was lost in this provincial rabble, the little undistinguished woman, with a common lorgnette in her hands, yet she filled his whole life; she was his grief, his joy, his only happiness, and he longed for her; and through the noise of the bad orchestra with its tenth-rate fiddles, he thought how dear she was to him. He thought and dreamed.

With Anna Sergueyevna there came in a young man with short side-whiskers, very tall, stooping; with every movement he shook and bowed continually. Probably he was the husband whom in a bitter mood at Yalta she had called a lackey. And, indeed, in his long figure, his side-whiskers, the little bald patch on the top of his head, there was something of the lackey; he had a modest sugary smile and in his buttonhole he wore a university badge exactly like a lackey's number.

In the first *entr'acte* the husband went out to smoke, and she was left alone. Gomov, who was also in the pit, came up to her and said in a trembling voice with a forced smile:

'How do you do?'

She looked up at him and went pale. Then she glanced at him again in terror, not believing her eyes, clasped her fan and lorgnette tightly together, apparently struggling to keep herself from fainting. Both were silent. She sat, he stood; frightened by her emotion, not daring to sit down beside her. The fiddles and flutes began to play and suddenly it seemed to them as though all the people in the boxes were looking at them. She got up and walked quickly to the exit; he followed, and both walked absently along the corridors, down the stairs, up the stairs, with the crowd shifting and shimmering before their eyes; all kinds of uniforms, judges, teachers, crown-estates, and all with badges; ladies shone and shimmered before them, like fur coats on moving rows of clothes-pegs, and there was a draught howling through the place laden with the smell of tobacco and cigar-ends. And Gomov, whose heart was thudding wildly, thought:

'Oh, Lord! Why all these men and that beastly orchestra?'

At that very moment he remembered how when he had seen Anna Sergueyevna off that evening at the station he had said to himself that everything was over between them, and they would never meet again. And now how far off they were from the end!

On a narrow, dark staircase over which was written: 'This Way to the Amphitheatre,' she stopped.

'How you frightened me!' she said, breathing heavily, still pale and apparently stupefied. 'Oh! how you frightened me! I am nearly dead. Why did you come? Why?'

'Understand me, Anna,' he whispered quickly. 'I implore you to understand. . . .'

She looked at him fearfully, in entreaty, with love in her eyes, gazing fixedly to gather up in her memory every one of his features.

'I suffer so!' she went on, not listening to him. 'All the time, I thought only of you. I lived with thoughts of you. . . . And I wanted to forget, to forget, but why, why did you come?'

A little above them, on the landing, two schoolboys stood and smoked and looked down at them, but Gomov did not care. He drew her to him and began to kiss her cheeks, her hands.

'What are you doing? What are you doing?' she said in terror, thrusting him away. . . . 'We were both mad. Go away to-night. You must go away at once. . . . I implore you, by everything you hold sacred, I implore you. . . . The people are coming——'

Someone passed them on the stairs.

'You must go away,' Anna Sergueyevna went on in a whisper. 'Do you hear, Dimitri Dimitrich? I'll come to you in Moscow. I never was happy. Now I am unhappy and I shall never, never be happy, never! Don't make me suffer even more! I swear, I'll come to Moscow. And now let us part. My dear, dearest darling, let us part!'

She pressed his hand and began to go quickly downstairs, all the while looking back at him, and in her eyes plainly showed that she was most unhappy. Gomov stood for a while, listened, then, when all was quiet, he found his coat and left the theatre.

IV

And Anna Sergueyevna began to come to him in Moscow. Once every two or three months she would leave S., telling her husband that she was going to consult a specialist in women's diseases. Her husband half believed and half disbelieved her. At Moscow she would stay at the Slaviansky Bazaar and send a message at once to Gomov. He would come to her, and nobody in Moscow knew.

Once as he was going to her as usual one winter morning—he had not received her message the night before—he had his daughter with him, for he was taking her to school which was on the way. Great wet flakes of snow were falling.

'Three degrees above freezing,' he said, 'and still the snow is falling. But the warmth is only on the surface of the earth. In the upper strata of the atmosphere there is quite a different temperature.'

'Yes, papa. Why is there no thunder in winter?'

He explained this too, and as he spoke he thought of his assignation, and that not a living soul knew of it, or ever would know. He had two lives: one obvious, which every one could see and know, if they were sufficiently interested, a life full of conventional truth and conventional fraud, exactly like the lives of his friends and acquaintances; and another, which moved underground. And by a strange conspiracy of circumstances, everything that was to him important, interesting, vital, everything that enabled him to be sincere and denied self-deception and was the very core of his being, must dwell hidden away from others, and everything that made him false, a mere shape in which he hid himself in order to conceal the truth, as for instance his work in the bank, arguments at the club, his favourite gibes about women, going to parties with his wife—all this was open. And judging others by himself, he did not believe the things he saw, and assumed that everybody else also had his real vital life passing under a veil of mystery as under the cover of the night. Every man's intimate existence is kept mysterious, and perhaps, in part, because of that civilized people are so nervously anxious that a personal secret should be respected.

When he had left his daughter at school, Gomov went to the Slaviansky Bazaar. He took off his fur coat downstairs, went up and knocked quietly at the door. Anna Sergueyevna, wearing his favourite grey dress, tired by the journey, had been expecting him to come all night. She was pale, and looked at him without a smile, and flung herself on his breast as soon as he entered. Their kiss was long and lingering as though they had not seen each other for a couple of years.

'Well, how are you getting on down there?' he asked. 'What is your news?'

'Wait. I 'll tell you presently. . . . I cannot.'

She could not speak, for she was weeping. She turned her face from him and dried her eyes.

'Well, let her cry a bit. . . . I 'll wait,' he thought, and sat down.

Then he rang and ordered tea, and then, as he drank it, she stood and gazed out of the window. . . . She was weeping in distress, in the bitter knowledge that their life had fallen out so sadly; only seeing each other in secret, hiding themselves away like thieves! Was not their life crushed?

'Don't cry. . . . Don't cry,' he said.

It was clear to him that their love was yet far from its end, which there was no seeing. Anna Sergueyevna was more and more passionately attached to him; she adored him and it was inconceivable that he should tell her that their love must some day end; she would not believe it.

He came up to her and patted her shoulder fondly and at that moment he saw himself in the mirror.

His hair was already going grey. And it seemed strange to him that in the last few years he should have got so old and ugly. Her shoulders were warm and trembled to his touch. He was suddenly filled with pity for her life, still so warm and beautiful, but probably beginning to fade and wither, like his own. Why should she love him so much? He always seemed to women not what he really was, and they loved in him, not himself, but the creature of their imagination, the thing they hankered for in life, and when they had discovered their mistake, still they loved him. And not one of them was happy with him. Time passed; he met women and was friends with them, went further and parted, but never once did he love; there was everything but love.

And now at last when his hair was grey he had fallen in love—real love—for the first time in his life.

Anna Sergueyevna and he loved one another, like dear kindred, like husband and wife, like devoted friends; it seemed to them that fate had destined them for one another, and it was inconceivable that he should have a wife, she a husband; they were like two birds of passage, a male and a female, which had been caught and forced to live in separate cages. They had forgiven each other all the past of which they were ashamed; they forgave everything in the present, and they felt that their love had changed both of them.

Formerly, when he felt a melancholy compunction, he used to comfort himself with all kinds of arguments, just as they happened to cross his mind, but now he was far removed from any such ideas; he was filled with a profound pity, and he desired to be tender and sincere. . . .

'Don't cry, my darling,' he said. 'You have cried enough. . . . Now let us talk and see if we can't find some way out.'

Then they talked it all over, and tried to discover some means of avoiding the necessity for concealment and deception, and the torment of living in different towns, and of not seeing each other for a long time. How could they shake off these intolerable fetters?

'How? How?' he asked, holding his head in his hands. 'How?'

And it seemed that but a little while and the solution would be found and there would begin a lovely new life; and to both of them it was clear that the end was still very far off, and that their hardest and most difficult period was only just beginning.

GOUSSIEV

I

It was already dark and would soon be night.

Goussiev, a private on long leave, raised himself a little in his hammock and said in a whisper:

'Can you hear me, Pavel Ivanich? A soldier at Soushan told me that their boat ran into an enormous fish and knocked a hole in her bottom.'

The man of condition unknown whom he addressed, and whom everybody in the hospital ship called Pavel Ivanich, was silent, as if he had not heard.

And once more there was silence. . . . The wind whistled through the rigging, the screw buzzed, the waves came washing, the hammocks squeaked, but to all these sounds their ears were long since accustomed and it seemed as though everything were wrapped in sleep and silence. It was very oppressive. The three patients—two soldiers and a sailor—who had played cards all day were now asleep and tossing to and fro.

The vessel began to shake. The hammock under Goussiev slowly heaved up and down, as though it were breathing—one, two, three. . . . Something crashed on the floor and began to tinkle: the jug must have fallen down.

'The wind has broken loose . . .' said Goussiev, listening attentively.

This time Pavel Ivanich coughed and answered irritably:

'You spoke just now of a ship colliding with a large fish, and now you talk of the wind breaking loose. . . . Is the wind a dog to break loose?'

'That's what people say.'

'Then people are as ignorant as you. . . . But what do they not say? You should keep a head on your shoulders and think. Silly idiot!'

Pavel Ivanich was subject to seasickness. When the ship rolled he would get very cross, and the least trifle would upset him, though Goussiev could never see anything to be cross about. What was there unusual in this story about the fish or in his saying that the wind had broken loose? Suppose the fish were as big as a mountain and its back were as hard as a sturgeon's, and suppose that at the end of the world there were huge stone walls with the snarling winds chained up to them. . . . If they do not break loose, why then do they rage over the sea as though they were possessed, and rush about like dogs? If they are not chained, what happens to them when it is calm?

Goussiev thought for a long time of a fish as big as a mountain, and of thick rusty chains; then he got tired of that and began to think of his native place whither he was returning after five years' service in the Far East. He saw with his mind's eye the great pond covered with snow. . . . On one side of the pond was a brick-built pottery, with a tall chimney belching clouds of black smoke, and on the other side was the village. . . . From the yard of the fifth house from the corner came his brother Alexey in a sledge; behind him sat his little son Vanka in large felt boots, and his daughter Akulka, also in felt boots. Alexey is tipsy, Vanka laughs, and Akulka's face is hidden—she is well wrapped up.

'The children will catch cold . . .' thought Goussiev. 'God grant them,' he whispered, 'a pure right mind that they may honour their parents and be better than their father and mother. . . .'

'The boots want soling,' cried the sick sailor in a deep voice. 'Aye, aye.'

The thread of Goussiev's thoughts was broken, and instead of the pond, suddenly—without rhyme or reason—he saw a large bull's head without eyes, and the horse and sledge did not move on, but went round and round in a black mist. But still he was glad he had seen his dear ones. He gasped for joy, and his limbs tingled and his fingers throbbed.

'God suffered me to see them!' he muttered, and opened his eyes and looked round in the darkness for water.

He drank, then lay down again, and once more the sledge skimmed along, and he saw the bull's head without eyes, black smoke, clouds of it. And so on till dawn.

II

At first through the darkness there appeared only a blue circle, the port-hole, then Goussiev began slowly to distinguish the man in the next hammock, Pavel Ivanich. He was sleeping in a sitting position, for if he lay down he could not breathe. His face was grey, his nose long and sharp, and his eyes were huge, because he was so thin; his temples were sunk, his beard scanty, the hair on his head long. . . . By his face it was impossible to tell his class: gentleman, merchant, or peasant; judging by his appearance and long hair he looked almost like a recluse, a lay-brother, but when he spoke he was not at all like a monk. He was losing strength through his cough and illness and the suffocating heat, and he breathed heavily and was always moving his dry lips. Noticing that Goussiev was looking at him, he turned toward him and said:

'I'm beginning to understand. . . . Yes. . . . Now I understand.'

'What do you understand, Pavel Ivanich?'

'Yes. . . . It was strange to me at first, why you sick men, instead of being kept quiet, should be on this steamer, where the heat is stifling and stinking, and the pitching and tossing must be fatal to you; but now it is all clear to me. . . . Yes. The doctors sent you to the steamer to get rid of you. They got tired of all the trouble you gave them, brutes like you. . . . You don't pay them; you only give a lot of trouble, and if you die you spoil their reports. Therefore you are just cattle, and there is no difficulty in getting rid of you. . . . They only need to lack conscience and humanity, and to deceive the owners of the steamer. We needn't worry about the first, they are experts by nature; but the second needs a certain amount of practice. In a crowd of four hundred healthy soldiers and sailors, five sick men are never noticed; so you were carried up to the steamer, mixed with a healthy lot who were counted in such a hurry that nothing wrong was noticed, and when the steamer got away they saw fever-stricken and consumptive men lying helpless on the deck. . . .'

Goussiev could not make out what Paul Ivanich was talking about; thinking he was being taken to task, he said by way of excusing himself:

'I lay on the deck because when we were taken off the barge I caught a chill.'

'Shocking!' said Pavel Ivanich. 'They know quite well that you can't last out the voyage, and yet they send you here! You may get as far as the Indian Ocean, but what then? It is awful to think of. . . . And that's all the return you get for faithful unblemished service!'

Pavel Ivanich looked very angry, and smote his forehead and gasped:

'They ought to be shown up in the papers. There would be an awful row.'

The two sick soldiers and the sailor were already up and had begun to play cards, the sailor propped up in his hammock, and the soldiers squatting uncomfortably on the floor. One soldier had his right arm in a sling and his wrist was tightly bandaged so that he had to hold the cards in his left hand or in the crook of his elbow. The boat was rolling violently so that it was impossible to get up or to drink tea or to take medicine.

'You are an orderly?' Pavel Ivanich asked Goussiev.

'That's it. An orderly.'

'My God, my God!' said Pavel Ivanich sorrowfully. 'To take a man from his native place, drag him fifteen thousand miles, drive him into consumption . . . and what for? I ask you. To make him an orderly to some Captain Farthing or Midshipman Hole! Where's the sense of it?'

'It's not a bad job, Pavel Ivanich. You get up in the morning, clean the boots, boil the samovar, tidy up the room, and then there is nothing to do. The lieutenant draws plans all day long, and you can pray to God if you like—or read books— or go out into the streets. It's a good enough life.'

'Yes. Very good! The lieutenant draws plans, and you stay in the kitchen all day long and suffer from home-sickness. . . . Plans. . . . Plans don't matter. It's human life that matters! Life doesn't come again. One should be sparing of it.'

'Certainly, Pavel Ivanich. A bad man meets no quarter, either at home, or in the army, but if you live straight, and do as you are told, then no one will harm you. They are educated and they understand. . . . For five years now I've never been in the cells and I've only been thrashed once—touch wood!'

'What was that for?'

'Fighting. I have a heavy fist, Pavel Ivanich. Four Chinamen came into our yard: they were carrying wood, I think, but I don't remember. Well, I was bored. I went for them and one of them got a bloody nose. The lieutenant saw it through the window and gave me a thick ear.'

'You poor fool,' muttered Pavel Ivanich. 'You don't understand anything.'

He was completely exhausted with the tossing of the boat and shut his eyes; his head fell back and then flopped forward on to his chest. He tried several times to lie down, but in vain, for he could not breathe.

'And why did you go for the four Chinamen?' he asked after a while.

'For no reason. They came into the yard and I went for them.'

Silence fell. . . . The gamblers played for a couple of hours, absorbed and cursing, but the tossing of the ship tired even them; they threw the cards away and lay down. Once more Goussiev thought of the big pond, the pottery, the village. Once more the sledges skimmed along, once more Vanka laughed, and that fool of an Akulka opened her fur coat, and stretched out her feet; 'Look,' she seemed to say, 'look, poor people, my felt boots are new and not like Vanka's.'

'She's getting on for six and still she has no sense!' said Goussiev. 'Instead of showing your boots off, why don't you bring home water to your soldier-uncle? I'll give you a present.'

Then came Andrey, with his firelock on his shoulder, carrying a hare he had shot, and he was followed by Tsaichik the cripple, who offered him a piece of soap for the hare; and there was the black heifer in the yard, and Domna sewing a shirt and crying over something, and there was the eyeless bull's head and the black smoke. . . .

Overhead there was shouting, sailors running; the sound of something heavy being dragged along the deck, or something had broken. . . . More running. Something wrong? Goussiev raised his head, listened, and saw the two soldiers and the sailor playing cards again; Pavel Ivanich sitting up and moving his lips. It was very close, he could hardly breathe, he wanted a drink, but the water was warm and disgusting. . . . The pitching of the boat was now better.

Suddenly something queer happened to one of the soldiers. . . . He called ace of diamonds, lost his reckoning, and dropped his cards. He started and laughed stupidly and looked round.

'In a moment, you fellows,' he said and lay down on the floor.

All were at a loss. They shouted at him but he made no reply.

'Stiepan, are you ill?' asked the other soldier with the bandaged hand. 'Perhaps we'd better call the priest, eh?'

'Stiepan, drink some water,' said the sailor. 'Here, mate, have a drink.'

'What's the good of breaking his teeth with the jug,' shouted Goussiev angrily. 'Don't you see, you fatheads?'

'What?'

'What!' cried Goussiev. 'He's snuffed out, dead. That's what! Good God, what fools! . . .'

III

The rolling stopped and Pavel Ivanich cheered up. He was no longer peevish. His face had an arrogant, impetuous, and mocking expression. He looked as if he were on the point of saying: 'I'll tell you a story that will make you die of laughter.' Their port-hole was open and a soft wind blew in on Pavel Ivanich. Voices could he heard and the splash of oars in the water. . . . Beneath the window someone was howling in a thin, horrible voice; probably a Chinaman singing.

'Yes. We are in harbour,' said Pavel Ivanich, smiling mockingly. 'Another month and we shall be in Russia. It's true; my gallant warriors, I shall get to Odessa and thence I shall go straight to Kharkov. At Kharkov I have a friend, a literary man. I shall go to him and I shall say: "Now, my friend, give up your rotten little love-stories and descriptions of nature, and expose the vileness of the human biped. . . . There's a subject for you."'

He thought for a moment and then he said:

'Goussiev, do you know how I swindled them?'

'Who, Pavel Ivanich?'

'The lot out there. . . . You see there's only first and third class on the steamer, and only peasants are allowed to go third. If you have a decent suit, and look like a nobleman or a *bourgeois*, at a distance, then you must go first. It may break you, but you have to lay down your five hundred roubles. "What's the point of such an arrangement?" I asked. "Is it meant to raise the prestige of Russian intellectuals?" "Not a bit," said they. "We don't let you go, simply because it is impossible for a decent man to go third. It is so vile and disgusting." "Yes," said I. "Thanks for taking so much trouble about decent people. Anyhow, bad or no, I haven't got five hundred roubles as I have neither robbed the Treasury nor exploited foreigners, not dealt in contraband, nor flogged any one to death, and, therefore, I think I have a right to go third class and to take rank with the intelligentsia of Russia." But there's no convincing them by logic. . . . I had to try fraud. I put on a peasant's coat and long boots, and a drunken, stupid expression and went to the agent and said: "Give me a ticket, your honour."

'"What's your position?" says the agent.

'"Clerical," said I. "My father was an honest priest. He

always told the truth to the great ones of the earth, and so he suffered much.'"

Pavel Ivanich got tired with talking, and his breath failed him, but he went on:

'Yes. I always tell the truth straight out. . . . I am afraid of nobody and nothing. There's a great difference between myself and you in that respect. You are dull, blind, stupid, you see nothing, and you don't understand what you do see. You are told that the wind breaks its chain, that you are brutes and worse, and you believe; you are thrashed and you kiss the hand that thrashes you; a swine in a racoon pelisse robs you, and throws you sixpence for tea, and you say: "Please, your honour, let me kiss your hand." You are pariahs, skunks. . . . I am different. I live consciously. I see everything, as an eagle or a hawk sees when it hovers over the earth, and I understand everything. I am a living protest. I see injustice—I protest; I see bigotry and hypocrisy—I protest; I see swine triumphant— I protest, and I am unconquerable. No Spanish inquisition can make me hold my tongue. Aye. . . . Cut my tongue out. I'll protest by gesture. . . . Shut me up in a dungeon—I'll shout so loud that I shall be heard for a mile round, or I'll starve myself, so that there shall be a still heavier weight on their black consciences. Kill me—and my ghost will return. All my acquaintances tell me: "You are a most insufferable man, Pavel Ivanich!" I am proud of such a reputation. I served three years in the Far East, and I have got bitter memories enough for a hundred years. I inveighed against it all. My friends write from Russia: "Do not come." But I'm going, to spite them. . . . Yes. . . . That is iife. I understand. You can call that life.'

Goussiev was not listening, but lay looking out of the port-hole; on the transparent lovely turquoise water swung a boat all shining in the shimmering light; a fat Chinaman was sitting in it eating rice with chop-sticks. The water murmured softly, and over it lazily soared white sea-gulls.

'It would be fun to give that fat fellow one on the back of his neck . . .' thought Goussiev, watching the fat Chinaman and yawning.

He dozed, and it seemed to him that all the world was slumbering. Time slipped swiftly away. The day passed imperceptibly; imperceptibly the twilight fell. . . . The steamer was still no longer but was moving on.

IV

Two days passed. Pavel Ivanich no longer sat up, but lay full length; his eyes were closed and his nose seemed to be sharper than ever.

'Pavel Ivanich!' called Goussiev, 'Pavel Ivanich!'

Pavel Ivanich opened his eyes and moved his lips.

'Aren't you well?'

'It's nothing,' answered Pavel Ivanich, breathing heavily. 'It's nothing. No. I'm much better. You see I can lie down now. I'm much better.

'Thank God for it, Pavel Ivanich.'

'When I compare myself with you, I am sorry for you . . . poor devils. My lungs are all right; my cough comes from indigestion. . . . I can endure this hell, not to mention the Red Sea! Besides, I have a critical attitude toward my illness, as well as to my medicine. But you . . . you are ignorant. . . . It's hard lines on you, very hard.'

The ship was running smoothly; it was calm but still stifling and hot as a Turkish bath; it was hard not only to speak but even to listen without an effort. Goussiev clasped his knees, leaned his head on them, and thought of his native place. My God, in such heat it was a pleasure to think of snow and cold! He saw himself driving on a sledge, and suddenly the horses were frightened and bolted. . . . Heedless of roads, dikes, ditches, they rushed like mad through the village, across the pond, past the works, through the fields. . . . 'Hold them in!' cried the women and the passers-by. 'Hold them in!' But why hold them in? Let the cold wind slap your face and cut your hands; let the lumps of snow thrown up by the horses' hoofs fall on your hat, down your neck and chest; let the runners of the sledge be buckled, and the traces and harness be torn and be damned to it! What fun when the sledge topples over and you are flung hard into a snowdrift; with your face slap into the snow, and you get up all white with your moustache covered with icicles, hatless, gloveless, with your belt undone. . . . People laugh and dogs bark. . . .

Pavel Ivanich, with one eye half open, looked at Goussiev and asked quietly:

'Goussiev, did your commander steal?'

'How do I know, Pavel Ivanich? The likes of us don't hear of it.'

A long time passed in silence. Goussiev thought, dreamed, drank water; it was difficult to speak, difficult to hear, and he was afraid of being spoken to. One hour passed, a second, a third; evening came, then night; but he noticed nothing as he sat dreaming of the snow.

He could hear someone coming into the ward; voices, but five minutes passed and all was still.

'God rest his soul!' said the soldier with the bandaged hand. 'He was a restless man.'

'What?' asked Goussiev. 'Who?'

'He's dead. He has just been taken upstairs.'

'Oh, well,' muttered Goussiev with a yawn. 'God rest his soul.'

'What do you think, Goussiev?' asked the bandaged soldier after some time. 'Will he go to heaven?'

'Who?'

'Pavel Ivanich.'

'He will. He suffered much. Besides, he was a priest's son, and priests have many relations. They will pray for his soul.'

The bandaged soldier sat down on Goussiev's hammock and said in an undertone:

'You won't live much longer, Goussiev. You'll never see Russia.'

'Did the doctor or the nurse tell you that?' asked Goussiev.

'No one told me, but I can see it. You can always tell when a man is going to die soon. You neither eat nor drink, and you have gone very thin and awful to look at. Consumption. That's what it is. I'm not saying this to make you uneasy, but because I thought you might like to have the last sacrament. And if you have any money, you had better give it to the senior officer.'

'I have not written home,' said Goussiev. 'I shall die and they will never know.'

'They will know,' said the sailor in his deep voice. 'When you die they will put you down in the log, and at Odessa they will give a note to the military governor, and he will send it to your parish or wherever it is. . . .'

This conversation made Goussiev begin to feel unhappy and a vague desire began to take possession of him. He drank water —it was not that: he stretched out to the port-hole and breathed the hot, moist air—it was not that; he tried to think of his native place and the snow—it was not that. . . . At last he felt that he would choke if he stayed a moment longer in the hospital.

'I feel poorly, mates,' he said. 'I want to go on deck. For Christ's sake take me on deck.'

Goussiev flung his arms round the soldier's neck and the soldier held him with his free arm and supported him up the gangway. On deck there were rows and rows of sleeping soldiers and sailors; so many of them that it was difficult to pick a way through them.

'Stand up,' said the bandaged soldier gently. 'Walk after me slowly and hold on to my shirt. . . .'

It was dark. There was no light on deck or on the masts or over the sea. In the bows a sentry stood motionless as a statue, but he looked as if he were asleep. It was as though the steamer had been left to its own sweet will, to go where it liked.

'They are going to throw Pavel Ivanich into the sea,' said the bandaged soldier. 'They will put him in a sack and throw him overboard.'

'Yes. That's the way they do.'

'But it's better to lie at home in the earth. Then the mother can go to the grave and weep over it.'

'Surely.'

There was a smell of dung and hay. With heads hanging there were oxen standing by the bulwark—one, two, three . . . eight beasts. And there was a little horse. Goussiev put out his hand to pat it, but it shook its head, showed its teeth, and tried to bite his sleeve.

'Damn you,' said Goussiev angrily.

He and the soldier slowly made their way to the bows and stood against the bulwark and looked silently up and down. Above them was the wide sky, bright with stars, peace and tranquillity—exactly as it was at home in his village; but below —darkness and turbulence. Mysterious towering waves. Each wave seemed to strive to rise higher than the rest; and they pressed and jostled each other and yet others came, fierce and ugly, and hurled themselves into the fray.

There is neither sense nor pity in the sea. Had the steamer been smaller, and not made of tough iron, the waves would have crushed it remorselessly and all the men in it, without distinction of good and bad. The steamer too seemed cruel and senseless. The large-nosed monster pressed forward and cut its way through millions of waves; it was afraid neither of darkness, nor of the wind, nor of space, nor of loneliness; it cared for nothing, and if the ocean had its people, the monster would crush them without distinction of good and bad.

'Where are we now?' asked Goussiev.

'I don't know. Must be the ocean.'

'There's no land in sight.'

'Why, they say we shan't see land for another seven days.'

The two soldiers looked at the white foam gleaming with phosphorescence. Goussiev was the first to break the silence.

'Nothing is really horrible,' he said. 'You feel uneasy, as if you were in a dark forest. Suppose a boat were lowered and I was ordered to go a hundred miles out to sea to fish—I would go. Or suppose I saw a soul fall into the water—I would go in after him. I wouldn't go in for a German or a Chinaman, but I'd try to save a Russian.'

'Aren't you afraid to die?'

'Yes. I'm afraid. I'm sorry for the people at home. I have a brother at home, you know, and he is not steady; he drinks, beats his wife for nothing at all, and my old father and mother may be brought to ruin. But my legs are giving way, mate, and it is hot here. . . . Let me go to bed.'

V

Goussiev went back to the ward and lay down in his hammock. As before, a vague desire tormented him and he could not make out what it was. There was a congestion in his chest, a noise in his head, and his mouth was so dry that he could hardly move his tongue. He dozed and dreamed, and, exhausted by the heat, his cough, and the nightmares that haunted him, towards morning he fell into a deep sleep. He dreamed he was in barracks, and the bread had just been taken out of the oven, and he crawled into the oven and lathered himself with a birch broom. He slept for two days and on the third day in the afternoon two sailors came down and carried him out of the ward.

He was sewn up in sail-cloth, and to make him heavier two iron bars were sewn up with him. In the sail-cloth he looked like a carrot or a radish, broad at the top, narrow at the bottom. . . . Just before sunset he was taken on deck and laid on a board one end of which lay on the bulwark, the other on a box, raised up by a stool. Round him stood the invalided soldiers.

'Blessed is our God,' began the priest; 'always, now and for ever and ever.'

'Amen!' said three sailors.

The soldiers and the crew crossed themselves and looked askance at the waves. It was strange that a man should be sewn up in sail-cloth and dropped into the sea. Could it happen to any one?

The priest sprinkled Goussiev with earth and bowed. A hymn was sung.

The guard lifted up the end of the board, Goussiev slipped down it; shot headlong, turned over in the air, then plop! The foam covered him, for a moment it looked as though he was swathed in lace, but the moment passed—and he disappeared beneath the waves.

He dropped down to the bottom. Would he reach it? The bottom is miles down, they say. He dropped down almost sixty or seventy feet, then began to go slower and slower, swung to and fro as though he were thinking; then, borne along by the current, he moved more sideways than downward.

But soon he met a shoal of pilot-fish. Seeing a dark body, the fish stopped dead and sudden, all together, turned and went back. Less than a minute later, like arrows they darted at Goussiev, zigzagging through the water around him. . . .

Later came another dark body, a shark. Gravely and leisurely, as though it had not noticed Goussiev, it swam under him, and rolled over on its back; it turned its belly up, taking its ease in the warm, translucent water, and slowly opened its mouth with its two rows of teeth. The pilot-fish were wildly excited; they stopped to see what was going to happen. The shark played with the body, then slowly opened its mouth under it, touched it with its teeth, and the sail-cloth was ripped open from head to foot; one of the bars fell out, frightening the pilot-fish and striking the shark on its side, and sank to the bottom.

And above the surface, the clouds were huddling up about the setting sun; one cloud was like a triumphal arch, another like a lion, another like a pair of scissors. . . . From behind the clouds came a broad green ray reaching up to the very middle of the sky; a little later a violet ray was flung alongside this, and then others, gold and pink. . . . The sky was soft and lilac, pale and tender. At first beneath the lovely, glorious sky the ocean frowned, but soon the ocean also took on colour—sweet, joyful, passionate colours, almost impossible to name in human language.

A MOSCOW HAMLET[1]

I AM a Moscow Hamlet. Yes. I go to houses, theatres, restaurants, and editorial offices in Moscow, and everywhere I say the same thing:

'God, how boring it is, how ghastly boring!'

And the sympathetic reply comes:

'Yes, indeed, it is terribly boring.'

This goes on through the day and the evening; and at night when I come home and lie down in bed and ask myself in the dark why I am so tormented with boredom, I have a restless, heavy feeling in my chest, and remember how in one house a week ago, when I began to ask what to do for my boredom, an unknown gentleman, obviously not a Moscow man, suddenly turned to me and said, with irritation:

'Oh, you take a piece of telephone cord and hang yourself on the nearest telegraph pole! That's all that's left for you!'

Yes, and all the while at night it seems to me that I am beginning to understand why I am so bored. Why? Why? This, I believe, is the reason . . .

To begin with, I know absolutely nothing. I studied something once, but damn it, is it because I have forgotten everything, or because my knowledge is good for nothing, that it turns out that I am discovering America every minute? For instance, when I am told that Moscow needs main drainage, or that whortleberries don't really grow on trees, I ask in astonishment: 'Is that so, really?'

I have lived in Moscow since I was born, but, heavens above, I don't know the origin of Moscow, what it exists for, why, what's the good of it or what it needs. At the meetings of the city council I discuss the management of the town with the others, but I don't know how many square miles there are in Moscow, how many people, the number of births and deaths, the income and expenditure, how much trade we do, or with whom. . . . Which city is richer, Moscow or London? If it's London, then why? God only knows. And when a question is raised on the council, I tremble and am the first to shout: 'Hand it over to a committee! A committee!'

[1] This feuilleton was published in No. 5667 of the *Novoye Vremya*, 7th December 1891, under a pseudonym.

I murmur to business men that it is time Moscow opened up trading relations with China and Persia, but we don't know where China and Persia are, or whether they need anything beside damped and worm-eaten raw silk. From morning till evening I gobble at Tiestov's restaurant and don't know what I'm gobbling for. Sometimes I get a part in a play, and I don't know what's in the play. I go to the opera to hear *The Queen of Spades*, and only when the curtain goes up do I remember that I haven't read Pushkin's tale, or I've forgotten it. I write a play and get it produced, and only after it has come a smash do I realize that a play exactly like it was written by V. Alexandrov, and by Fedotov before him, and by Shpazhinsky before him. I cannot speak, or argue, or keep up a conversation. When a conversation arises in company about something I do not know, I simply begin bluffing. I give my face a rather sad, sneering expression, and take my interlocutor by the buttonhole, and say:

'This is *vieux jeu*, dear fellow,' or 'My dear man, you are contradicting yourself. . . . We'll settle this interesting question some other time, and come to some agreement; but now, for heaven's sake, tell me: have you seen *Imogen?*' . . . In this matter I have learned something from the Moscow critics. When I'm present at a conversation about the theatre or the modern drama, I understand nothing about it, but I find no difficulty in replying, if I am asked my opinion: 'Well, yes, gentlemen. Suppose it is. . . . But where's the idea, the ideals?' Or, after a sigh, I exclaim: 'O immortal Molière, where art thou?' and, gloomily waving my hand, I go into the next room. There's a certain Lope de Vega, a Danish playwright, I fancy. I sometimes stun the audience with him. 'I'll tell you a secret,' I whisper to my neighbour, 'Calderon stole this phrase from Lope de Vega. . . .' And they believe me. . . . Well, let them verify! . . .

On account of my utter lack of knowledge I am quite uncultured. True, I dress according to the fashion, I have my hair cut at Théodore's and my establishment is *chic*, yet I am an Asiatic and *mauvais ton*. With a writing desk, of inlaid work, which costs about four hundred roubles, velvet upholstery, pictures, carpets, busts, tiger skins—lo, the flue in the fireplace is stopped up with a lady's blouse, or there's no spittoon, and I and my friends spit on the carpet. From the staircase comes a smell of roast goose, the butler's face is heavy-eyed, there's dirt and filth in the kitchen, and under the beds and behind the wardrobes there are dust, cobwebs, old boots covered with green mould, and papers smelling of cats. There's always something wrong in the house; the chimneys smoke or the lavatory is draughty, or the ventilator does not shut, and in order that the snow should not come flying from the street into my study, I hasten to stop up the ventilator with a cushion. At times I go to live in furnished apartments. I lie down on the sofa in my room, thinking on the subject of boredom, and in the next room to the right the German woman lodger fries cutlets on a kerosene stove; and in the room to the left little ladies drum with beer bottles on the table. From my room I am studying 'life,' I am looking at everything from the point of view of furnished apartments, and I write solely about the German woman, the little ladies, dirty serviettes; or I play the part exclusively of drunkards and fallen idealists; and the most important problem I consider that of doss-houses and of the intellectual proletariat. Yet I feel nothing and observe nothing. I quite readily reconcile myself to the low ceilings, black-beetles, the dampness, drunken friends who settle themselves on my bed with their dirty boots on. Neither the pavements, covered with a yellow-brown slime, nor the dust-heaps, nor the filthy gates, nor the illiterate sign-boards, nor the ragged beggars—nothing offends my aesthetic sense. I sit, shrivelled up like a hobgoblin on a narrow sledge, the wind gets at me from all sides, the driver blindly whips me with his whip, the scabby horse hardly trots—but I take no heed of it all. It's all of no consequence! They say that the Moscow architects have erected soap-boxes for houses and have thereby spoilt the city. But I don't think that those soap-boxes are bad. They say that our museums are beggarly, unscientific, and useless. But I do not go to museums. They complain that there used to be one decent picture gallery, and even that one has been closed by Tretyakov. Well, let him close it if he pleases. . . .

The second cause of my boredom is that I believe I am very clever and extraordinarily important. Whether I enter a house, or speak, or keep silent, or recite at a literary soirée, or gobble at Tiestov's, I do it with the greatest aplomb. There is no discussion I would not intervene in. It's true. I can't speak, but I can smile ironically, shrug my shoulders, interject. I, an ignorant and uncultured Asiatic, at bottom, I'm satisfied with everything; but I assume an air of being discontented with everything, and I manage this so subtly that sometimes I believe it myself. When there's a funny play on at the theatre, I long

to laugh, but I hasten to give myself a serious, concentrated air.
God forbid I should smile! What will my neighbours say?
Someone behind me is laughing. I look round sternly. A
wretched lieutenant, a Hamlet like myself, is put out, and says,
apologizing for his fit of laughter:

'How cheap! Merely a Punch and Judy show!'

And during the interval I say aloud at the bar: 'Hang it all,
what a play? It's disgusting.'

'Yes, a regular Punch and Judy show,' someone answers,
'but it's got an idea. . . .'

'Well, the motive was worked out ages ago by Lope de Vega,
and, of course, there can be no comparison! But how boring,
how incredibly boring!'

At *Imogen* my jaws ache with suppressed yawns, my eyes sink
into my forehead for boredom, my mouth is parched. . . . But
on my face is a blissful smile.

'This is a whiff of the real thing,' I say in an undertone; 'it's
a long while since I had such real pleasure.'

At times I have a desire to play the fool, to take part in a
farce, and would do it gladly, and I know it would be the very
thing for these gloomy times; but—what will they say in the
offices of *The Artist*?

No, God forbid!

At picture exhibitions I usually screw up my eyes, shake my
head knowingly and say aloud:

'Everything seems to be here, atmosphere, expression, tones.
But where's the essential? . . . Where's the idea? I ask you,
where is the idea?'

From the reviews I demand honest principles, and above all,
that the articles should be signed by professors, or by men who
have been exiled to Siberia. No one who isn't a professor or an
exile can have real talent. I demand that Mme Yermolov shall
play only idealistic girls, never more than twenty-one. I insist
that classical plays must absolutely be staged by professors—absolutely. I insist that the most minor actors, before taking a part,
should be acquainted with the literature on Shakespeare, so that
when an actor says, for instance, 'Good night, Bernardo,' the whole
audience shall feel that he has read eight volumes of criticism.

I get into print very often indeed. Only yesterday I went
to the editor of a fat monthly to ask whether he was going to
publish my novel of nine hundred pages.

'I really don't know what to do,' the editor said in embarrassment. 'You see, it's so long . . . and so tedious.'

'Yes,' I say, 'but it 's honest.'

'Yes, you 're right,' the editor agrees in still greater embarrassment. 'Of course, I 'll publish it.'

My girl and women friends are also unusually clever and important. They are all alike; they dress alike, they speak alike, they walk alike. There 's only this difference, that the lips of one of them curve in a heart shape, while the mouth of another opens as wide as an eel-trap when she smiles.

'Have you read Protopopov's last article?' the heart-shaped lips ask me. 'It 's a revelation.'

'You must agree,' says the eel-trap, 'that Ivan Ivanovich Ivanov's passionate convictions remind one of Belinsky. He 's my only hope.'

I confess there was a *she*. I remember our declaration of love so well. She sat on the divan. Lips heart-shaped. Badly dressed, 'no pretensions'; her hair was stupidly done. I take her by the waist; her corset scrunches. I kiss her cheek—it tastes salty. She is confused, stunned, bewildered. 'Good heavens, how can one combine honest principles with such a trivial thing as love? What would Protopopov say if he saw us? No, never! Let me go! You shall be my friend.' I say that friendship is not enough for me. . . . Then she shakes her finger at me archly and says:

'Well, I 'll love you on condition that you keep your flag flying.'

And when I hold her in my arms, she murmurs:

'Let us fight together . . .'

Then, when I live with her, I get to know that the flue of the fireplace is stopped up with her blouse, that the papers under her bed smell of cats, that she also bluffs in arguments and picture exhibitions, and jabbers like a parrot about atmosphere and expression. And she too must have an idea! She drinks vodka on the quiet, and when she goes to bed she smears her face with sour cream in order to look younger. In her kitchen there are beetles, dirty dish-clouts, filth; and when the cook bakes a pie, she takes the comb out of her hair and makes a pattern on the crust before putting it into the oven; and when she makes pastry she licks the currants to make them stick on the paste. And I run! run! My romance flies to the devil, and *she*, important, clever, contemptuous, goes everywhere and squeaks about me: 'He betrayed his convictions.'

The third cause of my boredom is my furious, boundless envy. When I am told that So-and-so has written a very

interesting article, that So-and-so's play is a success, that X won
two hundred thousand roubles in a lottery, and that N's speech
made a profound impression, my eyes begin to squint. They
close right up, and I say

'I'm glad, awfully, for his sake; of course, you know he was
tried for theft in '74.'

My soul turns into a lump of lead. I hate the successful
man with all my being, and I go on:

'He treats his wife very badly. He has three mistresses.
He always squares the reviewers by dining them. Altogether,
he's an utter rogue. . . . His novel isn't bad, but he's certainly
lifted it from somewhere. He's a blatant incompetent. . . .
And, to tell the truth, I don't find anything particular in this
novel even. . . .'

But if someone's play is a failure, I'm very happy and hasten
to take the writer's side.

'No, my dear fellows, no!' I shout. 'In this play there's
something. It is literature, at all events.'

Do you know that all the mean, spiteful, dirty things that are
being said about people of any reputation in Moscow were
started by me? Let the mayor know that if he managed to
give us good roads, I should begin to hate him, and I'd spread
the rumour that he's a highway robber. . . . If I am told a
certain newspaper already has fifty thousand subscribers, I'll
tell every one that the editor is kept by a woman. The success
of another is a disgrace, a humiliation, a stab in the heart for
me. . . . What question can there be of a social or a political
consciousness? If I ever had one, envy devoured it long
ago.

And so, knowing nothing, uncultured, very clever and exces-
sively important, squinting with envy, with a huge liver, yellow,
grey, bald, I wander from house to house all over Moscow, dis-
colouring life, and bringing with me into every house something
yellow, grey, bald. . . .

'God, how boring!' I say with despair in my voice. 'How
ghastly boring!'

I'm catching, like the influenza. I complain of boredom,
look important, and slander my friends and acquaintances from
envy, and lo, a young student has already taken in what I say.
He passes his hand over his hair solemnly, throws away his book,
and says:

'Words, words, words . . . God, how boring!'

He squints, his eyes begin to close, like mine, and he says:

'The professors are lecturing for the famine fund now. I'm afraid half the money will go into their own pockets.'

I wander about like a shadow, doing nothing; my liver is growing, growing. . . . Time passes, passes. Meanwhile, I'm getting old, weak. One day I'll catch the influenza and be taken off to the Vagankov cemetery. My friends will remember me for a couple of days and then forget, and my name will no longer be even a sound. . . . Life does not come again; if you have not lived during the days that were given you, once only, then write it down as lost. . . . Yes, lost, lost.

And yet I could have learned anything. If I could have got the Asiatic out of myself, I could have studied and loved European culture, trade, crafts, agriculture, literature, music, painting, architecture, hygiene. I could have had superb roads in Moscow, begun trade with China and Persia, brought down the death-rate, fought ignorance, corruption and all the abominations which hold us back from living. I could have been modest, courteous, jolly, cordial; I could have rejoiced sincerely at other people's success, for even the least success is a step towards happiness and truth.

Yes, I could have! I could have! But I am a rotten rag, useless rubbish. I am a Moscow Hamlet. Take me off to the Vagankov cemetery!

I toss about under my blanket, turning from side to side. I cannot sleep. All the while I think why I am so tortured with boredom, and these words echo in my ears until the dawn:

'You take a piece of telephone cord and hang yourself on the nearest telegraph pole. That's all that's left for you.'

AT THE CEMETERY

'THE wind is rising, and it's getting dark already. Hadn't we better be getting home?'

The wind walked over the yellow leaves of the old birch trees, and a hail of big drops scattered down upon us. One of the company slipped on the clayey ground, and clutched at a large grey cross to save himself from falling.

'Yegor Griasnorukov, Privy Councillor and Knight,' he read. 'I knew the gentleman. . . . He loved his wife, wore the order of Stanislav, read nothing. . . . His digestion was perfect. . . . That was a life worth living. One would have thought he had no need to die, but, alas! a mischance was on the look-out for him. . . . The poor man fell a victim to his genius for observation. Once, while he was listening at the keyhole, the door hit his head so hard that he got concussion and died. Under that cross lies a man who loathed verses from his very cradle. . . . As if to deride him, the whole monument is plastered with them. . . . Here's somebody coming.'

A man in a worn-out overcoat, with a clean-shaven bluish face, came up to us. He had a bottle of vodka under his arm, and a parcel with sausage in it stuck out of his pocket.

'Where is the grave of Moushkin, the actor?' he asked in a hoarse voice.

We led him towards it. Moushkin had died two years before.

'Are you a government clerk?' we asked him.

'No, I'm an actor. Nowadays one can't distinguish an actor from a clerk of the archives. You've noticed it, quite right. It's curious—though not exactly flattering to the officials.'

Moushkin's grave was hard to find. It had grown rank; it was covered with weeds, not like a grave at all. A cheap, little cross, drooping, mossed over, frost-blackened, looked old, dejected, and sick.

' . . . forgettable friend, Moushkin,' we read. Time had wiped away two letters and corrected the lie of man.

'Actors and journalists collected for a monument and drank it away. . . . Good lads.' The actor sighed, bowing down to the ground; his knees and hat touched the wet earth.

'What do you mean, they drank it away?'

'Quite simple. They collected the money, put the lists in the papers, and drank it away. . . . I don't say it to blame them, but that's how it was. . . . Your health, gentlemen. Here's to your health, and to his everlasting memory.'

'There's not much health in boozing, and everlasting memory is a sad business. Let's hope God has a temporary memory; as for an everlasting one—well.'

'That's perfectly true. Moushkin was a famous man; they carried a score of wreaths behind his coffin, and he's forgotten already. He's forgotten by those who liked him, and remembered by those he wronged. I shall never forget him, never, never, for I never had anything from him except wrong. I don't like him.'

'What wrong did he do you?'

'A great wrong.' The actor sighed, and an expression of bitter injury spread over his face. 'He was a rogue and a robber, rest his soul. By looking at him and listening to him, I became an actor. By his art he lured me away from home; he seduced me with artistic vanity; he promised so much, and gave me only—tears and sorrow. . . . The actor's bitter fate. I lost everything—youth, temperance, the likeness of God. . . . Not a farthing to bless myself with, boots down at heel, fringes to my trousers, my face just as if dogs had gnawed it all over. . . . Free-thinking and folly in my head. He took away my faith, the robber. It would be all right if I had some talent, but no, I've been lost for nothing. . . . It's cold, gentlemen. Won't you have a drop? There's enough to go round. Br-r-r. Let us drink to the repose of his soul. I don't like him, he's dead; all the same he's the only one I have in the world, like one of my own fingers. This is the last time I shall see him. . . . The doctors said I shall die of drink soon, so I came to say good-bye to him. We must forgive our enemies.'

We left the actor to talk to the dead Moushkin, and walked away. A drizzle, cold and fine, began to fall.

Where the main path turned, covered with rough gravel, we met a funeral procession. Four bearers in white cotton belts and dirty boots, hung round with leaves, carried a brown coffin. It was getting dark, and they hurried, stumbling and swinging the bier.

'We've only been a couple of hours walking here, and this is the third they have brought in. . . . Let us go home.'

AT THE POST OFFICE

THE other day we went to the funeral of the wife of our old postmaster, Sladkoperzov. After the lady had been buried, according to the custom of our fathers and grandfathers we gathered at the post office to 'commemorate.'

When the pancakes were put on the table, the old widower cried bitterly, and said: 'The pancakes are just as rosy as my dear wife was. Just as beautiful. Pre-cisely.'

'It's true,' the company agreed. 'She was beautiful . . . first class.'

'Ye-es. Every one was amazed when they saw her. . . . But, gentlemen, I did not love her for her beauty or her gentle disposition. Those qualities belong to the nature of woman; one often finds them in this world below. I loved her for another quality of her soul. I loved her—God rest her soul—because, in spite of all the liveliness and playfulness of her character, she was faithful to her husband. She was true to me although she was only twenty and I shall soon be past sixty. She was faithful to me, an old man.'

The sexton, who had been eating with us, coughed eloquently.

'You don't seem to believe it?' the widower turned to him.

'It's not that I don't believe,' the sexton said in confusion. 'But . . . you see . . . young wives nowadays are so often what d' you call it . . . *rendezvous* . . . *sauce provençale* . . .'

'You don't believe it. I'll prove it to you. I kept up her faithfulness by various strategical methods, as you might say, a kind of fortification. With my cunning behaviour, my wife could not possibly have been unfaithful to me. I employed cunning to safeguard my marriage bed. I know some words, a sort of passwords. I had only to say those words and—*basta*, I can sleep in peace as far as unfaithfulness goes.'

'What were the words?'

'Quite simple. I spread a wicked rumour in the town. You know it, I'm sure. I used to tell every one: 'My wife, Aliona, is the mistress of Ivan Alexeyich Salikhvatsky, the Chief of Police.' Those words were enough. Not a single man dared to make love to Aliona for fear of the anger of the Chief of Police. If any one happened to catch sight of her, he would run away for dear life, in case Salikhvatsky should get the idea into his head. Ha ha ha! You try having something to do with that whiskery idol. You won't get any fun out of it. He'll write five official reports about your sanitation. If he saw your cat in the street, he'd write a report as if it was straying cattle.'

'So your wife didn't live with Ivan Alexeyich, then?' we said in a slow-voiced amazement.

'Oh, no! That was my cunning. Ha ha ha! I took you youngsters in properly. That's what it comes to.'

Three minutes passed in silence. We sat and were silent, and we felt insulted and ashamed for having been so cleverly cheated by the fat, red-nosed old man.

'Pray God you marry again,' muttered the sexton.

SCHULZ[1]

A FRAGMENT

IT was a cheerless October morning, and large flakes of snow were drifting from the clouds. It was not yet winter—cart wheels still rattled loudly on the pavement. The snow that settled on Kostya Schulz's long, gown-like overcoat melted quickly, and turned to fine drops. Kostya, a pupil of the first form, was full of gloom. Partly the weather was to blame, partly the fable of 'The Monkey and the Glasses.' He had not got the fable by heart, and he pictured the scene in the classroom; the teacher of Russian, tall, corpulent, spectacled, standing so close to him that Kostya could study the little buttons of his waistcoat and his watch-chain with its cornelian stone. The teacher would ask in that little tenor voice: 'Well, you haven't learned it? . . .' Partly, the nurse was to blame. Before leaving home he was rude to her; to spite her he refused to take cutlets for his lunch. Already he regretted the cutlets, for he was hungry.

At the end of the street the school came in view. Twenty to nine by the watchmaker's! Kostya's heart contracted. Goodness! What a change! In August when mamma took him to the entrance exam.—the first lesson days—how keen he was, how he dreamed of school, how bored he felt on feast days and Sundays! Now, in October, all was hard, stern, cold!

[1] Taken from the Russian six-volume edition of Tchekhov's letters.

Three houses ahead of him walked Serguey Semionovich, the arithmetic teacher. In his top-hat he seemed so secure, solid; his high leather galoshes scratched the pavement so sternly, implacably. How much did the shoemaker charge him for those galoshes? And when making them did he know they would express so perfectly the character of the man now wearing them? . . .

LIFE IS WONDERFUL[1]

LIFE is quite an unpleasant business, but it is not so very hard to make it wonderful. For which purpose it is not enough that you should win 200,000 roubles in a lottery, or receive the order of the White Eagle, or marry a beautiful woman—all these blessings are transitory and are liable to become a habit. But to feel continuously happy, even in moments of distress and sorrow, the following is needed:

(*a*) To be satisfied with your present state; and

(*b*) To rejoice in the knowledge that things might have been much worse.

When your matches suddenly go off in your pocket, rejoice and offer thanks to heaven that your pocket is not a gun-powder magazine.

When your relations come to pay you a visit during your holiday in the country, don't get pale, but exclaim triumphantly: 'How very lucky it is not the police!'

If you get a splinter in your finger, rejoice that it is not in your eye.

If your wife or sister-in-law practises scales on the piano, don't lose your temper, but be grateful for the joy that you are listening to music, and not to the howling of jackals, or to a cat's concert.

Rejoice that you are not a tram-horse, nor a Koch bacillus, nor a trichina, nor a pig, nor an ass, nor a bear led by a gipsy, nor a bug.

[1] This article appeared in the original in No. 17 of the humorous paper *Oskolki* in 1885, when Tchekhov, then only twenty-five, was being paid literally in farthings for his contributions. *Life is Wonderful* has not been included in Tchekhov's collected works.

Rejoice that at the moment you are not a prisoner in the dock; that you are not interviewing your creditors, and that you have not to arrange the question of fees with Turba, the editor.

If you live in a place not so remote as Siberia, can't you feel pleased at the idea, that by mere chance you might have been deported there?

If you have pain in one tooth, rejoice that it is not all your teeth that are aching.

Rejoice that you can afford not to read the *Daily Citizen*; that you have not to drive a sewage cart, nor to be married to three women simultaneously.

If you are removed to a police cell, jump for joy that it is not the fiery gehenna that you have been taken to.

If you are flogged with a birch rod, kick your legs in rapture, and exclaim: 'How very happy I am that it is not nettles I am being flogged with!'

If your wife has been unfaithful to you, rejoice that she has betrayed merely yourself, and not your country.

A FAIRY TALE

THE HISTORY OF 'THE BET'

IN 1899 Tchekhov sold the copyright of his works to Marx, the well-known Russian publisher of the popular illustrated weekly the *Niva*, for the sum of 75,000 roubles. Under this agreement Tchekhov had to collect his works, scattered in various periodicals over a period of nearly twenty years, in order to supply the publisher with material for the original ten-volume edition.[1] Speaking of the labour of preparing the material for the ten-volume edition Tchekhov says, in his letter to Nemirovich-Danchenko of 24th November 1899: 'Marx's proofs are drudgery; I have hardly finished the second volume; and if I had known beforehand how hard it would be, I should have asked Marx not for seventy-five but for one hundred and seventy-five thousand roubles.' Apart from the labour of collecting and selecting, Tchekhov worked very earnestly on editing the material. The seriousness with which he went through the old stories, which were to be included in the collected works, may be gathered from the following example.

One of the stories which appeared in this collection is *The Bet*. This story as we now know reproduces *two* chapters of a story called *A Fairy Tale*, which was originally published in *three* chapters in the *Novoye Vremya*, No. 4613, 1889. In preparing *A Fairy Tale* for inclusion in his collected works, Tchekhov struck out the third chapter and changed its title to that of *The Bet*. By so doing he deliberately turned *A Fairy Tale* into its antithesis.

In *The Bet* a rich banker discusses with a young man, a lawyer, the question of capital punishment. The banker maintains that a man would prefer death to a long term of imprisonment.

[1] The ten-volume edition of Tchekhov's collected works was published by Marx during the years 1899–1901. In 1903 Marx published a new edition in sixteen volumes, giving it as a supplement to the subscribers to his weekly *Niva*. All the material for those two editions was selected and edited by Tchekhov himself. In 1911 Marx published twelve more volumes of Tchekhov's writings. These volumes include nearly all the work of Tchekhov's early period—work not selected by the author—as well as his latest work, as, for instance, *The Cherry Orchard* and *The Bride*.

The young man is willing to bet that he can endure solitary confinement for fifteen years. A sum of 2,000,000 roubles is offered by the banker on condition that if the prisoner leaves his prison even a couple of hours before the stipulated term, he is to forfeit the stake. Fifteen years pass, the day of liberation comes. During those years all that is known about the prisoner is that he had asked for a great number of books on various subjects, and that all these books have been supplied to him. During that time the affairs of the banker have grown worse, and finding it difficult to pay the 2,000,000 roubles, he steals into the prisoner's room on the very eve of his liberation, with the intention of killing him. But this is what he finds:

In the prisoner's room a candle is burning dim. The prisoner himself is sitting at the table. Only his back, the hair on his head, and his hands are visible. On the table, on the chairs, on the carpet—everywhere—open books are strewn. . . . On the table before his bended head lies a sheet of paper, on which something is written in a tiny hand. The banker takes the sheet from the table and reads as follows:

'To-morrow at twelve o'clock midnight, I shall obtain my freedom and the right to mix with people. But before I leave this room and see the sun, I think it necessary to say a few words to you. On my own clear conscience and before God who sees me I declare to you that I despise freedom, life, health, and all that your books call the blessings of the earth.

'For fifteen years I have diligently studied earthly life. True, I have seen neither the earth nor the people, but in your books, I have drunk fragrant wine, sung songs, hunted deer and wild boar in the forests, loved women. . . . And beautiful women, like clouds ethereal, created by the magic of your poets' genius, have visited me by night, and have whispered to me wonderful tales which have made my head drunken. In your books I have climbed the summits of Elbruz and Mont Blanc and have seen from thence how the sun rises in the morning, and in the evening floods the sky, the ocean and the mountain ridges with a purple gold. I have seen from thence how above me lightnings glimmer cleaving the clouds; I have seen green forests, fields, rivers, lakes, cities; I have heard sirens singing, and the playing of the pipes of Pan; I have touched the wings of beautiful devils who came flying to me to speak of God. . . . In your books I have cast myself into bottomless abysses, worked miracles, burned cities to the ground, preached new religions, conquered whole countries. . . .

'Your books have given me wisdom. All that unwearying human thought created in the ages is compressed to a little lump in my skull. I know that I am more clever than you all. . . .

'And I despise your books, despise all earthly blessings and wisdom. Everything is void, frail, visionary, and elusive like a mirage. Though you be proud and wise and beautiful, yet will death wipe you from the face of the earth like the mice underground; and your posterity, your history, and the immortality of your men of genius will be as frozen slag burnt down together with the terrestrial globe.

'You are mad and have gone the wrong way. You take a lie for truth, and ugliness for beauty. You would marvel if by certain conditions there should suddenly grow on apple and orange trees, instead of fruit, frogs and lizards, and if roses should begin to breathe the odour of a sweating horse. So do I marvel at you, who have bartered heaven for earth. I do not want to understand you.

'That I may show you indeed my contempt for that by which you live, I renounce the two millions, of which I once dreamed as of paradise and which I now despise. That I may deprive myself of my right to them, I shall come out from here five minutes before the stipulated term, and thus shall break the agreement. . . .'

The banker having read that sheet, kissed the man's head, and went back to his house. Next morning the night watchman came running to him to tell him that the prisoner had been seen climbing through the window into the garden, rushing to the gate and disappearing. The banker and his servants went to the prisoner's room and established the fact that the prisoner had escaped. To prevent the circulation of possible rumours the banker took away the paper with the prisoner's renunciation of the two millions, and, going back to the house, locked it in his safe.

That is how *The Bet* ends. Now we give its continuation, Chapter III, as it first appeared in the *Novoye Vremya*, under the title *A Fairy Tale*.

CHAPTER III

A year passed. The banker was giving a party. Many learned men were present at the party and interesting conversations were carried on. Among other things, the conversa-

tion turned on the purpose of life and on the destiny of man.
They spoke of the rich young man, of perfection, of gospel love,
of vanity of vanities and so on. The guests, mostly consisting
of very rich men, almost all proclaimed the worthlessness of
riches. One of them said: 'Among those whom we consider
saints or geniuses, rich men are as rare as comets in the sky.
Hence it follows that riches are no necessary condition for the
perfection of the human race, or to put it briefly, riches are not
at all needed. And all that is not needed, is only an obstacle. . . .

'Quite so!' another guest agreed. 'Therefore the highest
expression of human perfection, though in a crude form (a more
refined has not yet been invented), is monastic asceticism, that is,
the most complete renunciation of life for the sake of an ideal.
It is impossible at one and the same time to serve God and the
Stock Exchange.'

'I can't see why it should be so!' a third guest broke in with
irritation. 'To my mind, in renunciation of life there is nothing
resembling the highest perfection. Do understand me! To
renounce pictures means to renounce the artist; to renounce
women, precious metals, wine, good climate, means to renounce
God, since all these were created by God! And, surely, ascetics
serve God!'

'Perfectly true!' said the old millionaire, the banker's rival
on the exchange. 'Add to this too that ascetics exist only in
imagination. There are no such people on earth. True, old
men happen to give up women, *blasé* men—money, disappointed
men—fame; yet I have been living on this earth for sixty-six
years and not once in my life have I come across a healthy, strong,
and not stupid man who, for instance, would refuse a million. . . .'

'Such men do exist,' said the host, the banker.

'Have you met them?'

'Fortunately I have. . . .'

'Impossible!' replied the old millionaire.

'I assure you, I know such a poor man who has on principle
refused two millions.'

The millionaire laughed, and said:

'You have been mystified. I repeat, there are no such men;
and I am so deeply convinced of this that I am willing to bet
any amount on it, say, a million. . . .'

'I bet three millions!' the banker exclaimed.

'Agreed! I bet three millions!'

The banker's head swam. He was so sure of his victory that
he felt sorry at not having made the stake five millions. That

amount would be just sufficient to improve his affairs on the exchange.

'Hands on it!' the millionaire exclaimed. 'When will you give us the proof?'

'At once!' the banker said triumphantly.

He was going to his study to get out of his safe the paper with the renunciation; but the butler then entered and said to him:

'There is a gentleman who wishes to see you.'

The banker apologized to his guests and left the room. No sooner had he entered the reception-room than a well-dressed man rushed up to him. Amazingly pale and with tears in his eyes he caught the banker's hand and began in a trembling voice:

'Forgive me . . . Forgive me! . . .'

'What is it you want? asked the banker. 'Who are you?'

'I am the fool who has wasted fifteen years of life and re-nounced two millions.'

'What do you want then?' the banker repeated, growing pale.

'I made an awful mistake. The man who does not see life, or who has no power of enjoying its blessings, should not judge of life. The sun shines so brightly! Women are so fascinat-ingly lovely! Wine is so palatable! The trees are so beautiful! . . . Books are only a feeble reflection of life, and that shadow has robbed me!

'My dear sir,' the lawyer went on, dropping on his knees, 'I do not ask you for two millions, I have no right to them; but I implore you, let me have a hundred or two hundred thousand roubles! Or I shall kill myself!'

'Very well!' the banker said in a dull voice. 'To-morrow you shall have what you want.'

And he hurried back to his guests. He was seized by an inspiration. He passionately wished this very moment to declare to all in a loud voice that he, the banker, deeply despised millions, the exchange, freedom, love of women, health, human words, and that he himself renounced life, and to-morrow would give everything to the poor and retire from life. . . . But as he came into the drawing-room it occurred to him that he owed more than he possessed, that he had no longer the strength to love women and to drink wine, and that therefore his renunciation would in the eyes of men have no meaning—he remembered all this, and exhausted, he dropped into a chair and said:

'You have won! I am ruined!'